KU-523-524

BARBARA TAYLOR BRADFORD

THE TRIUMPH
OF KATIE BYRNE

HarperCollins*Publishers*

HarperCollins*Publishers*
77–85 Fulham Palace Road,
Hammersmith, London w6 8jb

www.fireandwater.com

Special overseas edition 2001
This paperback edition 2002
1

First published in Great Britain by
HarperCollins*Publishers* 2001

ISBN 978-0-00-780837-3

Set in Sabon by Palimpsest Book Production Limited,
Polmont, Stirlingshire

Printed and bound in Great Britain by
Clays Ltd, St Ives plc

This book
is for my husband, Bob,
with my love and thanks
for making everything
always so special.

Contents

PART ONE

Kiss of Death

Connecticut, 1989

'. . . break off this last lamenting kiss,
Which sucks two souls, and vapours both away.'

JOHN DONNE

'The coward does it with a kiss.'

OSCAR WILDE

Chapter One

The girl sat on a narrow bench, centre stage, her body bent forward, one elbow on her knee, a hand supporting her head. The thinker, deeply thinking, her body language seemed to convey.

She was dressed very simply, boyishly, in a loose, grey, knitted tunic cinched by a black leather belt, worn with black tights and ballet slippers. Her long, reddish-gold hair was plaited, the plaits wound tightly around her head, so that the finished effect was like a burnished-copper cap gleaming under the pin-spot shining down. The girl's name was Katie Byrne and she was seventeen: acting was her entire life.

She was about to act for her favourite audience – an audience of two: her best friends, Carly Smith and Denise Matthews. They sat on straight-backed wooden chairs in front of the makeshift stage in the old barn which belonged to Ted Matthews, Denise's uncle. Both girls were the same age as Katie, and had been friends since childhood; all three were members of the amateur acting group at the high school in the rural Connecticut area where they all lived.

Katie had chosen to perform a speech from one of Shakespeare's plays at the school's upcoming Christmas concert. It was only two months away, and she had recently begun to rehearse the piece; Carly and Denise were also perfecting their chosen speeches for the same concert, rehearsing with her in the barn almost every day.

Now, at last, Katie lifted her head, stared out into space, and focused her blue eyes on the back wall of the barn, as if she saw something visible only to herself. Taking a deep breath, she began.

'To be, or not to be, that is the question: Whether 'tis nobler in the mind to suffer the slings and arrows of outrageous fortune, or to take arms against a sea of troubles, and by opposing, end them. To die –'

Abruptly, Katie stopped.

She jumped up off the bench, walked to the edge of the stage, looked down at her friends. Shaking her head, she seemed unexpectedly uncertain of herself, she who normally had such confidence and self-possession.

'I'm not getting it right,' Katie wailed.

'Yes, you are, and you're wonderful!' Carly cried, rising, stepping closer to the stage, the stage on which they had started to act when they were children. 'Nobody does Shakespeare the way you do it. You're the best, Katie.'

'Carly's right,' Denise agreed as she went to join Carly near the stage. 'It's the way you *act* the words, *say* them.

You make sense out of them, and there's never been a Hamlet like you.'

Katie burst out laughing. 'Thanks for your compliment, Denny, but there were a few others before me . . . Laurence Olivier and Richard Burton, to name a couple of them . . . they were the greatest classical actors on the English-speaking stage, just as Christopher Plummer is the greatest classical actor today. And listen, I keep telling you, it's all to do with understanding the *meaning* of the words, the motivation and intention behind them. And also with *punctuation*, knowing when to run the words on without pause, and *when* to pause to breathe . . .' She let the sentence trail off, knowing now was not the right time to give Denise another acting lesson.

Returning to the bench, she seated herself, adopted the thinker's position, which was comfortable for her, and sat ruminating for a moment or two.

Whatever her friends said, however much praise they lavished on her, Katie knew that her performance *was* slightly off today. Her concentration was not what it usually was, and she wasn't sure why. Unless it was because she felt guilty at being here this afternoon. Her mother wasn't well, and she was needed at home to help out. And yet, selfishly, she had decided to steal this time at the barn in order to rehearse the speech from *Hamlet*, and persuaded her friends to come with her after school.

Then rehearse, a small voice inside her head instructed. She took several deep breaths, relaxed her throat, let the stillness of the stage envelop her, calm her.

Within minutes she was ready, and she launched herself into Hamlet's soliloquy, her natural self-confidence perfectly in place once more.

Listening attentively, Carly was transported by Katie's voice, as she always was. There was a lovely resonance to it, full of nuances and feeling. No wonder, Carly said to herself, thinking of the way Katie practised, was endlessly training her voice. They all knew how serious she was about acting. Katie was dedicated, disciplined, and very determined to succeed. Somehow, Katie knew how to act the parts she had chosen without having had too many lessons, while Denise and she sort of stumbled along as best they could. Fortunately, they were improving, thanks to Katie's relentless coaching and encouragement.

They had first started acting together seven years ago, ten-year-olds with stars in their eyes. Denise's Uncle Ted had let them make use of the old barn at the far end of his property, and they had created a makeshift theatre out of it. At that time they had made a promise to each other, had vowed they would go to New York one day and start their acting careers in earnest. Making it to Broadway was their big dream. Katie kept promising that the three of them would move to the city once they finished high school, and that eventually they would be stars on the Great White Way. Carly hoped this would come true, that they *would* have their names in lights, but sometimes she was filled with doubts.

Denise had no doubts whatsoever, and as she sat next to Carly, watching Katie on the stage, relishing her performance, she was absolutely positive that their dreams would soon materialize. Katie was brilliant, there was no question, and they themselves were getting better and better, mostly because of Katie's intense lessons. When they went to New York they would find an apartment to share, go to acting school, and become professional actresses. It was all going to work, the dream would become reality, she was convinced.

Katie suddenly stood up, moved downstage right, and continued, 'To die, to sleep – No more, and by a sleep to say we end the heartache and the thousand natural shocks that flesh is heir to: 'tis a consummation devoutly to be wish'd. To die, to sleep – To sleep, perchance to dream . . .'

Flawlessly, and without faltering once, Katie went on to complete this most famous of Shakespearean speeches, her well-modulated voice rising and falling as she gave emphasis to certain words, less importance to others. And the quality of her acting was superb; after her initial hesitation, her seeming loss of confidence, she had gone forward sure-footedly.

When Katie was finally finished, she remained motionless for a second or two, her cornflower-blue eyes still focused in the distance, and then she blinked several times before glancing at Carly and Denise. And then she smiled at them broadly, sure in the knowledge that she had managed to get the speech right at last.

Her friends began to clap and cheer and they bounded up onto the stage enthusiastically, hugged her, congratulated her.

'Thanks,' she said, grinning in return, and hugging them back. 'But don't you think I should rehearse again tomorrow, just to make sure?'

They both drew away and gaped at her in astonishment.

Denise cried, '*You* don't need another rehearsal! But we do. And you've got to help us tomorrow. I'll never get my Desdemona speech right, and Carly's still having trouble with her Portia, aren't you, Carly?'

'I am a bit.' Carly sounded miserable. Then her voice changed, became more positive as she added, 'As for you, Katie Byrne, you're just *awesome*.'

'We're not going to let you hog the stage tomorrow,' Denise announced with a grin, adding in a mock-threatening voice, 'You're going to rehearse *us*, because we still need it. And if you don't, you might find yourself going off to be a Broadway actress all by yourself!'

'*Never*. You'll both be with me,' Katie declared, pulling the girls closer, putting an arm around each one of them, glancing at Denise admiringly. Her velvet-brown eyes, full of hidden depths, were sparkling. She was never anything but high-spirited and happy, bubbling with laughter and good humour. She had a kind of golden radiance about her, with her long blonde hair and pink-and-white porcelain skin. She was a genuine All-American beauty, slender, shapely and long-legged.

In contrast, Carly, who had been Katie's closest friend since they were toddlers, was very different. She was quieter, had a more introspective demeanour, was a little fey at times, and her seductive, rather dramatic looks belied her retiring, gentle nature. Eyeing her, Katie thought that even in her school clothes she looked voluptuous. Carly had a beautiful diminutive figure, and with her short dark curls and pansy-violet eyes had the look of a young Elizabeth Taylor.

With a sudden rush of emotion, Katie felt her abiding friendship and love for them both flowing through her . . . they were her dearest, her very best friends.

'It's the three of us or nothing!' Katie exclaimed emphatically. 'And I'll be glad to rehearse with you tomorrow. But listen up you two, you're much better than you think. Just remember that.'

Carly and Denise beamed on hearing these words, but neither girl made a comment and, arms linked, the three of them left the stage together.

As they always did, they went through the long-established ritual of sitting at the table drinking a bottle of Coke each. Today they were intent on dissecting Katie's performance, and generally discussing their parts, their set pieces for the concert. It was Carly who changed the subject, when she suddenly straightened in her chair and said to Katie, 'Do you think your Aunt Bridget will be able to find us an apartment in New York? Do you really think it's all going to happen for us?'

Katie nodded. 'I do. *Absolutely*. And she said we can stay with her at the loft in Tribeca for as long as we want.'

Denise interjected, 'Mrs Cooke is sure we'll be able to get into the American Academy of Dramatic Arts. She even said she'll help us.' Denise reached out, squeezed Carly's arm. 'Don't be such a worry wart.'

Carly let out a sigh, then she leaned back in the chair, relaxing, sipping her Coke. After a moment, she said in a reflective voice, 'Just think, next year at this time we'll be in the big city, attending drama classes and camping out at Aunt Bridget's fancy loft.'

'Hey, it's not all that fancy,' Katie exclaimed, grinning at her. 'But it's comfortable, I'll say that.' She jumped up, headed towards the curtained alcove which they used as a changing room. Pulling the curtain open, she stepped inside, then swung her head, explained, 'I've got to hurry, I'm really late to help Mom with supper.' She eyed the Portia and Desdemona costumes and other items strewn around haphazardly, and shook her head. 'I just don't have time to help you tidy up, I'm sorry.'

'That's no problem,' Carly assured her. 'Anyway, it

doesn't matter if it's messy in here. Nobody ever comes to the barn except us.'

'Uncle Ted says that after all these years it's ours.' Denise looked from Carly to Katie and grinned, then reached for the copy of *Othello* which lay on the table. She started to flip through the pages of the play looking for the part she was learning.

Katie disappeared behind the curtain; Carly opened *The Merchant of Venice*, wanting to study Portia's famous 'quality of mercy' speech, wondering if she would ever master it, worrying about it again, as she had for several weeks.

Within seconds, Katie was stepping out of the curtained alcove, wearing her school clothes and struggling into her jacket. 'See you in class tomorrow,' she said, as she rushed across the floor to the door.

Denise flashed her bright smile and Carly, looking up, asked, 'Can you please bring the long black wig tomorrow, Katie? I think it might work for my Portia.'

'Yes, it'll look great on you. I'll bring it to school, Carly.' She waved nonchalantly over her shoulder as she left the barn.

Chapter Two

Katie closed the heavy barn door behind her and shrugged deeper into her jacket. It had turned cold and she shivered as she hurried up the hill leading to the highway. Her mind was still on Carly and Denise. They were so much better than they realized, good actresses who were accomplished and knew what they were doing. But they didn't give themselves enough credit, genuinely needed to gain more self-confidence, that was their main problem.

Mrs Cooke, their teacher, who ran the drama group and taught acting at the high school, predicted great things for them all in the next few years, because of their talent, dedication, and willingness to work hard. It pleased Katie that Heather Cooke believed in them with such conviction that she was encouraging their ambition to work in the theatre.

Katie trudged on up the steep slope, continuing to think about her best friends, imagining what it would be like to be living in New York and studying at the academy. She could hardly wait for the time to come and she knew Carly and Denise felt the same way.

Suddenly, out of the corner of her eye, she saw rapid movement close to the mass of rhododendron bushes growing in profusion on the hillside. She stopped abruptly, half turned, stood frowning in puzzlement at the clump of dark-green bushes. But everything was still, silent, and there was no sign of life.

Shrugging dismissively, Katie continued on up the slope, deciding that the dark flash must have been a deer. There were a great number of them in the Litchfield hills, and they were becoming bolder. Everyone's gardens, her mother's included, attested to that fact.

Within minutes, the hillside flattened out into a piece of barren land that stretched all the way to the highway. This cut through New Milford, ran up to Kent and the small towns beyond.

Katie paused at the side of the road to let a truck pass, and then ran across to the other side. A second or two later she was on the dirt track that led through the wide meadows behind Dovecote Farm, a local landmark with its picturesque red barns and silos, and, in the summer, lush fields of rippling golden wheat.

At one moment, as she walked along, she glanced up. The sky had turned the colour of old iron, bitter, remote, and forbidding. Dusk was slowly descending and the meadows were beginning to fill with shadows. Wanting to get home as fast as possible, she began to jog down the track, and found herself plunging deeper into the fields.

But soon she realized she must slow down. A faint mist was rising, wispy and vaporous, floating in front of her like a grey veil; trees and hedges were rapidly becoming blurred, turning into weird inchoate shapes looming all around her. Having tramped this dirt track from early childhood, her feet knew it well. Nevertheless, she found herself moving at a snail's pace, growing more cautious, afraid of stumbling in the thick fog.

Far off, in the distance, she heard cows lowing, and even farther away a dog was barking. These distant sounds were reassuring in their familiarity, yet still she felt a loneliness pervading the deserted fields, a strange sense of melancholy, and she was unexpectedly uneasy. It had grown even colder. She pulled her jacket around her chest, moving faster again, growing conscious of the time, as usual worrying about her mother.

It did not take Katie much longer to reach the end of the dirt path, and she finally came to the wide road which led into the area where she lived with her parents and her two brothers, Niall and Finian.

Malvern had been founded in 1799, and it was called a town, but it wasn't even a hamlet, not really. It was a scattering of houses, a couple of shops, a cemetery, a white church with a steeple, poised on top of the hill, and a recreational hall near the church. To Katie, the white church had always seemed like a brave little sentinel standing guard above the houses nestled so cosily below in a hollow of the hills.

It was with a sense of relief that she hit this main road. She stepped out onto the smooth tarmacadam surface, glancing back at the mist-laden meadows as she did, and she suddenly realized how glad she was to be leaving them behind. There had been something strange, almost ghostly, about those empty fields.

Slowing down as the road swept upwards to the church, Katie began her climb, her pace steady. When she reached the top she stood for a moment looking down at Malvern. She could make out the twinkling lights shining in the windows of the houses scattered across the hillsides, and the mingled smell of woodsmoke and damp leaves floated to her on the chill night air. She was suddenly struck by a sense of an early autumn, and she smiled. Fall was her favourite time of year, when the foliage turned gold and russet and red, and her grandmother baked upsidedown apple tart and cinnamon cakes, and the entire family prepared for Thanksgiving and Christmas. Fall was the beginning of the holiday season which her mother loved so much. As Katie passed the forest of Scotch pine trees on the right side of the road, her nose twitched, assailed as it was by the sharp, pungent smell of pine.

How reassuring everything was now that she was out of the damp meadows. Soon she would be home, where her mother was waiting for her. They would prepare supper for the family, set the table together and serve the food. A loving smile flickered across Katie's wan face, giving it a touch of radiance, lighting up her blue eyes.

Although Katie loved her two girlfriends and was devoted to them, it was her mother who was the most special person in her life, to whom she was the closest, and whom she idolized. She thought of her mother as a faerie princess from Ireland. Certainly she was beautiful, with her flowing red hair and the bluest of eyes, which Katie had inherited. To Katie, her mother's voice was mellifluous, warm, soft, resonant, touched with a hint of lilting brogue.

These thoughts of her mother galvanized her, and she began to run once more, her feet flying as she sped down the hill.

Chapter Three

As her parents' house came finally into full view, Katie was filled with a sudden rush of warmth, a sense of homecoming, and she continued to run, speeding down the road towards home as fast as she could.

Medium in size, and compact, the house sat atop a small hillock set back from the main road, and it was the only home Katie had ever known. She loved it dearly, as did her parents and her two brothers.

Tonight bright lights gleamed in some of the downstairs windows and plumes of grey smoke spiralled up from the chimneys; the house wore an air of friendliness, of welcome, and it appeared to beckon beguilingly.

Katie's glance swept over it as she climbed the flight of stone steps; these cut down through the green lawn which sloped away from the flagged terrace at the front facing the road.

For a moment she paused to admire the house, and her pleasure in its appearance brought a quick, bright smile to her face. New England Colonial in style, it had a white-painted clapboard façade, dark-green shutters and a slanted, black roof.

The original house dated back to the 1880s, and although its good bones had been retained throughout, some of the interior rooms had either been restored or remodelled by her father.

Michael Byrne prided himself on his knowledge of Colonial architecture, which he had always loved, and, in fact, he had turned his boyhood passion into a profitable business a few years after leaving school. He was one of the few local contractors who had a superior knowledge of Colonial design, and because of this he had managed to find plenty of building and restoration jobs, once he had established himself in business.

Katie's father and her elder brother, Niall, kept the house looking pristine, and devoted a great deal of their free time to its care and upkeep. It seemed to Katie that they never had a paintbrush out of their hands, and even her younger brother, Finian, the intellectual with his nose permanently in a book, did occasionally put the book down to dip a brush into a pot of white paint. It struck her often that twelve-year-old Finian was now as addicted as the other two males in the family.

When Katie reached the terrace she veered to her right, headed for the side door and went into the house. A blast of lovely warm air hit her in the face as she stepped into the back hall and closed the door behind her. Once she had hung her jacket on a wall peg, she hurried down the corridor to the big family kitchen. This had always been the hub of the house, the spot where everyone congregated, and it was a congenial and comfortable room. This evening it was filled with a warm rosy glow which emanated from the old Victorian glass lamps, placed strategically around the room, and the pile of logs blazing in the big stone fireplace.

Pieces of copper and brass winked and gleamed in this lambent light, and the room was alive with the most cheerful of sounds . . . the fire crackling and sputtering in the hearth, the kettle whistling atop the stove, the clock ticking on the mantel, and, in the background, soft music playing on the radio.

And even the air itself was special, weighted with the most delicious mixture of mouthwatering smells . . . an apple pie put out to cool on a board near the sink, loaves of bread baking in the oven, an Irish stew simmering in a huge pot and emitting fragrant wafts of steam.

For a split second, Katie stood in the shadows by the door, breathing all this in, wallowing in the sheer joy of the familiar and much-loved atmosphere . . . the cosiness, the smell of her mother's appetizing cooking, the warmth after the cold meadows. But most of all she relished the feeling of safety, the sense of belonging that came from being a cherished member of her family.

Her best girlfriends were not so lucky, she knew that, which made her appreciate her own family that much more. Carly, more often than not, went home to an empty house, because her mother worked at an old people's home and kept most peculiar hours, and her father was long dead.

As for Denise, she was in much the same situation, in a sense. Her parents owned a small bar and restaurant in nearby Kent, and they were always there cooking and serving their customers at all hours of the day and night. Even so, it wasn't all that profitable, according to Denise. Katie often wondered why they bothered to keep it open; she supposed it was the only way they knew how to eke out a living.

Of the three of them, Katie had long realized that she was the one who was the most fortunate, the one who had been truly blessed. Even though her mother also worked, she did so at home, keeping the books and doing the paperwork for the Byrne family business. She had a small office at the top of the house, and so she was always there for Katie and Finian. Niall, who was nineteen, was already working with his father in the building company.

At last Katie took a step forward and moved into the kitchen. Her mother was standing near the stove with a spatula in her hand, and she straightened and glanced over her shoulder on hearing the sound of footsteps.

At the sight of her daughter, Maureen Byrne's face lit up. 'Well, there you are, Katie Mary Bridget Byrne! But late again, so I see.'

'I'm sorry, Mom, I really am. I got caught up with

another rehearsal.' Rushing across the floor, Katie flung her arms around her mother and hugged her tightly. Maureen Erin O'Keefe Byrne was the best. The very best.

Against her mother's hair, Katie whispered, 'I'll make up for it, Momma. I'll finish the cooking and set the table and do the dishes later. Just say you're not angry with me.'

Drawing away, Maureen stared into her daughter's bright blue eyes, twin reflections of her own, and said with a light laugh, 'Oh don't be so silly, mavourneen, of course I'm not mad at you. And don't worry, there's nothing much left to do, at least there's no cooking anyway. Still, you could be setting the table for me . . . that's a grand idea.'

Katie nodded and exclaimed, 'I do feel awful, Mom, letting you down this way. You've had to do everything yourself and you're not well yet. I should have been home earlier.' She bit her lip, guilt-ridden, knowing her mother was still debilitated after her six-week bout with bronchitis.

'Oh get along with you, Katie, 'tis not important, and I'm feeling much better today. Besides, Finian helped me.' Her lilting laugh rang out again. 'Why, that boy's becoming the perfect little assistant, I can tell you.'

Katie laughed with her, peered around the kitchen and asked, 'And where is our little scholar?'

'I suspect he's off watching TV in the back room. I

told him he could, once he'd peeled the vegetables, put out the garbage, and washed the pans in the sink. He's a good boy really.'

Thinking out loud, Katie murmured, 'I wonder why Finian has suddenly decided to become such a paragon of virtue, Mom? Could there be an ulterior motive?'

Maureen nodded. 'I'm sure of it, Katie. He's trying to please me for some reason.' She smiled indulgently. 'He's a nice boy, but he's brilliant, and like you I also think he's plotting something. But what that is I can't imagine. 'Tis not important, darlin'.'

'I guess not,' Katie agreed, knowing that her mother was correct about Finian's brilliance. He had an extraordinary mind for a boy of twelve, and in some ways he was old beyond his years.

Maureen, meanwhile, brought her attention back to the stove, began to stir the onions she was frying in the skillet, explaining, 'I'll pop these in the lamb stew for a bit of extra flavour, then I'll help you set the table. After that we can –' Maureen did not finish her sentence. She broke off, unexpectedly afflicted with a violent attack of coughing. Putting the spatula down quickly, she dug into her apron pocket for a tissue and covered her mouth with it.

The coughing went on for so long Katie became alarmed, and she eyed her mother with apprehension. 'Are you all right, Mom? Can I get you anything? What can I do?'

Maureen was unable to answer; she simply averted her head.

Katie cried, 'Why don't you sit down? I'll finish everything.'

Gradually Maureen became quieter, and she finally murmured, 'I'm fine, Katie darlin'. Don't fuss so.'

'Take it easy now, Momma. I can set the table by myself,' Katie answered in a more assertive voice, and immediately strode over to the Welsh dresser in the corner of the room. After taking down the white plates they used every day, she carried them over to the large square table near the picture window. The table had already been covered with a red-and-white checked cloth, and once she had deposited the plates, she went to get the other items they needed for supper.

Maureen had completely recovered, and she began to spoon the onions into the stew. Without looking up, she remarked, 'Once you've set the table, it would be nice if you made a cup of tea for us, Katie. I'd like that.'

'Yes, Mom, I will.'

Eventually Maureen walked over to the hearth and stood with her back to it, observing her daughter flitting around the kitchen. The girl was her pride and joy. She doted on her, spoiled her, yet she tempered her love with a great deal of discipline. Maureen was a hard taskmaster, especially when it came to school, homework, and household chores.

How alike we are in so many ways, especially physically, Maureen thought, yet we don't have the same character or personality. We're entirely different on that score. She's more ambitious and driven than I was, and she wants so much more than I ever did. Katie wants the world in her arms . . . she wants the stage, the bright lights, the excitement, the applause, the success, and the fame. Yes, she wants it all, and of course she'll get it, I've no doubts about that.

For a moment or two Maureen thought about her own life. I got what I wanted, thank God, so why shouldn't Katie? Her dreams and desires, hopes and aspirations are very different from mine, but hers are just as *real* as mine. I craved marriage and a family, and I was fortunate that I found a good man, a man who loved me, still loves me, and whom I love. And I have fine, healthy, drug-free, responsible children, and a comfortable home, a beautiful garden, and a happy life in the country with my family. That was *my* greatest ambition, the dream I dreamed, and it did come true. I've been so blessed since I came to America.

The year had been 1960 and she had been exactly the same age as Katie was now – just seventeen. And her sister Bridget had been nineteen. They had emigrated with their parents, Sean and Catriona O'Keefe, and settled in New York. They had been lucky in that they had all found work relatively quickly; Bridget had opted for a career in real estate and had joined a small but prestigious firm, and Maureen had become the showroom model for the great designer Pauline Trigère, who, once she had seen her, had decided her long, lean figure was ideal for the elegant and superbly-cut clothes the designer created.

Her mother, Catriona, had also gone into fashion, in her own way; she had become a saleslady on the designer floor at Bloomingdale's department store. Her father, Sean, a master craftsman, had found a job with a custom-design furniture maker down on East Tenth Street, and had rapidly made a name for himself.

Looking back now, Maureen realized she had truly fond memories of their days in Forest Hills, where they had had an apartment. They had carved out a nice life for themselves and had forever rejoiced in the fact that they had had the courage to start their lives all over again by coming to America. But as the years passed they had begun to grow weary of the city, wanted to escape the hurly-burly, yearned to find a quiet spot that was reminiscent of the Irish countryside they loved. It was while they were visiting friends, who had recently moved to northwestern Connecticut, that they recognized they had found what they called God's country. 'This is it!' her mother had said that day, and they had all agreed with Catriona. A decision was made on the spot: this was where they belonged.

It took over a year, but finally she and her parents moved to New Milford, where they had found a house that had charm and comfort and wasn't overpriced. Bridget, captivated by her wheeling and dealing in real estate, elected to remain in the city during the week, and came out to Connecticut at weekends.

She had been twenty-three when they moved to the country, and she had met Michael Byrne within the first few months of her arrival in New Milford. It had been love at first sight for both of them. He was the type of man she had always pictured in her mind's eye as being right for her ... tall, dark, nice-looking, and kind, with a loving nature. They had married when she was twenty-five and Michael twenty-seven, and it had worked. It was still working.

I got married *twenty* years ago, she suddenly thought, a small frown pinching her eyebrows together, making a tight knot above the bridge of her nose. How fast the time has flown. I can't believe I'm forty-five already. She didn't feel it, and she knew she didn't look it. She sighed, remembering all of the things she still wanted to do in her life. I must do them before I'm too old, before Michael's too old, she added, reminding herself to talk to him about that long-promised trip to Ireland.

Glancing across the kitchen, Maureen saw Katie was now standing by the stove, filling a brown teapot with water. They might be different in character and personality, but there was no question that they were mother and daughter. They were practically identical in appearance, with the same colouring and build.

Sitting down in the wing chair next to the fireplace, Maureen settled herself comfortably against the chair back, her gaze still on Katie, her middle child and her only daughter. She had always known deep within her Celtic soul that Katie was different from other children. Her daughter's personality and character were already in place the day she was born. Even as a toddler of three years Katie had known exactly who she was and what she wanted, and she had been determined. Maureen had frequently told Michael that their daughter had an unusual awareness of herself, which was manifested in an amazing inner confidence. But he knew that without having to be told; she was unusual. Yet Katie had never been bratty nor had she been precocious in an objectionable way. There had been moments when Maureen had looked at her three-year-old daughter and seen the woman she would become, so well defined was the child's personality and character.

Maybe we're all like that, Maureen thought, only perhaps it's not so obvious in every one of us. She cast her mind back to Niall's childhood, and to Finian's as well, but they had been ... well, just ordinary little boys, and certainly not particularly self-possessed or as definite and determined as their sister.

Thoughts of her sons were interrupted when Katie came over to the fireside with two cups of tea. After handing one to her mother, she sat down in the other wing chair next to the fire.

'Thank you, darlin',' Maureen said and took a sip of the tea. 'It's good,' she murmured, smiling across at her daughter. 'So, you were at the barn rehearsing, were you?'

Katie nodded. 'I think I've got my Hamlet right at last. I always thought the soliloquy was easy, but it's not, Mom. Not if you're going to do it properly.' Katie sighed and made a face. 'I say I've got it, but there's lots of room for improvement.' She nodded to herself. 'There's always room for improvement, and perfection is hard won.'

Maureen smiled, wondering whom Katie was quoting now. There were times when her girl sounded like a little old woman, especially when she'd been dipping into the classics. She asked, 'And what about the others? How're Carly and Denise doing?'

'They're good, Momma, *I* know that. The trouble is, *they* don't. I *think* I'm getting them to believe in themselves more. It's all to do with self-confidence.'

Which you've never lacked, Maureen thought, but said, 'You should have brought them back to supper, Katie. There's always enough for everyone, and especially when it's Irish stew. Your father says I always make enough to feed Cox's army.'

'I thought about asking them, but I decided it'd be too much for you. You've been so sick.'

'I'm much better, darlin'.'

The door at the other end of the kitchen flew open,

and Finian came rumbling in. 'Hi, there, Katie!' he cried.

'Hi, Fin.'

'I prefer Finian,' the twelve-year-old announced.

'Oh, sorry,' Katie replied, hiding her amusement. This was something new with him.

'That's okay. But Finian *is* my name.' He glanced at his mother. 'Do you need me to help again, Mom?'

She shook her head. 'No, Fin . . . er, Finian. But thanks for asking. Do you want a mug of tea?'

'No thanks.' He shook his head and went over to the refrigerator. 'A Coke'll be great.'

'What about your homework, Finian?' his mother asked.

He swung around and gave her a long look. 'I've done it.'

Slightly puzzled and frowning at him, Maureen asked, '*When?*'

'Just now. When I was in the back room.' He shrugged nonchalantly, explained, 'I didn't have a lot of it tonight. Just math.'

Nodding, Maureen gave him the benefit of a pleased smile and drank her tea.

Katie sat bolt upright in the chair looking at her mother askance. 'Am I stupid!' she cried in a shrill tone. 'I left my school bag at the barn! Oh Mom! My homework! What am I going to *do*?' As she spoke she jumped up. 'I'll just have to go back.'

'Not now, Katie!' Maureen exclaimed. 'It's far too dark already, and you know very well I won't let you walk across the fields alone, so you can forget that!'

'But I need my books, Mom,' Katie wailed, her expression woeful.

'Yes, I know you do. But you'll just have to wait for Niall to get home. He'll go with you. Better still, he'll run you down to the barn in his pickup. That'll be the quickest. Fin, go and turn off the stew, please, and I'd better take the bread out of the oven.'

'It's *Finian*, Mom,' the boy muttered. 'My name's Finian, like in *Finian's Rainbow*. That's a musical.'

Maureen stared at him, wondering what he would come out with next.

Chapter Four

Katie kept herself absolutely still, remained quiet as she sat next to her brother in his pickup truck. She felt certain he was annoyed because he had to drive her to the old barn, so that she could retrieve her school books.

When he had arrived home from work a short while ago, he hadn't appeared to be put out by their mother's request, and had agreed readily enough to run her to the barn. But he had been totally silent as they had driven away from the house and headed in the direction of the highway.

Several times Katie stole a glance at Niall, wondering whether to start chatting or not. Usually he was talkative, discussed all sorts of things and confided in her, as she did in him. He was only two years older than her and they had always been close when they were growing up, best friends. The two of them had treated Finian as the baby, being either condescending or indifferent. Until he had become too clever by far to ignore. Although they had eventually accepted him, treated Finian amiably enough, they had never really let him in, and he hadn't seemed to care, much to their surprise.

Katie and Niall knew each other inside out, and now, as she cast another glance at him, she realized how preoccupied he looked. His normally smiling face was set in serious lines as he drove on at a steady speed, and she wondered what was going on in his head. Perhaps he was having trouble with his girlfriend, Jennifer Wilson. Women were attracted to Niall, usually threw themselves at him, and no wonder. He was as handsome as their father with his black hair, green eyes, and angular, masculine face. Niall's features were well defined, as were their father's, and their very macho looks harked back to their Byrne ancestors, who had come over from Ireland in the nineteenth century to settle in Connecticut.

It was Niall who finally broke the silence and interrupted her thoughts when he said, 'You're very quiet tonight, Katie.'

Startled, she sat up straighter, and exclaimed, with a small laugh, 'I could say the same about you, Niall! And you're certainly looking serious. Is there something wrong?'

'No, no, nothing . . . I was just thinking . . . about you.'

'What about me?'

'Mostly your plans to go to New York next year. Do you really think Mom and Dad'll let you?'

'Of course they will.' She half turned in her seat, stared at her brother in the dim light, and went on swiftly, 'Have they said something to you? I mean about *not* letting me go? Come on, tell me, Niall. We've never had any secrets before.'

When he remained silent, she said in a softer, pleading tone, 'Please tell me.'

'They haven't said a word, honest,' Niall responded truthfully. 'But I know they're not too happy about the idea.'

'Why not?'

'Come on, Katie, don't be dumb, that's not like you. It's obvious. They think you're too young to go off by yourself to the big city.' He sneaked a look at her out of the corner of his eye, then brought his gaze back to the road. 'I'm sure they want you to put it off for a couple of years.'

'Mom's never said anything like that to me, and neither has Dad. And why are you suddenly bringing it up tonight?' she demanded, sounding heated all of a sudden.

'I guess I wouldn't have said anything if you hadn't asked me if something was wrong. I was just being honest with you, because that's what I was thinking about . . . you going off to New York. And I suppose it came into my mind because we're on our way to the barn, where you spend most of your time playing actress.'

'I understand. But hey, listen up, Niall . . . I'll be with Carly and Denise in New York. And don't forget that Aunt Bridget's there, and we'll be staying with her.'

Niall exclaimed, 'And for how long? Aunt Bridget's got a big job in real estate and a life of her own. She's not going to want the lot of you under her feet . . . at least not for very long.'

A fast denial sprang to Katie's lips but she thought better of voicing it. Instead she took a deep breath and settled back in the seat, wondering if her parents *had* discussed this matter with him. But if they had, why wouldn't he admit it? He had never held things back in the past. Finally, she asked in a low voice, 'Tell me the truth, like you always have, Niall. Did Mom and Dad talk to you about my going to New York?'

'No, they didn't, Katie. Honest to God they haven't mentioned it. I'm only telling you what I personally think. I know what they're like. They're both very protective of you, and they're right to be. I feel the same way myself.'

'Traitor,' she muttered. 'You've never mentioned that before, and you always said I should go to the academy once I graduate high school. Now, suddenly, you're singing a different tune. All I've ever wanted to do is act, you know it's my life.'

Niall let out a small sigh. He might have known she would adopt this attitude; he was beginning to wish he'd never said anything to her, never voiced his thoughts.

'Let's not quarrel, honey,' he soothed gently. 'Look, I'm sorry I brought it up. Forget it. Forget I ever said anything. When the time comes I'm sure they'll agree, and let you go, especially if Aunt Bridget backs you up. And you'll be with Denise and Carly, and that'll help as well. After all, it's not as if you're going to New York by yourself.'

'No, I'm not, and I hope Mom and Dad *will* agree,' Katie answered, and began to relax. Also, knowing it was better to let the matter drop, she adroitly changed the subject. 'How's Jennifer? You haven't mentioned her lately.'

'I'm sort of cooling it,' he muttered, and then laughed in an odd way. 'She's getting to be a bit of a pest, if you want the truth, Katie. Can you believe she wants to get married?'

'*To you?*' Katie asked, her voice rising.

'Who else?'

'You're too young, Niall.'

'You bet I am. Anyway, Jennifer's nice enough, don't get me wrong, I just don't want to start getting serious with her. She's not the girl for me. I haven't found *her* yet.'

For a split second Katie was silent, and then she murmured, 'Funny, I thought you had once.'

Niall did not answer her but his hands tensed on the wheel.

Eventually Katie said, 'I used to think you were crazy

43

about Denise last year. The look on your face was . . . *unmistakable*. I was sure you had fallen for her. I was positive you'd finally seen the light, discovered what she was really like, what a special person she is.'

'I guess I had . . . The problem was with Denise, not me. She's hell bent on being an actress, having a career, going to New York with you and Carly. That's what she wants, not me or any other guy, as far as I can see. When I was taking her out last year, did she ever mention me? Say anything to you?'

Katie shook her head. 'No, I've told you that before. All she said was that you were nice.' Katie frowned. 'And I did repeat that to you at the time.'

Niall murmured, 'I guess you did. Denise doesn't want a boyfriend, at least not right now. What she wants is fame in capital letters. Her name in lights on a theatre.'

'I think so,' Katie agreed. 'But Denise *is* so beautiful and sweet, and Jennifer Wilson can't hold a candle to her . . .'

'I know that.'

Niall slowed down as they came to the entrance to Ted Matthews's land, where the old barn was located. He turned in and headed across the flat barren area, then rolled slowly down the hill to the dell at the bottom. It was here the barn sat nestled against a backdrop of trees.

As the pickup truck drew closer to the barn, Niall

said, 'Denise and Carly must still be here, Katie. The lights are on.'

Katie was not surprised, and she explained, 'They often stay here long after I'm gone. They like to rehearse, work together, and sometimes they do their homework, Niall. There's nothing much for them at home, with everyone working.'

'Yeah, I know.' Niall brought the pickup truck to a stop in front of the barn, and braked.

Katie opened the door and jumped down to the ground. It was cold and she shivered, huddled into her jacket as she ran forward. When she reached the barn door she was surprised to see it stood open.

Pulling it back, she went in, smiling and exclaiming, 'Carly! Denise! What's going on? Why's the door open on a cold night like this?'

No one answered. The barn was empty.

Taken aback, Katie stood for a moment frozen to the spot. Her eyes scanned the room swiftly, and straight away she noticed the disarray. Two straight-backed chairs had been turned over, lay on their sides. The shade on the old pottery lamp was lopsided, looked as if it had been hit with force, and the blue cloth on the table where they drank their Cokes had been pulled to one side, so that it hung off the edge of the table. As her eyes continued to scan the barn she saw their coats hanging on the wall pegs, and on the floor, nearby, were their school bags. And hers as well, although she didn't remember putting it there. She was sure she had thrown it in a corner, haphazardly. All three were neatly lined up, side by side. How odd.

Sudden fear clutched at Katie.

She swung her head as Niall came inside.

'Where's Denise? Carly?' he asked, and automatically took hold of her arm, immediately noticing the overturned chairs, and other signs of disruption.

Katie swung to face him. 'I don't know.' She bit her lip. 'They must be somewhere . . . outside . . .'

'Without their coats?' he frowned, staring hard at her.

For a moment Katie could not speak. The fear inside her seemed to intensify and her legs suddenly felt weak, as if they would give way beneath her. All of her instincts were alerted to trouble, and in a shaking voice she said slowly, 'There's something wrong, Niall.'

'Yep, there is.' Her brother took a deep breath, went on: 'We'd better go outside and look for them. They must be around here somewhere. It's very dark, but I've got a flashlight in the truck.'

'And there's one in the drawer of the table. I kept it for emergencies,' she explained.

'Then get it, Katie, and let's go.'

Chapter Five

It was chilly and damp outside and darker than ever. Heavy clouds obscured the opaque moon, and an ominous feeling floated in the air. It was palpable, something Katie felt she could reach out and touch.

She was taut and fearful. Her mind raced; dire thoughts rushed unchecked through her head. Nothing was normal any more, and her instincts told her something bad had happened here. Something evil. A strange sense of doom, a foreboding, persisted even though she tried to push it away.

The dampness seeped through her jacket into her bones, and she shivered as she stood waiting for her brother. Niall had gone to get the flashlight from his pickup, and she was clutching the one she had taken from the barn. Her mother had given it to her a long time ago, and Katie was glad she had thought to replace the batteries recently.

Unexpectedly, Niall's headlights flashed on and she started in surprise. The area in front of the barn where she was standing was suddenly illuminated, and at least she could see better. Niall ran towards her, waving his flashlight, and when he was by her side he took hold of her arm protectively. In a rush of words he said, 'Listen to me, Katie. We're going to stick close together. Real close. I don't want you wandering around here on your own. Okay?'

'Yes. And anyway that's the last thing I'd do,' she answered, her voice low, and she edged closer to her brother. There was a hesitation on her part, then she ventured, 'There are only two possibilities, Niall. They either left in a great hurry or they were taken.'

'*Taken*,' he repeated, and frowned, his slate-green eyes suddenly troubled. 'Who'd take them? And where?'

'I don't know. But what we *do* know is that there was an intruder, or intruders, because things have been moved around, disrupted in there.' She half turned, nodded her head at the barn. 'Carly and Denise might not be here at all, you know. They could be far away by now. If they've been . . . taken. *Kidnapped*.'

'Jaysus, what're you saying, Katie?' Niall muttered, sounding exactly like Grandfather Sean, whom he loved and emulated. 'Why would anyone take Denise and Carly? What are you getting at?'

'There're a lot of weirdos around, you know that as well as I do. Crazed druggies. Sex fiends. Whackos. Serial killers.'

Niall gaped at her, obviously startled by her words; a mixture of concern and fear washed across his face.

'Let's not waste any more time. We'll look at the back of the barn first.' As he spoke he hurried her towards the stands of trees that shaded the ramshackle building on its north side.

Katie said, 'They might have made for Ted Matthews's house, Niall.'

'Yeah, that's a possibility.'

Together they walked around the back of the barn, waving their flashlights from side to side, directing the beams of light at the trees and bushes, calling, 'Carly! Denise!'

No one answered and there was nothing untoward to be seen. No sign of trampled grass, broken twigs, smashed bushes or footprints in the earth. And certainly there was no sign of the girls.

At one moment, Niall paused, swung Katie to face him. He stared at her. 'We both believe somebody entered the barn. Unexpectedly. Uninvited. Whoever it was either took the girls by force, or frightened them so badly they fled. Correct?'

Katie nodded. 'And if they ran out, were really scared, they'd probably go to Ted's farm. It's not that close, but it is nearer than our house or their own homes.'

Niall was puzzled. 'Why wouldn't they run up the hill to the highway?'

'No, no, they'd never do that,' Katie responded quickly, shaking her head. 'It's tough running uphill. They probably rushed outside and just ran straight ahead, right into the wood facing the barn door. Once they were through the wood they'd be on flat ground all the way to Ted's farm. It's easy to run across fields quickly, they'd be there in no time.'

'You're right about that, so we'll search the wood next. It could be that Denise and Carly are hiding in there, afraid to come out. If we don't find them, we can call Ted from the pay phone on the highway.'

Katie took hold of her brother's hand. She was nervous, agitated inside. All of a sudden, a surge of apprehension flooded her and she felt slightly sick. She was certain something had gone wrong after she had left, and she prayed that Carly and Denise were all right, that they were safe.

Niall gripped her hand firmly as they made their way to the front of the building, where his pickup was parked, and went into the wood opposite. It was not large, but it was densely packed with trees, and very dark. The path through the trees was cut so narrowly it was necessary to walk single file; Niall insisted Katie went ahead of him so that his eyes were on her at all times. He wasn't prepared to take any chances.

Once they were moving along the path at a steady pace, Katie called out, 'Carly! Denise? It's me, Katie! Are you in here?'

Niall pitched his voice even louder. 'Denise? Carly? Where are you?'

There was no response.

The two of them kept to the path, waving their flashlights from side to side, peering about in the dim light. Suddenly, Katie stopped and held up her hand. She said quietly, over her shoulder, 'Did you hear that, Niall?'

'What?'

'A rustling sound just ahead of us.'

'No, I didn't. It was probably an animal. A deer.'

Katie's breath caught in her throat, and she held herself absolutely still as she remembered the dark flash caught on the periphery of her vision earlier that day. Near the rhododendron bushes on the hillside when she was going home. I shouldn't have left them alone in the barn, I should have made them leave with me. But they often stay late, that's nothing new. As long as they were at the barn they had each other for company, instead of being at home alone.

Had there been someone lurking near the rhododendron bushes? She swallowed hard. Her mouth went dry and she wondered if the intruder had been there on the hill this afternoon. If that was so, she had passed very close to him. Or them. She shivered.

'I can hear something now,' Niall muttered, leaning closer, putting his hand on her shoulder.

To Katie, the disturbance, whatever it was, seemed much louder, clearer, and it sounded as though somebody was plunging through the undergrowth, charging forward, and in the process rustling leaves and breaking branches. If it was an animal it was a large one.

'Who's there?' Niall shouted.

'Carly, Denise, it's me! And Niall,' Katie yelled through hands cupped around her mouth.

No one responded but the noise instantly stopped.

There were no sounds at all, only silence.

The two of them did not move for a moment or two. They stood waiting, listening, straining their ears. Nothing moved, not a leaf stirred. The wood was wrapped in total stillness.

Katie took a deep breath – and a step forward.

Niall followed her, even more disturbed. But not wishing to alarm Katie further, he murmured reassuringly, 'It was a deer, honey. Or a stag. Yes, a stag, that's more like it, and that's all it was, Katie. An animal.' Though he spoke confidently, he wasn't sure he believed his own words.

Katie certainly didn't; she had other ideas altogether. Taking several more deep breaths, steadying herself, she stepped out purposefully.

Katie saw Carly first. She was waving her flashlight from side to side when the cold, white beam of light fell across Carly's body. Her friend was in a small clearing to one side of the path, near a clump of bushes. She was stretched out on her back and lay very still.

'It's Carly,' Katie called and ran forward, driven by

anxiety, shining the light on her friend's face. Instantly she recoiled in horror. Carly's face was covered in so much blood her features were barely visible.

Katie screamed, called Niall's name, and remained rooted to the spot, unable to move.

When Niall reached her she grabbed hold of him and shouted in a very loud, unnatural voice, '*Carly's covered in blood*. Oh, God! Oh, God! She can't be dead! Can she? Who's done this terrible thing to her?' Katie leaned against her brother and the uncontrollable shaking began. She could barely stand up, thought her legs would buckle, and she pushed her face against his shoulder, wanting to block out Carly's bloody face.

Niall levelled his own flashlight on Carly, and he instantly looked away, as sickened and horrified as Katie.

After a moment, he said quietly, 'I want to look at Carly more closely. Can you stand on your own, Katie? Let me take you over there, you can rest against the tree. Okay?'

'Okay,' Katie answered through her sobbing.

Niall had to move his sister almost bodily, but once he had her leaning against a tree he hurried across the clearing to Carly. The stench of blood assailed him, and he averted his face, gulped air, and somehow managed to hold onto his composure. At last he bent over her, and realized that the blood was coming from her head, oozing out from her hairline, running down over her forehead and cheeks. It suddenly occurred to him there was very little damage, if any, to her face. She had obviously been hit on the head a number of times. Her eyes were closed, but now he noticed a faint pulse in her neck, and she was breathing, if only shallowly. She was alive, he was almost positive of that. Niall fumbled for her wrist. A faint pulse confirmed that she wasn't dead.

Straightening, Niall stepped back onto the path. Looking across at Katie, who was still clinging to the tree, he said, 'Carly's alive. I'm going to see if Denise is anywhere nearby.'

'Thank God.' Katie began to sob again, but this time it was with relief.

Within the space of several seconds Niall found Denise. She was about fifty feet away, and she too lay on her back on a patch of dry grass, off to one side of the path.

'Denise,' he murmured, kneeling down next to her, shining his flashlight on her face. He drew back at once, and his throat constricted, tears leaping into his eyes. A trembling took hold of him, and he knew even without taking her pulse that she was no longer alive. Those soft velvet brown eyes which he knew so well were wide and staring, and empty of life. Death was on her.

An involuntary sob bubbled in his throat, and he stood up swiftly, filled with sudden overwhelming grief. The tears ran down his cheeks unchecked and he wiped them away roughly with the back of his hand. When he looked at Denise again he saw for the first time that her skirt was pulled up to her waist and her tights were ripped. Niall snapped his eyes shut and pressed his hand to his mouth, filled with fury. Denise had been raped. *Bastard. Son of a bitch*, he muttered under his breath and he began to sob. Who had done this vile, unspeakable thing to her? Who had raped and killed her? Lovely, innocent Denise. Only seventeen. A whole life to live snuffed out. Just like that. *Bastard.*

Niall wanted to pull her skirt down, cover her with his jacket, give her a little respect and dignity in death. But he knew better than to do that. Trying to take control of his swimming senses, Niall walked back down the path on trembling legs, wondering how to break the news to Katie.

Quietly, holding his emotions in check, Niall said, 'Denise . . . she's gone, Katie, she's been . . . killed.' His face was contorted by pain and a terrible anger filled his voice.

A wracking sob broke free from Katie and she clutched at him. 'No, Niall! No! It can't be. Oh God, no.'

He wrapped his arms around her and held her close. After a moment, Katie whispered, 'I want to see her.'

'No, you don't.'

'I do. I must.' She broke free of his embrace and ran down the path, the spot of light from the flashlight bobbing around in the dark as she ran. She did not stop until she reached Denise's body. Her eyes widened, clouded with grief. She gazed down at her friend, and then she turned away, bending double, wrapping her arms around herself, consumed by a searing pain. Tears coursed down her cheeks and she cried out, 'Not Denise, oh God, not Denise! It's not fair! *It's just not fair.*'

Chapter Six

Katie screeched to a standstill, pulled on the brake and jumped out of the pickup truck. Sprinting to the pay phone in the rest area, she grabbed the receiver off the hook and dialled 911.

Immediately, the emergency operator came onto the line and Katie asked for the ambulance service. Before she could even blink she was talking to the Litchfield County Dispatcher for Fire and Ambulance in the Litchfield area.

'I need an ambulance! My friend's injured! It's a matter of life and death!' Katie exclaimed, her voice echoing with urgency and anxiety. 'She's been beaten over the head. She's bleeding. But she's still alive. *Just.* Please send an ambulance. As quickly as possible.'

'Where are you calling from?'

'I'm at a pay phone on Route 7. Up above Malvern, between New Milford and South Kent,' she swiftly answered, and then gave her the exact details of where she was.

'What's your name?' the female dispatcher asked.

'Katie Byrne. From Malvern.'

The dispatcher asked a few more questions, which Katie answered as precisely as she could, and then, voice trembling, she told the dispatcher, 'My other friend, Denise . . . well, she's dead.' Her sentence finished in sobs.

'Hang in there, Katie,' the dispatcher said in a kindly tone. 'And hold on. I'm putting you through to the state police. Give them all the details, tell them everything you know. The ambulance is being dispatched now.'

Katie stood clutching the phone, and a minute later a man's voice announced, 'State Police Dispatcher, Troop L, Litchfield. Tell me exactly what happened, Katie.'

'One of my friends has been badly injured. The other one is . . . dead,' she responded quietly, trying to be as calm and concise as possible. 'My brother and I found them a while ago. About fifteen minutes ago. But we don't know what happened. Or how it happened. We need an ambulance for Carly.'

'It's already on its way. Give me your exact location, Katie.'

Katie did so, shivering in the cold wind, thinking that she was living a nightmare. She couldn't believe she was on this phone talking to the Connecticut State Police about Carly and Denise. Only a few hours ago, at four o'clock, the three of them had been laughing together in the barn, and planning their future in New York.

The state police dispatcher said, 'Please wait there,

Katie. Stay where you are. Don't leave. Responding state troopers will arrive as soon as they can. There are several patrolling in the area. It won't be long before one of them gets to you.'

'I'll wait on the highway. At the entrance to the road leading down to the barn,' Katie told him, and replaced the receiver. She leaned forward, rested her forehead against the phone, and closed her eyes for a moment, willing herself to be strong. And willing Carly to live. Please God, don't let her die, she whispered silently. Let her live. Fight, Carly, fight.

Still shivering and turning up the collar of her jacket, she ran over to the truck and climbed in. Instantly, she jumped out and raced back to the pay phone, remembering that Niall had told her to call their mother.

Dropping the quarter in, she dialled her home. 'It's me, Mom,' Katie said when Maureen answered.

'Where are you both?' Maureen asked, sounding put out, even cross. 'Your father'll be home any minute now, and I'll be wanting to serve supper. Finian's starving.'

'Mom, something's happened,' Katie began, and her voice faltered. She was unable to go on.

'What is it, Katie? What's wrong?' Maureen demanded, at once alerted to a serious problem, since Katie wasn't one to exaggerate.

'It's something . . . *terrible*, Momma. Carly's been badly injured, and Denise . . .' Katie stopped. She swallowed hard, but her voice choked up as she whispered,

'Mom, Denise is dead. Somebody raped her, and they killed her . . . and he really hurt Carly. It was after I left the barn this afternoon.'

'Oh my God! Oh my God! No, Katie! Those poor girls. Oh Lord, where are you? Are you all right? Where's Niall? Let me speak to him!' Maureen cried, her voice rising shrilly, sudden panic and shock now getting the better of her.

'He's not here, Mom. He stayed with Carly in the wood. That's where it happened . . . the attacks on . . . the girls.' Katie put a hand over her mouth to stifle her sobs, but she didn't succeed very well.

'Listen to me, Katie,' Maureen whispered, but it was a harsh whisper. 'Get Niall on the phone.'

'I *can't*, Mom! He's looking after Carly. He stayed with her just in case the attacker came back. He sent me to the pay phone on the highway to call for an ambulance. They put me through to the police and now they're all coming, bringing help.'

'Katie, Katie, *listen* to me. I want you to come home. *And immediately*. I don't want you there. Maybe it's not safe. We don't know who did this . . . the person could still be around, couldn't he? Maybe even looking for you. It was always the three of you, everyone knows that. And perhaps *he* does. Come home at once. Your father will be here in a moment or so, and he'll drive down and pick Niall up. Go and get into the pickup, and get yourself home at once. Do you hear me, Katie Byrne?'

'Yes, Mom, I do. But I can't. I'd like to, but I have to stay here. The barn can't be seen from the road, you know that, and so I have to wait for the ambulance and the police. I'll come home once Carly is in the ambulance and going to the hospital.'

'Please come home,' Maureen begged.

'I'm okay, Mom. Honest. I'll be home soon,' she promised and hung up.

Katie drove down the hill, parked in front of the barn and hurried towards the wood, clutching her flashlight. She walked a few feet down the narrow path and took a deep breath. 'Niall! Niall! I'm back!' she shouted at the top of her lungs, pitching her voice as far as she could, as she had trained herself to do for the stage.

In the distance, faintly, she heard his response. 'Okay, Katie. It's okay, I hear you.'

Swinging around, she returned to the truck and once again drove up the hill to wait for the ambulance and the police. Her head had begun to pound, and she felt sick again, as though she were going to throw up. She took a number of deep breaths, as she so often did when she stood in the wings, willing her stage fright to go away. This nauseous feeling wasn't caused by stage fright, though, but by genuine fear. What if the killer was looking for her, as her mother had suggested he could be?

She sat waiting on the highway, but she didn't have

long to wait. Within the space of five minutes she heard a siren, and a moment later a state trooper's car came into view. It raced along the highway at breakneck speed.

Since the state trooper was coming up Route 7, from the direction of Gaylordsville, he had to park on the opposite side of the road; he got out and hurried over to the pickup truck.

Katie rolled down her window and peered out at him, her face strained, her eyes bleak with pain.

'Are you Katie Byrne?' he asked.

'Yes, I am. Is the ambulance coming?'

'It should be here real fast. I was in the immediate vicinity, and answered the radio call at once. Where's the crime scene located *exactly*?'

'I'll show you.' Katie opened the door, jumped down and led the trooper across the short stretch of barren land. Pointing down the hill, she said, 'It's in the wood immediately opposite that old barn down there. My brother Niall's waiting in the wood. He thought he'd better stay with Carly, to protect her. Just in case the attacker was still around here –' Katie stopped. Her voice was wobbling and tears had welled in her eyes.

'Take it easy, Katie,' the trooper said.

Gulping, she nodded, and endeavoured to get control of herself. 'Shall I wait for the ambulance while you go down the hill? To show them the way?'

'You won't have to do that. It's about to arrive,' the state trooper answered, cocking his head at the sound of screaming sirens. The highway was filled with whirling red lights as the ambulance shot along the road, coming to a halt behind the state trooper's car.

Katie made for Niall's truck and got inside. She was chilled to the bone and unexpectedly exhausted. She watched as the trooper sprinted over to the ambulance and spoke to the driver, pointed down the hill and then went and got into his own car. The ambulance began to move.

Katie followed the ambulance.

The state trooper was immediately behind her in his police car, his red light turned on, his siren shrilling loud and clear.

After pointing the way through the wood, Katie stood to one side and watched as the medics raced down the narrow path, carrying a stretcher.

Within minutes they were returning with Carly, and she was still alive. It's a miracle, Katie thought. She had been teetering on the edge of despair, certain her friend could not last. But Carly had hung in there. She made it. Oh God, thank you, thank you.

The medics were huddled around Carly, checking her vital signs before putting her in the ambulance.

Katie clung to Niall; the two of them were standing together near the barn, just a few feet away from Carly. How pale she was, Katie thought. White as bleached bone, and so still. Still as death. But the medics had given the thumbs up sign a moment ago, and one of them had said, 'She's breathing.'

'She *is* going to live, isn't she?' Katie asked the medic who had just helped to lift the stretcher into the ambulance.

He glanced over his shoulder at Katie and nodded. 'I think so. I hope so.'

The ambulance left with Carly, and Katie took hold of Niall's hand, held it tightly in hers. He looked at her quickly, and asked, 'Did you call Mom?'

'Yes. I told her what's happened. She was distraught. I think I'd better go home now, Niall. I told her I would, once Carly was on the way to the hospital.'

'You'll have to stay here with me, Katie. The state trooper needs to talk to us when he gets back from looking at Denise's body –' Niall paused, listened. 'Sounds like sirens again. More state troopers arriving, I guess.'

Katie seemed uncomprehending for a moment.

Niall stared back at her, his eyes narrowing. 'Denise has been murdered,' he said, sorrow echoing in his voice. 'This place is going to be teeming with police in the next half hour.'

Chapter Seven

This was the type of crime he detested. Defenceless young girls mercilessly beaten and murdered. Easy prey, innocent prey, Mac MacDonald thought bleakly as he sidestepped the yellow police tape two state troopers were placing around the wood, to cordon off the crime scene and safeguard it.

John 'Mac' MacDonald, commander of the Major Crime Squad of the Connecticut State Police out of Litchfield, had long ago discovered that crimes of this nature inevitably turned him into a raging bull inside. But he knew better than to unleash his fury. He had schooled himself for years to exercise total self-control and discipline. But that didn't mean he held the rage in check all the time. Most weekends found him hitting a punching bag in his basement exercise room, imagining who the recipients of his intense pummelling might possibly be. It was a release of a kind for him, yet he was aware it did nothing to stop the senseless murder and rape of young women. He had two teenage daughters himself, and he worried about them constantly, drilled them relentlessly about being street-smart and careful. Images of their lovely young faces leapt into his head, but he pushed them away. He could not afford to be distracted. He needed total concentration. He must think about one thing only: *solving this case quickly.*

Mac paused to speak to one of the state troopers handling the yellow tape. 'You were the first here, weren't you,' he stated, his manner chatty, friendly.

The state trooper nodded. 'Yeah, I was, Lieutenant. I made certain the crime scene wasn't contaminated in any way, and the medics were careful, they didn't destroy its integrity either. They went straight in, got the injured girl and came straight out. One, two, three, just like that.'

'And the other girl was dead when you arrived.' This was again a statement, not a question.

'Yeah. Poor kid.' The trooper shook his head and his eyes were suddenly sad. 'What a lousy thing!' he muttered and half grimaced, turned away.

Mac sighed under his breath as he moved on towards the wood. He knew how the trooper felt. He also knew that as long as he lived he would always react strongly to violence against women. It made him want to teach the cowards who perpetrated these outrages a lesson they would never forget. Some son of a bitch had done a really foul job on two young women earlier, and the fury Mac felt brought a hard glint to his grey eyes, and his expression was grim and as cold as steel. He never let any other emotion show on his narrow, craggy face; that's why they called him Mac the Knife behind his back.

Adopting a brisker pace, Mac walked down the narrow path that led to the middle of the wood where he knew a seventeen-year-old girl lay dead.

He was also well aware that Doctor Allegra Marsh, the Medical Examiner, was already on the scene. She had arrived a short while before he had, according to two of his detectives who were in the barn. Also, her dark-green Cherokee jeep was parked next to the black van he knew came from her office.

Mac liked Allegra Marsh, admired her. For one thing, there was no bullshit about her. She always called it the way she saw it at a crime scene, and she was very forthright in every other way. They had worked on countless cases together, and she had gone the distance for him, gone beyond the call of duty, in a sense.

All of this aside, she was the most brilliant forensic scientist and pathologist he had ever known and worked with. In her own way, she was also a detective, just as he was; they simply used different methods. They were good friends, but it stopped there, even though he was long widowed and she was single. With Allegra there were certain boundaries, ones which he knew not to cross, although sometimes ... Well, that was another story.

Even if he hadn't been told she was here, the intense

beams of light from her battery-operated spotlights announced her formidable presence in the wood.

When he was about five feet away, Mac came to a standstill, and said, 'Not a happy night, Allegra.'

The Medical Examiner was kneeling on the ground with one of the forensic team, and she glanced up at him and shook her blonde head. 'Hi, Mac. And you're right, not happy at all.' She sighed and added, 'It was some angry man who paid a visit here earlier tonight, no doubt about that.'

'What've you found?'

'Death by strangulation. Manual strangulation. Her larynx is crushed. Very intense bruising around the neck area. A violent attack. And she was raped, but you most likely know that from your team.'

'Yeah, I do.' He was staring down at the body, and he muttered, 'Oh God, she was so young . . .'

'And a virgin,' Allegra said.

'She was?'

'Yes, I believe so. Obviously, I'll know for certain once I do the autopsy. But there was blood mixed in with the seminal fluid. I have a number of DNA samples from her body. Semen, blood, which I believe to be hers, hair follicles. Skin and flesh from underneath her fingernails. More hair. Different hair. And this.'

Allegra showed him the large tweezers in her right hand, which she generally used to lift off DNA samples from a body. They now held a cigarette stub. 'We just found this beauty partially hidden under her body.' She placed it carefully in the glassine envelope her assistant was now holding, and went on, 'I'm certain the girl was not sitting around here smoking, Mac. She was running for her life. This was an oversight on the assailant's part. He tossed it away and forgot it.' She sat back on her heels. 'Saliva, Mac, the perp's saliva. I hope.' Her dark eyes sparkled at this thought.

He nodded. 'Any idea yet of what time she died?'

'In the vicinity of six, six-fifteen. I'll be able to place the time more accurately, pinpoint it, after the postmortem. But it wasn't much later than six-twenty, I'm fairly sure.' As she was speaking, Allegra was putting items away in one of the two metal medical cases she favoured. Then turning to her assistant, she said, 'Let's get her into the body bag, Ken.'

'Right away,' he responded and reached for the bag nearby. He knelt closer to Allegra and they lifted and manipulated the body until it was inside the bag, and then Ken zipped it. They both rose at the same time; together they picked up the bag and put it on the stretcher.

Allegra said, 'Thanks, Ken, I'll send Cody to help you bring the body out. Afterwards you can dismantle the lights.'

'I will,' he said, and began to pack his own medical bag.

Allegra rolled off her latex gloves, balled them and put them in one of her metal cases, which she then picked up. Mac grabbed the other one, and the two of them walked away from the crime scene, hurrying down the path in single file.

Mac said, 'Not a very good crime scene for us . . .'

'I've seen better, Mac, but it's not *that* bad. The medics didn't disturb anything, and we've been scrupulous.'

'I know you have. Let's face it, though, a wood is not the easiest place to find clues to a brutal murder.'

'True. And the ground is very hard at the moment. There'll be no footprints. Have you spoken to the brother and sister in the barn?'

'Yeah, I did, but only briefly. I got here after you did, Allegra. The girl is shell-shocked, yet despite that she's very precise, clear about things. There's not much she or her brother can tell us about the attack, since they arrived here after it happened.'

They did not speak for a few seconds, just ploughed on through the wood until they came to the area in front of the barn. It was crowded with cars and police, and they dodged around them, walked over to Allegra's jeep at a brisk pace.

Mac suddenly said, 'Katie told me that she caught a flash of something dark when she was leaving this afternoon. It was about ten to five and already dusk.

She was going up that hill over there, thought she saw something and stopped, looked over at the clump of rhododendron bushes. She says she wondered what she had *almost* seen. Then she decided it had to be an animal, a deer most likely, and she didn't bother to investigate further. But I've got one of my men and a state trooper up there now, looking around.'

Allegra stopped, turned to Mac, and frowned as she exclaimed, 'It's just as well she didn't go over to the bushes, because it could have been the perp loitering. And he might well have beaten her up also.'

'Yes, you're right about that. I'm hoping that when Carly Smith recovers consciousness she'll be able to tell us what happened here today, and who it was. She's an eye witness, our only eye witness, and we're obviously banking on her.'

Allegra stared at him.

Noticing at once the concern spreading across her face, he asked quickly, 'What's wrong?'

The Medical Examiner was silent, then finally she said in a low voice, 'From what I understand, that poor girl took some terrible blows to the head. I'm praying for her recovery, but those head injuries could prove to be extremely serious.'

'What are you getting at, Allegra? Are you saying she might die?' Mac asked, his voice rising.

Allegra hesitated fractionally, then said, 'No, not that necessarily. But she could be left in a coma.'

'Oh shit!'

'Let's hope for the best, especially for the girl's sake,' Allegra murmured, and put her metal case in the back of the jeep.

Chapter Eight

Michael Byrne drove at breakneck speed up Route 7, his foot pressed hard on the accelerator. He was filled with tension and anxiety, and these feelings showed in his taut face and worried eyes, which were intent on the road ahead.

How he regretted now that he had been caught up with a client, going over extensive plans for a house he was currently remodelling. His appointment with Bill Turnbull had become not only involved but interminable. It had dragged on and on, had made him arrive home much later than usual, to be greeted on the back doorstep by Maureen, who had obviously been waiting anxiously for him.

He had known at once that she was distraught, and as she blurted out the story through her tears he had turned ice-cold inside. He could not stand the thought that his daughter might have been at risk, in harm's way.

The moment Maureen had finished speaking, he had told her to go inside and lock the door. And then he had rushed over to his jeep, shouting over his shoulder that he was going to the barn to get Katie and Niall.

The only thing he could think of, as he had pulled out, was that Katie was safe. Not injured. Not dead. But safe. It was a miracle of sorts. She was always at the barn rehearsing and if she hadn't left early today, to go home to help her mother, she would more than likely have been a victim too. That did not bear thinking about. An involuntary shudder ran through him.

Now all he wanted was to get to his daughter, to satisfy himself that she was really all right, and to bring her home with him. His Katie. He loved his sons Niall and Finian very much, but Katie was extra special to him, the light of his life, and had been since the day she was born.

In all truth, she reminded him of his sister Cecily who had died of meningitis when he was fifteen and she was only twelve; his young heart had broken with her dying. He had loved and protected that child all through her sweet short life; after her death it would often strike him that perhaps unconsciously he had somehow known she was not long for this world.

Cecily had been a redheaded leggy colt, just as Katie was, although there the physical resemblance between them stopped, since Katie was the spitting image of her mother. But in other ways he saw Cecily in his daughter . . . the feyness, the gaiety, the openness, and the warm personality. There was very little, if any, guile in Katie, and she had a pureness, an innocence that he had only ever seen in Cecily. And like her long-dead aunt, whom she had never known, Katie truly was a free spirit.

He was thankful Niall was with Katie at the barn; that was a most comforting thought to him. His mind instantly veered to Denise's family. There would certainly be no comfort for Peter and Lois Matthews, and none for Ted either, who was a widower and childless and adoring of his only niece.

Michael shuddered again at the thought of Denise's awful fate. He had known her since she was a child, and Carly, too, for that matter, but Carly was alive, thank God. He hoped her injuries were not too severe. Suddenly, thoughts of her mother, Janet, intruded. As a widow all alone she had striven hard to do her very best for Carly, after her husband had died. Barry Smith had been a good friend of his for a number of years, and like everyone he and Maureen had been shocked when Barry had died of lymphatic cancer. He had been far too young for the grave. After his tragic death it had been a struggle, an uphill battle for Janet, and she had been faced with so many difficulties. Maureen had often wondered aloud to him how she managed.

Bad days ahead for those two families, he thought, his mouth grimly set, but he and Maureen would do the best they could to help them through this painful and shocking ordeal. He sighed and his hands gripped the steering wheel that much tighter . . . burying a child was something he could not imagine, or contemplate. A murdered child, at that . . .

Michael slowed when he came to the entrance to the dirt road which rolled down the hill to the barn. He eased the car in gently and found his way instantly blocked by a state trooper's patrol car.

As he opened his window another state trooper suddenly appeared as if from nowhere, and was already peering in at him.

'Can I help you, sir?'

'I have to pass through here, trooper.'

'Sorry, sir, but you cannot. Not tonight.'

'But I must. My two kids are down there at the barn. They were the ones who discovered the bodies of their friends, Denise Matthews and Carly Smith.'

'What's your name, sir?'

'Michael Byrne. I live in Malvern.' Michael pulled out his driver's licence and showed it to him.

Once the state trooper had scanned it and was seemingly satisfied, he nodded. 'It's okay, you can go on down to the barn. Ask for the detective in charge, Lieutenant MacDonald.'

'As in Mac the Knife?' Michael asked, a dark brow lifting.

The state trooper grinned at him. 'So you know the lieutenant, do you?'

'I sure do. I went to school with him.'

*   *   *

As he drove slowly down the hill, Michael immediately became aware of the activity below him in front of the barn. There were five patrol cars, along with several unmarked vans, and a number of men both in and out of uniform.

He recognized at once that this was a major crime scene, and he felt cold chills running down his back because his children were involved, however inadvertently. But naturally it was a big deal if Mac MacDonald was here. His old pal was in charge of the Connecticut State Police Major Crime Unit in the Litchfield area, and known to be one hell of a tough cop. They hadn't seen each other lately, not for several years in fact, but he had read about Mac in the local newspapers, and noted his climb to success and fame in law enforcement. Michael was relieved to know that Mac was in charge, because the investigation would be handled with great skill and professionalism.

After he parked, Michael got out of the jeep and slammed the door. He could see Mac a few yards away, talking to a good-looking blonde who was leaning against a Cherokee. When Mac happened to glance across and spotted him, Michael raised a hand in greeting, then walked around the front of his jeep.

A moment later the two of them were shaking hands and slapping each other on the back. Once they had pulled away from each other Michael said, 'My kids are here, Mac. I've come to get them.'

'They're fine, Mike, and they're ready to leave. They've been giving their statements in the barn.'

'What's taken so long?' Mike asked, frowning, staring into Mac's cool silver eyes, lots of questions reflected in his own.

'My fault, Mike, I got here late. My guys wanted me to have a couple of words with them.' Mac turned quickly as Allegra Marsh approached them.

'Sorry to interrupt, Mac, but I have to be going. I just wanted to say goodnight.'

'Allegra, this is Mike Byrne, my old buddy from school. Katie and Niall are his kids. Mike, meet Allegra Marsh. The Medical Examiner.'

Stretching out her hand, Allegra shook Michael's and said hello.

Michael nodded, cleared his throat and muttered, 'I can't believe something like this happened here. It's always been a sleepy sort of place. Never any problems, at least not this kind, anyway.'

Allegra gave him a long look through compassionate brown eyes. 'I know what you mean. Tragedies such as this are always a dreadful shock, and heartbreaking.'

She sounded sorrowful and concerned, and Michael looked at her closely, saw a sympathetic woman in her forties who happened to be beautiful in a cool, restrained way.

Mac interjected, 'This is the worst kind of crime, Mike. Such a lousy thing to deal with. Allegra's right, it's heartbreaking, they were only young girls . . .' He cut himself off, remembering what a narrow and lucky escape Katie had probably had.

As if he was reading his thoughts, Michael remarked, 'My Katie left early today, and I can only say thank God she did.' He first eyed Allegra, and then Mac. 'Any idea who could have done it?'

'No,' Mac said laconically and took hold of his arm. 'Let's go and get your kids, so that you can take them home. It's been a rotten few hours for them, all considered. But they've held up well, Mike. Very well indeed.'

Allegra murmured, 'Goodnight,' and stepped away from the two men. Then she suddenly spun around, and added, 'I'll call you first thing in the morning, Mac, and just let's hope these golden hours really do turn out to be *golden*.'

'I'm praying they are,' Mac answered. 'Praying damned hard, I might add.'

'What does she mean by golden hours?' Michael asked as he and Mac walked over to the barn.

'We call the first seventy-two hours the golden hours, because that's when we really can determine if the crime is going to be solved quickly. If a crime is not solved within those two and a half days . . . well . . .' Mac shrugged.

Michael caught hold of his sleeve. 'Are you saying that if you don't solve this crime by Monday it won't get solved at all?'

'Yes, that's what I'm saying,' Mac answered. His face was bleak.

Stunned, Michael stared at him speechlessly. Recovering, he exclaimed, 'Seventy-two hours and then you give up?'

'No, we never give up,' Mac assured him. 'But if we haven't solved it in that time, we know we've got a bad crime scene. That means no evidence, no real clues, no leads . . . a hard job ahead of us. But, let me repeat it again, Mike, we never give up.'

Chapter Nine

The only thing Michael Byrne saw when he went into the barn was Katie's face. Everything else was a blur. His daughter looked pale and drawn, and her eyes held a haunted look. Her appearance made him draw in his breath, and as he stepped forward he noticed how taut she was in the chair, her tenseness and anxiety obvious. He hurried to her, concerned.

When Katie saw her father with Mac MacDonald her face changed and her blue eyes lit up. Instantly she leapt to her feet and ran across to him.

Michael held her close, his arms wound tightly around her, as if never to let her go. How could he let her go? How could he let her out of his sight ever again? The world out there was full of maniacs and criminals, and she was a sweet, innocent girl who was unprotected and defenceless when she was alone.

He looked at Niall, who was walking towards him. Michael's relief that he had both of his children in his sight was reflected in his green eyes, so like Niall's.

Draping an arm around Niall, Michael pulled his son

closer, drew him into the circle of his embrace with Katie, and the three of them clung together without saying a word. Finally they broke away from each other and stood huddled together, looking at the detectives in the barn.

Mac spoke first: 'Thanks, Katie, and thanks to you too, Niall. You've both been very helpful.'

'What happens next?' Niall asked, his eyes on the commander.

'We keep going with the investigation, with the gathering of evidence. We've got police everywhere, scouring the area, looking for anyone who might be behaving in a suspicious way. We've even put up some roadblocks for the same reason,' Mac explained. 'And early tomorrow morning we'll be back here checking every inch of the terrain again. After you leave, we'll be blocking off this whole area and posting guards to protect the crime scene.'

'Denise *was* strangled, wasn't she?' Katie spoke softly and her shaking voice betrayed her raw emotions.

Mac nodded, his eyes softening briefly as he looked at the girl. 'We'll know more about her death tomorrow, once I've spoken to Doctor Marsh, the Medical Examiner. And I'll also have the reports from the forensics techs who were here. Every bit of evidence, however small, will help us to solve this crime, and find Denise's killer, Katie.'

Katie nodded and exhaled. A deep sigh of sorrow and

anguish rippled through her, and although she tried hard to be totally controlled, her eyes filled with tears as she thought of Denise and Carly. She leaned against her father, striving to get a hold of herself, wanting to be strong and brave.

Niall said to Mac, 'Can we take Katie's school bag with us when we leave, Lieutenant?'

Mac MacDonald answered, 'Of course you can,' and then he looked across at Dave Groome. 'I'm presuming that's okay, Dave. The techs *have* taken fingerprints?'

'Sure have, Mac. From all the school bags. And we've finished with Katie's.' As the detective spoke he lifted her bag full of books off the table and took it to her, gave her a friendly nod as he handed it over.

'Thanks,' Katie murmured and glanced at the bag she was holding, and frowned. 'I've just remembered something,' she began and then paused.

Dave Groome stared at her. He trusted this girl, was prepared to listen to anything she had to say. He had taken her statement earlier, and he had been impressed with the way she had handled herself. She had been calm and very precise in the details she had given him; she was an articulate, intelligent young woman, and he felt a certain admiration for her. 'What is it, Katie? What've you remembered?' Dave probed.

Katie shook her head, still frowning, and taking a deep breath, she murmured, 'Well, it might not be anything really, but –' She stopped and stared across at the far wall where a row of hooks had been hammered into place for their coats. The two coats which had hung there previously had now been taken away by the police, and all the hooks were empty. A lump came into her throat, and tears welled.

After a split second, she went on in as steady a voice as she could muster, 'It's about my bag of books, Detective Groome. At home, earlier, when I realized I'd left the bag behind, I tried to think where I'd put it in the barn. I just couldn't remember. Then later, when Niall and I arrived, I saw my bag immediately. It was over there, against that wall, with Denise's bag and Carly's, all three standing on the floor underneath their coats. Except there was no coat above mine, since I was wearing it. The bags were neatly placed, and I thought, oh, three bags in a row, like that old nursery rhyme . . . *three pretty maids all in a row*. Then I suddenly remembered that *I* hadn't put it there, I'd thrown it down in the dressing area behind the curtain.' She indicated the curtain in the corner, and finished, 'And I couldn't help thinking . . . *how odd*. Who moved my bag? And who arranged all three of them like that, in such a neat row?'

'Do you think the assailant took your bag and put it with Carly's and Denise's? Is that what you're saying, Katie?' Dave asked.

Katie nodded. 'Yes, I am. Who else would have done that?'

Dave looked at her thoughtfully, and after a moment said, 'Perhaps one of the girls arranged the bags that way.'

Katie shook her head most emphatically. 'I don't believe so, Detective Groome. They never saw my bag after we arrived at the barn. You see, I was the only one who changed into a costume this afternoon, because I was the only one rehearsing. So they were never in the dressing area.'

'Couldn't they have noticed you didn't have your bag of books with you when you left?' he pressed.

Katie explained, 'They were too busy to notice anything, they were concentrating on their parts, and anyway I rushed out, I was in a hurry. No, no, they didn't notice, I'm sure of that.'

There was a silence.

Mac broke it when he said, 'Sorry, Katie. I'm afraid we'll have to keep your bag after all. The killer may or may not have handled it. We'll have to have it checked by the lab for trace evidence to be sure. If it's clean you can have it back.'

Katie nodded and gave him the bag. 'Have you heard anything about Carly, Lieutenant? Since she got to the hospital?'

'She's still unconscious, but she's stable,' Mac answered. 'And she's in good hands at New Milford Hospital.'

'Will I be able to go and see her tomorrow?' Katie asked.

'Hopefully you will, yes.'

'Thanks, Mac,' Michael said briskly, cutting in, wanting to get his children home. He edged Katie and Niall towards the door, and added, 'Let's get going, kids.'

Mac followed them to the door of the barn. He put his hand on Michael's shoulder. 'We'll solve this, Mike, I'm certain of that. And let's stay in touch.'

Once they were alone, Mac sat down on one of the chairs, leaned back and closed his eyes, concentrating his thoughts on the murder. And the events that most likely preceded it. What he needed was evidence; he also needed to talk to the two detectives who were here on the scene with him, and get their input.

Finally he sat up, and looked across at Charlie Graham. 'So what did you find up there by the rhododendron bushes, Charlie?'

'A couple of things, Mac. I had the techs bag a cigarette butt we'd spotted, and they also took away a bag of heavily trampled leaves. Some of the leaves were wet, probably with urine, we decided. It was a man up there, not a deer. Most likely the attacker.'

Mac nodded, and asked, 'What about the undergrowth and the brush at the end of the wood where the body was found? I'm assuming there were signs that someone had been there. Loitering. Or hiding.'

'That's right. The techs took away trace samples, as well as leaves and grass,' Charlie answered. 'It's my feeling the perp was still in the vicinity when Katie and Niall arrived and began to call the girls' names.'

'They saved Carly Smith's life,' Dave Groome asserted, walking over to join Mac and Charlie at the table. He sat down and went on, 'The perp was probably about to finish Carly off with additional blows to the head, when Katie and Niall showed up. She might easily have ended up dead like Denise Matthews.'

Mac nodded in agreement, turning cold inside when he thought about the dead girl and the fiend who had raped and killed her. Had he planned to do the same to Carly and been interrupted? Or had he simply wanted Carly dead? Shifting his weight in the chair, Mac thought out loud when he said, 'He wouldn't want a witness, would he? Someone who could identify him . . . as Carly could, and will, when she regains consciousness.'

'That's true,' Dave agreed, and looked off into the distance, frowning.

Mac said, 'I guess Keith and Andy aren't back yet.'

Charlie shook his head. 'It was a pretty tough mission you sent them on, Mac, going to see Denise's parents and Carly's mother. Keith radioed in a short while ago. They've taken Mrs Smith to the hospital in New Milford so she can be with her daughter. They're probably on their way back here already.'

There was a moment or two of silence; none of them spoke. All three men were lost in their thoughts, worried and concerned about the crime and solving it. Finally it was Dave who said in a quiet voice, 'What *do* you think happened here this afternoon, Mac?'

'Somebody was stalking the girls, in my opinion, hiding up there in the rhododendron bushes. Once Katie had left, whom I'm sure he saw, by the way, he came down the hill, and went into the barn. Some kind of altercation took place. The girls ran out frightened, and headed straight into the wood. He chased them, attacked them both, then he raped Denise, and strangled her.'

'What did the doc say?' Charlie asked.

'That it was a violent attack by an angry man. We'll know more tomorrow, after the autopsy's done.' Mac rubbed his chin thoughtfully with his hand, and looking from Dave to Charlie, he said, 'No weapon was found at the scene, which means that the perp took it away with him.'

'It could have been a piece of wood, a stone, something handy he found there,' Charlie suggested.

'Or he brought some kind of club with him,' Mac said.

'That's true,' Dave agreed, and continued, 'We'd better come up with a profile of this guy real fast. Was he after all three girls? Or only Denise? Was he a local? Or a stranger passing through? A serial killer on the loose? Who the hell is he? And where is he now?'

'I wish I could answer all your questions, Dave, then we'd be in clover. But I can't. Not yet. However, there is one thing . . . in my considered opinion, it's a local,'

Mac replied. 'Maybe not from Malvern or any of the towns close by, but he's from this area.'

'What makes you rule out a stranger, Mac? The idea of a drifter wandering around doesn't grab you?'

Mac shook his head slowly. 'No, Dave, it doesn't.'

Charlie said, 'Three pretty maids in a row . . . that's what Katie said.'

'What *do* you make of the school bags being lined up the way they were, Mac?' Dave cut in, and rose, walked over to the window, glanced out, then turned back to face Mac. 'Weird, eh?'

Mac lifted his hands in a futile gesture. 'I don't know what it means, if anything.'

Dave said, 'I kinda trust Katie's judgement. If she says her friends wouldn't have done that, then I tend to go along with her. Look, maybe the perp came back to the barn to check it out, to remove any evidence he'd left behind. Then he spotted the bags, lined them up.'

'*But why?*' Mac said.

Dave shrugged. 'Who knows? A message of some kind, if he's a whacko?' The detective sat down heavily in a chair as a thought struck him. He said, worriedly, 'Could Katie be in danger?'

'No, I'm sure not,' Mac answered confidently, then wondered if she could be. 'We'll know more when we get the lab report on the bag.' After a moment he added, 'The perp wouldn't stick his neck out, draw attention to himself. He's lying low, he probably thinks he's gotten away with murder.'

'Has he?' Charlie asked, looking unhappy.

'No, he hasn't,' Mac stated in a strong voice. He pushed himself to his feet and began to pace up and down. 'Tomorrow, first thing, we'll start a background check, talk to Denise's school friends, her known associates, and especially her boyfriends –'

'According to Katie, Denise didn't have any boyfriends,' Dave interjected. 'Except for her brother Niall, who dated Denise last year. Niall says it never went anywhere, never became a romance. I'm sure he's telling the truth. And by the way, he accounted for his whereabouts today.'

'So he has an alibi?' Mac asked.

Dave nodded. 'Oh yes. He finished work in Roxbury at about four-twenty, or thereabouts. He's working on a remodelling job over there. He then went to the hardware store in Washington Depot, where he purchased a special hook for a picture. Then he drove to Marbledale, where he met a pal at the pub. They had Cokes and a packet of crisps. He says he left the pub at about five-forty and drove home to Malvern, arriving there a couple of minutes after six. Apparently he turned around and drove Katie back to the barn only a few minutes after he'd arrived.'

'So Niall's not under suspicion. I'm glad to hear that,' Mac muttered, almost to himself.

'Even if the perp is from around here, he could be someone Denise didn't actually know,' Dave pointed out.

'Yes, that's true,' Mac agreed, and went on, 'Let's go outside and see what's happening. Then we should get back to base. I'd like to go over whatever evidence there is available. We must make the most of the golden hours left to us.'

Dave and Charlie followed Mac across the barn, and Dave said, in a low undertone, 'This looks as if it's going to be a tough case. Let's pray for a few breaks.'

Chapter Ten

Maureen Byrne glanced around the family kitchen, trying to draw a measure of comfort and reassurance from the familiar.

Everything was in its given place, as it had always been here. The old brass clock ticked away on the mantelpiece, the Victorian lamps cast pools of warming light, and the fire burned brightly in the great stone hearth.

Even the air was redolent with the delicious, mingled smells of the food she had cooked this afternoon ... Irish stew, breadcakes and a big apple tart. Only this afternoon, she repeated under her breath, but it seems eons away now, so much has happened in the last few hours.

For all its familiarity, the kitchen was no longer the same to her. It had changed, and it was different because pain and heartache, and so many other emotions, hung heavily on the air, dimming somehow its warm glow, cosiness and rustic beauty.

Sighing to herself, Maureen looked at each member

of her family grouped around the table, saying little, keeping their troubling thoughts to themselves, their faces etched in sadness. Worry and concern clouded her clear blue eyes. None of them was bothering to eat, not touching the stew she had served, not even Fin, and she understood the reason why. Not a morsel had passed her own mouth, and she had put her fork down a moment ago, knowing she had no appetite whatsoever.

The events of this terrible day had overwhelmed Maureen, overwhelmed all of the Byrnes. They had become submerged in the violence of Denise's murder and the vicious attack on Carly, and by the tragedy and sorrow of such horrendous events. These had been stunning and frightening in their suddenness, their unexpectedness, and shock still lingered in their eyes. Chaos had invaded their ordinary, uneventful, protected lives and turned them upside down. Nothing would ever be the same again, none of *them* would be the same, Maureen was absolutely convinced of that.

Her keen, perceptive eyes settled on her daughter. Katie concerned her the most, because she was so intimately tied to Carly and Denise, her friends since childhood, and her boon companions growing up. Katie's eyes were red-rimmed from crying and her face was puffy and swollen. How to help her, Maureen wondered desperately, how to help her get through this awful tragedy, how to get Niall and Fin through it. And Michael and herself, for they were as deeply affected and disturbed by it as their children were.

Suddenly, Maureen's nostrils were assailed by the fragrant scent of the coffee which had finally brewed. And instantly, she stood up, lifted her plate, and said to them briskly, 'Let's have a quick mug of coffee and then get off to the hospital. Nobody's going to eat supper tonight, none of us are hungry, and I for one can't swallow a mouthful. I'm sure you're all feeling the same. Come on, Katie, Fin, help me to clear the table. Many hands make light work.'

'Yes, we should get going,' Michael agreed, looking at his watch. 'It's ten to nine already.'

Katie rose, took her plate and Niall's, and walked over to the counter at the other end of the kitchen. The garbage pail was concealed in a cupboard under the counter, and once she had opened the door and pulled the pail out, she and Fin scraped the plates clean. Then Katie went back to fetch her father's plate, and the bread basket; Maureen poured steaming hot coffee into five mugs, and Fin and Katie helped her carry them back to the table.

But after only a few sips of coffee, Katie stood up again. 'I'm going to wash my hands and face, and get my coat, Mom,' she muttered, 'if you don't mind.'

'You're excused, Katie,' Maureen replied.

'We'd also better go and get ready, too,' Niall said,

looking down at Finian, and then rising himself. 'If you'll excuse us, Mom.'

Maureen inclined her head.

Niall hurried out, Finian close on his heels. 'I'll get the jeep out of the garage, Dad,' Niall said over his shoulder, and then stepped through into the back hall.

'Thanks, son, I'll be there in a minute,' Michael answered, and turned to Maureen. 'We'll clean up everything else later, when we get back. But we should get off now. I'm worried about Carly's mother. Janet must be beside herself, and I'm sure she's all alone at the hospital.'

'She probably is,' Maureen responded and rose. Looking at his drawn face, shadowed by worry, she felt a fleeting pang of guilt. When Michael had arrived home with Katie and Niall in tow, a short while ago, she had insisted they eat before going to the hospital, and would brook no argument. 'You need something warm inside you, some food to keep up your strength,' she had pointed out, immediately serving the stew.

At first, Michael demurred. He had wanted to drive them over to New Milford at once, without further delay, and Katie had agreed; Maureen had managed to persuade them to eat first. But he was right, she acknowledged to herself now. The food hadn't interested anyone, least of all herself, and in the end they had wasted valuable time hanging around the kitchen looking morose.

'I'm sorry, Michael, I was wrong. I should have listened to you earlier,' Maureen murmured. 'Forcing food on all of you was silly, was of no purpose. And if I hadn't done so we could have been there by now.'

Michael got to his feet, and his response was a quick, warm smile. Then gently he led her out to the back hall to get her coat.

Maureen sniffed the cold air, walking along with Michael to the jeep, which Niall had parked outside the garage. She lifted her head and looked up at the ink-black sky, sparsely littered with but a few misty stars tonight, and felt the first drops of cold rain on her upturned face.

Michael helped her into the back seat, where she usually sat with Katie and Fin, and just as he was closing the door a flash of bright white lightning streaked through the sky, and thunder rumbled far away, like distant cannons poised in the heavens.

'There's a storm brewing,' she said to Michael, once he was settled in the driver's seat, and she shivered and drew her quilted coat around her slender body.

Looking at her over his shoulder, Michael replied, 'I guess so, honey. But we must stop by the Matthewses' after we've been to the hospital, storm or no storm. They must be devastated, and I'm only sorry I couldn't get them on the phone earlier.' He wanted to help them in whatever way he could.

'Perhaps Peter and Lois are at Ted's, you know how

close they are,' Maureen ventured, and then she stopped abruptly as the door opened and first Katie, and then Fin, scrambled into the jeep. Maureen slid along the seat to make room for them, and once Niall had jumped inside next to his father in the front, Michael turned on the ignition and backed out of the drive.

Katie immediately bunched up to her mother, and put her arm through hers, wanting the comfort and security of her closeness.

Maureen was well aware of Katie's neediness tonight, and it was understandable. All of the girl's defences were down, and she was still in shock, vulnerable and hurting, and wanting to be with her parents, her mother in particular.

No one spoke.

Michael drove towards New Preston and lovely little Lake Waramaug, heading for Route 202 which would take them directly to New Milford and the hospital.

Usually when they were in the jeep together they chattered and laughed, told silly jokes, and sometimes they sang their favourite songs, for they were all musically talented. Niall, in particular, had a wonderful voice that made every one of them stop singing the instant he opened his mouth, so they could listen to him. Fin said Niall had missed his way and ought to be in musicals, or a pop star, but they just laughed at Fin, most especially Niall.

But this evening the jeep was quiet and sad, the baleful silence engendered by shock and worry. And fear, of course, on Maureen's part. She knew, deep down within herself, that she was terribly afraid for Katie's safety, although she had not voiced this to Michael, nor to Katie herself, as yet.

Maureen Byrne was nobody's fool, and she knew there was a deadly killer out there, on the loose. Perhaps he was some kind of madman, a psycho.

And how did they know that this psycho wouldn't seek out Katie next? Perhaps he had intended to kill all three girls, but had been cheated out of one. Yes, there was still one left to kill. Her Katie. Her beloved only daughter. Maureen's mouth went dry and there was a hollowness in the pit of her stomach as she contemplated the horrendous possibilities.

Such dire and troubling thoughts appalled Maureen, but she knew she must not push them to one side. Common sense told her she must deal with the situation in a direct manner, discussing it with Katie, as well as her husband. Despite her daughter's feyness, her artistic turn of mind, her innocence, and lack of experience of life, she did happen to have a practical side to her nature. This trait had always pleased Maureen, reassured her that her daughter had good judgement, and that this would help her to make the right choices in life.

It now struck Maureen that Katie would be the first

one to understand that she must be careful, that she must be street-smart, and not put herself at risk. Instantly, this realization brought a bit of relief, but she would have a proper talk with her about everything later, that was essential. At this moment, though, Carly's condition, and the seriousness of her injuries were uppermost in everyone's minds, and to discuss anything else would appear horribly selfish.

As if zeroing in on her mother's thoughts, Katie leaned closer to Maureen, and said, in such a low voice it was almost a whisper, 'Do you think Carly's going to die, Momma?'

Maureen turned to look at Katie, and then she put an arm around her daughter's shoulder and brought her closer.

'I hope not, mavourneen. But we must be honest with ourselves, accept the seriousness of her injuries, not push them under the rug because they frighten us. 'Tis important we face them. Head injuries of this nature can be fatal. On the other hand, they may be superficial, not as serious as we've been led to believe. The best thing is to be positive, and believe that Carly is going to get better. We're also going to pray that she's as good as new, not impaired in any way.'

Katie sat bolt-upright. 'Mom, I hadn't thought about that! Oh God, *brain damage*. Carly could end up . . . a vegetable.' An involuntary shiver shot through the seventeen-year-old girl, and she squeezed her eyes tightly shut, suddenly more than ever afraid for her dearest friend.

Maureen took hold of Katie's hand, and said, 'Try not to worry, Katie, darlin'. And don't forget what I've forever drummed into you . . . there's nothing worse than anticipatory despair, 'tis debilitating, for one thing, and a waste of precious time for another. So let's not start anticipating anything. Let's hold positive thoughts, and hope that Carly's going to be her old self in no time at all. And we must be there for her as much as we can.'

'Yes, Mom, we must. We'll all rally round for Carly,' Katie swiftly asserted, her natural courage coming to the fore.

'She could end up in a coma like that woman Sunny von Bulow,' Finian said, leaning forward around Katie, so he could look at his mother through his thick glasses. 'And *she's* never going to come out of it.'

'Be quiet!' Maureen hissed, waving her finger reprovingly at her youngest child. She never knew what he was going to come out with.

'There are a few press people over by the door,' Michael said to them as he drove up to New Milford Hospital and parked the jeep at the kerb. 'But they don't know who we are, or our involvement, so we'll just walk in quietly. Don't look at them, especially you, Fin. And all of you, stick close to me.'

'We will, Dad,' Finian promised, sounding excited.

'Come on then, let's go!' Maureen said. Quickly taking charge, she opened the door, got out, then waited for Fin and Katie to alight from the jeep. She immediately took hold of Fin's hand, even though he wasn't too happy about this, considering it babyish. He struggled; she held him.

The Byrne family, huddled together, went through the front door of the hospital in a tight-knit little group. Once inside, Michael walked over to the desk where a nurse was on duty; the others trailed along, stood waiting patiently behind him.

'Good evening,' Michael said.

The nurse glanced up at him, half smiled, nodded.

'We're friends of Mrs Smith,' he explained. 'Mrs Janet Smith. She's here because of her daughter, Carly, who's in intensive care.'

'Yes,' the nurse replied, and shuffled some papers on the desk.

'How is Carly? Do you know?'

'About the same, so I understand.'

'We'd like to see Mrs Smith, and Carly, if that's at all possible.'

'Can I have your name, please?'

'I'm Michael Byrne. From Malvern. This is Mrs Byrne . . .' As he spoke, Michael turned, took hold of Maureen's arm and brought her forward. 'And my children,' he added, indicating the trio alongside.

The nurse peered at them all over her spectacles, and then she looked down at one of the pieces of paper on the desk, as if she were checking something out.

After a few more minutes without any kind of response, Michael, growing impatient, said, 'Can we go and find Mrs Smith?'

'You don't have to *find* her,' the nurse replied. 'She's in the second waiting room, down that corridor.' She spoke somewhat grudgingly and looked ill at ease.

Katie at once noticed this and stepped forward, saying as she did, 'Hi, Mrs Appleby! Don't you remember me? Katie Byrne. I go to school with Florence.'

The nurse studied Katie for a moment, and when recognition finally dawned she knew exactly who Katie was, and exclaimed, 'You're that good little actress I've seen in the school plays and concerts! The friend of Carly and Denise.' Nurse Appleby leaned over the desk, and dropping her voice, added, 'Terrible thing about the murder, wasn't it?'

Katie drew back, turning cold inside, and said nothing.

Michael took hold of Katie's arm and, regarding the nurse, he smiled at her with great cordiality, and said in his most charming voice, 'Thanks very much, Nurse Appleby. We'll go and see Mrs Smith.'

They found their way to the second waiting room, halfway down the very long corridor.

Katie hurried forward, her eyes on Janet Smith.

She was sitting alone on a small two-seater sofa, looking worried and forlorn. Her short, platinum-blonde hair was all awry, as if she'd been running her hands through it endlessly. Her face was as white as a bleached sheet, and there were dark violet smudges under her pale grey eyes, which were bloodshot from crying and filled with terror. As always, she wore black wool slacks and a matching black sweater; her beige raincoat was thrown over the arm of the sofa, and she tightly grasped the handbag resting in her lap.

She looked up as Katie came to a standstill in front of her, and blinked rapidly, frowning, as if she didn't know who Katie was for a moment. Then she got a grip on herself, and said, in a hoarse whisper, 'Oh Katie, there you are . . .'

'I'm sorry we're so late in coming, Mrs Smith,' Katie apologized, and went on to explain swiftly, 'Niall and I had to help the police. They kept us for ages. We had to give statements, and then Dad came to get us and we went home together to get Mom and Fin.'

'We came as soon as we could, Janet.' Maureen spoke softly, and seated herself next to Janet, who looked at her through the corner of her eye, then nodded dourly.

'How's Carly doing?' Katie asked, crouching down next to Mrs Smith's knees, her face full of genuine concern, her blue eyes spilling sympathy.

'Thankfully, her skull has stopped bleeding, and although she's still unconscious, the neurologist says he thinks she'll regain consciousness in the next few days.'

Katie let out a huge sigh of relief, and she smiled for the first time in hours. 'Oh, this is good news, we've all been so worried about Carly. Do you think I can see her, Mrs Smith?' She gazed at her friend's mother expectantly.

Janet stared back, shaking her head, and made a moue with her thin mouth. 'No, they won't let you, I haven't seen much of her myself. She's hooked up to a lot of tubes and machines, and there are two policemen guarding her door.' Sudden tears sprang into her pale eyes, and she sucked in her breath, then gasped, 'It's terrible when you think of it . . . that she might be in danger still. My poor Carly, my poor little girl.'

Touched by Janet's plight, and worried about her, Maureen put a comforting arm around her. 'Look, she's going to be all right. It's just a precaution, the police being there.'

Katie rested her hand on Mrs Smith's knee. 'Carly *saw* him. So she can identify him, and that's why the police have posted guards. In case he comes to the hospital. But he won't come, and you mustn't worry, because the police are going to catch him.'

Janet looked distracted for a moment, glancing around the waiting room, and then she finally tried to look at Katie. 'Do you think they will? Catch him?'

'I really do. And listen, Carly's going to be fine. She's young and strong and healthy, and she's a fighter. She'll make it, Mrs Smith.'

Wiping the tears from her eyes with the back of her hand, Janet finally nodded. 'At least my Carly's alive, which is more than –' The rest of her sentence remained unsaid, but they all knew exactly what the unspoken words were.

Maureen leaned closer. 'Tell us what we can do to help you, Janet. You only have to ask, nothing's any trouble, and we're here for you.'

Janet nodded, then glanced at Michael and his sons, standing off to one side. 'It was nice of you to come, Michael. And you, too, Niall.' She tried to smile without much success. Moving closer to Maureen, she grasped her hand tighter. 'And you Maureen, and Katie, thanks for offering to help. But honest, there's nothing you or anyone else *can* do. It's up to the doctors.'

'All you have to do is phone us,' Michael said. 'Whatever it is you want. We just feel you should know you have friends.'

'In your time of need,' Fin said.

For the first time, Janet smiled weakly. 'Thank you, Fin.'

Maureen thought, the little scamp. But she made no comment, deeming it wiser.

Janet concentrated on Katie, peering at her. 'The police told me you found Carly. Found *them*. Tell me. Please tell me about it.'

'I'd forgotten my school books at the barn, and when Niall came home just after six he drove me back to get them. The lights were on, and I thought Carly and Denise had stayed late to rehearse, or do their homework. But they weren't there. And then we saw their coats, so Niall and I went looking outside,' Katie explained. 'We found Carly first, resting on her back in the little wood, and her head was bleeding. But Niall said she was definitely breathing, so we knew she was alive. A bit away from Carly, he found Denise. She was already . . . dead. Niall sent me to phone for the ambulance, and he stayed behind to look after Carly.'

Turning her head, settling her gaze on Niall, Janet Smith said, in a low voice, 'Thanks, Niall, for staying with Carly. You probably saved her life. Did she . . . *say* anything?'

Niall walked over to the sofa, shaking his head. 'No, I'm afraid she didn't, Mrs Smith. I think she was probably unconscious by then.'

Janet could only nod, and then she began to sob once more, bringing her hands to her face. And she wept and wept, the tears trickling through her fingers and down onto her handbag in her lap.

Her heart aching, Maureen wrapped both her arms around Janet and held her in a close embrace, endeavouring to comfort her. She understood totally how Carly's mother felt, understood how much she was suffering. Maureen could scarcely bear to think about the other mother involved in this tragedy, and the emotional turmoil *she* must be enduring. Poor Lois. Her beautiful daughter Denise was on a cold slab in the morgue. That was unbearable even to contemplate.

Eventually, Janet seemed to settle down and the sobbing slowly ceased. It was then that Maureen said, in a soothing voice, 'Janet, I know you probably don't feel like eating, but can we take you out for something, even if it's only a cup of coffee or a drink?'

'That's kind, Maureen. You and Michael have both been kind to me, ever since Barry died. But I'm not hungry. And since the doctors are forcing me to leave, I guess I'll go home. There's nothing I can do here and they won't let me see Carly again. Not tonight. They told me that. And I was in her room just before you arrived.' She shook her head, exhaling. 'Oh dear, I'm going to cry again.' Swallowing hard, she somehow managed to quickly get hold of her floundering emotions, and was able to continue. 'The police brought me here, so my car's at my house. Could you drive me home? That would be a help, Maureen.'

'Yes, of course. Of course we will.'

Outside, the storm was now raging. Thunder and lightning and hard rain sluicing down greeted them as they returned to the lobby of the hospital.

'Let me go first,' Michael said to them. 'So that I can unlock the jeep. And give me a second to pull up in front, then make a dash for it.' Glancing at his wife, he said,

'It'll be best if Janet squeezes in the back with you, Katie and Fin.'

'There's room enough for us all,' Maureen assured him.

Seconds later they were all rushing out through the front door and scrambling into the jeep, wiping their wet faces with tissues once they were settled inside.

Maureen and Michael tried to make conversation on the way to Janet's house, but it was desultory at best, and in the end they fell quiet, understanding she was in the wrong frame of mind for talking. At one moment, Maureen did ask her if she wanted Katie or herself to sleep over that night, but Janet declined, telling them that she wanted to be on her own.

In a short while they were pulling up at Janet's front door, and after thanking them again, she made a dash for it through the driving rain. Once she had opened the door, she turned, waved and disappeared into the house.

'I wish she'd let me stay with her; or you, Mom,' Katie murmured. 'I hope she's going to be all right.'

'Oh she will be,' Maureen answered. 'She's quite a strong person, tough. And let's face it, Carly's alive, and the doctor says she'll come out of her unconscious state by the weekend, thank the Lord.'

'Carly was lucky,' Niall interjected.

'Yes, lucky because you and Katie got there in the nick of time,' Michael added. 'Now, we'd better pass by the Matthewses', see what we can do to help them.'

It was only a short drive up the road to the house where Peter and Lois Matthews lived, and once he had brought the car to a standstill, Michael and Maureen alighted, and went to the door. The house was in total darkness, and Maureen said, looking up at the windows, 'Maybe they've already gone to bed.'

'I doubt it,' Michael replied, ringing the bell and banging the brass door knocker. No one answered, and after a couple of seconds, he took Maureen's arm and led her away. 'We're getting soaked to the skin. Come on, honey, let's go home.'

When they were back in the jeep, Maureen said, 'Do you think they're at Ted's house?' and took some tissues from the box Katie was offering, wiped her face.

'It's possible.' Michael turned on the ignition and pulled away from the kerb. 'But it's too far to drive there now, and also too late. I'll phone Ted when we get home.'

'We should keep an umbrella in this jeep, Dad,' Fin announced in his piping child's voice. 'Then Mom wouldn't get so wet.'

'I put one in the back the other day,' Michael told him. 'But, mysteriously, it's disappeared.'

'The wee faeries took it,' Fin shot back, mouthing a favourite phrase Maureen used when anything went missing.

They all laughed.

Then Katie said, 'All this rain isn't going to help the police, is it, Dad?'

'No, it's going to hamper their investigation, that's for sure. But Mac is a good cop, the very best, and if anybody can solve this crime he can.'

Chapter Eleven

Katie sat in front of the big stone hearth in the kitchen, wearing her pyjamas and warmly wrapped in a blue fleecy-wool dressing gown. She was nursing a mug of tea and staring into the fire, watching the red and amber flames leaping up the chimney, her mind befogged with a jumbled mixture of thoughts.

Once they had returned home from New Milford Hospital, her mother had made them all take off their damp clothes and get ready for bed. Then she had given them bowls of hot soup and turkey sandwiches in the kitchen, and even Katie had partaken of the soup, despite her lack of appetite. But she had no stomach for food.

Faintly, behind her at the kitchen table, she could hear her mother mildly chastising Fin for having eaten his turkey sandwich too quickly, and in the background a piano concerto was playing on the radio, turned down low. All too quickly the concerto finished, and she fell back down to earth, came back to reality with an uncomfortable bump. Her mind started to churn all over again, so many different thoughts jostling for prominence in her head.

There, in the dancing flames of the fire, she saw her dearest friends staring back at her . . . Carly and Denise, the two of them together. Carly's face, sexy, voluptuous but, oddly, also sweet and endearing. The glossy black curls, those irresistible dimples in her cheeks, and eyes the colour of pansies. Carly would be all right, she would make it; all at once, Katie felt absolutely certain of that. She knew her friend almost as well as she knew herself. Carly was a true survivor, a fighter who would battle through and win . . . Now Denise became more prominent in the flames, her exquisite face so calm and gentle, her eyes of velvet brown so soft and loving, and around that alluring face the shimmering hair falling to her shoulders, long smooth skeins of gold . . . Then she was gone . . . only Carly remained, only she was constant in the flames.

Katie let out a long sigh. It didn't seem possible, but it was true . . . Denise *was* gone. Lost to her, lost to all of them forever. A lump came into her throat and she swallowed. *Never to see Denise again.* Never to hear her laughter, never to share their dreams and hopes.

Death. She had never known death before. It hurt so much. Katie felt the tears welling and she closed her eyes, leaned back in the chair, sat perfectly still, reflecting.

Today had been the worst day of her life, and yet it had started out so well, had been so full of promise. She had walked to school this morning in the bright October sunshine, full of excitement about the school concert in December, and the start of the holiday season, beginning with Thanksgiving. Carly and Denise had been waiting for her at the school gates, and they had shared English literature and history lessons, which were their favourites. And later they had eaten lunch together, and in the afternoon, after school was out, the three of them had gone off to the barn. Happy, laughing, full of hilarity and excitement, making their plans; she rehearsing the well-practised soliloquy from *Hamlet*; Carly and Denise cheering her on, as always her greatest fans and boosters.

At the end of the afternoon, the long walk home alone, through the deserted fields shrouded in mist and so eerie in the fading light. And finally coming back into the warmth and brightness of this kitchen, coming home. Helping her mother with supper, and then going off with Niall to retrieve her books, unsuspecting, not tuned in to thoughts of tragedy since she was entirely focused on their elaborate plans for the coming year. Then finding Carly and Denise in the wood. It was unendurable to picture them there, her dearest friends damaged beyond belief, one horribly beaten, one murdered and raped.

Shuddering, Katie sat up, took a sip from the mug of hot tea she was holding, and pushed these images of them far away from her. In the background, the radio was still playing, a piece of music she did not recognize.

And then above the music she heard Niall's voice.

'I'm going to bed, Mom, Dad. I'm bushed.'

The sound of his footsteps as he crossed the kitchen, coming towards her, coming to say goodnight. Always the good brother, loving, kind. His hand on top of her head, a gentle touch, his face next to hers. He said, in a low voice, 'It's been a terrible day, Katie, but try to get some sleep. And try not to fret. Things'll be better tomorrow.'

She looked into his eyes and attempted a smile. 'It's got to get better, Niall. It couldn't get any worse than it is already, could it? And thanks . . . for looking after me tonight.'

He leaned down and kissed her cheek, and she touched his hand resting on her shoulder. There was nobody better than Niall. He smiled, very faintly, turned, and walked away.

She heard him say to Fin, 'Come on, sport, it's time for bed, let's go up together.'

Fin was scrambling out of his chair, saying, 'Niall, listen. Dad says Mr Turnbull is going to let me see the beaver dam down by his pond. Did you know that beavers have the sharpest teeth, incisors for cutting down whole trees? And they build underwater lodges where they live, as well as making dams.'

'Let's go, Fin, and you can tell me all about those industrious little beavers, once you're tucked up in bed.'

Her mother began to cough, and Katie glanced at her in alarm. But Maureen turned on the tap, filled a glass with cold water, drank some of it quickly, and seemed to be all right.

Katie sank back into the chair and stared into the fire. Soon her mother began to stack the dishwasher, and in a peculiar way there was something suddenly comforting, reassuring about the familiar noise. Katie stood up, and called, 'Do you want me to help you, Mom?'

'No, no, I'm almost finished,' Maureen answered. 'In a minute I'll come and have a quiet cup of tea with you, before I go to bed myself.'

A moment later her father was dialling the phone and then, after letting it ring and ring, he threw it back into the cradle in frustration, and exclaimed, 'Still no answer at the Matthewses'. It just doesn't make sense under the circumstances, Maureen.'

'And they're not at Ted's either,' her mother remarked, 'so perhaps they've checked into a motel. For a little bit of privacy.'

Katie exclaimed, 'Dad, I remember that Denise used to go off to stay with an aunt sometimes. Her mother's sister. It was in Litchfield. Aunt Doris. But I don't know her last name. Unfortunately. It could be that the Matthewses went there. Mrs Matthews must be devastated; perhaps she wanted to be with her sister, with her nearest and dearest, you know, for comfort.'

'That's a possibility.' Michael swung to Maureen. 'Is there any more tea, honey?'

'It's gone cold. But I'll put the kettle on and make a fresh pot for us all.'

A short while later Katie sat with her parents in front of the kitchen fire, sharing the fresh pot of tea with them. None of them spoke, and she herself was wrapped in silence, her mind still whirling with all kinds of troubling thoughts.

She muttered in a glum sort of voice, 'It was all wrong.'

'What was?' Maureen asked, staring.

'Seeing Carly's mother at the hospital.'

'What do you mean by *all wrong*?' Her father threw her a puzzled look.

'What I mean is, it didn't work. It was a waste of time. She didn't care whether we were there or not. She was just being polite, and she wouldn't have missed us if we hadn't gone.'

Michael looked at his daughter alertly, his black brows drawing together in a frown. His slate-green eyes were thoughtful. 'That's true, Katie. She *has* always been an odd duck. I was Barry's friend, you know, since our junior high days, and when he died, I tried to help Janet get through her grief, and so did your mother. But she never wanted us around, not really.'

'She's not a woman who likes intimacy or familiarity,' Maureen volunteered. 'At least, that's my opinion. 'Tis a pity, but she's kept everyone at arm's length, and by that I mean Barry's friends. But still, that doesn't make her a bad person, does it?'

'No. But there is something cold about her.' Katie looked from her mother to her father. 'Cool and collected.' Katie shook her head. 'In a way, I wish we hadn't gone. It was so . . . banal.'

'*Banal*,' Maureen repeated. 'What a funny thing to say.' She gave Katie a curious stare. Her daughter surprised her sometimes, in much the same way Finian did with the odd things he came out with.

'Trite, Mom. And it was certainly not very important to Mrs Smith. Even though she thanked us, in a way they weren't the right words, she didn't *say* the right words.'

Again startled by his daughter's insight, Michael said, 'Now that you mention it, Katie, I think you're probably right. But we had to go to the hospital, for Carly's sake. And our own. How could we have lived with ourselves, if we'd not gone? We've known Carly almost all of her life, and she's your dearest friend. It was the only decent thing to do. And I know your mother agrees.'

'Yes, I know she does, and I do, too, Dad. I was only trying to say that I don't think Carly's mother was at all grateful. She didn't appreciate our being there.'

'Perhaps she did, Katie darlin', we can't be sure,' Maureen remarked in a quiet tone. 'Janet's always been so . . . *contained*. In control. Revealing nothing. Although God only knows what she's been trying to hide.

Maybe nothing at all. Perhaps she just can't properly express herself . . .' Maureen broke off, shrugged. 'Well, we made the effort to go and comfort her, and that's what counts. And we shall go again to see how Carly is, and keep going to the hospital till that girl's on her two feet again.'

'Mom, Dad, did you notice Mrs Smith never made any reference to the Matthewses, or to Denise? Wasn't that peculiar?'

'She cut herself off when Denise's name was on the tip of her tongue,' Michael muttered.

'Yes, we all noticed that, I think.' Maureen gave a long sigh. 'It was a bit shocking, not a thought, not a word for Denise or her parents.'

A silence lay between them for a few minutes, but eventually Michael broke it when he looked across at Katie and said, 'Are you *really sure* Denise didn't have a boyfriend?'

Katie shook her head vehemently. 'She didn't, Dad! Just as Carly didn't, doesn't, and neither do I. You *know* that. You know how much we all wanted to go to New York, to go to acting school. It's all we've thought about, talked about and aimed for, and for years. Boys haven't figured into anything we did, Dad.'

'That's what I thought, *believed*, and that's what I said to Mac MacDonald.'

'And I told Detective Groome the same thing. He kept pressing me about Denise, asking me whether or not she had a boyfriend when he took my statement. And I kept telling him there was no boyfriend, and no secret admirer, either.'

A short while after this, her father went to lock the doors, and then the three of them trooped upstairs together. On the landing, her parents kissed her goodnight, and Katie went into her room and closed the door.

Within seconds she was in bed, curled up in a ball underneath the eiderdown, squeezing her eyes tightly shut, pressing back the sudden flow of tears with her fingertips. She sighed, and tried to settle down, wanting to go to sleep.

She was almost dozing off when there was a tap on the door, and her mother peeped in.

'Are you asleep?' Maureen whispered.

'Still awake, Mom.'

Maureen crept into the room, sat down on the edge of the bed and smoothed her hand over Katie's soft young cheek, her eyes overflowing with love for her daughter. 'I'm so sorry that you've had to go through such an awful thing as this. It's a terrible tragedy.' Leaning forward, Maureen put her arms around Katie and brought her close. 'You're devastated, I know. We all are, but we'll get through it somehow. You have to be strong, Katie, and very brave. The next few days are not going to be easy for you, nor the coming weeks and months. You'll be grieving for Denise, and you must grieve. 'Tis not a good thing to bottle grief up. That's what I came to say . . . let your grief come out, take as long as you want to mourn her. And be there for Carly, she's going to need you, Katie. She'll need all of us, in fact, and all the help she can get.'

'I know, Mom.' Her voice was muffled, her head still pressed into her mother's shoulder.

'And there's just one other thing . . . always remember that your father and I are here for you.'

'I know you are, Mom.'

Maureen released her.

Katie lay back against her pillows, looking up at her mother, then she reached out, touched her face gently with one finger. 'I love you, Momma.'

'And I love you too, Katie mine.'

Her mother quietly slipped out of the room and Katie closed her eyes and willed herself to go to sleep. But for the longest time she could only think about her friends, and disturbing images of them, in distress and needing her, floated around in her head . . . until at last she fell asleep from sheer exhaustion.

Katie awakened with a start.

She sat up in bed, looking around the room as though there were an intruder within its confines. But she was alone in the darkness, and yet something had made her come awake, sit up like this with a jolt.

The room was icy cold. The curtains were billowing

out from the window, which she had opened earlier. Throwing back the cover, she climbed out of bed and glided across the floor to close it, and then stood for a moment, staring out.

There was a full moon in the velvet-black sky, which was clear and without clouds, and the stars were crystal-bright and sparkling now that the storm had passed. How beautiful her mother's garden looked, everything washed with silvery moonlight. Closing the window, she turned away, and as she did she thought she saw a dark image darting across the lawn and into the trees.

Katie froze. She was unable to move, and she began to shake. What was it? A deer? Or a man?

Not again, she thought, I can't be seeing things again. She pressed her face against the window, staring out. But of course there was nothing, no one there. She snapped her eyes shut, then swiftly opened them again, and looked down at the garden, scanning it. There was no sign of life; it was totally deserted, filled only with moonlight and shadows.

She was so cold her teeth were chattering, and she ran back to the bed, climbed in and huddled down, wondering what that dark flash had been. She was not really frightened, because she was here in the safety of her home with her parents and brothers, and she knew that her father had locked every door in the house.

And yet . . . a sliver of fear edged its way into her

mind. Was someone stalking her? And if so, who? And who had attacked Carly and killed Denise? Was it someone they all knew? She had no answers for herself.

Chapter Twelve

Mac MacDonald pushed open the door of the autopsy room, went in, and stood just inside the door. 'Morning, Allegra.'

Allegra Marsh was bending over a gurney with a body on it, and she looked up, nodded. 'Good morning, Mac,' she answered, her voice slightly muffled by the mask she wore. Pulling the sheet up, she covered the body, then stepped away from the gurney, removing her mask and her latex gloves as she did, dropping them in the trash.

Mac glanced over at the gurney, and asked, 'Is that the victim from last night?'

'Yes, it's Denise Matthews. I finished the autopsy about fifteen minutes ago.'

Mac was glad the post-mortem was over. Although he was loth to admit it to anyone, especially Allegra, he always felt a bit squeamish when he was in the autopsy room. He had balked at coming here this morning, but he knew he had to see Allegra Marsh, and so he had steeled himself for the visit. Autopsy rooms and morgues were not his bag, although being in them was part of his job.

Stepping forward, now that the body was covered, Mac said, 'What've you got?'

'I'm afraid not very much more than I had. And you?'

'The same. It was a bad crime scene to begin with, and then the storm last night did us in. Washed away anything that we might have missed. Apparently it's very muddy over there at the moment.'

'I have the DNA samples I took last night. But without a suspect there's no one to match them with. Still, they are here and available, pending an arrest. Plus some wool fibres I found on the body. From a sweater, most probably.'

Mac nodded. 'Time of death was as you thought?'

'Yes, approximately six-fifteen last night.' Allegra walked around the gurney, and leaned against a cabinet a couple of feet away from Mac. She shook her head and a sad expression settled on her face. Then she took a deep breath, and there was a sudden flash of anger in her eyes, when she said, 'It was a violent strangulation, as I told you. Very heavy bruising, larynx totally crushed. A lot of bruises on her arms, her breasts –'

'But she was fully clothed,' Mac cut in peremptorily.

'Bruising through her clothes. There's no other expla- nation. I doubt that he undressed her then re-dressed her. He must have grabbed her hard, a vice-like grip. A strong man, I suspect. He was inordinately rough with her, Mac. Her shoulder was dislocated, as well.'

He shook his head, looking pained. 'Oh, Jesus,' he sighed.

There was a small silence before Allegra said, 'The blood in the semen . . . it wasn't hers, Mac.'

Mac recoiled fractionally, frowning. 'What are you saying?'

'Just that. The blood I found in the seminal fluid on the body was not Denise Matthews's blood. Therefore, it had to be the perp's blood –'

'The perp's blood,' Mac interrupted. 'How the hell did *that* get there?'

'Obviously, I can't say for sure, I can only *imagine* how, Mac. Perhaps she scratched him in the struggle. She had long nails and they were strong. I found flesh and skin underneath them, also particles of wool fibre. Maybe she scratched his lower extremities and he bled. Or she scratched his penis. Whatever, Mac, there was blood in the semen and the blood is his. It has to be his, because it's *definitely* not hers.'

'You said she was a virgin.'

'What I actually said was that I thought she might be a virgin, and that I would only be able to make a proper assessment when I did the autopsy today.'

'Well, was she or wasn't she?'

Allegra shook her head. 'How can I be sure, Mac . . .' She hesitated a split second before she went on slowly,

'Look, I don't believe she was a virgin, because she would have bled, if only a little bit, if she had been. Also, it's not her blood anyway, not her particular blood type. To be more precise, let me say there's usually bleeding when the hymen ring is pierced, and especially in young girls. I must repeat, Mac, there was none of Denise Matthews's blood in the seminal fluid I took from her vagina and her body.'

'So she must've had a boyfriend.'

'Yes, I would say so, at some time or other.'

'If only we knew *who*, it might help us. I wonder . . .' Mac rubbed his hand over his chin, his eyes turning thoughtful as he looked at Allegra. 'Perhaps the perp was her boyfriend . . . and he got nasty?'

'Maybe.' Allegra pursed her lips, frowning. 'What I do know is that there was considerable trauma and bruising to the vaginal area. He was rough with her. It was a forced entry, broken blood vessels present, even a slight tearing of the vaginal tissue. I told you last night, I thought it had been a violent rape. Let me clarify that, Mac . . . I believe it was fiendish. He attacked her in the most horrendous way, and that girl wasn't willing, not at all. She fought him.'

'Oh my God, the poor girl . . .' Mac began to pace up and down for a few seconds, and then he came to a sudden standstill in front of Allegra. 'Mike Byrne told me Denise didn't have a boyfriend, and that nor did Katie or Carly. He explained they were all dedicated to their acting. I trust Mike, I've known him most of my life. That guy's as straight as a die.'

'I'm sure what he says is true. He has no reason to lie to you, Mac. But I'm pretty certain Denise was intimate with a man, at some time in the last couple of years.'

'Mike's son, Niall, dated Denise last year. He says it never blossomed into anything romantic. A couple of dates and then a fast fizzle. I believe him. Like his father, the kid's honest, and I doubt he was the one who deflowered Denise.'

Allegra nodded her agreement, and said, 'You may turn up something important when you interview her friends and acquaintances at her school.'

'I have my guys over at the school right now, and when I leave here that's where I'm heading.'

'What about Denise Matthews's parents? I guess they couldn't help you in any way . . . What did they say?'

'Not very much, Allegra. They're shattered, grief-stricken. They're staying with her sister in Litchfield, for privacy. And they more or less reiterated what Mike said. Denise had no boyfriends, she was devoted to her acting and looking forward to going to New York to study next year.'

'So you've no leads at all?'

'Not a damned thing.' Mac slouched against the counter top, looking despondent. He sighed heavily, and added, 'It's frustrating. You have all these DNA samples, but as you said, they're useless to me until I have a suspect, somebody to match them to.'

'I can sort of . . . well, I might be able to pinpoint a *type* for you, from what I've found,' she ventured.

Mac stared at her, his expression suddenly eager, and he straightened up. 'Shoot,' he said. 'I'm all ears.'

'As I told you, he must have bruised her through her clothes. She has bruises on her arms, breasts, and on her back. That is indicative of great strength, to me. So the perp must be very strong, with a tremendous, and powerful, grip. I found pubic hair on her body, other than hers. Brown pubic hair. Also, several strands of brown hair. No doubt from the perp's head, since she was a blonde. The wool fibres are cashmere, according to the crime lab. So what I'm envisioning is a tall, probably heavy-set and very strong man, with brownish hair. One who favours cashmere sweaters. It's not very much, I know, Mac.'

'But it's something, Allegra. I'm still convinced we're looking for a local. It's gut instinct, but gut instinct's always served me well in the past. Also, no strangers have been spotted around the area in the past forty-eight hours, to the best of our knowledge.'

'Can you give me a quick scenario, off the top of your head, like you've done in the past, Mac?'

'I don't know. But something tells me that it's someone local. A stalker. Perhaps watching them constantly, possibly for weeks, without their knowledge. He zeroes in on one of them, or maybe all three of them. He finally makes his move, when he observes them walking to the barn again. He knows it's the one place they're vulnerable, because they're always there alone, and it's in a pretty isolated spot. But this is just speculation.'

'A psychopath?'

'Possibly . . .' Mac paused. 'Yeah. I'd say that's more than likely. But it could be someone who's leading what appears to be a very normal life, as far as the rest of the world is concerned. He may not have killed before, but this might not be the last time he'll kill.'

Allegra said nothing, merely shook her head, sorrow etched on her face as she walked over to a metal table. It was hard not to feel emotional when a beautiful young girl of seventeen had been murdered and raped so violently, and in such cold blood. Putting her feelings aside, she picked up several brown envelopes and looking over at Mac said, 'These are photographs of the body my team took last night, at the crime scene. And more, which they shot this morning, before and during the autopsy. Whenever you feel up to taking a look at them, they're here.'

Mac hesitated, then said quickly, 'Let's take a look now. Get it over with. Then I've got to be on my way. I'm anxious to get down to Malvern.'

Chapter Thirteen

The wintery sun had long since sunk below the distant horizon, and dusk was beginning to fall, cloaking the lawn and the garden with long shadows.

Katie sat at her small desk in her bedroom, staring out of the window at the darkening sky, thinking about the events of the day. Downstairs, the whole family was assembled in the big kitchen, drinking coffee or tea. They had all come here for an early supper after the funeral, and although she and her mother had set the table in the dining room, before leaving for the church service, they had not eaten in there in the end. 'It's much cosier in the kitchen, Maureen,' Grandma Catriona had said, and everyone had agreed, and so that is where they had eaten supper. Aunt Bridget had arrived from New York last night and was staying with them; and both sets of grandparents had come to the funeral as well, Sean and Catriona O'Keefe, and Patrick and Geraldine Byrne, her father's parents, and his sister, Mairead, a favourite of everyone's, and her husband Paddy Macklin. Aunt Moura was sick and unable to attend, and Aunt Eileen was in Los Angeles on business.

A small sigh escaped Katie's lips, and she leaned forward, put both elbows on the desk, and held her head between her hands. She had a terrible headache; her mind was buzzing with so many disparate thoughts, she wasn't sure if she'd ever sort them out. But as she sat there ruminating, she remembered her diary. Her mother had given it to her only very recently; it was bound in dark-green leather and on the front, embossed in gold, were the words Five Year Diary. So far, she had enjoyed writing in it, had taken great pleasure in expressing herself. Perhaps that's what she should do tonight . . . put down her private thoughts. That was one way of making sense of things, and so she opened the centre drawer of the desk and took the diary out. Once she found the first blank page, after her last entry, she picked up her pen and wrote:

November 1st, 1989   *The Day of Denise's Funeral*

When I got up this morning, I felt very sad, and I couldn't think why. And then I suddenly remembered. It was the day Denise was going to be buried.

Most of my family went to the funeral. All the men wore their dark suits, and the women were in black. My mother wore her best black coat and dress that she got eight years ago. My Aunt Bridget was also in black.

The weather was so beautiful this afternoon it brought a lump to my throat, because Denise would never see such beautiful days ever again. There was bright sunshine, and the sky was without a cloud. It was a crisp clear blue, and so smooth it looked as if it had been freshly painted. And against that unblemished blue splashed the vermilion and gold, russet, yellow, copper and pink of the fall trees. Everything was so vivid, so sharply defined it was heart-stopping.

After the service in the church, we went to the cemetery for the burial. So many people were there. Everyone in our class came, and some of our teachers. And Mrs Cooke, who taught drama, was present, too, with Jeff, her husband. Carly's Mom came, and she stood with us, next to Denise's parents and her older brother, Jim, who'd come up from Hartford with his wife, Sandy. Jim and his father had to support Denise's mother, who was near collapse, and sobbing with grief.

I kept thinking of Denise, seeing her face, and worrying about the last hour of her life. It haunted me. I couldn't get it out of my mind. She must have been so frightened when the man attacked her. Lieutenant MacDonald told my father she fought for her life. I can't bear it. Carly prostrate on the ground, unable to help her. Yes, Denise must have been terrified. And the assailant hitting Denise, and raping her, then strangling her. It hurts. How it hurts me just to think of it. I don't believe I'll ever get it out of my mind.

I should have been there at the barn, then it wouldn't have

happened. I'm sure the murderer wouldn't have attempted to tackle the three of us. We could have fought him off, I'm very strong, and the three of us would have escaped.

We sent white lilies to the funeral, and they were laid on the coffin with red roses from her parents, and a wreath of pink and white carnations from Mrs Smith. When Denise's coffin was lowered into the ground, I thought my heart was breaking. Never to see her again. I threw some lilies into the grave, and so did Niall, and then Denise's sister-in-law Sandy threw in a red rose.

How final it was, the sound of the earth being shovelled in, falling on top of the coffin and the flowers. I began to weep and my father led us all away and drove us home. We'd given our condolences to the Matthewses at the church. But I knew they weren't consoled. My mother said their sorrow was unendurable.

When we came back to the house, my father poured shots of whiskey for his father and Grandpa Sean and Uncle Tommy. Then my mother, who never drinks anything but sherry, asked for one, too. So Dad brought out the bottle again, and extra glasses, and poured for everyone, except Niall, Fin, and me. Even Aunt Bridget took one.

My mother had made her famous Poulet Grandmère, a chicken casserole, earlier in the day, and I went to help her reheat it. She wore a white apron over her black wool dress, and she looked so sorrowful and worried I choked up again. Several times, when we were working at the counter top, she put an arm around me and held me close to her. And when

I looked at her I saw that her bright blue eyes were full of tears. I know she's always thinking that I might have been a victim too, and that she's thanking God I'm alive. Every day, she thanks God.

The 'golden hours', as Mac MacDonald calls them, have long since gone. Dad says Mac is angry and frustrated because his team have hit a blank wall, so far, at any rate.

I went back to school last week, but things are not the same any more. Not without Denise and Carly. She is still in a coma in the hospital, and they don't say anything any more about when she'll wake up. I go to see her all the time, but it's like she's lying there dead.

I've been feeling so depressed without them . . . almost all of my life it was the three of us. Now I'm just one. I'm all on my own, and nothing matters any more.

I don't want to act now. I don't even want to do the school concert. Acting has become tainted, clouded with pain and grief and sorrow. I'm giving it up. I'm not going to the academy in New York next year. It wouldn't be the same without them. I should never have talked them into going to the barn that day . . . it's my fault Denise is dead. And that Carly's in a coma, and lies there like a vegetable.

I don't know what I'll do when I leave school. I told Mom I have to find something new. I might go to work with Aunt Bridget in real estate. In New York. My parents don't seem to mind if I go. I think they're scared the killer is lurking around, somewhere near Malvern, and that I could be a target. I think they'd be much happier if I left this area.

I know how they feel. Sometimes I'm frightened myself. I keep racking my brains, trying to imagine who could have raped and killed Denise, but I can't come up with a name. I have no candidate for her murder.

When I told my father about seeing someone in the garden, on the night of the murder, he called the police immediately and they came over. There were some footprints near the stand of trees at the end of the garden, because the ground was wet after the storm. The police took measurements and made casts, but nothing's happened since.

The same day, my father had an alarm system installed in our house, and now my Mom picks me up from school every day. Or Dad or Niall come to get me. They don't want to take any chances on these dark winter afternoons. And I'm glad, because I don't want to walk across the lonely fields.

At night I find it hard to fall asleep. I can't get Denise's face out of my mind. She was so lovely, so sweet, and I fill with tears constantly. My grief is never ending, very familiar to me these days. I know how her family must feel . . . to lose a beautiful daughter at seventeen must be heartbreaking.

When I go to see Carly, I hold her hand and talk to her and recite Shakespeare, because she loved his work so much, but there's nothing, not a flicker . . .

'Katie, Katie, come on down,' Maureen called up the stairs.

Katie put down her pen, closed her diary and slipped

it into the drawer. It was only then she realized her cheeks were wet with tears. She wiped her face with her fingertips and went out onto the landing.

'Yes, Mom? What is it?'

'Your grandparents are leaving, come down and say goodnight.'

'Yes, Mom.'

Dutifully, she ran downstairs, and when she reached the bottom, Grandma Catriona hugged her tightly, and so did Grandpa Sean. And when it was their turn, Grandfather Patrick and Grandmother Geraldine were as affectionate as they embraced their only granddaughter and said goodnight. Aunt Mairead and Uncle Tommy came forward and kissed her several times, and then Mairead squeezed her arm and gave her a loving smile.

And Katie knew what they were all thinking . . . they were thanking God she was alive.

PART TWO

Gift of Friendship

London – Yorkshire, 1999

'Friendship is Love without his wings.'
LORD BYRON

'. . . the most essential thing for happiness
is the gift of friendship.'
SIR WILLIAM OSLER

Chapter Fourteen

The young woman who hurried down the Haymarket on a cool Wednesday evening in October had no idea of the swathe she cut as she glided along. But more than one head, male and female, turned to look at her as she headed towards the Theatre Royal.

She was tall, lithe, very slender, and striking in her long, black wool cape worn over a tailored black trouser suit. The only touches of colour were her startlingly blue eyes in her pale, finely-boned face, and her mass of fiery auburn hair that framed that face in an aureole.

Once she reached the theatre, she went straight up to the box office and stood in line. 'Katie Byrne,' she said to the man behind the window, when it was her turn, and after a shuffle of envelopes he passed over her ticket.

A moment later she was being ushered down the aisle to a seat in the centre of the theatre, eight rows up from the stage. It was one of the best seats in the house, as she was well aware.

As always when she entered a theatre, Katie found

herself filling with excitement, experiencing a sense of great expectation. Every nerve in her body seemed to tingle as she sat there gazing at the red velvet curtain, eager for the moment when it would rise and she would be captured by the unfolding drama, swept away into another world.

But quite aside from her own feelings, there was an undercurrent of anticipation in the theatre tonight, and Katie picked up on it at once. The play was called *Charlotte and Her Sisters*, and it had opened two months ago to rave reviews. It was an immediate sell-out, a huge hit, one guaranteed to run for months, indeed years.

Much had been written about the play and the playwright, a young woman no one had ever heard of before, who had penned the play in her spare time. Her name was Jenny Hargreaves, and she came from Harrogate, where she worked as a feature writer on a local county magazine.

The play she had written was about the Brontë sisters, the nineteenth-century novelists and poets, who had lived in Haworth, a village on the windswept Yorkshire moors, and had produced such extraordinary works as *Jane Eyre*, *Wuthering Heights*, and *The Tenant of Wildfell Hall*.

Opening the programme she was holding, Katie scanned the details of the different acts, and then the cast list. Three very famous and talented British actresses were playing the roles of Charlotte, Emily, and Anne Brontë, and she could hardly wait to see their performances. She was fully ready and willing to experience the 'suspension of disbelief'. I *will* believe every word, Katie said to herself, as she inevitably did when she came to see a play. I *will* believe that it's really happening, that I'm witnessing real life being played out before my eyes.

Suddenly, the flurry of movement, of people edging along rows of seats already filled, and finally settling in their own seats, came to a stop. Silence filled the theatre. The lights dimmed. The curtain went up. And Katie, her hands clasped together, focused all of her attention on the stage.

Instantly, she was pulled into the drama, caught up in the lives of the three sisters, their talented yet decadent brother, Branwell, and their pious father, the Reverend Patrick Brontë, vicar of Haworth Parish in the West Riding of Yorkshire.

And there she sat, witnessing life in the parsonage on the bleak moors, where the cemetery edged up to the windows, and all the trees leaned the same way because the wind never stopped blowing in one direction. The acting was superb. The three women gave of themselves unstintingly, and they convinced her that they *were* the Brontë sisters. Katie was mesmerized by their performances, in awe.

In the interval, Katie sat perfectly still in her seat, didn't bother to go out and stretch her legs, not wanting to break the spell, lose the magic that had been created on stage and with such potency. She could hardly wait for the next act to begin, and when it did she was once again held spellbound by the playwright's words, the acting, the stage sets and the costumes, as was everyone else in the audience.

Katie did not want the play to end.

As she trooped out behind the other theatregoers, she could only marvel at the miracles that had been wrought on that stage tonight. She knew she had seen something truly remarkable, and it had moved and touched her beyond measure. And that's what it was all about, wasn't it?

Once she left the theatre and went out into the street, Katie looked around for the chauffeur she had been told would be waiting for her, to drive her to the restaurant for dinner.

Katie hurried towards him where he was waiting at the kerb, next to the Dawson car.

'Hello, Joe,' she said, smiling, remembering his courtesy the last time he had driven her to meet Melanie Dawson.

He smiled back, brought a hand to his cap. 'Good evening, Miss Byrne.' He opened the back door of the car for her and she got inside. 'It's the Ivy tonight,' he told her as he closed the door.

Katie sat back, relaxing, still thinking about the performances as the car pulled away towards Soho and the Ivy. She was so glad Melanie had offered to get her a ticket for this very hot play, but then Melanie had always shown her great kindness. They had been friends for four years, and Katie was flattered that a woman so highly thought of, so important in the theatre, so chic, sophisticated and successful would want to be her friend. She looked forward to seeing her for dinner, and couldn't wait to tell her what she thought of the play. Melanie always asked her opinion, and was interested in what she had to say about most things, not only the theatre.

Melanie Dawson spotted Katie being escorted through the famous show business restaurant, and stood up to greet her as she came to a standstill. The two women hugged, then sat down, and Melanie exclaimed, 'You look marvellous, Katie. London certainly does agree with you. But then I said that the last time Harry and I were here.'

Katie laughed, nodded. 'I guess it does, and I've been enjoying my classes at RADA. How's Harry?'

'He's great and he sends his best. Stuck in New York at the moment. He's got problems with a play. But knowing Harry, he'll solve them.' Melanie motioned to a waiter, looked at Katie and asked, 'What would you like to drink?'

Katie shook her head. 'You know I don't really drink. But tonight I'll have a glass of champagne, please. That's light enough.'

'Let's have a bottle of Veuve Clicquot,' Melanie said to the waiter, thanked him, and then turned back to Katie. 'And how did you enjoy the play?'

'I loved it. Thanks so much for arranging the ticket, Melanie. It was so kind of you to think of me.' She leaned across the table, and went on, 'I was very moved at times, and that's what the theatre's all about, having your emotions engaged, being touched, feeling what the characters are feeling, empathizing with them, living through their tragedies and heartbreaks and happier moments. And I thought the acting was superb. It's a marvellous cast.'

'I couldn't have said it better, but then you've always been a clever girl, Katie.'

Katie smiled, simply accepted the compliment in silence. She could not help thinking how smart Melanie looked tonight, in her dark-grey silk suit, obviously an expensive designer number, and her grey South Sea pearl earrings. She was a striking woman, with her well-shaped, stylish short brown hair and deep brown eyes. Katie thought she had great flair in the way she dressed, and everything she did, in fact.

The waiter was back in a jiffy with an ice bucket filled with ice, and the bottle of champagne, which he proceeded to pour.

A moment later the two women were clinking glasses, toasting each other. Once they had taken a sip of the wine, and put their glasses down, Melanie studied Katie for a moment, then asked, 'What did you think of Branwell?'

Katie shook her head slowly. 'I couldn't believe how utterly modern he was, in a sense . . . a drunk, a gambler, a drug addict, and a wastrel, especially of his talent. I never knew much about the Brontës and their personal lives, I only knew about their work, but the whole play was gripping, really fascinating. And Jonathan Rhyne is wonderful in that role. But they all are.'

'I agree, and I agree about the play. It is drama at its very, very best. However, of all of them, *my* favourite character is Emily, perhaps because I've always loved *Wuthering Heights*.'

'Yes, Emily is very interesting, and somewhat . . .' Katie paused, then bit her lip. 'I was going to say that she seems to be so mysterious in the play, and yet I'm not sure if I mean *that* exactly.'

'I hope you do, because she was a very mysterious person in real life, so reluctant to have anything she wrote published, guarding her privacy and her innermost being, her soul, in a way. A free spirit, mystical, in a certain sense, and perhaps the one Brontë who deserves the accolade of greatness. For what it's worth, I believe Emily Brontë was one of the great geniuses of English literature.'

'It's certainly made me want to read some of their books again,' Katie exclaimed, and stopped when a man came to a standstill at their table.

Melanie cried, 'Chris! How are you?'

The man grinned, and replied, 'I'm good, Mel, and you?'

'Couldn't be better. Chris, I'd like to introduce you to a friend of mine, Katie Byrne. Katie, this is Christopher Plummer, as I know I don't need to tell you.'

The actor smiled at her, and she smiled back, and gave him her hand, which he shook.

Melanie said, 'Any chance of lunch or dinner, Chris? How long are you here for?'

'A couple of days. Give me a call. Maybe we can get together.'

He smiled at them both and took his leave, and Katie said, 'Phew! What a treat! I never thought I'd meet Christopher Plummer, not in a million years. He's one of my favourite actors.'

'He's just the greatest, in my opinion.' Melanie picked up the menus, and handed one to Katie. 'I don't know what you feel like, but I'm having the fried fish and chips with mushy peas. It's awfully naughty, they're so fattening, but I can never resist them when I'm here.'

'I'll have the same.' Katie laughed. 'I can't resist them either, not that *I* come *here* very much.'

'It's a national dish, and I can understand why.'

After the waiter reappeared and took their order, he topped up their glasses, and hurried off.

Melanie said, 'How long are you intending to stay in London, Katie?'

'I'm not sure.' She shrugged lightly. 'That's a silly answer, because I am sure, well, to a certain extent, anyway. My parents are going to Ireland in November, and then they're coming to London for Thanksgiving. My brother Fin's at Oxford University, I think I told you that. He's the brainy one in the family. So, we'll all be here together . . . well, Niall, my elder brother, is not coming, as far as I know. But I guess he could surprise us. In any event, I have classes to finish at RADA, which will take me through until early December, and I know my parents are going to want me to go back to Connecticut for Christmas. I'm not certain of what I'll do in the new year, probably trot back to London. I do love it here.'

'Who doesn't,' Melanie agreed. Clearing her throat, she took a sip of champagne, and continued, 'I bought the play, Katie.'

Katie frowned. 'What play?'

Melanie chuckled. '*What play?* you ask. The one I wanted you to see tonight. *Charlotte and Her Sisters.*'

'You did!' Katie was completely taken aback and unable to conceal her surprise.

Melanie nodded. 'I made a deal for a firm option long before it opened, and a week ago I purchased the rights for the States from the British producer. I also bought the movie rights.'

'Congratulations! Isn't Harry thrilled?'

'Yes, he is. *For me.* I'm producing this one myself. I'm

opening it on Broadway sometime next year. I suppose you could say it's my contribution to the year of the Millennium.'

Katie gave her a warm smile. 'I know how much you've wanted to find something really dramatic. Now you have.'

The waiter arrived with their dinner; while they ate, the two of them continued to chat about London, acquaintances they had in common, the theatre in general. Once their plates had been cleared away and they were sipping camomile tea, Melanie startled Katie when she said, 'I want to have a serious talk with you about something.'

'Yes, what is it?' Katie asked, staring at the producer intently, wondering what she could possibly have on her mind.

'I told you I'm bringing the Brontë play to Broadway. I want you to play the part of Emily. That's what this is all about tonight, Katie. I'm offering you the second lead. That's why I wanted you to see the play. I wasn't just giving you a treat.'

Stunned, Katie sat gaping at her, rendered totally speechless.

'Well, say something, Katie. Yes, no, maybe?'

Taking a deep breath, Katie said, 'Melanie, how wonderful of you, what a fabulous offer.'

'So you're accepting it,' Melanie exclaimed, beaming at her, obviously thrilled.

'Not exactly,' Katie began and paused, shaking her head, grimacing. 'I think I'd like to do the play, but can I sleep on it, at least? I don't want to say yes, and then change my mind.'

Melanie Dawson sighed heavily. 'Like you did the last time? I'm not sure why you keep turning down the parts I offer you, but if you pass on Emily Brontë this will be the third time. Then I will really begin to wonder if you're serious about your acting career.'

'You know I am! Those other two parts weren't right for me, Melanie, and you know they weren't. And Harry agreed with me. I was too old for the girl in *Plainspeaking*, and I really didn't like the role in the musical. Harry was of the same mind, and besides, you know very well I'm not a good singer.'

'There was hardly any singing in that particular part, and you could have done a Rex Harrison and talked your way through the songs. But look, you're avoiding the issue. Don't you want a part in a Broadway show, Katie?'

'Naturally, I do. It's my dream, and it always has been. But I want it to be the right part. I'm an American, Melanie, and Emily Brontë was English, and I'm not so sure I can get it right. Also, there are other considerations.'

'Such as what? Give me one.'

'Well . . .' Katie glanced away, biting her lip, looked around the restaurant, and when she brought her gaze back to the producer, she murmured quietly, and very truthfully, 'I don't think I want to live in New York, Mel.'

'Oh, well then, that's a different matter.' Melanie eyed her carefully, thinking, for the umpteenth time, that there was something in her past that troubled Katie. She had asked her several times before if there was a problem, but Katie had always said there was not. Melanie prided herself on her psychological insight into people, as well as her shrewdness and acumen as a theatrical producer, and she was convinced there *was* a problem, a liability perhaps, of some sort. And Katie was apparently unwilling to share it. No actress in her right mind would turn down the role of Emily Brontë on Broadway, in a red-hot hit play from London. Not an actress of Katie's talent and calibre. Not unless there was . . . an impediment. There is, and that's why she doesn't want to come home to New York, Melanie now decided.

Taking a deep breath, the producer said, 'I'm signing Georgette Allison for the leading role of Charlotte, and Harrison Jordan for Branwell. Two big stars, as you well know, Katie. That wouldn't do you any harm, to be in a play with them, now would it?'

Katie reached out, put a hand on Melanie's arm. 'I'm so appreciative, I truly am, Melanie. I do want to do it . . . but I want to be really sure that I can, that I'm up to it before I say yes.'

Melanie nodded, her face softening. She and her husband were very fond of this young woman, and they believed she could be a great actress, a star. If she wanted to be. Melanie said, 'All right, darling. Let me know tomorrow.'

Chapter Fifteen

Xenia Leyburn paced up and down the floor of the study in her house in Farm Street, Mayfair, a cell phone pressed to her ear. She was in conversation with her business partner in New York, and at this moment she was listening intently. Finally, she responded, 'I'm sure I can do it quickly. I'll think about it, then I'll send you an e-mail or fax tomorrow, Alan. But what about the invitations? They have to be done immediately, don't they?'

She heard a noise, and while continuing to listen to Alan Pearson across the Atlantic, she walked over to the door of the study and looked out. At the sight of Katie Byrne she raised a hand in greeting, then brought her attention back to the phone call. 'Well, there's no problem then. None for me either, so let's talk tomorrow, Alan. Bye.'

Going out into the hall, Xenia watched Katie fastening the chain, shooting the bolt and double-locking the front door. At once she began to laugh, and exclaimed, 'You don't have to do that, Katie. This place is safer than Fort

Knox once the alarm's on! And you should know that by now.'

'Better to be safe than sorry,' Katie said, turning around, smiling at her friend. 'I always lock doors. It's a habit.'

'So I've noticed,' Xenia murmured, then, changing the subject, she asked, 'How was your evening?'

Throwing off her black cape and hanging it in the hall cupboard, Katie said, over her shoulder, 'The play was wonderful, really great, and then afterwards I met Melanie at the Ivy for supper.'

'Oh very nice indeed!' Xenia remarked, and heading towards the kitchen, she went on, 'How about a cup of tea before we go to bed?'

'I wouldn't say no.' Katie followed Xenia down the corridor, and into the kitchen. Seating herself at a small table in the middle of the room, she added, 'The cast was wonderful, and the play's really outstanding, a superb drama. I never knew very much about the Brontës, although I've always loved their books.'

After filling the electric kettle with water and turning it on, Xenia joined Katie at the table. 'In a way, their whole life was a drama,' she said, 'so I'm not surprised it translates well to the stage. Actually, they all had quite colourful lives, even though a great deal of their time was spent at Haworth.'

'Do you know a lot about the Brontës?'

'Course I do, Katie, it's local fodder. You haven't

forgotten I lived in Yorkshire for a great deal of my childhood, have you?'

'Yes, it had slipped my mind for a moment, since I think of you as International with a capital I.'

Xenia burst out laughing, and pushed her hand through her luxuriant brown hair. 'Oh yes, Miss Cosmopolitan, sophisticated little me.' She laughed again. 'You know very well I'm a country girl at heart.'

Katie shook her head. 'That's not *exactly* how I see you! Nor do the rest of your friends, I'm sure. You were travelling the world with your father at the tender age of six, staying in all the best hotels in London, Paris and New York, and living the high life.'

'Don't forget Cannes, Nice, Vienna, and L.A.' Xenia grinned, and then jumped up when the kettle began to whistle. Taking two mugs out of the cupboard, she added tea bags, turned off the kettle and poured hot water into the mugs. 'I made green tea, is that all right?'

'I prefer it, thanks.'

Xenia brought the mugs to the table, put one in front of Katie, and sat down. 'You know, when I was seventeen and just out of school, on my own for the first time, I found the world a difficult place to function in for a while. And I suppose I can only blame that on my father and hotel living.'

Katie frowned at her over the rim of the mug. 'What do you mean? I'm not really following you.'

Xenia leaned forward and explained: 'The concierge of every hotel we stayed in was my father's good right hand, and eventually also mine. Want a letter posted, a reservation made for a plane, a train, a car, a restaurant, a hairdresser, a hotel room in another city, or another country. Call the concierge, he'll fix it. That was my father's motto. He truly believed that if you knew the head concierge at the Dorchester in London and the head concierge at the George V in Paris, you didn't have to worry about a thing. The world was your oyster. Those beloved concierges would simply ease the way for you, wherever you were going or whatever your needs were.'

Xenia paused for a sip of tea, then continued, 'Do you know, I didn't have a clue how to post a letter for years. You see, I'd always given my letters to the front desk in a hotel, to a concierge, to be precise.'

Katie grinned. 'You sound so dismayed, but I think it's a cute story. Anyway, you weren't always with your father, if I remember correctly. You once told me that sometimes you were with your mother. Didn't she ever take you to a post office? Or show you how to cope with the real stuff in life?'

Shaking her head, Xenia explained. 'First of all, my mother's family home is in a remote area of Yorkshire, which is where she was living in those days, and where I lived when I was with her. We were staying with her brother, my Uncle William. And secondly, she wasn't very well when I was a little girl. I think it was her chronic ill health that actually came between my parents, because she couldn't function properly. Maybe her illness was psychosomatic ... I don't know. Anyway, because she wasn't well, I spent a lot of time with Timothy and his sister, Verity, when I was growing up. My mother had spent most of her own childhood with *their* father, so they were sort of like family to me. Tim, Verity, and I occupied a dream world at Burton Leyburn ... it's the most extraordinary house, unique really. Certainly my life there was something of a contrast to life with my fast-travelling, globe-trotting, high-rolling, movie-producer father.'

'I can well imagine. You must miss him,' Katie murmured sympathetically, knowing how much she would have missed her own father if he had died.

'Oh yes, I do miss him. A lot,' Xenia replied. 'He was a wonderful father, if a little crazy at times. He was very colourful, you know, Katie, and you'd have loved him. He was so handsome, a Russian émigré, taken out of Russia as a child, just before the Revolution, brought up in Paris and Nice by his mother, living in Hollywood eventually. And horribly addicted to London, Savile Row suits, gambling, and making movies. And to me, of course. He was very adoring of me.'

'He sounds like quite a character.'

Xenia merely smiled, sipped her tea, remembering with great love and much sadness her beloved father,

Victor Alexandrovich Fedorov, who had died when she was twenty-two.

They sat quietly together, drinking their tea in silence for a few moments. There had been an instant rapport between them when they were introduced by Katie's Aunt Bridget in New York; for the last two years they had been fast friends and room-mates in London for a year. Although they were from totally different backgrounds, they nevertheless understood each other very well. The silences between them were companionable; and they enjoyed being together.

'I know you grew up with Tim, but were you in love with him then? When you were a child?' Katie asked, breaking into Xenia's thoughts.

Xenia nodded. 'Oh yes, I was. I loved Tim forever.'

Katie noticed the sad, faraway look in Xenia's large, transparent eyes and, realizing they were on delicate ground, she changed the subject by saying, 'Guess what? Melanie introduced me to Christopher Plummer tonight. He was having dinner at the Ivy, and came over to say hello to her.'

'He's a remarkable actor,' Xenia answered. An elegant dark brow lifted, when she asked, 'Is he going to be in one of her plays?'

'I don't know, I don't think so.' Katie paused and there was a short silence before she cleared her throat, and went on, 'Actually, Melanie offered *me* a part tonight.'

'She *did*? What kind of part?'

'The second lead in *Charlotte and Her Sisters*. The part of Emily Brontë.'

'That's absolutely wonderful, Katie. Congratulations!'

'Don't say that yet. I don't know if I'm going to take it.'

'You don't. Whyever not? You should jump at it.' Xenia threw her a puzzled look, frowning and shaking her head. 'Why would you even hesitate?'

'I'm just not sure I can do it. Emily was English, I'm American and –' Katie cut herself off, looking troubled.

'Don't be so ridiculous,' Xenia chastised sharply. 'Of course you can do it! You're a talented and gifted actress, and a hard worker. This part's a snap for you, believe me.'

'Thank you. But I feel very uncertain about playing this part. I told Melanie I'd like to sleep on it, and give her an answer tomorrow.'

'I hope that's going to be in the affirmative,' Xenia swiftly responded. 'You've got to accept it. Listen, you're not actually signing the contract tomorrow. You can always get out of it later, if you feel you must. Just say yes for now.'

'I couldn't do that, it's not fair to Melanie.'

Xenia rose, began to walk up and down the kitchen, those beautiful grey eyes of hers growing thoughtful.

Finally, she came to a stop, put a hand on Katie's shoulder. 'This is what we're going to do. You'll give Melanie Dawson a ring in the morning, and tell her you're accepting the part. Then I'll take you up to Yorkshire tomorrow. For a few days. We'll get the morning Pullman train from King's Cross to Harrogate. And we'll stay with Verity at Burton Leyburn.

'On Friday or Saturday, I'll drive you over to Haworth. You can commune with the ghost of Emily Brontë on those wild, untenanted moors she loved so much and where she spent so much time with her dog, Keeper. We'll visit the Black Bull where Branwell always got horrendously drunk, and stroll around the village streets. We'll even walk over the moors to Top Withens. It's a long trek but worth it. It's a ruin now, but it's supposedly the house Wuthering Heights was modelled on. We can also spend an hour or so in the parsonage. That's now the Brontë Museum, and they have many of the Brontë manuscripts on display, including some of the Juvenilia, the stories of Gondal and Angria which they wrote when they were children. All very Byronic and melodramatic, and forerunners of their adult novels.' Xenia stared at Katie. 'So don't you think that sounds great?'

'Yes . . .' Again, Katie seemed hesitant.

'Listen to me, Katie Byrne. Once you've visited where they lived, seen the bleakness of the moors, the storm-filled skies, you'll understand the Brontës much better, especially Emily. That place is so windswept and harsh it had to have had an influence on them, on their characters, and ultimately on their writing. Also, there are a lot of books on the Brontës in the library at

Burton Leyburn, plenty of reading matter for you. So say you'll come.'

Katie was silent.

'Oh come on, say *yes*,' Xenia cried, growing impatient.

Katie was touched by Xenia's invitation to Yorkshire and she looked across at her, and finally nodded. 'It's really lovely of you to offer to do this for me. But what about your work? I thought you had to put together a big party for the Millennium, and were having problems?'

'And how,' Xenia replied. 'We had no venue for that party, and couldn't find anywhere that was suitable, or available on New Year's Eve. Alan and I were beginning to panic, and then today a New York couple who were giving a wedding anniversary party unexpectedly cancelled it. They're getting a divorce! We were having it at the Plaza Hotel ballroom, and so, *voilà*! Now we have an empty ballroom for our other client. Problem solved. What was worrying Alan a while ago was the theme for the Millennium bash. The Plaza ballroom is such a big room for a private party, but I believe I've come up with a theme he likes.'

'What is it?'

'I suggested turning the ballroom into a replica of the Winter Palace in St Petersburg. He wasn't sure about it at first, but then the client just flipped when she heard what I had in mind. I'll call him tomorrow and tell him I'll be in Yorkshire, in case he needs me. The great thing is that I can work on the party theme at Burton Leyburn; that house is bound to inspire me. When you see it, you'll understand what I mean.'

Katie suddenly realized how important it was to Xenia that they go to Yorkshire where she had spent so much of her childhood. It was obvious from the sudden flush on her normally pale cheeks, the sparkle in those unusual eyes that it had a special hold on her.

'All right,' Katie said. 'I'll come to Yorkshire with you, Xenia.'

'And you'll accept the part of Emily?'

Katie took a deep breath. 'Okay. I'll call Melanie and tell her I want to do it, that I'm going to Yorkshire to research the Brontës . . . I can always cancel when we get back to London.'

Over my dead body, Xenia thought, but she remained silent.

Chapter Sixteen

They spoke only sporadically on the first part of their train journey to Yorkshire the following day. Xenia was busy with office memos, and Katie was immersed in the homework she had to complete for one of her acting classes at the Royal Academy of Dramatic Art.

They ordered lunch about an hour after the train had pulled out of King's Cross, and when it was served some time later they finally looked up and smiled at each other over their first course.

'Time flies when you're doing something you enjoy, doesn't it?' Katie murmured with a light laugh.

Although Xenia at first laughed with her, her face quickly changed along with her tone, when she grumbled, 'I loathe paperwork. Unfortunately, with Bella out sick, I have to do her job as well as mine. On the other hand, I shouldn't be complaining, since we're doing so well. Just imagine, when I met you in New York two years ago, I had been in partnership with Alan for only a year. We've been really lucky to become what we have in three short years.'

'But the special events and parties you plan are exactly *that*, Xenia. Special, *very* special. Certainly they're unique, and you and Alan have a lot of flair between the two of you. So I'm not surprised the company's been a success.'

'Thanks, Katie, it's nice of you to say that.' Picking up a spoon, Xenia took a few mouthfuls of the oxtail soup she had ordered, then broke off a bit of roll and added a dab of butter.

Katie watched her, wondering how she managed to stay so slender. Xenia was thirty-four, seven years older than Katie, but she didn't look it. She had an extremely youthful, girlish appearance even though her manner was somewhat sophisticated, and international, in certain ways. She spoke four languages, Russian, English, French and Italian, and was extremely well educated, and knowledgeable about art and literature. And, of course, the movies, having grown up with a father who produced them.

Katie marvelled at her ability to stay slim despite a very healthy appetite. She managed to resemble a model from Paris, was bone-thin, with a boyish figure and long legs. Willowy was the word Katie usually applied to Xenia. Her thick chestnut hair, falling to her shoulders, and her wide-set, transparent grey eyes were her most striking features. Her rather pale heart-shaped face was finely boned, and she had high cheekbones that to Katie seemed to have a Slavic slant.

Or perhaps that's just my imagination, Katie now thought, eyeing Xenia surreptitiously as she plunged a fork into a piece of tomato and ate it.

Katie had frequently wondered about Xenia and her past, for it was obvious that parts of it were shrouded in mystery. Katie had only ever asked her one personal question – about her mother – and had been instantly rebuffed.

Ever since that time she had left it to Xenia to choose when to confide in her. And often she did. All of a sudden Katie felt an unexpected stab of guilt; who was *she* to mentally criticize Xenia? She had never been particularly forthcoming about her own life, and she supposed she might appear a bit mysterious and secretive to Xenia.

'I spoke to Verity. Early this morning,' Xenia suddenly announced, looking directly at Katie. 'She goes riding every day, usually at the crack of dawn, so I had to catch her before she went galloping off across those endless fields, jumping hedges and putting herself and her horse to the test. Anyway, she's glad we're coming, and she's sending Lavinia to pick us up at the station in Harrogate.'

'Who's Lavinia?' Katie asked curiously.

'The daughter of Verity's cook, Anya. She was born in the village and grew up at Burton Leyburn. Now she does a bit of secretarial work for Verity. And sometimes other little jobs, like collecting guests from trains, that sort of thing. But she's actually an artist by profession, and a good one, too.'

Katie nodded, picked up her glass of water, and sat back as the waiter removed her salad plate. When they were alone, she said, 'By the way, I took your advice, Xenia, and called Melanie Dawson. She was thrilled when I accepted the role of Emily Brontë. But I'm going to feel terrible if I don't take the part.'

'I'm not going to listen to such talk as that, my friend. So just shut up.' The moment these words left her mouth Xenia was embarrassed and looked chagrined. Shaking her head, she said, 'My Russian grandmother would turn over in her grave if she heard me speaking to you like that, Katie. I didn't mean to be so rude. I'm so sorry.'

'It's okay, and you weren't rude, Xenia.' Katie paused, and then asked, 'Did you spend a lot of time with your Russian grandmother?' She hoped Xenia would not snap her head off as she sometimes had in the past. Questions about Tim and her family in particular were apparently forbidden, and rendered her speechless.

'When I was little, yes,' Xenia responded in a level voice, and continued, 'My father used to take me to Paris and Nice to see her. She was quite remarkable, and very beautiful well, I could see how beautiful she'd been as a young woman. She was still rather striking, quite an imposing old lady in very many ways. A *grande dame* is the best way to describe her, I think. Grandmother died in Nice when I was seventeen, a few months after I'd left

Lady Eden's school in London . . .' Xenia grinned at her, and added, 'And oh boy, what a stickler *she* was about manners. Worse than my grandmother, if that's at all possible.'

The waiter returned with their omelettes and green salads, and their conversation became desultory once again as they ate their lunch. When they had finished the main course, they both skipped dessert, settled for black coffee, no sugar, and then went back to their papers.

Katie finished her homework quickly, but Xenia was engrossed in her office papers and did not lift her head for some time. Settling herself in the corner of her seat, Katie sat gazing out of the window, watching the countryside flying past as the express train rolled on towards Yorkshire.

At one moment she leaned her head back against the seat and closed her eyes, drifting with her myriad thoughts. She found herself wondering about this house where they were going to stay, which apparently meant so much to Xenia. Katie had no idea what to expect, although she did have the impression that it was large. When Xenia talked about it she usually did so in terms of people – Pell, Verity's gardener who had, not green thumbs, but magical green fingers. And there was Dodie, the housekeeper, who believed she had psychic powers, and Pomeroy, the ancient bootboy, who wasn't actually the bootboy any more, because there weren't that many boots to clean. And just a short while ago Xenia had mentioned Anya, the cook, and her daughter Lavinia, born in the village, living at the house, a secretary to Verity but really a painter. Seemingly, Verity lived alone, except for this odd assortment of helpers, and her long-standing boyfriend, Rex Bellamy, known to everyone as Boy, who sometimes stayed with her. Curious mixture, Katie thought, just before she dozed off, lulled to sleep by the rhythm of the train and the warmth in the carriage.

The train screeching to a halt and sudden activity in the dining car made Katie sit up with a sudden jolt. Blinking, she glanced across at Xenia. 'Are we there?' she asked. 'Is this Harrogate?'

'No, Leeds. Big industrial city. Used to be the centre of ready-made clothing until they started making cheap suits in Hong Kong, or whatever. Still, it's thriving again. Leeds, I mean. Financial centre of the north, and a very big student town. Leeds University has become one of the most coveted places to study.'

Katie nodded. 'Yes, I've read quite a lot about that.'

'Yes, it's happening here.' Snapping her briefcase shut, Xenia put it on the seat next to her, glanced around the carriage and then leaned forward over the table. Looking intently at her friend, Xenia said, 'There's something I want to tell you. Actually, in a sense I want to apologize to you, Katie, for not telling you the truth. Well, look, I didn't really lie to you, I simply omitted to tell you something, and Verity always says that that's a form of lying.'

Katie stared back at Xenia. 'I'm not sure if I agree with Verity, but tell me.' When Xenia didn't say anything, Katie said again, 'Tell me what it is.'

Xenia still remained silent, but her eyes did not leave Katie's face.

Feeling slightly uncomfortable under this sudden and peculiar fixed scrutiny, Katie murmured, 'You can tell me *anything*, I'd never be upset. Why do you look so worried? It can't be all that bad. Or is it?'

Swallowing, Xenia replied quietly, 'I'm not divorced from Tim.'

'Oh.' Katie sat back, astounded.

'I let you think that, Katie. Actually, you assumed I was divorced when I told you I used to be married,' Xenia rushed on. 'Of course, I allowed you to make that assumption because it was easier for *me*. For you to think I was a divorced woman saved me from having to say anything else. And I didn't –'

'You mean you're still married to Tim, is that what you're saying?'

'Oh no. No, not that at all. I don't mean that . . .' Taking a deep breath after this slight pause, she finished, 'Tim is dead. He was killed in a ghastly accident. But I never tell anyone this, because then the sympathy starts, and the condolences, and I get terribly sorrowful again, and weepy, and nothing gets done because I fall totally apart. But I wanted you to know now, because at Burton Leyburn everything is out in the open, obviously. And within hours, no, perhaps even minutes, you'd know Tim was . . . no longer alive, and then where would I be?'

Katie reached out, put her hand over both of Xenia's, clasped together on top of the table. 'I'm so sorry . . . it must've been heartbreaking for you. And you're not to say another word. When and if you feel like talking about it, I'm here for you. You're my friend, and I care about you, so if you want to unburden yourself feel free to do so.'

'You're very kind, Katie.' Xenia took hold of Katie's hand and squeezed it. 'You probably think I've been secretive.'

'Oh no, not at all,' Katie answered softly, knowing that she was the secretive one because she had not told Xenia anything about her past.

Chapter Seventeen

The young woman who met them at Harrogate railway station was so stunning, so arresting in appearance, Katie did a double take as she hurried towards them down the platform. She was about five feet seven in height, very slender and delicately boned, with dark hair cut short and sleek.

There was a gamine quality about her, and she seemed vaguely familiar to Katie, although they had never met before. Lavinia was dressed in black wool capri trousers, ballet slippers and a turtle neck, this all-black ensemble enlivened by a short swing jacket of bright red wool.

After Lavinia and Xenia had embraced affectionately, Xenia brought Katie forward and introduced the two young women. They shook hands, said a cordial hello, and as Katie stared into the pretty woman's smiling face she immediately understood why Lavinia appeared to be so familiar. She was a dead ringer for a young Audrey Hepburn, had the same large, expressive dark eyes, heavy, though shapely brows, and a soft fringe falling onto her forehead.

After their introduction, Lavinia waved her hand airily, and exclaimed, 'Come on, let's go! Verity instructed me to have you back in time for tea, and you know what her afternoon teas mean to her, don't you, Xenia? They're something of a ritual these days, and not to be ignored.'

Not waiting for Xenia's comment, she swung around, beckoned to the porter, who by now had stacked their luggage on a trolley, and propelled them along the platform like a bustling sergeant major. Her take-charge manner was still in evidence as she swept forward, leading the way out of the station and into the nearby car park.

Within seconds the porter was loading the luggage into the boot of a burgundy-coloured, vintage Bentley Continental drop-head coupé with a weathered beige leather hood. Katie noticed what looked like a small family crest painted on the rim of the driver's door, just below the window. She tried to make out the symbols without success, and was instantly filled with curiosity.

'Why don't you sit in the back, Xenia,' Lavinia now suggested. 'Then you will be able to point out special landmarks to Katie.'

'What a good idea,' Xenia agreed, glanced at Katie and winked, then promptly opened the car door.

'Wouldn't you prefer to be in the front with Lavinia?' Katie asked.

'No, I'd like to be your tour guide. And she and I will

catch up on the local gossip later. Lavinia loves to play chauffeur, don't you, darling?'

Lavinia's light laugh rang out in the cool October air, but she made no comment, got into the car and turned on the ignition, obviously anxious to be on her way. Once the others were settled in the back, she pulled off the brake, sailing forth out of the car park and into Harrogate's busy streets.

They were soon in the centre of town, and Xenia glanced at Katie, then tapped the window. 'Look, that's the Stray over there, a piece of common ground which has grown rather famous over the centuries. It looks awfully bare right now, but in the spring hundreds of crocuses bloom, make a carpet of purple, yellow and white. And just down there are the gates into the Valley Gardens, famous for their magnificent flowers in summer. I used to go for walks there with my mother when I was a little girl.'

Katie followed the direction of Xenia's gaze and simply nodded. She thought she had detected a note of sadness, or perhaps wistfulness, in her friend's voice when she'd mentioned her mother. Katie decided to change the subject, and, looking at Xenia, she said, 'I've been noticing the lovely architecture . . . Harrogate's quite old, isn't it?'

'Oh yes, and the terrace of houses we've just passed dates back to the Georgian period. Actually, Harrogate has a number of elegant terraces like that, and crescents and squares. Some are Victorian and Edwardian, as well as Georgian. The town was once a famous spa, Katie, and some really lovely houses and villas were built, along with *very* grand hotels.'

From the front seat, Lavinia interjected, 'Katie, did you ever see a movie with Vanessa Redgrave and Dustin Hoffman called *Agatha*?'

'I'm not sure,' Katie responded, frowning, trying to remember. It sounded familiar to her, but she couldn't place it. 'Anyway, why do you ask?'

'Because it was filmed in Harrogate, in the seventies,' Lavinia answered her. 'And the actual events it was based on really did happen here, fifty years earlier. The story goes that in 1926 Agatha Christie disappeared. There was a big hue and cry. No one knew where she was. Then a bit later she was spotted at the Old Swan Hotel here, where she was registered under the name of Theresa Neele. After she'd been found, her publishers said that overwork had caused her to have a nervous breakdown. And that when she had seen a travel poster, at a railway station, advertising the beauties of Harrogate, she had simply taken a train up here. It was all very mysterious, like one of her novels.'

Katie now stared out of the window again, admiring the beauty of this ancient country town, wishing they could stay longer to walk around the streets. It had an old-fashioned, quirky charm about it that captivated her. The only excursions out of London she had made in the year she had been living in England had been to Stratford-upon-Avon. Rural areas intrigued her and she wanted to explore the bucolic spots that abounded.

Xenia cut into her thoughts, when she remarked, 'The town is very old, Katie; in fact I think it dates as far back as the 1300s. In any case, mineral wells were discovered here in 1571, and that's when people started to come to take the waters. Eventually, the Royal Pump Room was built, also the Royal Baths, where people took treatments for all kinds of ailments. Eventually, Harrogate became the most advanced centre for hydrotherapy in the world. Apparently, there was also quite a smart social scene here, and anyone who was anybody visited Harrogate – kings, queens, princes, princesses, dukes and duchesses, maharajahs, politicians, actresses, singers, and writers. You name it, they all came to Harrogate. Even Byron was here once to take the famous mineral waters.'

'Is it still a spa?' Katie asked.

'Not any more. Everything closed down after the Second World War,' Xenia said. 'In a way, it's a shame the old mineral wells have been allowed to fall into ruin.'

'But the springs are still there, under the ground,' Lavinia cut in. 'At least, that's what Verity says.'

'Will the wells ever be restored?' Katie wondered out loud.

'I don't think so.' Xenia shrugged. 'Modern medicine and proper diets have made this kind of spa redundant.'

As they rolled down the hill and onto a flat tarmacadam road, Lavinia announced, over her shoulder, 'We're heading up into the Dales now, Katie. They're a great beauty spot.'

'How far is Burton Leyburn?'

'Not too far,' Xenia replied. 'About an hour and twenty minutes, Katie. So sit back and relax and enjoy the countryside.'

Even though it was October the Dales were still green, this gently rolling landscape cut into sections by drystone walls and dotted with sheep grazing. The leaves had not yet fallen and most of the trees were shady green bowers lining the road the car was travelling along at a steady speed.

Katie's nose was glued to the window, her eyes taking in everything. And she couldn't help thinking what lush country this was, not what she had expected at all. In her mind's eye, she had envisaged Yorkshire as bleak and forbidding, but then perhaps it was at Haworth, where the Brontës came from.

Xenia had told her on the train that she had made arrangements for them to go over there tomorrow. The thought of this excursion excited Katie, and she was praying she wouldn't lose her nerve at the last minute, and step away from the role in *Charlotte and Her Sisters*. She didn't have to be told it was her big chance at last.

Katie was well aware that if she turned down Melanie

Dawson yet again she might never be offered another part. The famed producer and her husband, Harry, had singled Katie out when they had spotted her in an off-Broadway play several years ago. And they had taken a keen interest in her career ever since then.

It was obvious that they appreciated her as an actress, believed she had talent, otherwise they would not have gone out of their way to keep in touch with her. They had even looked her up in London eight months ago, and shown her a great deal of kindness, taking her to plays, then for supper afterwards at the best restaurants.

Katie turned her head, looked out of the car window once more, her eyes on the countryside as they drove on, heading for Burton Leyburn. They had already driven through various villages and the ancient cathedral city of Ripon. Now they were almost at Middleham, at least so the signpost told her.

How calm it is here in these ancient places, she thought, and instantly envisioned New York. She bit back a sigh, and wished she didn't feel so reluctant about going back there. It was this which was at the root of her indecision about accepting the part in *Charlotte and Her Sisters*.

She knew very well that the role was a great one for her, the best she'd ever been offered. And, apart from her worry about adopting an English accent, she knew she could handle it. Certainly the role of Emily was exactly right for her; the other parts Melanie had dangled in front of her had been all wrong.

Yes, playing Emily Brontë on Broadway would truly launch her acting career into the big time. She just wished she was not so alarmed about returning to New York. Her chest tightened and the familiar fear rushed through her. She took a deep breath, tried to turn away from her troubled past, the painful memories, and sat staring out of the window blindly. She did not see the landscape any more, only the faces of Denise and Carly, gone from her in life but forever in her heart and mind. Taking another deep breath, she leaned back against the car seat, waiting for the anxiety to recede, as it would eventually.

Xenia said, 'When we get to the top of the next hill, just ahead of us, we'll be in Middleham. Quite a famous beauty spot around here, and an area of Yorkshire that's saturated in history.'

'I've heard of Middleham,' Katie answered, forcing her voice to sound normal. 'I know that Richard III grew up there at the castle, and somewhere I read that it was once known as the Windsor of the north.'

'That's right, and it was indeed the seat of power. A great deal of power, actually. And it was in the hands of one man, the most powerful man in England in those days. He was known as the Kingmaker, Richard Neville, the Earl of Warwick, a Yorkshireman, and the last of the great feudal barons and magnates. He really did have more power than King Edward IV, his young cousin, whom he put on the throne of England after the War of the Roses. You see –' Xenia cut herself off, and exclaimed, 'Look, Katie, over there! Those are the ruins. Slow down a bit, Lavinia, so Katie can see them properly.'

Lavinia dutifully did as she was told and brought the car almost to a standstill as they drove very slowly past the castle. She said, 'If you want to look around Middleham, I'll bring you back another day, Katie. But right now I've got to race back to the house. Verity's waiting for us.'

'I understand,' Katie replied, peering out of the window, straining to see the famous ruins. They appeared eerie and mysterious, the shattered battlements wrapped in deepening shadows as the cold northern light began to dim.

Involuntarily she shivered, drew herself into her loden coat, suddenly feeling chilled to the bone. She tried to throw off the irrational feeling of apprehension that suddenly gripped her.

Once they left the ruined castle behind them, the car began a steady climb up the hill which led out of Middleham. In a short while they were on a winding road that flowed across the top of the moorland. The sun of earlier had long since disappeared, but up here the sky was a soft, pale blue, and filled with great scudding white clouds blown along by the gusting wind. A few birds wheeled and turned against the puff-ball clouds, solitary inhabitants of the empty, rolling moors of Coverdale.

Eventually the twisting road straightened out, then slowly fell away, and they were descending into the lush green valley below. It was a valley marked by stands of ancient trees, and pastures sectioned by drystone walls. And through this verdant valley ran a narrow silver ribbon of a river wending its way towards the North Sea.

Ten minutes later the car was approaching another village. And this time the signpost announced that they were about to enter Burton Leyburn.

Katie glanced at Xenia quickly. 'We must be there!'

'Not yet. The house is outside the village.' She grinned at Katie. 'You sound impatient to get there.'

'I suppose I am. What you've told me about it has made me very curious.'

Xenia smiled enigmatically, but made no further comment.

Burton Leyburn was small, pretty, picturesque, a classical Yorkshire Dales village, clustered with houses made of local grey stone. Many of the gardens were filled with flowers which hinted at an Indian summer just passed, although the majority of the blooms were of russet, gold and amber hues, mostly chrysanthemums, a favourite at this time of year.

Katie noticed several small shops, a post office, a pub called the White Hart, and a lovely old grey-stone church with a square Norman tower and stained-glass windows. But there were very few people about and no cars in evidence: it looked to her like a deserted spot.

When she voiced this thought, Xenia and Lavinia both burst out laughing, and Lavinia said, 'But it's tea time, Katie, and everybody's at home tucking in.'

At the end of the main village street, Lavinia turned left, slowing her speed in order to ease the car down the narrow lane. But within seconds she was pulling onto a much broader road, and she did not slow her speed until they arrived at tall and elaborate black-iron gates. They were impressive, daunting, set between huge stone pillars, the latter surmounted by stone stags.

The gates were closed, and Lavinia exclaimed, 'Hang on a minute, Pell must have locked up already. I'll have to go and punch in the code.'

'I'll do it, it's easier,' Xenia exclaimed, and alighted swiftly. Skirting the bushes, she went to the metal stand which held a key pad and punched in numbers. A second later she was getting back into the Bentley.

Slowly the iron gates swung open.

Lavinia shot through them, and sped down the drive. This was very wide, actually an avenue, and it was lined on either side by ancient trees, many of their thick trunks covered in green moss. Among the trees, deer and fawns wandered around, some of them grazing, and the animals added a natural charm to the setting, which had a timelessness about it.

Xenia observed Katie staring at the deer. 'I forgot to tell you, but Burton Leyburn Hall is set in a deer park. There have always been deer here, ever since Queen Elizabeth I gifted the lands to Robert Leyburn, who eventually built the hall on them. These days we've got about fifty deer, stags, and fawns.'

Katie had been thinking about her mother's problems with the deer in Malvern, deer which ate all of her flowers, but she decided not to mention this now. Instead, she asked, 'How old is the house?'

'It's late Elizabethan. It was built in 1577, which is the date over the door, and that's probably when the house was actually finished. So it's over four hundred years old. But you'll see it in a moment. It's rather charming.'

The woods on either side of the wide drive soon gave way to a vast expanse of flat green parkland, and in the distance, poised against the blue horizon, stood the house. Katie realized that Xenia's description of it as being 'rather charming' was something of an understatement.

It did not look like a country house, or a manor house. Nor could it be termed a mansion. Burton Leyburn Hall was much, much more. It fell into the category of stately home, of that Katie was absolutely certain. Even from this distance she could see that it was magnificent.

But much to her disappointment, Katie did not get a chance to view the house properly in the way she wished to; as they approached the front façade, Lavinia suddenly, and rather quickly, veered off to the right.

She sped down a dirt road and turned into a large cobblestone yard, exclaiming, 'These are the stables, Katie,' and brought the vintage Bentley to an abrupt standstill.

'Come on,' she said, pulling on the brake and turning off the ignition simultaneously. 'We're late for tea. We'll deal with the luggage later.'

'So sorry to bring you through the back way,' Xenia apologized once they had alighted from the car. Taking hold of Katie's arm, she led her across the cobblestone yard.

Katie heard snorting and whinnying, and glanced over her shoulder. She saw two beautiful horses looking out over the stall doors. Then, a split second later, she was ushered into the house.

Chapter Eighteen

A cacophony of sounds greeted them as they came into the back entrance hall, which also served as a mudroom-cloakroom and was filled with a diverse collection of riding boots, green wellies, raincoats, and Barbours.

A woman's voice, singing in a foreign tongue, rose above the clatter of pots and pans, a dog barking, a kettle whistling and muted voices in conversation. All emanated from the nearby kitchen, from which delicious smells were wafting, reminding Katie suddenly of home.

'That's Anya singing, of course.' Xenia grinned as she shed her black coat and scarf, and hung both on a peg. 'I want you to meet her, but it'll have to be later. Right now I think we should join Verity for tea.'

Katie nodded, put her loden coat alongside Xenia's, then straightened the jacket of her wine-coloured trouser suit. She glanced at her watch and frowned 'It's almost five, aren't we a bit late?'

'No, only a few minutes.'

'But I thought the English always had afternoon tea at four.'

'Anywhere between four and five. And here it's always been later, around quarter to five, mostly because dinner's usually about eight-thirty or nine. But Verity doesn't mind if people are a few minutes late for tea.' She shook her head, added, 'It's Lavinia who always makes such a fuss about being on time for tea. Come on, follow me.'

Xenia left the mudroom and headed down a long corridor. This was somewhat gloomy, despite wall sconces which hung at intervals on the side walls. Katie, who was right behind her, soon found herself stepping into a large, square entrance hall filled with late-afternoon light, plus sparkling illumination from a huge, carved-wood chandelier dropping down from the ceiling. The sudden change made her blink, and she adjusted her eyes to the brightness.

Xenia turned, waved her hand in the air, and said, with sudden vivacity, 'This is where you *should* have come in, Katie, and isn't it a lovely entrance hall?'

'It certainly is, and very impressive,' Katie exclaimed, smiling with pleasure. Glancing around, she took in the four tall leaded windows, the high-flung, beamed ceiling, the stone urn of chrysanthemums and branches on an oak table, and faded but beautiful wall tapestries.

'In summer, it's a tradition to have tea either in the Blue Room, or on the terrace just outside it, depending on the weather. But at the end of September, it's always taken upstairs in the Great High Chamber, as it's called.

This custom was started by Verity's great-grandmother, who favoured that room,' Xenia explained. 'So we've got to go to the second floor.'

'That's no problem,' Katie answered.

Their footsteps echoed sharply as Xenia, making for the wide, curving staircase, guided Katie across the time-worn old flagstones in the carpetless hall.

Together, the two women mounted the grand staircase constructed of dark polished oak and with an intricately carved balustrade. The side wall was hung with family portraits of Leyburn ancestors, and Katie would have loved to pause for a moment really to look at the paintings. But Xenia, hurrying faster, was already ahead, her high heels clattering against the wide, wooden stairs.

When Katie reached the second-floor landing, Xenia was sitting on a bench, waiting for her, and she looked at her intently, frowning. 'Is there something the matter? You're looking rather odd.'

'No, nothing's wrong. I was just wondering about Verity's last name. You've never told me what it is. I don't know what to call her.'

'Her married name is Lady Hawes, but she doesn't like to be called that. Probably because she's divorced from Geoffrey . . . that's Lord Hawes. She prefers Verity.'

'I can't call her by her first name, that's so rude.'

'She doesn't mind, honestly.'

Katie shook her head. 'I can't. I shall call her Lady Hawes.'

Xenia smiled knowingly. 'Suit yourself, but you'll *see*, she won't like it.' Xenia now opened the large double doors on the landing, beckoning to Katie. 'This is the Great High Chamber.'

What an apt name, Katie thought, as she followed her friend inside.

The room was vast and high, with a soaring ceiling that was coffered, and heavily decorated with plaster flowers and medallions, each painted in soft pastel colours. But aside from its size and airy proportions, what was so stunning about it were the six windows which almost reached to the ceiling. All six were mullioned; three punctuated one wall. Two of these windows had window seats beneath them, while the third central window was in a curved bay, and was, in fact, an oriel window into which was set, in glass panes, the coat of arms of the Leyburn family. Two more tall windows flanked the fireplace, a sixth broke up the wall facing the bay with its oriel window.

Katie realized that because of the windows the room must be spectacular on a sunny day. But even now, late on this October afternoon, soft light suffused it. And this natural light, slowly fading as dusk came down, was underscored by the muted glow from the porcelain lamps, shaded with cream silk, which were placed around the room.

A fire blazed in the hearth, potpourri and candles scented the air, as did several tall vases of gold and russet chrysanthemums mixed in with copper beach leaves and yellow roses.

Overall, the room was essentially cream in colour, with soft accents of pale green, pink and a touch of black. Katie took in several large sofas and armchairs covered in cream silk-brocade, mixed with handsome antique chests and occasional tables. A beautiful Elizabethan writing table, intricately carved, stood behind one of the large sofas. Hanging on the cream walls were wonderful portraits of Leyburn ancestors, all of them female, and the vivid colours of their gowns enhanced the mono-chromatic scheme.

Katie's instant impression, as her eyes scanned the room, was one of charm and beauty, along with a feeling of welcoming warmth and comfort.

A woman was sitting near the fireplace and she rose, came forward to meet them, her face filled with smiles, her eyes sparkling.

'You must be the famous Katie Byrne. Whom I've heard so much about,' she said, extending her hand, taking Katie's in hers. 'I'm so glad Xenia asked you to come. I've been longing to meet you.'

'And I you,' Katie found herself saying with a wide smile. 'Thank you for having me, Lady Hawes.'

'Oh no, no, no, not that! It's Verity. That's the only name I answer to around here, Katie. Please call me Verity.'

Katie inclined her head. 'Verity, then.'

'Now, come and sit here near the fire, not that it's very cold out today. But I do like a fire. There's something rather comforting about one, don't you think?'

Katie simply nodded and sat down.

'And very welcoming,' said Xenia, embracing Verity and then lowering herself into an armchair. Leaning forward, looking at the tea tray on the large coffee table, Xenia began to laugh. 'Goodness, what scrumptious things, Verity, but oh so lethal! Clotted cream and Anya's homemade strawberry jam for the scones. Oh dear, and a sponge cake with cream and raspberry-jam filling. And chocolate eclairs. Everything does make my mouth water, but I think I'll settle for one of the nursery sandwiches and a cup of tea with lemon. What about you, Katie?'

'A cucumber sandwich will do nicely, thanks. I'm afraid all the lovely creamy things will go straight to my hips.'

'Neither of you have to worry,' Verity exclaimed. 'You're both as thin as sticks. Come along, tuck in, you must be hungry after the journey. And dinner is not until nine tonight.'

Reaching for the teapot, Verity filled their cups and her own, added lemon to Xenia's and asked Katie, 'Do you prefer milk?'

'No, lemon, please.'

The door burst open at this moment, and Lavinia came gliding into the room.

She had shed her red jacket and freshened up, and once again Katie couldn't help thinking how much she resembled the late Audrey Hepburn, as the star had looked when she had first gone into movies. And it was that essentially gamine quality that was so appealing about Lavinia, and gave her such individuality.

Lavinia was carrying a folder. 'I'm sorry, Verity,' she said, 'I forgot to give you your letters before I went to Harrogate. I'll put them here on the table. You can sign them later, and I'll post them tomorrow.' She placed the folder in the middle of the Elizabethan table behind the sofa, and then came to join them in front of the fire.

'I ran into Pell, and he says we're in for a cold snap tomorrow, Xenia. You and Katie will have to wrap up well when you go to Haworth. It can be bitter up on those moors.'

'I thought you'd planned to take Katie to the Brontë Museum on Saturday?' Verity said swiftly, looking across at Xenia. 'I really need to go over a number of important matters with you, and very frankly, I'd set aside tomorrow morning to do that, since I have a busy day on Saturday . . .' Her cultured voice trailed off and she sat back in her chair, crossed her legs.

'Oh that's not a problem, we can go to Haworth on Saturday, Verity. And tomorrow Katie can immerse herself in all the Brontë books in the library here. Right, Katie?'

'Yes, I'd like that. It doesn't matter when we go to Haworth. Sunday would be fine, if you prefer that.'

'And miss one of Anya's smashing Sunday lunches, oh no,' Xenia laughed.

Lavinia poured herself a cup of tea, placed a slice of sponge cake on a plate and carried both over to the hearth. Here she sat down on a low bench, and took a sip of tea.

A silence fell between the four of them.

Katie leaned against the sofa cushions, relaxing, enjoying the warmth and beauty of this extraordinary room, so filled with the past, the history of this family, and she felt its peacefulness, its lovely tranquillity flowing around her. There were no sounds at all except for the crackle of the logs in the fireplace and the faint ticking of a large brass carriage clock on a nearby chest of drawers. The clock was surrounded by many silver-framed photographs and she wished she could go and look at them, but she knew she couldn't do that. It would be far too rude. Perhaps later, if she were alone here, she would sneak a look.

Her eyes shifted to her hostess, and for a few seconds she studied Verity surreptitiously. She was a lovely-looking woman in a soft, understated way. Her hair was pale blonde, almost silver-gilt, and she wore it in a pageboy style which fell just above her shoulders. Her face was very clean cut, almost sharp in its planes and angles, and her pale-blue eyes were large and expressive under arched brown brows. Of medium height, Verity was trimly built and slender, and she looked good in the expensive, well-cut grey trousers, and a man-tailored white silk shirt. Katie noticed that she wore a watch on one wrist, and a collection of narrow gold bracelets on the other, but no rings at all. A long string of large pearls and pearl studs on her ears were her only other pieces of jewellery. But despite her simple clothes and the simplicity of her appearance, Katie thought she was one of the most intensely glamorous women she had ever seen, and she was intrigued by Verity, longed to know more about her.

Xenia broke the silence when she said to Lavinia, 'Do you want to come with us to Haworth? You're very welcome.'

'Thanks, but no thanks, Xenia. I'm going to paint on Saturday and Sunday.'

'The Hudson Gallery in Harrogate is giving Lavinia a show,' Verity announced with a smile. 'And although she has a number of paintings finished, she still needs quite a few more to make a full show.'

'How wonderful. Congratulations!' Xenia exclaimed.

'Yes, congratulations, Lavinia,' Katie murmured.

'I hope you'll both come up for it,' Lavinia said, looking from Xenia to Katie. 'The show's in January.'

'When in January?' Xenia asked.

'Towards the end of the month,' Lavinia replied. 'Penny Hudson, the owner of the gallery, hasn't set the actual date. But she was thinking of the twenty-fifth, something like that. When all of the Millennium celebrations have calmed down.'

Xenia nodded. 'I'll probably be back in London by then. I have to be in New York for the New Year, we have a number of events we're organizing.' She looked at Katie and said, 'And you'll be rehearsing, won't you?'

'Yes,' Katie said quickly, and picked up her cup of tea, suddenly not wanting to talk about the play. How angry they would all be with her if she should change her mind. I'm not going to do that, she thought. That would be cowardly on my part. She said to Lavinia, 'I'm sorry I'll miss the show, but I would love to see some of your paintings, if you'd like to show them to me this weekend.'

'Hey, that's a great idea, Katie!' Lavinia cried, full of enthusiasm, her exuberance bubbling to the surface. 'Perhaps you'll have a chance to come and see them tomorrow. Verity lets me use an old barn for a studio, and it's not far from the Hall, near the Home Farm. It's a nice walk, but if you prefer, I'll come and fetch you in the landrover.'

'I'd enjoy that,' Katie murmured. Once again, her curiosity rose to the surface and she wondered what Lavinia's story was, and how Anya, a Russian woman, had come to be the cook here. She would ask Xenia later.

After eating the cream cake and a chocolate eclair,

Lavinia jumped up, announcing, 'I'd better be off. Thanks so much for tea, Verity. I'll be in the office for another hour, if you need me.'

'I don't think I will, darling,' Verity said, smiling at the younger woman. 'And thanks for all your hard work today, and for fetching Xenia and Katie from the train.'

Lavinia simply smiled at her, and hurried out of the Great High Chamber, saying as she left, 'See you tomorrow, ladies,' and closed the heavy door behind her with a bang.

Verity laughed. 'Oh to be twenty-two again and full of vitality, as she is.'

'You're no slouch yourself,' Xenia exclaimed with a laugh. 'Look at you ... out every morning at the crack, riding your horse, and jumping hedges. Running the estate and the village and everything else in sight. Overseeing the Home Farm. Looking after Leyburn interests in general. Why you're ... a ... veritable tycoon. And very successful at what you do, which is a lot.'

Verity smiled. 'Not really, and you're just prejudiced.'

Xenia laughed, and said, 'I'm loth to break up our little tea party, but I think I ought to retrieve the luggage and take Katie to her room, if you don't mind.'

'Of course, you must do that, and you should both have a rest, relax a bit before dinner. And I'm sure you'll find your suitcases have been brought up from the stables by Pell's boy. Lavinia will have asked Jamie to do that earlier. You know what a sergeant major she's become.'

Chapter Nineteen

'I asked Verity to give you this bedroom, because it's my favourite, after my own, that is,' Xenia said. 'And I hope you like it as much as I do, Katie.' As she spoke Xenia flung open the door, placed her palm on Katie's back and gave her a gentle push into the room.

Katie almost gasped out loud as she stood in the middle of the bedroom, glancing about her. 'Oh Xenia, it's really beautiful!' she cried, and when she turned to look at her friend her face was wreathed in smiles.

Xenia walked in and stood leaning against a small, elegant armoire, watched Katie moving across to the tall, mullioned windows. 'You won't be able to see much tonight, it's already dark outside, but trust me, the view's spectacular,' Xenia remarked. 'Tomorrow you'll see just how spectacular – the gardens, the terrace, and the parterres below. And across the lawns there are views as far as the eye can see . . . all the way to the ornamental lake.'

Katie nodded then turned away from the window and stood staring at everything, her eyes missing nothing as they flicked around the room. The walls were wood-panelled, but they had been painted a soft green: not celadon, not lime, but a peculiar sort of faded tone, which was somewhere in between these two hues. What was unique was the painting on each central panel on all the walls. Each one had been decoratively painted with chains of pink and red roses looped together with ribbons and bows.

A white marble fireplace, Robert Adam in style, had a gilded French mirror hanging above it, and the four-poster bed was dressed with pale green taffeta; the same fabric hung on either side of the mullioned windows, sewn into swagged and tied-back draperies. There was no carpet on the floor, except for two rugs on either side of the bed, obviously because no one wanted to hide the lovely, honey-coloured parquet floor set in an intricate pattern.

Turning to Xenia, Katie exclaimed, 'It has a distinct French feeling to it. Certainly it's not a bit Elizabethan.'

'True,' Xenia agreed with a grin. 'And guess what, it's called Frenchie's Room. Verity's great-grandmother, the one who started the tradition for tea in the Great High Chamber, was a Frenchwoman, and this was her room. Almost a hundred years ago, she had it designed, decorated and furnished to her taste.'

'And the family has kept it that way all these years. I'm not surprised they did. It's a lovely room.' Katie walked over to the kidney-shaped dressing table with a pale-green silk skirt, and stared down at the pretty objects on it, admiringly.

Xenia continued, 'From what I understand from Verity, her great-grandmother was a favourite with everyone. Very beautiful, charming, and flirtatious. Her name was Lucile, but her husband and her close friends called her Frenchie, hence the name of the bedroom.'

'I'm glad you picked it for me, Xenia, it's a room with a happy feeling to it.'

Xenia nodded in agreement, then indicated the door on the far side of the bedroom. 'The bathroom's in there, quite grand actually. And over there you have a big walk-in closet.' Xenia went over and opened it and looked inside. 'Verity was correct, your suitcase was brought up and Dodie's already unpacked it for you. Probably when we were having tea.' Swinging to face Katie, she asked, 'Now, is there anything you need?'

Katie shook her head. 'I was going to ask for some water, but I see there's a carafe on the bedside table.'

'Yes, and a bowl of fruit over there on that little table by the side of the armchair. And in that china biscuit barrel are Anya's home-baked chocolate cookies.'

'Thanks, but no thanks,' Katie laughed.

Xenia strode across to the door, opened it, then swung around. 'I'm not far away, just one room down, so you know where I am if you need anything.'

'Thanks, Xenia, and what time should I be ready for dinner?'

'About eight-thirty, for a drink in the Great High Chamber.' Xenia blew a kiss as she closed the door behind her.

Immediately, Katie turned the key in the lock and then walked over to a chest, began opening drawers, trying to ascertain where Dodie had put her things.

But Xenia, standing on the other side of the door in the corridor, did not move for a moment, stood gazing reflectively at the door, asking herself yet again why Katie had such a compulsion for locking herself in rooms. She did it continually at the London house, and now she was doing it here at Burton Leyburn. She was afraid, of course . . . but of what? Or whom?

Baffled, Xenia turned away, walked down the corridor to her own room, realizing that Katie's strange behaviour was beginning to trouble her.

Once she had familiarized herself with the bedroom and bathroom, Katie took off her suit and sweater, hung them in the wardrobe and put on her dressing gown.

After drinking a glass of water, she took her Five Year Diary out of her carryall, found a pen in her handbag and went over to the *bûreau plat* in a corner of the room.

Seating herself at the desk, she opened her diary, realizing as she did that the events of the past five years hadn't taken up that many pages after all.

She flicked through her diary, reading a page here and there, and discovered that mostly she had written about her acting career, such as it was. There were quite a few pages about the professional things that had preoccupied her since she had left the American Academy of Dramatic Arts when she was twenty-two.

Suddenly, Katie saw Grant Miller's name, and she stiffened, stared hard at it, frowning. Then she began to read the pages on which she had recounted their first meeting, their first date and the beginning of their love affair.

Sighing deeply, Katie finally sat back in the chair, biting her lip, wondering what to do about him.

Nothing, she thought. I'll do nothing about him.

Deep down she hoped her lack of interest would send him a potent message, and that he would finally go away. Poor Grant, he tried so hard to please, and managed in the process only to irritate her. And irritation was hardly conducive to a good relationship.

But it had never been all that good anyway, and she wondered now why she had ever became involved with him. She who was so very wary of all men, and distrusting of them.

Initially, she had been attracted to him because of his looks. Yes, a physical attraction then, she knew that only too well. But there was also his extraordinary talent as an actor. She admired him on a stage. Off the stage he was . . . *dull*. No two ways about that. Grant was only interesting when he was playing the part of someone else. Perhaps that was why he was such a good actor.

In real life he was a little bland, a cipher of sorts, but as a cipher he could so easily lose himself in a role, make the person he was playing really come alive. He could take on the persona of any character he wished, because he had no persona of his own.

She frowned again, thinking this was truly a damning condemnation of someone, but however unpalatable, it was the truth. I'll die of boredom and irritation if I stay with Grant Miller, she thought. Fortunately he was far away in New York, working in a play on Broadway. And so she didn't have to cope with the problem of Grant and his constant pursuit of her right now.

Once she returned, *if* she took the role of Emily Brontë, it would be a different matter. He would be there, seeking her out, and he would be an unwanted suitor.

I'm not going to think about Grant tonight, she told herself, and pushed all thoughts of him to one side.

Turning to a new page in her diary, Katie wrote:

October 21st, 1999   *Burton Leyburn Hall*
                                                    Yorkshire

I want to put everything down while my first impressions are fresh in my mind.

Xenia has told me several times in the last year that Burton Leyburn Hall is special to her, the beloved house where she spent so many happy days as a child. Yet she has never really told me about the house, as a house, I mean. What it looks like, how old it is, those kinds of things.

And so I was momentarily startled when I first saw it this afternoon . . . rising out of the faint mist at the end of the long, wide avenue of trees. It stood alone against the horizon, unencumbered by trees or hills or mountain tops, its chimneys and turrets precisely outlined against the backdrop of that fading pale sky.

From a distance it seemed so . . . dreamlike . . . magical, and I couldn't wait to see it properly. And then Lavinia drove us to the stables instead, and I missed a close-up view of the front of the house. I was so disappointed.

Lavinia is going to take me to her studio tomorrow morning to see her paintings, but before she does I am going to take a walk around the outside of the house. In the ten months I've lived in England I've become interested in architecture, just like Dad. He favours American Colonial, although ever since he's been coming to Ireland and England with Mom for the past nine years, his tastes have grown and expanded. Like me, he has developed a passion for Georgian and Elizabethan houses.

I feel the timelessness of this house . . . and when I stepped into the front entrance hall I sensed the weight of its history and of this family. When Yenia took me into the Great High Chamber, I thought of that phrase, 'if only walls could talk'. Cliché though it is, it's so very true . . . I can only imagine what the walls of this house have witnessed. Four hundred years of one family living here . . . Marriages, births, deaths.

Pain and suffering, joy and happiness, sorrow and heartbreak. Life eternal, from one generation to the next . . .

My room is beautiful, a mixture of soft greens, and mostly French antiques, at least the pieces look French. I want to see a portrait of the woman called Lucile, known as Frenchie, who came here as a foreign bride and put her own stamp on this house, in certain ways. Yes, Frenchie intrigues me.

So does Verity. She was such a surprise. Xenia has mentioned her sister-in-law, but she's never described her, nor had I seen a photograph of her. Xenia's house in London is short on photographs, so I've noticed. I wonder if Verity knows how glamorous she is? She has a natural glamour that comes from her classical blonde looks, the way she moves and talks, and presents herself with such grace. Xenia told me Verity's forty-one, but she doesn't look it. Xenia and she are more like sisters, but then they spent a lot of time together as children.

When Xenia confided on the train that she's a widow I was really taken aback at first. But it has always been apparent that she loved Tim so much, it didn't really make sense to me that they had been divorced. Now I understand why she's not particularly interested in men . . . she must still be grieving . . .

Katie put down the pen, sat staring at the wall for a split second, then she pushed back the chair and rose. The room was suddenly icy cold and she felt chilled. Walking across the bedroom and into the bathroom, she turned on the taps of the huge tub, then seated herself on a small, white-painted chair to wait for the bath to fill. A good soak would do the trick, she decided, then wondered, absently, how they kept warm here in winter.

There was a full-length mirror on the wall at the far end of the walk-in closet, and Katie stood in front of it, checking herself out before leaving the bedroom.

She had dressed in a dark, fir-green crushed velvet jacket, long and loose and falling just below her hips. With it she had teamed a silk shirt of the same fir-green colour, and a pair of narrow, black silk trousers. High-heeled black silk pumps and pearl earrings completed the ensemble.

I don't look *too* bad, she thought, staring at herself critically, her head on one side. She had tied back her fiery red hair, fastened the pony tail with a black satin bow, and although the style gave her a certain severity, she liked the look it gave her . . . a touch of elegance, she thought.

Turning quickly, she went back to the bedroom, and immediately noticed her diary on the *bûreau plat*, where she had abandoned it earlier. After returning it to her carryall, she picked up a small black evening purse and left the bedroom.

Katie walked down the wide staircase to the second-floor landing, and pushed open the heavy oak door of the Great High Chamber.

The room was empty, and she hesitated for a moment

just inside the doorway, before walking across to the fireplace, where a huge log fire blazed on the stone hearth. The scented candles were still burning, Mozart played softly in the background, and there was a tray with drinks sitting on an antique chest.

Glancing at her watch, she saw that it was exactly eight-thirty, but the carriage clock on the chest near the fireplace read ten minutes earlier. Maybe her watch was fast. Stepping closer, she leaned forward to look at the photographs arranged around the clock, which she had caught a glimpse of during tea.

There was one of Verity in an elegant, pale-blue suit and a navy-blue picture hat, obviously quite recent. She had her arm linked through that of an attractive young man with a shock of blond hair like hers. He must be her son, whom Xenia had once mentioned.

Verity appeared in other photographs, with lots of different people. Then Katie spotted a picture of Tim with a small boy. She leaned even closer, her eyes resting on it for a moment, frowning slightly. The child bore such a strong resemblance to Xenia, Katie was startled. Had Xenia and Tim had a child?

'You got down before me,' Xenia said from the doorway, her voice sounding more clipped and English than usual as she strode into the room.

Katie swung around and nodded, feeling inexplicably embarrassed. Had Xenia seen her fascination with the picture? Would she think her rude for prying?

Xenia came to a stop at the drinks tray on the chest, asked, 'How about a drop of bubbly? Or do you prefer white wine?'

'White wine tonight. Thanks, Xenia.'

A moment later Xenia was handing Katie the glass. Her face was very pale, stark almost, and she was unsmiling. Her transparent grey eyes were sadder than Katie had ever seen them, and her manner was subdued.

Taking the glass quickly, Katie went and sat in one of the armchairs, her embarrassment now turning to discomfort. It was as though she had been caught with her hand in the cookie jar. Perhaps she had been. Suddenly, she knew that Xenia had seen her staring at the photograph of Tim . . . And her child? The boy in the picture was so like Xenia, Katie was suddenly convinced it was her son. But where was he? At school? And why had she never mentioned him?

Xenia poured herself a glass of champagne and joined Katie near the fireplace. She said, 'It's just the three of us for dinner tonight. Verity did ask her friend Rex Bellamy to join us for the weekend, but he won't arrive until tomorrow. You'll like him, he's very nice.'

Nodding, Katie took a sip of wine and said, 'Cheers.'

'Cheers.' Xenia sipped from the champagne.

'Why is he called Boy?' Katie asked.

'Because his father was also named Rex and when he was a child everyone referred to him as The Boy, or

Rex's Boy, and it became a nickname.' Xenia shook her head, faintly smiled. 'The English have such a penchant for giving each other nicknames, some of them most peculiar, I'm afraid.'

Katie merely nodded, and then glanced at the door as it opened. Verity smiled at her as she came forward, exclaiming, 'I've just sent Dodie up to turn on the heat in your room, Katie. It only just occurred to me that you must have been frightfully cold while you were dressing for dinner.'

'It did get a bit chilly,' Katie replied, smiling back. 'But I took a hot bath and that did the trick.'

'The room will be nice and cosy when you go to bed,' Verity murmured, and added, 'My apologies for being so thoughtless.'

'It's all right,' Katie assured her, 'really it is. I'm fine.'

Xenia said, 'I've been looking at one of the maps in the library, Verity, trying to plot the best route to Haworth on Saturday. I guess Harrogate then across to Ilkley and down to Keighley.'

'I think you might be better off going from Harrogate to Skipton, but you can ask Rex tomorrow. He'll give you the best route. He's rather good at things like that.'

After this exchange, Verity poured herself a glass of champagne, then strolled over to the fireplace, stood in front of it.

Katie, watching her, thought she looked stunning in a long, red-wool skirt, cut straight and slender, worn with a red turtleneck cashmere sweater. A collection of gold chains hung around her neck; she wore gold hoop earrings and the many narrow gold bracelets which tinkled when she moved her right arm.

Katie thought that in contrast Xenia looked somewhat sombre in a dark-grey suit and matching sweater. Xenia wore no jewellery at all, which wasn't like her, and she seemed out of sorts. She's not her usual buoyant self, Katie decided, leaning back in the chair, observing her friend from the corner of her eye. It struck Katie that Xenia was sadder tonight than she had ever seen her, and she wondered why.

Verity lifted her champagne flute in the air. 'Cheers,' she said.

The other two women responded, also lifting their glasses.

After taking a sip of champagne, Verity said, 'It's rather dull here in the country, Katie, so I thought I might invite a few people for dinner on Saturday –'

'Oh no, don't do that!' Xenia exclaimed, interrupting her.

Verity stared at Xenia, obviously puzzled.

Katie, turning from Verity to Xenia, recognized the expression of horror sliding across Xenia's face, immediately understood that the idea of a dinner party appalled her.

Quickly, Katie interjected, 'You don't have to make a dinner party for me, Verity, although it's very nice of you to think of doing so. I'm very happy to be alone with you and Xenia.'

'All right. Then it will be just the four of us, since I've invited Rex to come over from York to spend the weekend with us.'

Chapter Twenty

Ten minutes later the three women went downstairs for dinner. Verity led the way.

'Thanks,' Xenia whispered in Katie's ear, as they followed their hostess down the stairs.

Katie nodded, smiled at her, but made no comment.

When they arrived in the grand front entrance hall, Verity took hold of Katie's arm, led her across the floor. 'There's a formal dining room over there: it seats a hundred people. But we rarely use it these days. The smaller one is perfect for us, for family dinners,' Verity explained. Opening the door, she ushered Katie inside.

Katie saw at once that it was a charming room, and quite unusual. Circular in shape, its walls were upholstered in red brocade and hung with beautiful classical landscape paintings. The round dining table, skirted in red taffeta, was teamed with three antique dining chairs, upholstered in black silk. Other matching chairs were placed against the walls; two flanked a sideboard, another one stood next to an inlaid wood chest. A crystal chandelier sparkled above the table, which was set with four silver candlesticks holding white candles, standing around a bowl of dark-red flowers. Crystal goblets and silverware completed the setting.

A fire in the grate and the candlelight added to the cosy, welcoming feeling of the red dining room, which Katie was silently admiring.

'Sit here,' Xenia murmured, indicating a chair. 'Verity always takes the middle chair.'

Katie did as she was told, and she was spreading the linen napkin on her knee when a door at the far end of the room opened.

A plump, grey-haired woman with apple-rosy cheeks, wearing a black dress and a white organdie apron, came into the room. Moving quickly, she went straight over to the sideboard and took a bottle of white wine from the ice bucket. 'I thought I'd serve the wine now, m'lady.'

'That's fine, Dodie,' Verity said. Glancing at Katie, she went on, 'This is Dodie, who looks after us all so well. And Dodie, this is Miss Byrne.'

Dodie nodded, smiled. 'Pleased to meet you, Madame,' she said, walked around the table and poured wine into Katie's crystal goblet.

'I'm pleased to meet you too, Dodie,' Katie said. 'Thank you.'

For a split second Dodie seemed unexpectedly flustered. She looked intently at Katie, then swiftly, almost jerkily, stepped back. She inclined her head politely, but she was no longer smiling.

Katie, staring at her retreating figure, couldn't help wondering what had wrought the sudden change in the housekeeper's demeanour. Dodie had backed away from her as if she had a bad smell.

Once Dodie had poured wine for Verity and Xenia, she returned the bottle to the silver ice bucket, and then left the dining room swiftly, closing the door quietly behind her.

Katie stared across the table at Xenia, instantly realized that her friend had noticed Dodie's odd behaviour.

Xenia merely shrugged her shoulders, appeared baffled.

Verity, who missed nothing and had seen the change in Dodie, sat back in the chair, a thoughtful look settling on her face. 'Dodie believes she's psychic, Katie. From the way she acted, I think she picked up some vibes from you.'

'But she behaved as though they were not good ones.' Xenia gave Verity a knowing look. 'She did sort of . . . well, back away from Katie.'

'I've never been told I give off bad vibes!' Katie exclaimed, and let out a forced laugh self-consciously. 'Just the opposite.'

'Don't pay any attention,' Verity murmured in a kindly tone. 'I've known her since I was a child. She's lived here all her life, and though she can be a little strange, she's really quite harmless. Isn't she, Xenia?'

'Of course she is. She's always been daft.'

They were interrupted by the sound of voices and

the clatter of dishes; almost immediately the door flew open again. A cook dressed in a chef's white jacket and trousers came into the room carrying a large tray, and Dodie was with her.

Katie recognized Anya, Lavinia's mother. She was tall, dark-haired and athletic, had a look of Lavinia, but was not quite as pretty as that younger version of herself.

Dodie took a small, white soufflé dish on a plate off the tray, placed it in front of Katie, then gave one to Xenia and one to Verity.

As the two women moved away from the table, Anya said, 'This is the only way to serve, m'lady, what with Jarvis being off tonight.'

'It's not a problem, Anya.'

Anya nodded and left the dining room, and Dodie was quick to follow on her heels.

'Anya makes the best soufflés,' Xenia told Katie. 'Eat it at once before it falls. Oh, and by the way, I asked Verity to order your favourite plaice and chips for the next course.'

Katie laughed, feeling at ease with them again, and dipped her fork into the soufflé.

It was almost midnight when Katie and Xenia made their way upstairs to bed. They hugged outside Katie's room, and she said, 'Thanks for inviting me up here, Xenia. Verity's so nice . . . it's been such a lovely evening.'

Xenia smiled at her. 'Breakfast starts at eight and it's

on the go until ten. So get up when you wish. It's served in the garden room, and you'll find it easily enough, if I'm not down. But I probably will be. There's tea, coffee, rolls, and things like that already put out. But you can have a cooked breakfast if you prefer. You just have to ask. Jarvis will be hovering solicitously.'

Katie shook her head. 'I don't think so. We'll both be getting fat up here, if we're not careful.'

'Only too true,' Xenia agreed with a half smile.

Katie went into her room, closed the door, and locked it.

Xenia, standing outside in the corridor, heard the key turn as it had earlier that day. For a moment she hesitated, and then she lifted her hand and knocked on the door.

There was no response.

She knocked again.

Katie's voice echoed through the door. 'Yes? Who is it?'

'It's *me*.' Xenia wondered who Katie could possibly think it was, if not her.

Katie turned the key and opened the door.

Xenia, staring at her intently, said a trifle sharply, 'I don't understand you. Jarvis may be off tonight, but he always goes around the house locking the outside doors. And even if he didn't, Verity would. You have a ridiculous obsession about locking yourself in . . . it's . . . *crazy*.'

'No, I don't!' Katie exclaimed heatedly. 'It's just a habit, I guess. And I'm not crazy.'

Fractionally, Xenia hesitated, and then she said, 'Can I come in for a minute? I want to talk to you. Or would you prefer to talk in my room? There are other pictures there you could peer at.' Suddenly, her voice had an edge to it.

Katie felt herself flushing and she shook her head, said with vehemence, 'I wasn't prying, Xenia. *I wasn't*. And I'm so sorry you're upset. I just happened to notice the picture of Tim and the little boy . . .' Her voice trailed off helplessly. She was at a loss.

'I know, I know,' Xenia muttered, and pushed the door, walked purposefully into the room. 'I wouldn't have invited you up here to Burton Leyburn if I'd wanted to hide my past. I was going to tell you certain things tomorrow. But before I got the chance, you saw the photograph, which I'd forgotten was there on the chest in the Great High Chamber –'

Cutting herself off, Xenia closed the door behind her, looked keenly at Katie. 'Do you mind? Can I stay for a few minutes? Talk to you, Katie?'

'Yes, of course. And you don't have to tell me anything. You're my friend, I care about you, and I certainly wouldn't pry into your past. It must be painful for you . . . to discuss.'

Xenia sat down in one of the chairs. She bent forward, put her head on her knees, sat immobile like that for a few minutes. Eventually, she straightened, took a number of deep breaths. Then she began, 'Justin was six when it happened. Tim was taking him to Harrogate. It was June, not winter, not bad weather. No rain. It was a fine, sunny day. No reason for a huge lorry to skid, to go out of control. But it did.'

Xenia stopped abruptly, compressed her lips, screwed her eyes shut and looked up at the ceiling. Her hands were clenched into fists, and her body trembled. Taking deep breaths, she swallowed hard, pushing back the tears. She was so choked up she could not speak. Finally, she opened her eyes. 'The lorry slammed into the car. They were killed instantly. My husband, my son. Nine years ago. I suppose I still haven't . . . got over it . . . so sorry . . . to break down like this.'

Xenia pressed her fingers to her eyes as the tears leaked out, slipped through her fingers, slid down her cheeks.

Katie went to her, knelt on the floor next to her knees and encircled Xenia with her arms. 'I'm sorry, I'm so very sorry. You didn't have to tell me . . .'

Without saying a word, Xenia clung to Katie, held onto her very tightly, trying to regain her composure. After a while she did so, and released Katie from her grip; she groped in her pocket for a tissue. After blowing her nose, she said quietly, 'As long as I don't talk about it, I'm all right.' She cleared her throat, went on, 'I can function fairly well these days . . . Is that the way it is for you?'

'What do you mean?'

'It's often struck me that there's some sort of tragedy in *your* past, Katie. And that you don't talk about it, so you can get on with a relatively normal life. As I try to do.'

Katie sat down heavily in the other chair.

She did not answer at first. Then finally, she replied: 'I suppose so. I haven't been able to talk about . . . what happened. Not for years, not without falling apart. But I think about it every day. It never leaves me.'

'I know. Can you tell *me* about it?'

Chapter Twenty-one

Katie sat quietly in the chair, trying to marshal her thoughts so that she could speak coherently about the murderous attack on her girlfriends in Malvern long ago.

Part of her balked at dredging up the past, speaking out loud about it to Xenia, because it was painful for her to do this even now, years later.

She lived with the memories of Carly and Denise on a daily basis, and they were forever with her. It was usually in that quiet time just before she fell asleep, or was fully awake in the morning, that their faces were most vivid in her mind's eye. She had never forgotten them or what had happened, but to recount everything to Xenia would almost be like living through it all over again.

Yet, in a sense, she was boxed in, because Xenia had been so open with *her* about the untimely deaths of Tim and Justin. Katie felt that if she did not confide about her own past the relationship between them would somehow be damaged, and irretrievably so. And that was the last thing she wanted.

Xenia was the first real friend she had made in all these years, and she was important to her. In many ways, Xenia had stepped into the gap left by Denise and Carly; certainly no one else had ever been able to fill it.

Tell her about it, a small voice at the back of her head whispered. Tell her everything. Maybe it will help you if you unburden yourself.

Leaning forward slightly, her hands clasped together, Katie took what was a giant leap for her, when she said: 'It all happened when I was seventeen.'

She paused for a split second, staring off into the distance, then quickly brought her eyes back to Xenia, adding, 'It was in October of 1989. Exactly ten years ago.'

Xenia simply nodded. She sensed that Katie had an upsetting tale to tell, and deemed it wiser not to say one word, lest it put her off. But she shivered involuntarily, intuitively knowing that she was about to hear something awful. Sinking further down in the armchair, she focused her attention entirely on Katie.

'When you and I first met two years ago, I told you that I had always wanted to be an actress since I was a child. What I didn't tell you was that I had two friends who harboured the same ambitions, Carly Smith and Denise Matthews. The three of us had been friends since we were little. We were the same age. We grew up together, went to the same kindergarten, the same high school, lived in the same area around the little town of Malvern in northwestern Connecticut. We planned to go to New York when we were eighteen, to attend the American Academy of Dramatic Arts. We were going to live with Aunt Bridget, who had a loft in Tribeca in those days, until we became accustomed to New York and the academy. Then she was going to find an apartment for the three of us to share. We were inseparable . . . everyone knew that, knew how close we were.'

Katie stopped, appeared to hesitate.

Xenia said quickly, 'Go on, Katie, I'm listening.'

Slowly, and with great care and deliberation, Katie continued her story. She told Xenia about the old barn and how Denise's Uncle Ted had let them use it. She spoke of the years the three of them had spent rehearsing there, and of the school concerts every Christmas. Until finally she was recounting the events of that fateful day in October of 1989.

She explained how she had left the barn early that day, gone home to help her mother, had remembered later that she had left her bag of school books behind, and had returned with her brother to retrieve them. And then she told Xenia about the disarray in the barn, the missing girls, and how she and Niall had searched for them.

'It was Carly I saw first, lying there in the wood, her face covered in blood,' Katie said, her voice shaking more than ever. 'But Niall found a pulse, and she was alive, and I was so happy, *relieved*. He left me with Carly, went off to look for Denise . . .' Katie paused, took several deep breaths to steady herself. 'Poor Denise . . . She was dead, Xenia. Raped and strangled.'

'Oh my God!' Xenia's eyes were wide with horror as she stared at Katie. 'To be struck down like that, both so young, with their lives stretching ahead of them. How terrible for them, and for you, Katie.' She shook her head. 'And what about Carly? She did live, didn't she?'

'Oh yes –'

'So she was able to point a finger . . . identify the attacker.'

'No, no, she couldn't. Carly never regained consciousness. She went into a coma.'

For a moment Xenia seemed uncomprehending, and she threw Katie a puzzled look, frowning. 'And she never came out of it? Is that what you're saying?'

'That's right. Carly has been in a coma for the last ten years. She's in a hospital in Connecticut.' Katie's mouth trembled, and her eyes filled suddenly with tears. She brushed them away with both hands, took hold of herself and added, 'But she's also dead, in a certain sense. Lost to us all, trapped in the coma.'

Xenia sat back, not speaking for a moment. At last she murmured softly, sympathetically, 'I'm so very sorry, Katie darling. So dreadfully sorry this happened to you. What a heartbreaking thing for you to bear. Did the police catch the murderer?'

'No, they didn't. It's an unsolved case. Mac MacDonald,

the detective in charge of the major crime squad in the Litchfield area, has never closed the case. It's still open, *it's still on the books*, that's the way *he* puts it.'

'So you're in touch with him about the case even now?'

'I'm not, but my father and he went to school together. Ever since they met again, through the . . . the murder, they've become close friends. Mac believes something will happen, come to light, and that he'll solve the case one day. Dad says it really bugs him that he was never able to arrest the murderer at the time.'

'Why didn't he?'

'Because he didn't know who it was. Mac told my father that it was a really bad crime scene, no clues at all. The Medical Examiner did get DNA samples off Denise's body, but they were of no use.'

'Whyever not? I thought DNA samples helped to solve crimes,' Xenia asserted.

'That's true, yes. But you have to have a suspect to match to the DNA samples. And if you don't, all you've got are . . . DNA samples.'

'So no one was ever suspected or caught.'

'That's right. According to Dad, Mac has always thought that it was someone who knew us. A man who more than likely was leading a very normal life. On the surface. But one who was a psychopath in reality. A man who stalked us, targeted us . . . the three of us.'

'But he only got two of you, and that's why you're so afraid.'

Katie could only nod.

Xenia muttered, 'No wonder you're always locking doors.'

'At first, just after the murder happened, it made me feel safer, and then it did truly become a habit,' Katie responded. 'You see, my parents were certain there was somebody out there watching me, waiting for an opportunity to get me. In a way they were torn about what to do . . . they wanted me to be with them in Malvern, so they could protect me, watch over me. Yet at the same time, they wanted to get me out of the area.'

'I fully understand that,' said Xenia, clasping her hands, leaning forward. 'It's a very natural reaction. And is that why you went to live with Bridget in New York?'

'Yes. But I didn't leave home immediately, I stayed on in Malvern until I was nineteen,' Katie explained. 'For one thing, I wasn't sure I wanted to be an actress any more. Not without Carly and Denise. It didn't seem to be the same. I thought that acting was tainted, because of their deaths. And anyway, the spark had gone out of me. I felt so guilty because *I'd* talked them into going to the barn that day, and I'd left early. Left them alone. If I'd been there, perhaps we could have fought him off, and maybe the outcome would have been different.'

'Survivor guilt,' Xenia ventured softly. 'I know all about *that*, and only too well. I was supposed to go with Tim and Justin to Harrogate that morning in June, but I changed my mind at the last minute. I stayed here to help Jarvis sort stuff in one of the storage rooms. And that's why I'm alive and they're dead. I've always felt that I should be dead too, you know.' She shook her head. 'I'm alive because of a pile of old junk.'

Katie nodded her understanding. 'As I just said, the spark had gone out of me, and I discovered I couldn't act any more. It was literally impossible for me to walk on a stage. I had developed the worst kind of stage fright. I just shook all the time and my legs trembled. The year the attack happened, I dropped out of the Christmas concert at school. I'd been going to do the soliloquy from *Hamlet*, but I just couldn't. That's what I'd been rehearsing the day they were attacked. Anyway, I guess I retreated into . . . a shell.'

'And how did you manage to pull yourself out of it?'

'I didn't, not really. It was my mother who dragged me up from the depths of despair. She was wonderful. She insisted I go to New York and enrol in the academy, and she came with me to hold my hand. She stayed with Bridget and me for a few months, and slowly I began to enjoy classes. I also managed to shed some of my fear.'

'But not all of it?' Xenia lifted a brow quizzically.

'No. I did get a bit paranoid at one point, and I was

always looking over my shoulder. I guess it's never gone away completely . . . the fear. Nor has the idea that I was the only one who escaped. Mac thinks that he, the perp as he calls him, may have moved out of the area, gone far away to avoid eventual capture. I want to believe Mac's right. Besides, New York is a big city.'

'It is indeed, but you *are* an actress, Katie, and bound to be seen, and known, in the limelight, so –' Xenia immediately cut herself off, shaking her head. 'I suppose I don't have to tell you anything, do I?'

'No, you don't,' Katie answered. 'And I do sometimes worry about being up there on a stage . . . a target, a sitting duck.'

'Is that the reason you've turned down so many big parts?'

'I honestly don't think so. The ones Melanie Dawson offered me certainly weren't right. All wrong for me, in fact, and her husband Harry agreed.'

'You're not hesitating about taking the part in *Charlotte and Her Sisters* for that reason are you . . . the fear, I mean?'

'I don't think so . . . I just don't know, to be honest,' Katie admitted ruefully. She rose, walked over to the tall, mullioned window and looked out across the gardens. It was dark and she could barely see anything.

The velvet-black sky was littered with crystal stars and high up, in one corner, there was a crescent moon. It was a friendly sky, benign.

Turning around, walking back to the chair, Katie continued, 'What happened ten years ago has really affected my life, Xenia, changed me in so many ways. It's made me a bit paranoid, admittedly, and even afraid. For a time it turned me off acting. And men. Still, I did come back to acting. I do get a lot of satisfaction from performing.'

'But you're still very wary of men, that I do know.'

Katie nodded, made no response.

'I hope you don't mind me saying this, but Grant Miller is not for you. I know he's a wonderful actor, but he's just not up to snuff, not good enough for you.'

'Oh I know. And it's over, at least as far as I'm concerned.'

'Does Grant know that?'

'I've tried to tell him, and I made it very obvious when he came to London six months ago. I hope it's sunk in, that he won't be pestering me if I go back.'

'I hope you take this part. It'll be the making of you, Katie. I feel this deep down ... call it ... gut instinct.'

'I want to do the play, Xenia, as long as I can master the character of Emily,' Katie admitted. 'Because I want to succeed. Not just for me, but for them. For Carly and Denise ... they wanted to be actresses so much, so I want to do it for them as well as for myself. Being on Broadway ... well, you know, it was their dream as well as mine. Do you understand what I mean?'

'I do. I think you're very brave.'

Chapter Twenty-two

Katie stood at the end of the avenue of trees, looking towards the front of the house, admiring its imposing beauty on this cold Friday morning. Although she was not an expert on architecture like her father was, she could easily recognize that Burton Leyburn Hall was an extraordinary example of the late Elizabethan style.

It was built of the pale-grey stone that seemed to be prevalent in Yorkshire, and which worked so well with the surrounding landscape. The roofline was crenellated, and the house was a lovely combination of bays and recesses, gables and battlements, tall chimneys, and many mullioned windows, all of them soaring and elegant, glinting in the bright sunlight.

When she had arrived yesterday afternoon, the house had looked mysterious in the fading light. But on this early morning it seemed to be just the opposite. Steadfast, stalwart, made to last, were the words which instantly sprang into Katie's mind. And it *was* built to last, she thought; obviously it hasn't flinched for four hundred years.

Walking back up to the house and around to the south side, she came to a wide terrace with a balustrade which ran the entire length of the house. The rail and row of balusters beneath it were broken in the middle, to permit a flight of wide stone steps to flow down to the parterre, the beds and paths of this ornamental flower garden arranged to form an intricate pattern of elegance.

About fourteen feet beyond the parterre, the lawns began and these swards of green stretched all the way to the ornamental lake, which was just visible in the distance. On either side of the lawns were stands of huge trees, and with their broad, gnarled trunks and great spreading branches they added shelter to the gardens and offered shade in summer.

Once again Katie experienced that sense of timelessness which she had felt when arriving here. History abounded in this ancient house and on these lavish lands, gifted to the Leyburn family by the great Tudor queen. She couldn't help wondering what it was that Robert Leyburn had done for Elizabeth to make her favour him with such an extravagant gift. She made a mental note to ask Verity.

Since it was still not yet eight, which was when breakfast was put out, Katie decided to walk down to the ornamental lake. As she walked she thought about Xenia and their revealing conversation last night. She was pleased they had shared confidences; she felt, in her heart, that it had brought them closer. Although they hadn't known it before, they had both endured a traumatic experience earlier in their lives. Now that they had recounted their experiences to each other, they understood each other better than before. At least, that's what Katie felt. She considered it a bond of sorts.

Katie had not gone very far when she heard her name being called. Turning, shading her eyes with her hand, she looked up the path, saw Xenia sprinting towards her.

Xenia was dressed in a grey track suit and running shoes, her chestnut hair tied back. When she came to a standstill next to Katie she was perspiring and out of breath. Taking the towel from around her neck, she wiped her face and tried to say something without success.

'Hey, take it easy, don't try to talk for a minute,' Katie exclaimed, noting her exertion.

After a few seconds, when she was finally breathing more evenly, Xenia said, 'I decided to go for a quick jog down the front avenue, but I'd forgotten how long it is.' She leaned against a tree, exhaled several times. 'Either that or I'm out of condition. I was coming back up to the house when I ran into Pell, the gardener. He told me he'd seen you setting off down here, going to the lake, he assumed.'

Katie was surprised. 'I never saw anyone.'

'Oh, you wouldn't.' Xenia smiled knowingly. 'Pell lurks around the garden doing his various jobs, but he's invisible, when he wants to be. Do you mind if I walk with you for a bit, Katie? Then we can go in and have breakfast together at eight.' She laughed, shook her head. 'I have a feeling Anya and Jarvis are putting on quite a spread for you. The works, a real Yorkshire breakfast, country style.'

'Well, I must admit I'm a bit hungry, and I'd like to try some of the local dishes. I was up early myself and so I got dressed and came downstairs. I wanted to see the front of the house.'

'It's beautiful, don't you think?'

'Fantastic, Xenia, and I love this grey stone. It's local, isn't it?'

'Yes, it is. I doubt you'll ever see a red-brick stately home in Yorkshire, God forbid.'

The two young women walked on for a while in a companionable silence, but just before they arrived at the ornamental lake, Xenia said, 'You know, Katie, I've been wondering if I'm doing the right thing . . . taking you to Haworth tomorrow, force-feeding the Brontës to you.'

'What are you getting at?'

'It struck me in the middle of the night that I'm pushing you to take the part of Emily in the play, and in the process I'm probably pushing you into danger.'

Coming to an abrupt stop, Katie turned to stare at

her friend. Her bright-blue eyes swept over Xenia's face, and after a split second, she said, 'I know what you're getting at, but no, you're not propelling me into any danger. Nothing of the kind. The attack on Carly and Denise was ten years ago. That's a long time. And for the last four years, after I left the academy, and before I came to England, I was appearing in plays. Admittedly, off-Broadway, rather than on Broadway, but I was on a stage and visible. And nobody's taken a pot shot at me. Yet. I go along with Mac MacDonald's theory that the murderer left the East Coast soon after he attacked Carly and killed Denise.'

'Why does the policeman think that?' Xenia asked.

'According to Dad, Mac has always believed that the murderer would have been afraid of giving himself away to family and friends, if he had stayed in Malvern, or in the general area, in one of the local towns, such as Kent or Cornwall Bridge.'

'He may well have gone to New York,' Xenia pointed out.

'Only too true. He could be anywhere. Listen, once I'd decided to go back to acting, I knew that I'd be earning my living on a stage one day, and that I'd be very much on view, so to speak. So I took a deep breath and got on with my life. I've tried very hard to stop being paranoid, forever looking over my shoulder. I've also tried to put my fear to one side.'

'I think you've done awfully well under the circumstances.' Xenia eyed her friend carefully, her expression thoughtful and caring.

Katie suddenly began to laugh. 'I know just what you're thinking. That I still have a terrible compulsion to lock doors.'

Xenia laughed with her, slipped her arm through Katie's as they walked on at a steady pace. 'Old habits die hard perhaps,' Xenia murmured. 'You know, Katie, I'm so happy we're friends. It's comforting to have a girlfriend like you.'

'I feel the same, Xenia.'

'After I married Tim when I was eighteen, I was wrapped up in him and in this house, which was such a big part of his life, the running of it, you know, with his father. Then I became wrapped up in my child when Justin was born. It was inevitable that I would lose touch with my girlfriends from school. Then one day I found myself entirely alone . . .' Xenia's voice trailed off.

Katie chose not to say anything, having heard the note of sadness creeping into Xenia's voice.

But after only a brief moment, Xenia went on, 'My reasons for being, for living, were gone, snatched away from me just like that.' She snapped her thumb and finger together. 'Death is so final.' She took a deep breath. 'Well, there I was, all alone. The only person I had was Verity. I shut myself up here for years, licking my wounds like a sick dog. And trying to keep myself from going entirely mad. But it was five rather long years, now that I look back.'

'I understand,' Katie replied quietly, her voice sympathetic. 'The circumstances of my grief are very different from yours, but for two years I became pretty reclusive myself.' Stealing a glance at Xenia, Katie now said, 'What made you finally leave here and go to London?'

'It was Verity, actually. She'd come back to live here after her divorce from Geoffrey, almost fifteen years ago now. Stephen, her son, was away at boarding school, and anyway she had nowhere else to go. And this *was* her childhood home. Her father, the Earl, invited her to live with us all, and I was happy to have her companionship, and so was Tim. And she adored the baby. Anyway, after Tim and Justin were gone, I sort of clung to Verity. She was all I had. The Earl was devastated by Tim's death, and it was at that time that he started to spend months on end in the south of France. He has a lady friend with a beautiful château, and he's mostly there these days. But getting back to Verity . . . One day she decided to shove me out. For my own sake.'

Xenia paused, shook her head, and chuckled as if laughing at herself. 'I was so reluctant to leave here. But I was helping her with her catalogues, and she said I had to go to London to attend the gift shows, do her buying for her. It was a good ruse really. She believed I had to get away from Burton Leyburn and the memories, especially the sorrowful ones. Just as my father-in-law had. Poor Uncle Thomas, losing Tim and Justin aged him considerably.'

'Is the Earl really your uncle?'

'Not actually, no. He's my father-in-law. But my mother and he were always very close, all their lives, and so I'd called him Uncle Thomas from being a child.'

'Doesn't he ever come back to Yorkshire? Visit the estate?'

'Yes, in the summer. He's not a well man, and the climate in the south of France is milder in winter, it suits him better. And Veronique, that's his friend, looks after him well.'

'So you went to London and started to buy for Verity's catalogues. But when did you get the idea for the business you started yourself?' Katie ventured.

Xenia came to a standstill and turned to face Katie. 'When Verity wanted me to leave, I was a bit hurt at first, but I'm not a stupid person and I suddenly understood her reasons. So I did as she suggested. I had the house in Farm Street, and that became my base. And hers too, since she had to come up to town on business quite frequently. The house had belonged to Tim for years, he'd inherited it from his mother when she died, and I inherited from him. Anyway, I worked on the catalogues and came up here for weekends occasionally. Then one day I had a brainstorm . . . the idea for Celebrations. I contacted Alan Pearson, who was living in New York, and had a similar business, planning conventions. The idea of planning fancy parties instead appealed to him no end. We were old family friends, Alan had been at school with Tim, and so we became partners. We'd been in business for a year when I met you at Bridget's dinner party for Alan's birthday.'

Xenia started walking again, and Katie hurried to keep pace with her. She said, 'You've mentioned Verity's catalogues before, but you've never gone into details. What does she sell?'

'All sorts of things. Verity created the mail-order catalogues about ten years ago, but it's only been in the last few years that they've become a big success. Real moneymakers, thank goodness. You see, she's been clever about the items she's chosen to sell, and how she presents them. That's what did the trick.'

Again Katie asked, 'But what does she *sell*?'

'Well, let's see, she has a catalogue called *Home Comforts from Burton Leyburn Hall*, which offers all kinds of scented candles, beeswax candles, cushions, flowerpots, linens, sheepskin slippers, and things for the home. Then there's another, *Lady Verity's Bath*, and that's a line of shampoos and bath gels, potpourri, scented sachets, body lotions, soaps. The third is *Lady Verity's Kitchen*. That offers honey, jams, jellies, pickles, dried herbs that are bottled here. Basically she sells items that won't spoil, that have shelf life.'

'That's quite an undertaking,' Katie exclaimed, sounding impressed.

'Yes it is. Everyone works for the catalogues, including me. I still do some of the buying for Verity. I enjoy it. It's a local business.'

'Do you mean everyone in the house works for the catalogues? Or everyone in the village?'

'Both. Verity's a bit of a tycoon in her own quiet way. She employs quite a few of the local women, who are only too happy to make a few extra quid for themselves, and she also employs Lavinia, Anya, Barry Thwaites, who's married to Anya and runs the Home Farm, Pell, and Jarvis, of course.'

'I thought Jarvis was the butler.'

'He is, although Verity calls him her general factotum these days. I suppose because he has his fingers in everything here. Jarvis is her good right hand. Anyway, he's been at Burton Leyburn for donkey's years, and he loves the estate as much as she does. You see, Katie, all of the money which is made from the catalogues is used for the upkeep of this place. That's why Verity and I open the house and gardens to the public in summer. The admission fees help to pay for the gardens. And there's the shop, which is another moneymaker, where we sell all of the products in the catalogues.'

Katie didn't say anything for a moment or two. Then she nodded. 'It hadn't occurred to me, but I guess a great house like this, these vast grounds and gardens, cost a lot of money to maintain.'

'The upkeep is crippling, ducks,' Xenia answered.

'And there's not a lot of inherited family money. Which is why everyone is thrilled about Verity's success. I don't know what we'd do without the three catalogues. I suppose the Earl would have to give the place to the National Trust, or do something like that, which none of us would really be happy about, since we couldn't live here then. The house would become a museum.'

'I understand,' Katie said softly, thinking that nothing was ever the way it seemed.

'We call it a lake, but actually it's a pond really,' Xenia said and, pointing to the centre of the water, she added, 'There's a fountain in the middle, but it's only turned on in the spring and summer.'

'It's a lovely spot, and the lake is so perfectly positioned it appears to float into the horizon, into the sky.' Katie squinted against the sunlight, shaded her eyes with her hand, and continued, 'I guess it's also a haven for wildlife. I see quite a lot of water fowl on the other side of the water.'

'Yes. That's one of the reasons I love coming down here to the lake. So many different species of birds settle, if only for a while, on the water. Why, we've often seen seagulls flying around, even though the sea is not all that close.'

'Who built the ornamental lake?'

'It was the eighteenth-century Leyburns who created what are known as the pleasure gardens here. Adam

Leyburn, and his son, Charles, in particular had the energy, creativity and money to do it, not to mention the time. The entire park looks as it does today because of them and their immense vision. They were rather brilliant when it came to the river, the Skell, which runs through the valley, just beyond those trees. By damming the river at various intervals they created weirs, lakes, stretches that are straight and canal-like in form, and ornamental ponds. Uncle Thomas has always said the park is a triumph of eighteenth-century romantic landscaping. He's right.'

'Do you get a lot of visitors?'

'Oh yes, I'll say. People come from all over the country and Europe to see the gardens and the park. And I'll tell you this, Katie, there are some truly spectacular things to see. The rhododendron walk is sheer bliss in summer, and then there are surprise views and vistas, and people do adore the deer park and the animals. The bambi park, some of them call it.'

'Does it bother you and Verity? Opening the place to the public, I mean?' Katie glanced at Xenia from the corner of her eye.

'No, not at all. Firstly, it's an absolute necessity. We very genuinely need the money that comes from the admissions and the guidebooks we've had printed, and which most people buy. And then secondly, I think it's nice that others can share the beauty of Burton Leyburn, view the gardens, walk through the grounds, and visit the pleasure gardens in the valley. And they also get a chance to see the treasures inside the house as well.'

Katie nodded, but remained silent. She had always assumed that Xenia was a rich young woman, since she gave off the aura of wealth. But the truth was something different, as she was coming to realize.

Suddenly Xenia swung away from the edge of the ornamental lake, and grabbed Katie's arm. 'Come on, let's go back to the house. I don't know about you, but I'm positively ravenous.'

'Yes, I am too,' Katie admitted with a grin.

Chapter Twenty-three

Ten minutes later Xenia was ushering Katie into the front entrance hall and leading her towards the garden room. 'Breakfast is served in here, as I told you.' She flung open the door, added, 'I'll be down in a few minutes, after I've showered and changed. Don't wait for me. Tuck in immediately.'

'Thanks, I will,' Katie replied, walking into the room. She saw that the walls were a soft lime-green, and someone, probably Lavinia she decided, had painted elegant tropical trees on them. The trees were filled with colourful, exotic birds, and the lovely murals helped to give a three-dimensional look to the room. Plants filled the window area, and were also arranged on a long table set against a side wall, hence the name of the room, she supposed.

'Hi there, Katie!' Lavinia exclaimed only a moment later, as she came into the room through a swing door. 'No one else is down yet. I expect they're ligging in.'

'Good morning, Lavinia. Xenia's down. Or rather, she's been down, and outside for a run, and a walk with me. But now she's gone back upstairs to shower and change.'

'I wish I'd known she was going jogging, I'd have gone with her. And come for a walk with the two of you, if you'd have let me.'

'Naturally we would . . . what does that expression mean . . . *ligging in*?' Katie inquired, as always fascinated by language.

'It means lying in bed. It's old Yorkshire. Jarvis told me it comes from the Vikings, who invaded the north of England centuries ago. That's why there are so many blue- and green-eyed blonde people around here, don't you know? Anyway, Jarvis is the expert.'

'And what am I an expert in?' Jarvis asked from the doorway.

'Yorkshire dialect, and old sayings, among many other things.' Lavinia turned to smile up at him. 'This is Miss Katie Byrne from America, Jarvis.'

He inclined his head. 'Good morning, madam.'

'Good morning, Jarvis,' Katie said, thinking what a pleasant-looking man he was, with his silver hair and weather-beaten face. He was slim and of medium height, looked to be in his late fifties, perhaps early sixties. As befitting a butler in a house like this, he wore the grey-striped trousers, black jacket, white shirt and grey tie that constituted the standard daytime uniform of the proper English butler.

'Which would you prefer, Miss Byrne, orange or grapefruit juice? It's freshly squeezed.'

'No juice, thanks, Jarvis.'

'Tea or coffee, madam?'

'Coffee, please.'

Jarvis nodded, and walked around to the sideboard, where several hotplates held silver chafing dishes; alongside them were an electric coffee maker and a large teapot under a quilted tea cosy.

Lavinia jumped up and went to join him at the sideboard. 'I think I'm going to have a cooked breakfast this morning, Jarvis. What do you recommend?'

'You like everything that's here, Lavinia. There's fried black pudding, grilled tomatoes, pork sausages, grilled bacon, scrambled eggs, and your two favourites, kippers and finnan haddie. Also, your mother toasted some pikelets.'

'Oh goodie, Mam's done us proud.' Lavinia lifted the lids of various dishes, peering inside.

'What's black pudding?' Katie asked, looking across the table at Jarvis.

'It's a Yorkshire delicacy,' he told her. 'A blood sausage that's made by the butcher in Ripon. It can be eaten cold, but Anya usually slices it and fries it with thinly-sliced potatoes. Would you like to try it?'

'I don't think so,' Katie answered. 'But thanks. I'd prefer a sausage, a piece of bacon, and perhaps a grilled tomato. And toast. Thank you, Jarvis.'

Jarvis picked up the coffee pot and filled a cup, brought it to the table. Katie thanked him again.

Lavinia said, 'Have some finnan haddie, Katie.' Then she immediately asked, 'Do you know what it is?'

'Not really.'

'Smoked haddock from Scotland.' Lavinia put a piece on a plate and brought it to show her. 'Look, it's pale yellow, because of the smoking. My mother poaches it in a little milk and then serves it with a pat of butter and parsley on top. Would you like this piece?' She offered the plate.

Katie shook her head. 'Thanks, but not really. But you can tell me what a toasted pikelet is.'

Lavinia laughed, and explained, 'It's a round flat type of bread with little holes punched in the top, and when it's toasted and buttered it's delicious.'

'Some people call it a crumpet,' Jarvis volunteered as he arrived at the table with Katie's plate of food.

'Thanks,' Katie said.

'I understand Lavinia's going to show you her paintings after breakfast, Miss Byrne. She's very talented,' Jarvis murmured, sounding proud.

Lavinia beamed at him from the sideboard, where she was filling her plate.

'I'm sure she is, Jarvis,' Katie responded, glancing at the lovely young girl. To Katie, she looked as if she had just stepped out of the sixties this morning, wearing a red plaid shirt, blue jeans, white socks and loafers. She had tied a white silk kerchief around her neck and wore gold hoop earrings.

Before she could stop herself, Katie said, 'You look very Audrey Hepburn-ish this morning, Lavinia.'

Lavinia smiled with obvious pleasure, preening slightly.

Jarvis said, 'Oh please, Miss Byrne, don't tell her that. It always goes to her head when the resemblance is remarked upon, which seems to be rather frequently these days.'

'Morning, Jarvis,' Xenia said from the doorway and walked into the room. She had changed into a yellow twin set and beige trousers, looked scrubbed and fresh-faced, with her hair tied back in a black silk bow.

'Good morning, Miss Xenia,' Jarvis said. 'What would you like to have?'

'Just a slice of toast, please, Jarvis. Oh, and you can add a sausage. And tea, of course. Thanks.'

Turning to Katie, Xenia went on, 'I have to rush. Verity's already in the office, and the accountant's arriving within minutes. I'll be busy with them all morning, apparently. So I do hope you'll be all right . . .'

'Of course I will. Don't worry about me.'

'Lavinia will look after you, won't you, ducks?'

'I'm going to show Katie my paintings in the studio, Xenia. And we can go for a walk, there's lots to do.' Lavinia gazed across at Katie and asked, 'Do you ride?'

'I'm afraid not,' Katie answered. 'I'm a bit timid around horses.'

'We have a lovely old mare called Jess, you could try

her. She's very friendly and docile,' Lavinia murmured.

Katie merely smiled.

Xenia said, 'Now, Lavinia, don't press Katie, she obviously doesn't want to go riding.'

Jarvis interrupted. 'Lavinia, will you do the honours? Help Miss Byrne to anything else she wants.' He turned to Xenia, and added, 'I'm afraid I have to go over to the packing barn. I've got a crew coming from the village in a few minutes. Four lads are going to help wrap packages. So if you'll excuse me, Miss Xenia . . .'

'No problem, Jarvis. And I have to leave myself in a moment.' As she spoke she gulped down the last of her tea, and rose. 'See you later,' she said, squeezing Katie's shoulder before she hurried to the door.

Katie nodded.

Jarvis departed also, and Lavinia refilled Katie's cup with coffee, and then, a moment later, the swing door opened and Anya came into the garden room.

'Oh Katie, you haven't officially met my mother!' Lavinia exclaimed, jumping up.

'Mam, this is Miss Byrne from New York.'

Anya came forward, her hand outstretched, a smile spreading across her face. 'Good morning, Miss Byrne. I hope you enjoyed your breakfast.'

'Good morning, Anya, and yes, I did, it was delicious,' Katie answered, standing, shaking her hand.

Anya went over to the sideboard and began to look in all of the dishes. 'Such a lot of food left over,' she muttered, clucking to herself. 'Oh well, never mind. Pell and Jamie are always ready for a snack, such big appetites they have, and Pomeroy just came up to the kitchen for his morning sandwich. Plenty here for them, and some left over. Oh dear, I made too much again.'

'Don't worry, Mam, Jarvis told us there's a crew coming up from the village to wrap packages,' Lavinia said. 'They'll make inroads on the rest of the breakfast, given half a chance.'

'Yes, that's a good idea, I'll make sandwiches for them.' Anya swung around, murmured, 'I do hate to waste food when half the world's starving.'

'I know what you mean.' Katie nodded in agreement.

'I must be getting along,' Anya announced. 'I'm in the middle of preparing the vegetables for lunch.' As she spoke she picked up two of the chafing dishes and carried them out.

When they were alone, Katie said, 'Your mother must have lived here a very long time. In England, I mean.'

'She has. But why do you say that, Katie?'

'Her English is perfect.'

'Oh, but she came here as a child. To London. She was born in Paris. You see, my grandparents were Russian but lived in France, because of the Revolution. Then they came to England. My mother married a Yorkshireman, David Keene, from Burton Leyburn. He brought her back to live in the village twenty-five years ago. I was born here, you know. My father died when he was only thirty, of a heart attack. I was just three.'

'I'm sorry,' Katie responded. 'He was very young, wasn't he? How awful for you and your mother.'

'It was, but Mam's strong. A survivor, that's what she calls herself. She's been working here at the hall for nineteen years. And she loves it, loves to cook. She believes that's the secret of her success, loving what she does, wanting to make delicious food for people to eat. It's important to love your work, don't you think?'

Katie nodded. 'Yes, it is, Lavinia. I love acting, always have, and I know Xenia loves running Celebrations, creating those wonderful parties of hers.'

'Yes, I know she does. She's asked me to draw some interiors for her this weekend, of the Winter Palace in St Petersburg at the turn of the century. They're for a party in New York at the end of the year. I'll enjoy doing the drawings.'

'Do you know what the Winter Palace looked like at the time of the Tsars?'

'Oh, yes, we've got some really fantastic picture books in the library. They belong to Xenia, her father gave them to her.' She smiled, and stood up. 'It's good research material. Anyway, shall we go, Katie? I've got the old landrover outside in the stable yard.'

Katie also stood up, and glanced down at her oatmeal wood trousers and fisherman's sweater. 'I'm sure I don't need a coat, I didn't earlier.'

'Oh no, it's warming up even more. Even though Pell said there was going to be a cold snap, he's sometimes wrong.'

The landrover turned out to be the English equivalent of a station wagon, and it was somewhat old and dilapidated. But with Lavinia at the wheel it shot up the dirt road at full speed, behaving just like a modern sports car.

'The barn's not far, just beyond the woods,' Lavinia explained, handling the car expertly as she went up the rutted track. 'It's near the Home Farm. That's where we live. Dad runs it, well, he's my stepfather, but he's always treated me like his own. And he's looked after Mam and me very well. He sent me to Leeds College of Art.'

'Oh, so you studied up here in Yorkshire, not in London.'

'That's right. It's a good college, and anyway, I didn't want to go and live in London. I love it here.'

'That's not surprising, Lavinia. Yorkshire's beautiful, and the hall is something else, out of this world.'

'Thanks to Verity!' Lavinia exclaimed. 'She's the one who keeps everything running smoothly. Dad says she's a really good administrator.'

'And she's obviously very enterprising.'

'Oh yes, and a clever businesswoman.' Lavinia looked at Katie quickly, then brought her eyes back to the dirt track she was driving along. 'The Earl sort of . . . gave up when Tim and Justin were killed. His son and heir, and his grandson and heir, both of them gone just like that . . . in the blink of an eye. It was a terrible shock. Mam says he's never really recovered, and that's why he finds it hard to live here now.'

'I understand,' Katie murmured quietly, imagining the Earl's overwhelming grief. 'And who will inherit the title and the estate?' she then wondered out loud.

'Verity's son, Stephen. When his grandfather dies, Stephen will become the Earl of Burton Leyburn. Right now he's studying at Cambridge.'

'I see.' Katie leaned back against the worn leather seat, thinking about the family's sorrow. It was so hard to come to grips with sudden and unexpected death, especially when it was touched with violence. She knew that only too well. It struck her now that Xenia had made a wonderful recovery. She functioned very well, and if, at times, she appeared sad and morose it was understandable. But for the most part, Xenia was fully in control of herself. Five years was not very long to come to grips with the loss of a husband and a child.

Katie looked at the passing landscape. The long fields gave way to woods filled with great old trees, and beyond were more fields cut into a patchwork design by the low, drystone walls. As she peered ahead Katie soon saw the beginning of a huge stretch of farmland, and a farmhouse and out-buildings were just visible in the distance. Wide pastures surrounded the farmhouse, and in one of them a herd of Guernsey cows grazed lazily in the bright October sunlight. A white horse and its foal were gambolling together in another pasture, and helped to complete what was a truly pastoral scene, Katie thought.

Ten minutes later, Lavinia was turning onto a wide road that ran behind the farmhouse up towards the moors etched against the pale-blue sky. Straight ahead of them, at the foot of the moorland, was a barn.

'That's it, my studio!'

Katie walked with Lavinia towards the barn, and she couldn't help thinking of that other barn, far away in Connecticut. She felt a sudden, involuntary shiver pass through her. Troubling memories, forever fresh, flashed before her eyes, and she quickly pushed them to one side. But thankfully that other barn no longer existed; after Denise's murder Ted Matthews had torn it down and flattened the ground where it stood. However, it still existed in Katie's mind, and she knew it always would.

Lavinia pushed open the door, and cried, '*Voilà*! Here it is, Katie. Isn't it great?'

Katie had to agree. The barn was of medium size, with a cathedral ceiling; at the opposite end, the wall had been removed and replaced with a sheet of glass. This allowed bright daylight to flood into the barn so that it became the perfect place to paint.

'Dad put the big picture window in, but it's really

a French window. It slides open,' Lavinia explained. 'I have easy access to the outside. Come on, Katie, I want to show you my paintings.'

The paintings hung on two walls of the barn, and they were very well illuminated by pin-spots that shone down from beams in the cathedral ceiling. Katie knew at once that they were not merely good, but quite extraordinary. Jarvis is right to sound so proud, Katie thought; this girl is talented beyond belief.

The first painting that Katie lingered in front of was of a young girl sitting on a bale of hay in front of a haystack. It reeked of a hot summer's day. Lavinia had brilliantly captured all of the inherent elements of high summer: a cerulean-blue sky, white puff-ball clouds, and golden hay. And sunshine spilled forth from the large-sized canvas. The laughing, dimpled girl with gypsy-black curls and cheeky black eyes was simply enchanting. The sleeves of her red shirt were rolled up to show her plump arms, which were as tanned as her merry face, while her luscious ripe mouth echoed the red of her shirt. Katie was captivated.

Lavinia painted in the Impressionist style, and she had obviously mastered it well. It happened to be the school of painting Katie had always preferred, especially the great French Impressionists, such as Renoir, Monet and Degas, and so she understood how talented Lavinia was.

'They're all fantastic!' Katie exclaimed, when she had finally viewed the entire collection. 'I think your art show at the gallery in Harrogate is going to be a smash hit, Lavinia.'

'Oh, I do hope so, and I'm glad you like my paintings, Katie. Rex Bellamy thinks some of them are like those from the Newlyn School. That was a group of painters who worked in the 1930s, and they were tremendously popular. He keeps talking about those painters, and he actually thinks some of my work is a little bit like that of Dame Laura Knight . . . Well, I don't know about that. I'm flattered he thinks so of course, but I just paint what I love, the images I want to get on canvas, because they touch my . . . soul.'

Katie nodded her understanding, and pointed to another. 'I like this as well,' she murmured, hovering in front of a painting of two children sitting under a willow tree, next to a large body of water. 'Who are these children? They're beautiful. Did you have real models? Or are they from your imagination?'

'They're the grandchildren of Jarvis and Dodie.'

'*Oh*.' Katie stared at her, speechless for a moment, and then she asked, 'Are you saying that Jarvis is married to Dodie?'

'Yes. They have a daughter, Alicia, and she's married to Alex Johnson, and these are their children, Poppy and Mark. They're adorable, aren't they? And I'll tell you something, Katie, they were such good kids when

I was painting them. They sat really still, and behaved like little angels.'

Katie smiled, but there was a perplexed look in her eyes. 'I just can't connect Jarvis and Dodie, somehow . . .'

'I know what you mean, they don't seem to work together, do they? But they've been married for donkey's years. And they both grew up on the estate here. Jarvis's father was the butler before him, and Dodie's mother was the cook for a while. So in a way I suppose they're like family to Verity in one sense. Certainly they're really part of this place.'

'And tell me, Lavinia, do you think Dodie's psychic?'

Lavinia burst out laughing. 'I don't know what to think. I'm not really into hocus-pocus, that kind of thing, if you know what I mean. But for what it's worth, my mother is absolutely certain she is, and so is Dad.'

'I see. You know, I have a feeling that Verity is a believer, too.'

'Oh yes, I agree. Course she is.'

Chapter Twenty-four

It was the juvenile writings of the Brontës which Katie found fascinating. After a full tour of Haworth Parsonage, where they had grown up, she lingered in the parlour. Xenia was with her, and the two of them stood looking down at manuscripts penned by Charlotte, Emily, and Anne, and their brother, Branwell.

Known as the Juvenilia, these particular manuscripts were housed in glass cases, and to Katie one of the most remarkable things about them was their size. None of them was any bigger than a standard matchbox; the tiny pages, handstitched together by the Brontës, were about three inches in size, and the handwriting on the pages was minuscule. In fact, it wasn't really handwriting at all, but tiny print-writing, which the Brontë children had adopted in order to make their manuscripts look more like real printed books.

'How extraordinary they are,' Katie murmured, leaning closer to the glass case in order to see them better.

'Listen, when Mrs Gaskell, Charlotte's friend and

biographer, first held them in her hand, she was astonished, truly startled that the children's imagination had been the source for the material in them. Later she wrote that they gave one the idea of creative power carried to the verge of insanity,' Xenia said. 'And from what I've read about the Brontës, the imaginary world of Angria did become the centre of interest for Charlotte and her siblings for a long time. She was the driving force behind all of them and their writing, by the way.'

'What about Gondal? Wasn't that important to them?'

'To Emily and Anne, absolutely. You see, first came the stories of the Glasstown Confederacy, by Branwell and Charlotte. Later, all four children shared that imaginative world,' Xenia explained. 'Eventually it was split into two separate entities . . . one they called the kingdom of Angria, the other the kingdom of Gondal. Emily and Anne took Gondal for themselves, and many of Emily's great poems, written later, are Gondal poetry.'

'I see. But for the most part, I've noticed only Angrian material here in the museum. Weren't there many Gondal stories, or more of the little books?'

'I believe there were, but they were penned in later years by Emily and Anne, although Anne began to lose interest before Emily did. The story goes that Charlotte destroyed the manuscripts after Emily's death.'

'But *why*?' Katie exclaimed, sounding puzzled. 'Was Charlotte jealous of her sister's greatness as a writer, do you think?'

Xenia shook her head. 'No, I don't. On the other hand, how will we ever really know the truth? The theory put forward by scholars and experts on the Brontës is that Charlotte was only following Emily's wishes, her overriding desire for privacy. Charlotte believed Emily wrote only for herself, and didn't want anything read by others, especially strangers, i.e. the public.'

Katie murmured, 'What you're saying is that she wrote because she had to, in order to be fulfilled as a human being.'

'Exactly. She remains a tantalizing figure, mysterious and mystical. Emily was driven by her own demons . . . She's one helluva part for you to play, Katie.'

Straightening up, turning to face Xenia, Katie smiled, and nodded. 'Oh, I know that. And the more I see of Haworth, the more I'm intrigued.' Glancing around the parlour, she walked over to the window, stood there for a moment, her eyes resting on the graveyard. Then she sighed to herself. 'Not much of a playground for children, was it?'

Xenia joined her at the window, also looked out at the bleak scene, the gravestones. 'No,' she agreed. 'But there is a little garden in the back, and Emily apparently used to take her lap desk out there, and sit and write under the shade of a tree. It seems she didn't like to stray far from Haworth . . . this house, the garden, and the moors. I suppose she felt safe here . . . secure and unafraid.'

'I can't imagine that Emily Brontë, the creative genius who wrote *Wuthering Heights*, was *timid*.'

'I didn't say that.'

'The implication's there, Xenia.'

'Perhaps. You know, at one point Charlotte and Emily went to Mme Heger's school in Brussels. Professor Heger, who taught at the school, and whom Charlotte fell in love with, once wrote to the Rev. Brontë to say that Emily seemed to have lost some of her timidity while at the school. But it was well known by the family and friends that she really did want to remain in Haworth, did not wish to step out into the greater world, although she did actually go away a few times.'

'Perhaps, like most writers, she was selfish, and just wanted to stay in a familiar environment in order to write,' Katie suggested.

'That's true. I think she was hell-bent on perfecting her art, her craft.'

'And what became of Charlotte's romance with Professor Heger?'

'Oh, it never blossomed into a real romance, as such. He was a married man, remember. There was Madame Heger, who owned the school, and she was awfully suspicious of Charlotte and her husband at one point. I think it was during Charlotte's second visit to Brussels that Madame Heger cottoned on.'

'Do you think that the professor reciprocated Charlotte's romantic interest in him?' Katie asked.

'No. Now why am I saying that? How do we know anything?' Xenia muttered, shaking her head wonderingly. 'We weren't there. We weren't witnesses. And anyone who was is now dead and buried. Let's face it, Katie, there's no saying what men and women will do when driven by that all-consuming, overwhelming feeling of sexual passion and romantic love.'

'Almost anything, I guess,' Katie responded. 'You know what men are.'

Xenia burst out laughing. 'It takes two to tango, Katie. Don't forget, a man can't do it all by himself; he needs a woman. A partner. And there's something else to consider. Without Professor Heger in Charlotte's life, if only as a teacher, we would not have had those two marvellous books, *The Professor* and *Villette*.'

'Those I haven't read. But I did read *Shirley* and enjoyed it. Charlotte was much more prolific than Emily, wasn't she?'

'Oh yes, and very much the professional. And also the promoter. What I mean is, she was the one who got them published, who was actually out there in public, doing her stuff like a modern-day press agent. And she sort of stage-managed them all, in a sense. If she hadn't had the energy and drive, and the ambition, to make their lives better, the world might never have heard of the Brontë sisters.'

A short while later, Xenia and Katie left the Brontë Parsonage Museum, and went out into the cobbled streets. Since Xenia knew Haworth well, she led the way past the church with its square tower and clock, up to the top of this Yorkshire hill village, poised high above the industrial valley of the West Riding far below.

Within minutes, the two of them stood looking out across the wild, untenanted moors. These stretched away in an endless, unbroken line towards the distant horizon, a sea of dun browns and purples for as far as the eye could see.

'They're stunning,' Katie said, feeling slightly awed by the harsh implacability of this bleak and desolate scenery. 'But kind of forbidding.'

'Yes, I tend to agree with you.' Xenia shaded her eyes with her hand, went on: 'I've always thought that this landscape was daunting, although quite breathtaking in its windswept loneliness, its emptiness.' She smiled to herself. 'I suppose it's an acquired taste. A lot of people think it too harsh altogether. And I must admit, I'm really sorry you're not seeing the moors in August and September, when the heather is in full bloom. Then they're magnificent. Right now, you're getting the end of the season, the last of ling.'

'What's ling?'

'The local heather. It's not quite as bonnie as the Scottish heather,' Xenia said. 'It's about three miles to Top Withens, which is supposedly the setting for *Wuthering Heights*, as I told you before. However, a lot of scholars believe that the old farmhouse itself was never the actual *model* for the Earnshaw home, that Emily used the much grander High Sunderland Hall for her descriptions of Wuthering Heights, but that she put High Sunderland Hall in the location where Top Withens stands; that's a ruin now. But if you wish, we can take a walk over the moors. I'm game.'

Xenia paused, lifted her head, glanced up at the pale-blue sky. 'Well it's still clear, a fair day. But you never know what might happen up here on the moors. The weather is unpredictable. It can change within seconds, easily start pouring. That's why I brought an umbrella.' She patted her shoulder bag as she spoke.

'I would like to walk across the moors,' Katie responded. 'But we don't have to go all the way to Top Withens. I don't need to see the ruined farm. I just want to get a feeling of the landscape, a sense of this place, because Emily *did* spend so much time up here.'

'Then let's go!'

The two women began walking along the dirt track in silence, both lost in their thoughts.

Katie was contemplating Emily Brontë, a woman who had seemingly been so enigmatic she appeared, at times, to be unfathomable. To play the part of Emily, Katie knew she must truly understand her character and personality; if she were to succeed in the role she had to be fully aware of Emily's motivations, intentions, passions, desires, and even her dreams.

The prospect was frightening, in a way, but she knew there were a number of books in the library at Burton Leyburn Hall which would be helpful. Verity had taken down several biographies and studies of the Brontës, as well as some of the novels the sisters had written. Verity had shown them to her, and told her she could borrow them, as long as they eventually came back to the library. 'Because they're all catalogued,' Verity had explained.

Katie now made up her mind to read as much as she could about Emily while still in Yorkshire, and, if necessary, she would take some of the books to London with her.

For her part, Xenia's mind was on the party her company was to prepare for clients on New Year's Eve. Alan, her partner, had phoned from New York yesterday, and confirmed for the second time that she should definitely go ahead and use the Winter Palace in St Petersburg for the decorative theme.

And so now she was thinking about the drawings Lavinia would do for her this weekend, scenes taken from some of her own photographic books in the library at Burton Leyburn. Her father had given them to her years ago, at the time he had taken her on a trip to Russia.

It was going to be a challenge to re-create the ballroom of the Winter Palace, at the time of the Tsars, in the ballroom of the Plaza Hotel in New York. But it was one she looked forward to enormously. Challenges helped her to keep her mind off the loss of her child and her husband, helped to subdue her continuing grief. Challenges held pain and anguish at bay. For a short time, at least.

They had been walking for twenty minutes when the weather unexpectedly changed, just as Xenia had predicted it could. Without warning, thunderheads suddenly rolled in across the high-flung sky, the diffused pale blue darkening to leaden grey in an instant, and in the distance there was the loud rumble of thunder.

'I think we ought to turn back,' Xenia exclaimed, glancing up at the sky. 'It's going to pour. I can promise you that.'

'Yes, we'd better go. At least I've seen a bit of the moors.' Katie felt the splash of raindrops on her face, and added swiftly, 'Come on, Xenia!'

The two of them started to run along the dirt road, heading for Haworth village. They had just reached the end of the moorland when the rain began to come down in a steady stream. Huddling together under Xenia's umbrella, they flew down the main street, their feet clattering on the wet cobblestones as they ran.

'That was definitely a close call.' Xenia wiped her wet face with tissues and handed the box to Katie. 'A few minutes longer on the moors and we'd have been soaked to the skin.'

'Thanks.' Katie pulled out a bunch of tissues, also dried herself off, and then sat back in the car seat. 'I'm sorry our visit was cut short, but you were right to insist I come, Xenia. It's given me a much better picture of Emily.'

'I thought it would.'

Xenia turned on the ignition and drove the vintage Bentley out of the car park, which was virtually empty on this cool October Saturday. Most visitors came to Haworth in the spring and summer, or when the heather bloomed in August and September.

Xenia pulled out onto the main road to Keighley, which would take them to the motorway leading to Skipton and Harrogate. She drove along at a steady speed, from time to time exchanging the occasional comment with Katie.

At one moment, she said, 'If you need a little more insight into Emily Brontë you should talk to Rex Bellamy. He's something of an expert on the family.'

'Is he really. But then it doesn't surprise me, he sounded quite knowledgeable about their novels and poetry last night.'

'I didn't hear him talking about the Brontës.'

'No, you wouldn't have. It was when you went upstairs to get your sweater.'

'I see.'

'What does he do? He looks like an academic. *Is* he a teacher?'

Xenia laughed. 'No. And don't be taken in by that donnish air of his . . . it's very misleading, as no doubt he fully intends it to be.'

'So what does he do?'

Xenia was silent.

Katie waited for a moment, eyeing her surreptitiously, wondering why she was suddenly being mysterious about Rex. After a second or two, she pressed, 'Isn't he a professor then?'

'No.' There was a pause before Xenia said, 'He's a spy.'

'*A spy*? What do you mean?' Katie sounded startled.

'Just that. He's a spy, in my opinion anyway. I believe he's with MI6.'

'MI6 . . . but what exactly is that?' Katie asked.

'MI6 is like your CIA, in that it operates outside Great Britain. MI5, on the other hand, operates within this country, much like your FBI.'

'I see.' Katie pondered for a moment. 'I didn't know a spy let people know he was . . . I thought spies kept their profession a secret.'

'Oh goodness, Rex doesn't go around *telling* people he's a spy, not at all. Actually, he likes to give the impression he's an academic, just as you thought he was, and a writer. Certainly he's very scholarly, well informed about the arts and literature. But he's a spy, of that I'm fairly certain.'

'Does Verity think that too?'

'Sometimes she does, at other times she's in denial about it. He used to work for army intelligence when he was in the army, and now I believe he's with MI6. He's away a lot, he's very mysterious about his travels, where he goes, and he knows too much about certain things. You know, he lets snippets drop by mistake, then makes an attempt to cover up.'

'Is he Verity's boyfriend?' Katie ventured carefully.

'Well, they're not romantically involved, if that's what you mean. But he's her closest male friend. I guess you could say they're chums, you know, best pals. They've been friends for donkey's years, and now that he's divorced he spends more time at the hall. He lives in Yorkshire part of the time. His mother has a beautiful Georgian house, near York actually, but I think I told you that.'

'And the rest of the time he's travelling for MI6?'

Xenia chuckled. 'I think he is, but he does have a flat in London. In Chesterfield Street. But listen, if you ask Rex what he does he'll be relatively honest with you, Katie. He'll tell you he works for the British government, that he's with the Foreign Office, and that his office is in Whitehall. All true. But as I just said, *I* believe he's with British intelligence.'

'Why is Verity uncertain? Why is she in denial sometimes?'

'Because she doesn't want anything to happen to him, I suppose. And look, don't get me wrong, I like Rex enormously, and I don't give a hoot if he *is* with British intelligence. He's kind, civilized, good-looking, and charming. And Verity is very fond of him. So am I, for that matter.'

'Why is he an expert on the Brontës?'

'I'm not sure. But they're *the* great Yorkshire writers, and he's very much a dyed-in-the-wool Yorkshireman.' She chuckled again. 'He's very proud of his Yorkshire heritage. And as it happens, he does have a strong literary bent. But you can ask him about his interest in the Brontës. He's very forthcoming. Just don't ask him if he's a British agent,' she cautioned.

'As if I would, Xenia! I'm not *that* dumb.'

Xenia glanced at her and nodded. 'You're one of the brightest people I know, Katie.'

Chapter Twenty-five

The library at Burton Leyburn Hall was a long room, somewhat like a gallery, Tudor in style, with a beamed ceiling and stone fireplace. Bookshelves lined all of the walls from ceiling to floor, and in front of the fireplace a large leather sofa and several comfortable chairs were grouped together.

Katie walked across the floor to the refectory table in front of one of the mullioned windows, and once again looked at the books Verity had previously selected for her. Her gaze lingered on one about Emily Brontë, written by the novelist Muriel Spark, and a collaborator, Derek Stanford.

As she turned away from the window, making for the sofa with the book, she almost jumped out of her skin when Rex Bellamy rose from a wing chair near the fireplace.

Immediately, he smiled apologetically. 'I'm sorry, Katie, I obviously startled you. Do forgive me, my dear.'

'It's all right, Rex,' she said, smiling back at him. 'I didn't know anyone was in here.'

'Ah, I see you have the Muriel Spark book in your hands. It's very well done, marvellous stuff. Now tell me, how was your trip to Haworth this morning?'

'Interesting, and I'm glad Xenia talked me into going. I know a lot more about Emily Brontë than I did yesterday. So it was really worthwhile.' She hesitated fractionally. 'Xenia told me you know a great deal about the Brontë family,' she finally went on. 'She said you could give me a few insights into them, especially Emily. Would you mind, Rex?'

'I'd be happy to talk to you. Do you have the time now, Katie? If so, perhaps we can spend a little time chatting before tea is served.'

Katie nodded, and sat down on the sofa; she placed the book on a nearby side table.

Rex lowered himself into a wing chair, and looked across at her expectantly, as if waiting for a question.

Katie asked, 'If it's not rude of me to ask, what led you to have such an interest in the Brontës?'

'It's not rude, it's a perfectly normal question. I got interested in them because of my sister, Eleanor. Years ago, when she was still at school, she was making a study of them for a school paper, for an exam. I became . . . well, I suppose I became *intrigued*.' Rex leaned forward slightly, his hands on his knees, his dark eyes full of quickening interest. 'You see, Katie, I love a mystery, and it struck me all those years ago that the Brontës, as a family, were surrounded in mystery. And so I began to read some of Eleanor's books, and became even more fascinated. Studying them has been a quiet little hobby of mine off and on over the years.'

'Are you in the literary field? I mean, are you a professor of literature? Something like that?' Katie asked, wondering how he would answer. Her eyes were on him intently; Rex was a good-looking man with a narrow but well-defined face. He had high cheekbones, a broad brow, and a full head of dark hair turning grey at the sides, and brushed straight back; his wide-set black eyes sparkled with intelligence and humour. Tall, lean, with long legs, he was an elegantly-turned out man, his clothes casual, but obviously expensive.

After a moment, Rex said, 'No, I'm not an academic. I work for the British government. I'm with the Foreign Office.'

'Oh really, what do you do there?'

'I'm in the information business . . . intelligence, you might call it.'

'*Oh*,' Katie exclaimed, wondering if she sounded as startled as she felt.

Rex began to laugh, his expression amused, those dark eyes more humorous than ever. 'I'm quite certain that Xenia told you I'm a spy — a British agent. But that's not true. I have an office job, I'm tied to a desk shuffling papers, not playing the trade of spy out in the field. Although Xenia loves the idea that I am. Anyway, in some ways, it's a very boring job really.'

Katie laughed with him, and not wishing to betray her friend, she lied. 'Oh no, Xenia didn't discuss your work. She just told me you have a lot of knowledge about the Brontës. I think she hoped you might enlighten me a bit. I told you last night that I'm considering taking the role of Emily in the hit play *Charlotte and Her Sisters*, and you did say you'd seen it.'

Rex nodded, 'Oh yes, I wouldn't have missed it for the world. And whilst I don't want to influence you, I think I can say I enjoyed the play but wasn't entirely satisfied with the way Emily was interpreted.'

'What do you mean?'

Rex hesitated. After a moment's careful reflection, he replied, 'Later I'll give you a critique about the part of Emily as she is being re-created on the stage at the moment. But right now I think I ought to tell you a little about the Brontës, as *I* see them.'

She nodded. 'I'm very grateful that you're talking to me about them.'

He leaned back in the wing chair, and said, 'From our talk last night, I realize you know a few things about them already.'

'Yes, and Xenia filled me in a bit today.'

'Then let me give you a quick summary of them as a family. The four children were close, yet also divided into two pairs. Charlotte and Branwell, and Emily and Anne. Although later, in their adult lives, Charlotte became truly awed by Emily's immense gifts.

All four were extraordinarily talented writers and had the most vivid imaginations. Branwell was also a painter. In fact, he studied painting. He was a drunk, as no doubt you know, and eventually a drug addict. He took laudanum. He wasted his life and he died far too young. His three sisters had mixed feelings about him. They loved him, of course, but they were also awed, enraged, frightened, fascinated, and thrilled by him as his escapades kept coming to light, and latterly when debt-collectors gathered on their doorstep in Haworth they were fearful.' Rex paused, cleared his throat, and finished. 'To sum up, he was the proverbial black sheep of the family.'

'And spoiled by his sisters, no doubt,' Katie volunteered.

'At times, yes. But not always. Their mother had died young, of tuberculosis, and the Rev. Brontë was somewhat of an absentee father, in that he was always in his church, writing his sermons or lost in his own thoughts. There was only Aunt Branwell to keep an eye on them when they were young. And Charlotte, but she was only a year older than Branwell. There wasn't much difference in any of their ages, as a matter of fact, they were just over a year apart. Oh, except for Anne, who was almost two years younger than Emily.

'Charlotte was their . . . *promoter* I guess you could call it,' Katie said. 'The one who was out hustling, getting their work published.'

'Yes, indeed. Charlotte was the eldest and by far the best novelist of the four of them, and the most prolific. However, Emily was the true genius, with six great epic poems and that one extraordinary novel to her credit. But Anne was also a good novelist and poet, and emotionally close to Emily. But getting back to Charlotte, she did act as their agent, in a sense, and she did get them published by first paying for a book of their poems to be printed. Only two copies were sold. But there was one review, a good one, and it was of Emily's poetry, who was otherwise known as Ellis Bell. Anne being Acton Bell, and Charlotte was Currer Bell. You see, they did not want the world to know they were three sisters called Brontë.'

'Yes, I knew about that.'

'Charlotte pushed them all to write books which would sell, i.e. novels. She was very ambitious for them, wanted them all to do well in the world.'

'But Emily didn't care about that, did she?'

'No. She herself made no effort to get her work published, or to gain public recognition. *Her* genuine anxiety was about *perfecting* her work. She was very committed to her writing, and in that way she was professional,' Rex explained. 'I believe she destroyed a lot of her writing for that reason. She was not satisfied with it. Especially after *Wuthering Heights* was published. And possibly Charlotte destroyed some of it after her death, protecting her sister's privacy.'

'What do you think of *Wuthering Heights*?'

'Not what the world thinks, that's a certainty!' he exclaimed.

'Would you tell me your opinion?'

'The world sees it as a great love story. But it's not that at all,' Rex said. 'Basically it's a very violent book about revenge and hatred, about a Byronic hero, Heathcliff, getting his revenge on Cathy Earnshaw and the Earnshaws.'

'I understand what you're saying, but surely it's a love story in a certain sense, isn't it?' Katie asserted, a brow lifting quizzically.

'Not in the way we think of love stories, no,' Rex answered. 'It is so very violent, almost demonic, and sombre, dark. The so-called lovers are never united in physical passion. They are always celibate, although, to be honest, they are passionate in other ways. I believe it is a paean to death, as only Emily Brontë could write it, and a book of some complexity. It has energy, enormous narrative drive, and the most unique narrators in Nelly Dean and Mr Lockwood. I never tire of reading it again. It always gets to me.'

'And Emily? What do you make of her?'

'She was a relatively normal young woman,' Rex said. 'By that I mean she was fairly down to earth, practical. Her family and her friends said she was always homesick when she was away from Haworth. And this may well be true. But the truth is, she liked being at home doing the housekeeping, because it *enabled her to make her own rules*, and she was able to slip away to write whenever she wanted. And that's what *she* was all about, Katie. Homesick? Maybe. But in my opinion, she wanted to be in Haworth running the parsonage, instructing the domestic help in their duties, and *doing as she pleased*. You see, when Charlotte and Anne were away being governesses, and Branwell was working for the railway in Luddenden Foot, she was in charge of everything. She was the boss, and the boss spent most of her time writing.'

Katie smiled. 'The selfish artist, is that what you're saying?'

'In a way, yes,' Rex acceded. 'To be successful as an artist, whether as a painter, writer or actor, there has to be dedication. And if that means being selfish, so be it. I came to these conclusions about Emily after reading Charlotte's letters to her girlfriends Ellen Nussey and Mary Taylor, also Charlotte's letters to Emily, and vice versa.'

'Why do you think Emily was normal? What I mean is, she is always depicted as being odd, certainly enigmatic and mystical.'

'I think she was those things, Katie,' Rex was swift to assert. 'But she was a normal young woman in that she could write a very matter-of-fact letter about her daily doings, sounding ordinary and happy, and yet earlier that same day she had spent hours writing high drama.

In other words, she got into the head and heart of a character, became that character during the time she was writing. But when she put down her pen and left her desk she became herself again, became Emily Jane Brontë, vicar's daughter, running a house and looking after her father.'

'I think perhaps I might have to reassess my ideas about Emily. For the play I mean. *If* I take the part.'

'Oh you mustn't turn it down, Katie. It's perfect for you, I feel quite positive about that. I will make a few notes for you later,' Rex said. 'They will cut down on your reading, although I think you ought to read the Muriel Spark book about Emily. My notes will be something of a short cut, perhaps.' He leaned forward, stared at her intently, and finished, 'Please don't turn down the part of Emily Brontë. I've only just met you, but I do have strong feelings about you playing her.'

He sounded so fervent as he said this that Katie said, 'I did tell the producer I would do it. I just want to be sure of myself, sure I can portray Emily.'

'You can, my dear.'

The door of the library opened and Rex jumped up at once as Verity came rushing into the room. 'There you are, darling,' he said as she hurried to his side. Embracing her, he hugged her to him tightly, and kissed the top of her silver-gilt hair.

Katie saw the look of love on his face, the warmth

and tenderness in those dark eyes, and she knew without question that these two were very close, extremely attached to each other, whatever Xenia thought.

Verity pulled away from Rex's loving embrace, and smiling, she turned to Katie. 'I hope Rex has been able to give you a few tips about Emily. He's the great expert on the Brontës, you know.'

'Not exactly!' Rex laughed and shook his head.

'Around these parts you are,' Verity shot back, and said to Katie, 'Xenia tells me you had a grand trip to Haworth but got rained out. Never mind, you probably saw more than enough to help you. Now, shall we all go up for tea?'

The cold spell that Pell, the gardener, had been predicting finally came to pass. Katie felt the terrible coldness in the front entrance hall when they went up the grand staircase together for tea.

Verity remarked about the sudden chilliness in the house as she pushed open the double doors and went into the Great High Chamber. 'Cool on the outer fringes, but it'll be warm enough by the fireplace, thank goodness,' she said. 'I'm quite certain of that. Pell's promise of early frost has been fulfilled finally. I must say, that man's usually right.'

'Of course he is. He's a dyed-in-the-wool countryman,' Rex responded. 'You can always rely on them to pinpoint the weather every time. Harold, my mother's gardener at Great Longwood, is exactly the same way. I keep teasing him, suggesting he should be on the telly doing the weather spot.'

The big silver tea tray, and another tray of delicious sandwiches and pastries, had already been brought up by Jarvis, and placed on the big square coffee table in front of the fire. Verity took up her position near the teapot, and Rex sat down next to her, while Katie settled in an armchair immediately opposite them.

A moment later, Xenia came whirling into the room, and within seconds of her arrival Lavinia appeared in the doorway, looking as pretty as always. This afternoon she was dressed in a fire-engine-red wool jump suit and red ballerina slippers.

Verity poured the tea as usual, and Lavinia and Xenia passed the cups; they then offered around the tiny nursery sandwiches which were all different, filled with egg salad, potted meat, smoked salmon, cucumber or sliced tomatoes.

Katie loved the little sandwiches, which Xenia had told her were invented here in the British nursery years before, but limited herself to one of egg salad, another of smoked salmon, and a third of potted meat. Even though Rex urged her to make it a round figure of six at least, she resisted the temptation.

She then sat back, munching on the sandwiches, enjoying the marvellous warmth of the big roaring fire, the comfort and cosiness of this lovely old room. And it was cosy, despite its grand size. Her thoughts jumped around in her head as she reviewed the last couple of days, and she realized that she had been busy every minute. Today had probably been her most fruitful, in regards to her work, because of the visit to Haworth and then her discussion of the Brontës with Rex.

She stole a quick look at him. Katie thought Rex Bellamy was a nice man, and she liked him a lot. Just as she liked everyone in this room, even though they were all a bit odd, in their own way. It seemed to Katie that each of them had some kind of secret. She laughed inwardly. Didn't everyone have secrets of some sort? Skeletons in the closet?

Katie brought her attention back to Xenia, and her ears pricked up when she heard her friend say, 'I've no idea where it is, Rex. I looked for it last night, actually. I wish we could run it. Laurence Olivier is great as Heathcliff and Merle Oberon is a most beautiful Cathy Earnshaw. Odd, but she didn't look *chichi*, which she was, of course.'

'What's *chichi*?' Lavinia asked.

'Anglo-Indian,' Rex answered.

Xenia went on, 'At times one has the feeling bits of it were shot on the Hollywood backlot, but for the most part it has great authenticity.'

'Are you talking about the film of *Wuthering Heights*?' Katie asked.

'Yes,' Verity replied. 'We have a video of it, but

apparently it's been lost. Anyway, why watch it, since Xenia just put the kibosh on it.'

'No, I didn't!' Xenia exclaimed. 'And it's a classic now. Certainly it's a hundred times better than those awful remakes of the last few years. Nobody ever gets it right, you know.'

'I would've loved to have seen it,' Katie murmured, sounding disappointed.

'I think I know where the video is,' Lavinia announced, standing up as she spoke. 'I'm sure I saw it on a shelf in the library, and not long ago either.'

'The library! What on earth is it doing there? I always keep the videos in the study off my office,' Verity said, sounding puzzled.

'I *know* I saw it in the library,' Lavinia cried, and went out. She was obviously intent on retrieving it, not listening to Verity, who was telling her to look for it later.

'Have you never seen the film, Katie?' Rex asked. 'Not ever?'

She shook her head. 'No, I haven't, but I'm a big Olivier fan. He was the greatest, wasn't he?'

'A most superb actor,' Rex agreed, and offered Katie a plate of pastries.

Against her better judgement, she took a piece of cream sponge, and reminded herself to go on a diet the moment they got back to London. All of this wonderful home cooking was definitely going to her hips.

Within minutes of her rushed departure, Lavinia came racing back into the room, excitedly waving the video in her hand. She handed it to Xenia, and went back to her seat by the fire, murmuring to Verity, 'I just *knew* I'd seen it in the library.'

'What a cast!' Xenia looked up from the video and stared at Katie. 'Just listen to this list of actors. Laurence Olivier, Merle Oberon, David Niven, Flora Robson, Geraldine Fitzgerald, and Donald Crisp. It was directed by William Wyler, produced by Sam Goldwyn and written by Ben Hecht and Charles MacArthur. Gee whiz, I'd forgotten what an illustrious crew was involved with it! Smashing that you found it, Lavinia.' Xenia looked across at Verity, and said, 'Shall we watch it after dinner tonight?'

Verity smiled at her. 'I think that's a grand idea. It'll be a treat for Katie. And by the way, talking of all these wonderful old actors reminds me of the Wainrights' party in November, Rex. You are going to escort me, aren't you?'

'Of course, although I'm damned if I know who I'll go as. Movie stars of the past. What a theme! I do detest these fancy dress things.'

'But you promised,' Verity said, throwing him a reproachful look.

'You could go as Harry Lime in *The Third Man*,' Xenia suggested. 'I don't mean as played by Orson Welles in the movie, but as played by Michael Rennie in the British television series. You do look a bit like him, you know.'

'I take that as a compliment,' Rex said, bowing. 'And I have an idea for you, Verity.' Looking across at her, he said, 'Try this one on for size, darling. Ann Todd, the way she was in *The Seventh Veil*.'

'A bit before my time,' Verity said, laughing. 'But I vaguely remember Ann Todd. She was a favourite of Daddy's, and he was always watching her old movies. I bet if we look through the videos later we'll find some of hers.'

Chapter Twenty-six

Even though the heating system was turned on, the sudden cold spell had brought a distinct chill to her room. Katie noticed it the moment she returned to her bedroom after tea.

Shivering slightly, she ran over to the fireplace. Kneeling down in front of it, she brought a match to the newspaper and chips of wood which had been placed in the grate. Once these were burning fiercely, she added several logs, then hurried into the adjoining bathroom.

A long soak in a hot bubble bath brought a tingle of warmth to her body; after towelling herself dry and putting on her robe, she returned to the bedroom.

Katie now took her diary out of her carryall and sat down at the *bûreau plat* in the corner. The fireplace was quite close to the little French desk, and Katie felt the warmth, enjoyed the flare of the flames, the crackle of the logs as the fire leapt up the chimney.

Reaching for a pen, she opened her Five Year Diary and found a new page. She sat back for a moment, endeavouring to marshal her thoughts, and eventually began to write.

October 23rd, 1999   *Burton Leyburn Hall*
                                                    Yorkshire

I have to put a few things down here because I don't want to forget this weekend in Yorkshire. I can't remember when I had such a nice time. A lot of it has to do with my own frame of mind . . . I have been much more relaxed than I usually am in this old house with some very nice people.

They're all highly individualistic, certainly different from anybody I've ever met. Even a bit odd, if I'm honest. And mysteries seem to abound. Still, I do love it here.

I'd love to know the truth about various relationships, but I don't suppose I ever will. To begin with, there's Lavinia. She's treated like a beloved member of the family, but she isn't even related to Verity or Xenia. She's the daughter of the cook and an employee herself. She does secretarial work for Verity, runs errands, picks up guests at the station, things like that. And yet Verity treats her like her own daughter.

I mentioned this to Xenia yesterday, but she threw me such a peculiar look I clammed up. Then a bit later on she obviously felt she had to say something, so she told me Verity was extremely democratic in the way she did things here, that she didn't even want to use her title, play the lady of the manor. But, in fact, she is the lady of the manor, in her father's absence. When I was at the studio yesterday, Lavinia explained that Verity was born Lady Verity Leyburn, because as the daughter of an earl she had her own honorary title. Then she married Lord Hawes, and became Lady Hawes, so she's a lady twice, according to Lavinia. When she was married to Geoffrey Hawes she was called Lady Verity Hawes, though, because being the daughter of an earl entitles her to use her first name. If she had been just a plain Miss when she married Lord Hawes, she would have been known as Lady Hawes. No first name allowed in the title when you're a simple Miss before marriage to a lord.

Lavinia took ages to explain this, but as an American I find it all a bit complicated. Not Lavinia though. She seems to put great store by it. But then she's half English and grew up here at the hall.

Then there's Rex. He's very nice, kind, and charming, and I'm really grateful that he's going to make notes for me about Emily Brontë. But he's a true mystery. Xenia says he's a spy, he says he isn't, but would he admit that? Who knows. Still, he did tell me of his own accord that he worked in intelligence. Also, I think he's in love with Verity, and she with him, no matter what Xenia thinks. They look at each other in a very intimate way.

I am sure that they are having a thing. That they're lovers. Something I noticed at tea today was Rex's behaviour with Lavinia. He seems to be very paternal and loving, and Verity was looking on adoringly. If I hadn't known differently I would have thought they were her parents.

Lavinia confided that the Earl, Verity's father, stayed away because of his grief, and she sounded a bit strange when she said this. It seems odd to me, sort of neglecting his duties here on the estate. I saw a photograph of him in the library; Xenia told me it was her Uncle Thomas. He was in a Royal Air Force uniform, and she said it was taken during the Second World War and that he was quite a hero, one of the young flyers who did so much in the Battle of Britain. He was also very handsome when he was young. Xenia told me he still is; Lavinia says he's having an affair with this woman in France called Veronique.

Lavinia's definitely a bit of a chatterbox. She told me all kinds of other things, when I was up viewing her paintings. It's true that the family don't have a lot of money these days, and that it's Verity's ingenuity that keeps everything running. Lavinia said the catalogues have helped, but that Verity sold off a lot of family jewellery and paintings, although the Earl hadn't been too happy about it. She also told me that Xenia will never fall in love again, because she won't let herself, that she's 'the keeper of the flame', was the way she put it. I also found out that Xenia has a title too, because Tim, the only son of the Earl, was Viscount Leyburn. But she doesn't use it.

I don't care about any of their idiosyncrasies, or their complicated relationships. I just know that I like them all very much, and they've been so welcoming, so kind to me, especially Xenia. It's wonderful to have such a true friend, a real girlfriend again after all these years. She'll never be able to replace Carly and Denise in my heart, but I know she is a good person, and that she cares about me, as I do her. I love Xenia. She's special. I hope Lavinia is wrong and that she will fall in love again one day.

Denise is gone, but Carly is there, lying in that hospital bed in the hospice in Connecticut. I haven't seen her for over a year now, but Mom has been every month or so, as she always has for the last ten years. Mom's been very devoted to her. Carly looks the same. In some kind of coma . . . lost to us all, is the way Mom puts it.

I'm still ambivalent about taking on the role of Emily Brontë. For a lot of reasons, really. I'm still not sure I can play the part; and then again, I know that deep down I truly dread going back to New York. It's not that I'm afraid about my safety, because I'm not. Yes, there's a murderer roaming free out there, a man who literally got away with murder. But I don't think he's after me, even if he did target me all those years ago. The reason I dread going back is because I was never happy in New York. These months I've spent in London have only pointed this up even more . . .

There was a loud knocking on the door. Katie stopped writing and put her pen down. Rising, she hurried to see who was there.

Dodie, the housekeeper, was standing in the corridor with an armful of towels. 'I'm sorry to disturb you, Miss Byrne, but I thought you might need these . . . just freshly laundered.'

'Thanks, Dodie.' Katie opened the door wider, and the housekeeper came in and headed towards the bathroom.

A moment later she was back in the bedroom; she looked across at Katie, who was standing with her back to the fireplace.

'Oh, I see you started the fire,' she said. 'I'll send Pell's boy up with some extra logs.'

'Thanks.'

Dodie nodded, walked towards the door, and then stopped abruptly. She closed the door with some deliberation and came back to the fireside. In a low voice she asked, 'Could I have a word with you, Miss Byrne?'

'Yes, of course.' Katie frowned slightly, a puzzled look settling on her face.

'It's like this, miss. I acted funny, sort of odd, on Friday, when I first saw you. And I know you noticed, so did her ladyship. And Miss Xenia, she noticed too.'

Katie nodded, not sure how to respond to this statement.

Dodie was silent, stood staring at her intently.

Feeling suddenly uncomfortable under this concentrated scrutiny, Katie said, 'It's all right, Dodie. Please don't worry about it.'

Dodie took a small step forward, peered into Katie's face. 'I've lived here all my life, I was born here . . . in the village. I'm like part of the family.'

'Yes,' Katie murmured, nodding.

'So you know I'm not a crazy person. What I mean is, her ladyship trusts me, she knows me inside out, miss. Lady Verity is aware I'm psychic. Miss Xenia knows it too, but she doesn't always accept it. She thinks I'm daft, but I'm not. Far from it, miss. I told Lord Tim not to go to Harrogate that day. I had bad feelings. I saw death. But he didn't listen. And then they were in that . . . crash.'

Katie stared at the housekeeper, wide-eyed, wondering what was coming next.

'On Friday night, when I stood near you, I picked up on you, Miss Byrne . . . your aura . . . You are full of pain. You hide it. But I see it. I see it all around you.'

Katie swallowed hard, continuing to gape at Dodie, but she made no comment.

'There's violence in your past . . . violence changed your life . . . you must go home, Miss Byrne.'

'To New York?'

'To America. You must go. There is unfinished business . . . you are needed.'

'Who needs me?'

Dodie shook her head. 'Please, Miss Byrne, go home. *Home*.' She repeated this word, stressing it. 'It will all be clear.'

'I was planning to go for Christmas.'

'No. Sooner.'

'Dodie, are you all right?'

'Yes, miss.'

'Are you sure? You look very pale,' Katie said, frowning again.

Dodie came closer, and she placed her hand on Katie's arm. 'Listen to me, miss. Your future . . . I can see it all around you. It's in America. And there's unfinished business, like I said. Years old. I mean you no harm, miss.'

'Oh I know that, Dodie. But I can't leave London immediately. I have classes to finish at RADA . . .' Katie's voice trailed off under Dodie's unwavering gaze.

Dodie went on, 'Soon. Go soon. That's best.' She walked across the floor, added, 'I'll tell Verity what I've told you . . . I always tell her when I've *seen* . . . something.' She paused at the door, turned around and said in that same matter-of-fact voice, 'I'll send the boy up with the logs.'

PART THREE

Touch of Love

New York – Connecticut, 2000

'Alas I have grieved so I am hard to love.
Yet love me – wilt thou? Open thine heart wide . . .'
ELIZABETH BARRETT BROWNING

'With the first dream that comes with the first sleep
I run, I run, I am gather'd to thy heart.'
ALICE MEYNELL

Chapter Twenty-seven

Katie stood alone in the middle of the stage, staring out into the empty auditorium. It was in darkness, and the stage was also dark, except for one pin-spot shining down on her red hair, illuminating her delicate face.

Taking several steps, she sat down on the bench and leaned forward, her right elbow on her knee, her chin resting on her right hand. After a moment, she began:

'To be, or not to be, that is the question: Whether 'tis nobler in the mind to suffer the slings and arrows of outrageous fortune, or to take arms against a sea of troubles, and by opposing, end them. To die, to sleep – No more, and by a sleep to say we end the heartache and the thousand natural shocks that flesh is heir to; 'tis a consummation devoutly to be wish'd. To die, to sleep – To sleep, perchance to dream – ay, there's the rub, for in that sleep of death what dreams may come, when we have shuffled off this mortal coil, must give us pause; there's the respect that makes calamity of so long life . . .'

Katie paused for an instant, to take a quick breath, and

in that infinitesimal moment of silence sudden applause broke out in the auditorium.

Startled, she looked up, her mood of intense concentration broken. She rose and peered out into the darkness, saw sudden movement in the stalls, and then a slender figure came forward, walking slowly down the aisle towards the stage.

A moment later Katie recognized Melanie Dawson.

'I didn't know you were there!' Katie exclaimed. 'I was certain I was totally alone in the theatre.'

'Remind me to cast you in the leading role, if ever Harry and I produce *Hamlet* again. That's one of the best renditions of the soliloquy I've ever heard. How about that? Not a bad idea, eh? A female playing Hamlet.'

'I'd love it,' Katie replied. 'But you've only heard half of the speech.'

'I know that. You're very gifted, Katie, and I'm both thrilled and relieved you took the part of Emily Brontë. Thrilled because I know you're going to be great in my show; relieved because I would've hated to see that talent of yours go to waste.'

'Thanks for saying that, Melanie, your opinion of me as an actress is so important.'

Melanie was now looking across the proscenium, her face serious, as was her voice, when she said, 'This part of Emily Brontë couldn't be more perfect for you, Katie. You'll see what it'll do for your career.'

'I'm glad you like the way I've been playing her. I was

worried at first, because my interpretation is not quite the same as Janette Nerren's is in London.'

'No, it's not. But I've liked what you've been doing, right from the start of rehearsals. It's the way *you* visualize Emily that makes your performance different. You've made *your* Emily Brontë a very modern woman, I guess that's what appeals to me. But I've told you this before. And you know, you were explaining to me why you're playing her the way you are a couple of weeks ago, and then we were interrupted as usual. So tell me now.'

'It was a friend in Yorkshire, Rex Bellamy, who helped me to see Emily differently. He's an expert on the Brontës, and he gave me some insight into her. He didn't tell me how to play Emily, of course. But he did explain a great deal about her, what she was *really* like, not what others have turned her into over the last hundred years or so.'

'In other words, he showed you the *real* woman, the woman behind the myth.'

'Exactly.'

'It's working, Katie, as you well know. You're doing something special up there on that stage.'

'Emily was very modern, Melanie. Before her time. Independent, extremely go-ahead. She thought she was superwoman, that she could do anything, achieve anything, because of her strength of will. And she emancipated herself, in a sense.'

'Sounds like quite a few women I know.' Melanie began to chuckle, looking amused.

Katie joined in that laughter and then she said, 'I'll come down off the stage.'

'No, no, I'll come up there, and walk back to the dressing room with you.'

A couple of seconds later the two of them were heading backstage, and Melanie was saying, 'I was looking for you when I got stopped by Paul Mavrolian. He wanted to talk about the lighting. You know what tech week is like. I saw you, out of the corner of my eye, heading for the stage. And when I was finally able to follow you, I realized you were about to perform, so I went down into the auditorium to watch.'

'I see. But why are you looking for me? Do you want to talk to me about something?'

'Yes. You'll have to meet Selda Amis Yorke tomorrow. For your final costume fittings. You should go to her studio tomorrow morning, then get back here as soon as you can for rehearsals.'

'Okay, I will. And thanks again, Melanie.'

'You've already thanked me.'

'I know, but I am so aware of your faith in me . . . I promise I won't let you down.'

'I know you won't.'

Maureen Byrne was busy dusting the living room of Katie's small apartment in New York when the phone began to ring. Immediately she picked it up and said, 'Hello?'

'Is that you, Katie?'

'No, it's her mother. Who's this?'

'Oh *hello*, Mrs Byrne. How *are* you? This is Grant . . . Grant Miller.'

'Hello Grant . . . Katie's not here. She's at rehearsals.'

'Of course, how stupid of me. I keep forgetting she's in the Brontë play. What time do you expect her?'

Maureen hesitated. She really couldn't stand Grant Miller, and it took a great deal of her self-control to be civil to him. He was a bore with a face. His claim to fame, no doubt, although Katie had always said he had talent. Clearing her throat, her good manners kicking in, Maureen finally answered. 'I guess she gets out of rehearsals about six.'

'That sounds about right . . . ten until six. Those mandatory eight hours the producers make one work, tough, tough, Mrs Byrne. And I can only say, oh boy, am I *glad* I've moved out of the theatre and into the *movies*.'

'Have you really, Grant?' Maureen tried to keep the sarcastic tone out of her voice, but she wasn't sure that she had. 'Can I give Katie a message?'

It was his turn to clear his throat. 'Well, er, I'm not really sure, Mrs Byrne . . . I hate leaving a message. I really should talk to Katie about this . . .'

There was a sudden silence.

Maureen could hear him breathing at the other end of the phone. Reaching for the pen, sliding the small white pad towards her, she said in a brisk voice, 'Give me your number, please. I'll have her call you when she gets home. If she's not too tired.'

'I'm in Beverly Hills,' he replied, and rattled off ten digits. 'But as I just told you, Mrs Byrne, I don't like to leave a message about a sensitive subject, so –'

'You never said it was a sensitive subject, Grant,' Maureen cut in.

'It is though, you see . . . Look Mrs Byrne, maybe I should explain to you, and then you can give me *your* input, tell me what you think.'

'Go ahead, Grant.'

'It's like this Mrs Byrne . . . I'm getting married. Now this will come as something of a shock to Katie, I know, and I don't want her to take it too hard, get upset.'

Maureen was silent.

After a moment, he cleared his throat again, more nervously than before, and asked, 'Are you there, Mrs Byrne?'

'I am, Grant.'

'It's just . . . Well, look, I don't want Katie to be hurt. How will she react?'

With relief, I'm certain of that, Maureen thought. But she said, in a no-nonsense tone, 'Oh, don't worry about Katie's reaction, she's totally involved with the play right now. She'll be the first to wish you much happiness. As I do. Goodbye, Grant.'

He was mumbling his goodbye as she hung up swiftly.

Good riddance, Maureen thought, staring at the phone, and then she whirled away, gaily flicking the feather duster over the bookcase, suddenly feeling like humming a tune for the first time in ages. But instead of humming she began to laugh. Michael had always said Grant Miller was pompous and he had just proved it.

How like Grant Miller to imagine Katie would be upset because he was about to marry. Ego, she thought, what an ego that man has. She and Katie were as close as they had always been, if not closer these days, and her daughter had confided, over a year ago now, that the relationship with Grant was going nowhere, that it was over, as far as she was concerned.

And Katie had moved on. Not to another man, unfortunately, but she had finally taken a decisive step and accepted a part in a Broadway show at long last.

Maureen was relieved about that; also relieved that Katie had returned to America. She had understood her daughter's need to get out of New York, her desire to go to London to study at the Royal Academy of Dramatic Art. Katie was very enamoured of English acting and actors, wanted to hone her own acting talent in the place she considered the best.

She and Michael had been more than willing to support her financially through this period, just as they had taken over this apartment while Katie was absent.

Her sister, Bridget, had found it for Katie, when she had first come to New York to study. It was on West End Avenue in the Seventies, in a small building with a doorman, safe, very convenient, and accessible to Broadway.

When Katie had announced her intention to go to London last year, Bridget had cautioned Maureen not to allow Katie to vacate the apartment. 'She'll be back before you know it, and this is rent-controlled, a bargain she'll never find again. It will even be a bargain if and when the building goes co-op. And that *will* happen, you'll see. So hang on to it, even if you have to take it over yourself.'

She and Michael had listened to Bridget and done exactly that, which had turned out to be an excellent move on their part. In the past year, during Katie's absence, they had frequently driven into Manhattan to spend the weekend, go to the theatre or the movies, to shop, and have a meal with Bridget. And even Niall used the apartment from time to time, on quick trips to the city on business.

Niall. Her eldest child. Maureen worried about him. He was twenty-nine and still not married, much to her disappointment. She'd always thought that by now she would've had at least one grandchild. But Niall wasn't even courting anyone special. Lots of girlfriends, though. Safety in numbers.

She didn't worry about Fin. Her youngest was twenty-two and loved Oxford University, where he would graduate next year. He always struck her as being totally in harmony with himself, in control, at ease with his academic accomplishments, which were considerable. Not taking them for granted *exactly*, but accepting them in the most natural way. A bit of a loner, of course, but then Katie and Niall had made him that, not always allowing him into their tight circle of two. Fin was forever going forward, though. No, he's not a worry at all, she thought. But then again, Fin was not as badly affected by the tragic events of ten years ago as Katie and Niall were.

Maureen sighed, and glanced at the photograph on one of the bookshelves.

Katie, Carly, and Denise.

The photograph had been taken when they were sixteen. At Katie's Sweet Sixteen Party. She put the duster down on the desk, reached for the photograph in its dark wood frame, held it in both her hands, staring down at their faces. So young, so innocent, so tender.

Unexpectedly, tears sprang into Maureen's deep blue eyes as she thought of their great promise . . . it had been stolen from them so viciously.

Katie was alive, but the violence had left its terrible

and very damaging imprint on her daughter. And on Michael and Niall and Maureen herself.

The violence *had* shattered their lives, turned everything upside-down, but she and Michael had managed eventually to recoup. And if Michael had thrown himself into work, as an antidote to pain, then they had all reaped the benefits of his actions ultimately. Because he had made a grand success. That little building and contracting company he had started all by himself, when he'd left school, wasn't so little any more; if anything they had too much work, according to Niall. He was a full partner now with his father, and a very astute businessman as it turned out.

There were many newcomers in their area, mostly New Yorkers who sought weekend homes in the Litchfield hills, and traditional American Colonial was the favoured architectural style. Whether it was a remodelled old home brought up to modern standards, or a brand-new version, it was designed by Michael and built by their thriving family company.

Maureen was well aware that her daughter was the one who had suffered the most, never really recovering from the horror and grief of Denise's murder, Carly's unconscious state. It had stalled her acting career, slowed her down . . . in all ways. Until now.

At last Katie had found the courage to take this part, and perhaps now her whole life would change for the better. And it had struck Maureen, only the other day, that Katie seemed to be accepting New York for what it was . . . a great and exciting metropolis, like no other place on earth.

Katie had not been happy in New York in the past, mostly because she had no special friends, in Maureen's opinion. In many ways, she had clung to her aunt. Bridget had been happy to take her niece under her wing, and they had grown close. Bridget had never married, and so Katie had been like the daughter she had never had.

Maureen was grateful that her sister had looked after Katie. But it had never really worried her that her daughter was out on her own, living in the big city. Katie was sensible, smart, and she could look after herself very well. It was Katie's presence in Connecticut that caused Maureen concern, put her on edge. For unlike Michael and Mac MacDonald, and even Katie herself, Maureen did not believe the murderer had left the Malvern area.

She knew, deep within her Celtic soul, that he was still there, somewhere close, leading the life he had always led. Whether he had killed any more young women she did not know. Certainly there had been no more murders in the area, to her knowledge. And in any case, Mac would have told Michael if there had been. Still, that did not necessarily mean he hadn't killed again in the past ten years. *Somewhere else.*

Maureen touched Carly's face in the photograph, very gently with one finger, as she always did when she went to visit her at the hospice. There was never any reaction or response from Carly, but nevertheless it made Maureen feel better to go and see her, and she could only hope it helped Carly somehow. The nurses said they weren't sure if she knew Maureen was there in the room. Nevertheless, Maureen hoped Carly could hear her voice, and that she was aware, however dimly, of her presence, aware of the love she felt for her.

Janet, Carly's mother, went every week to see her, Maureen knew that. But the Matthews family never did. It was probably too difficult for them, she thought. They had moved away not long after Denise's funeral; they had sold their house and the restaurant in Kent and gone. No one knew where. It must have been unbearable for them to go on living in the Malvern area, with so many memories to haunt them. Maureen understood that.

Placing the photograph back in its place on the shelf, her expression bereft, she retrieved her duster and went out into the kitchen, trying to push the heartache to one side, as she always did. Somehow you lived with it, but it was hard at times.

Automatically she filled the kettle and put it on the stove top. Katie would be home soon, and she always liked a cup of tea when she got back from rehearsals.

Suddenly the telephone shrilled, and she jumped, startled. Then she reached for the wall phone. 'Hello?'

'Hello, Mrs Byrne. It's Xenia.'

'Yes, I recognize your voice. How are you, Xenia dear?'

'Fine, and you?'

'Not so bad. Katie's not here, she hasn't returned from rehearsals yet. Where are you? Can she call you back?'

'Not really. I'm in Chicago and just about to have a meeting with a client. But I'm coming to New York next week, just for a couple of days. I hope I'll be able to see Katie.'

'I'm sure you will. Shall I tell her you'll call her later?'

'Yes, please. How's the play going?'

'Great, from what she says. I'm so glad you helped her to come to the decision to do it, Xenia. I think it'll change her life.'

'I know it will.'

'This week is tech week, you know, dealing with lighting and sound, all that kind of thing. But she's very excited, since they're in the theatre for the first time. Next week it'll be dress rehearsals.'

'The play's at the Barrymore Theatre, isn't it?'

'That's right. It's one of the smaller theatres, of course, but perfect for an intimate dramatic play like this. Katie tells me a musical house with eighteen hundred seats would've been too big.'

'I can well imagine. And I can't wait to see Katie in the play. When is the opening?'

'In about a month, three weeks of previews first, and

the opening is near the end of February. Sunday the twentieth. Black tie, and a party afterwards at Tavern on the Green. Very fancy. Katie told me the invitations have just gone out. I hope you can come, Xenia.'

'Absolutely. I'll be there with bells on! Looking forward to seeing you that night, Mrs Byrne.'

'Me too, Xenia.' As she spoke, Maureen leaned over and turned off the kettle.

They said goodbye and Maureen hung up; she went through into the small living room, sat down on the loveseat, thinking about opening night. That was one of the reasons she had come to New York. She owned one elegant evening gown, a long, slender sheath made of black wool, another of her treasured Trigères. She had bought the gown fifteen years ago, just before Miss Trigère had closed her showroom; rarely worn, it was in perfect condition. Maureen had come into the city to buy black silk shoes and a new black evening bag. Bridget had taken her shopping for them, and it was only then that the reality of it all had finally sunk in.

It was really happening at last. The fulfilment of Katie's childhood dream . . . the dream of being on a Broadway stage in a show. How exciting it was. They all felt the excitement . . . Bridget, their parents Sean and Catriona O'Keefe, and her in-laws. The entire family was coming in from Connecticut for the opening and the party, and everyone's expectations were riding high.

There were moments when Michael worried about his

darling Katie, worried about her ability to carry this off. But she didn't, not at all. She had total and absolute faith in her daughter, a faith so strong it left no room for doubt. It will be a triumph . . . the triumph of Katie Byrne, Maureen thought. And it's been so hard won.

Maureen leaned back against the loveseat and closed her eyes, her thoughts turning to Xenia. If not for her, Katie's Broadway debut might never have come about. How glad she was her child had a girlfriend at last. All these years she had shunned overtures from other young women, had become something of a loner. Because of them, because of Carly and Denise. She didn't want to have a girlfriend because she thought it would signify disloyalty to them, to their memory. And it was guilt, too. That played a part in all this.

Why had she never realized that before . . . The sound of the key in the lock made her turn her head just as Katie came into the tiny entrance hall. 'Hi, Mom!'

Maureen got up, and went towards her daughter, her face wreathed in smiles. She kissed her cheek, and said, 'Hello, honey. You look frozen, let me turn on the kettle.'

'I wouldn't say no to a cup of tea,' Katie declared brightly, unwinding various pale-blue and purple pashminas from around her neck, struggling out of her black coat. After hanging them all up in the hall closet, she followed her mother to the minuscule kitchen, leaned against the door jamb, looking in.

'How was your day, Mom?'

'Busy. I cleaned the apartment.'

'You shouldn't have; anyway, it wasn't dirty,' Katie protested.

'Just a bit dusty,' Maureen murmured, taking mugs out of the cupboard. 'Your old friend Grant Miller called.'

'Oh God, no! I hope he's not in New York.' Katie's expression was one of horror as she stared at her mother.

Maureen began to laugh. 'No. He called from Beverly Hills, left his number. He'd like you to call him back.'

'No way.'

'Oh, I think you probably should, honey.'

'Why? What for? I can't stand him.'

'He's getting married. The least –'

'Whoopee! Isn't that great.'

'I started to say the least you can do is congratulate him.'

'I suppose,' Katie mumbled and grinned at her mother.

'He says he's now in the movies. Given up the theatre.'

'It wouldn't surprise me. He's very photogenic.'

Maureen filled her in about the entire conversation, and Katie laughed and said, 'What a jerk.'

'Xenia called. She's in Chicago. She'll phone later.'

'I wonder if she plans to come to New York? Didn't she say anything else, Mom?'

'Yes, she'll be here for a day or two next week. She

hopes to see you. And she definitely plans on being at the opening.'

'That's great!'

'Yes, it is.' Maureen picked up the two mugs of tea and followed Katie into the living room. After handing a mug to her, she sat down on the loveseat.

Katie seated herself in a chair opposite, and said slowly, carefully, 'I've often thought you didn't really like Xenia, Mom.'

Maureen nodded. 'I've been in two minds about her from time to time, especially when you first met her.'

'Why? She's very nice.'

'I suppose I thought she was a bit fancy for you, 'tis such a high falutin background she has . . . the two of you are as different as chalk and cheese. I didn't think a friendship was feasible.'

Katie began to laugh. 'Because I'm an ordinary country girl, a nobody from the sticks, is that what you mean?'

'Sort of, yes. Although I don't think you're *ordinary*.'

'Xenia's not a snob, Mom, and she and her sister-in-law work very hard. They have to, they don't have inherited money, trust me on that. She and I . . . well, we just clicked the first time we met. We genuinely liked each other, and then I discovered we have certain things in common.'

Curious, Maureen asked, 'Such as what, mavourneen?'

'Tragedy in the form of sudden, unexpected death. Grief, pain, suffering.'

Maureen gaped at her daughter. 'Xenia has experienced things like that?'

'Yes, she has. Let me tell you her story, Momma.'

Chapter Twenty-eight

A rehearsal was in progress.

Charlotte and Anne Brontë, as played by Georgette Allison and Petra Green respectively, were sitting in the Victorian parlour of Haworth parsonage. Through the open window could be seen a thunderous, overcast sky and a vista of the wild Yorkshire moors.

The set on the stage of the Barrymore Theatre had great verisimilitude, and was authentic down to the last detail. The respected set designer, Larry Sedgwick, was an Englishman and veteran Tony Award winner, and so he had made sure that his reputation for brilliance was preserved. The set spoke of a time gone by.

The two women sat at a table with open books in front of them. Their faces were serious. Charlotte was enunciating her lines.

Katie stood in the wings, waiting for her cue.

Finally she walked out onto the stage, confident, ready to play her part as Emily Brontë. Blinking for a moment under the bright lights on stage, she said clearly, in a very English voice, 'I've been thinking on what you said to me, Charlotte, and I have made a decision. We cannot publish under our real names. Put very simply, I will not permit it.'

Charlotte responded in a gentle tone. 'Now, now, Emily. You know perfectly well I cannot abide this stubbornness of yours.'

Anne, leaning forward slightly, leapt in when she said, 'Charlotte dear, Emily is *right*. It would not be . . . seemly to use our own names.'

Charlotte replied.

But Katie did not hear her lines. Nor did she speak her own.

Georgette was no longer Georgette playing Charlotte.

She was Carly Smith. Her black hair glistened under the pin-spot, her violet-blue eyes were shining, full of life.

And Petra had become Denise, that long blonde hair flowing over her shoulders, the rich brown eyes soft and beguiling.

Was it a trick of the lights? For a split second Katie thought it was. She blinked several times and took a step closer to them, peering. Then she opened her mouth to speak, but no words came. She stood in the middle of the stage, speechless, floundering, lost. She was no longer able to rehearse. Immediately she broke out in a cold sweat, began to shake.

It was Carly and Denise in the barn on that last day when they had all been together. Sitting at that

little table. Learning their lines for the school concert.

Snapping her eyes closed, Katie endeavoured to get
a grip on herself, to stop shaking. But to no avail.
There were other flashes now, coming at her fast and
furious. Flashes of Carly and Denise as she had last seen
them, images of them in the wood. Carly with her head
smashed in, blood streaming down over her face; Denise
spreadeagled on the ground, her skirt flung around her
waist. Raped, murdered. More flashes . . . of violence,
of death . . .

Katie stood there in the middle of the stage, shaking,
unable to move backwards or forwards. Frozen.

Dimly, in the distance, she suddenly heard a man's
voice. It was Jack Martin, the director. 'Are you all
right? What is it? What's wrong?'

Swaying slightly, blinking, she managed to mumble, 'I
don't know . . . I'm sick . . . dizzy . . . I feel nauseous.'

A split second later he was by her side, his arm
around her waist. Now he was leading her offstage.
Into the wings. Down to her dressing room. Sharp
footsteps followed them. High heels clicked against the
hard floor. It was Melanie. She knew it was Melanie.

She had let her down. She hadn't meant to, but
she had.

'Try to explain what just happened out there,' Jack
Martin said, sounding very irritable. But then he was not

313

only renowned for his extraordinary directorial skills, but his irascibility as well.

Katie shook her head, one hand clinging to the arm of the chair where she sat in her dressing room.

Jack stood looking down at her, his face furious, his blue eyes dangerously cold. He glared at her. 'Cat got your tongue? It certainly had on stage. Come on, Katie, *what happened*?'

'I don't know. Honestly, I don't, Jack.' She leaned back in the chair, trying to keep herself from weeping.

'Are you coming down with a bug? Hot damn, we start dress rehearsals this week. This is a bitch. All I need is a lame second lead. *Jesus!*'

Pulling herself together, Katie said, 'I'm feeling better. I'll go back on stage, finish the scene.'

'No, you won't, Katie,' Melanie Dawson interjected, and handed her a box of tissues. 'You're perspiring heavily, and it's not all that warm in the theatre. I hope you're not getting the flu. That you haven't got it.'

Katie wiped her neck, patted her face. She shook her head again. 'I don't think so . . . I am beginning to feel better. Could I have some water please.'

Melanie handed her the glass of cold water she was holding. 'Here it is, drink it up.'

'Thanks, Melanie.'

Jack stormed over to the door, his annoyance now verging on anger. 'I'd better get this show on the road! Take the rehearsal without my second lead.'

'Good idea, Jack.' Melanie gave him a reassuring look, smiled at him. 'It's going to be all right, and I'll be there shortly.'

He glanced over at Katie. 'Feel better.' He dashed out, slamming the door behind him.

Once they were alone, Melanie sat down on a small chair near the dressing table. Staring at Katie, her gaze direct, she said, 'I *know* you, and I know you didn't forget your lines. So what *really* happened out there on stage?'

'I don't know, Melanie. I just suddenly felt ill, unable to continue. Honestly, I'm telling you the truth.'

Melanie seemed perplexed and she frowned, clasped her hands together and leaned forward slightly. 'If you're ill you *must* tell me. We're close to the previews and the opening. I can't afford to have anything go wrong at this stage. So please tell me.'

Katie was silent. She bit her lip; her eyes filled.

Melanie continued, in a low, very kind voice, 'You're not stupid, Katie. Far from it. You're very, very bright, and intelligent. So you *know* there's a lot of money involved, millions of dollars, in fact. I have several very important and generous backers who trust me to put on a good play. No, not merely good. A *sensational* play. And most of all, a *hit* play. I have a fiscal responsibility to them, and to Harry, who is putting up a lot of money as well.' Melanie paused. 'And you have a responsibility to me. I can't have a dud opening, with you missing your lines and freezing on stage. Do you understand me?'

'Yes, I do, and I'm sorry. Really sorry. It won't happen again.'

'*What* is it that won't happen again? Come on, confide in me, Katie. You owe me that.'

'I do, yes. You've been very good to me.' Katie hesitated for only a split second. She was filled with chagrin and sudden guilt, knowing she had disrupted rehearsals and created an inflammatory situation. She must be honest with Melanie, who had always been good to her, and had believed in her.

Clearing her throat, Katie began, 'I don't know how to explain this . . . explain what occurred on stage. It was like . . . a *flashback*. That's the only word I can use –' She broke off abruptly.

'Go on.'

Katie sat staring at Melanie, chic as always in a black suit and white silk shirt, the short, dark-brown hair elegantly cut and coiffed. Melanie Dawson, Broadway producer *par excellence*. Box office certainty. Critics' favourite. Multiple Tony winner. Her good friend. Her mentor. Her champion. Katie knew she owed her the truth. 'Something happened one day, ten years ago. I don't really know why, but parts of that day started . . . started flashing through my head out on stage just now. It was like . . . being there, living it again.'

'And it was a terrible thing, wasn't it, Katie?'

'Yes.'

'I've always felt there was something in your past that

troubled you . . . that this . . . *event* had propelled you to London, and that it also prevented you from returning to New York.' She nodded as if to herself, as if confirming something in her own mind. Her brow furrowed. 'I felt there was some sort of . . . impediment . . .' Melanie's voice trailed off.

Taking a very deep breath, Katie told her story.

'Oh my God!' Melanie sat gaping at Katie. Not having anticipated anything quite as dreadful as this, she was momentarily at a loss for words. Finally, she said softly, 'What a truly horrendous thing to happen to those poor girls. And an awful burden for you to bear.'

'It was that particular afternoon that flashed back to me, out on stage . . . I'm not sure why, though.'

Melanie was quiet, reflective for a long moment. 'Has it ever happened before? This kind of flashback?'

'No, and certainly not on a stage. And as you know, I'd been working solidly for four years before I went to RADA in London.'

'It's a terrible memory, a traumatic experience that you can't shed, obviously. Have you ever talked to a psychiatrist about it, Katie?'

'No.'

'Maybe you should.'

'I don't think so, I really don't, Melanie. No one can help me, I can only help myself, I suppose.'

'Talk to *me*, Katie, unburden yourself to *me*. God

knows, I'm not a psychiatrist.' She half smiled. 'But sometimes I think I am, though, dealing with the free-floating temperament and emotion that's around all you talented actors every day. So talk, get it off your chest . . . I do have a good listening ear, a strong shoulder to cry on, if necessary.'

And so slowly, carefully, Katie told the producer everything about her girlfriends, the deep and loving relationship the three of them had, their dreams and hopes and ambitions. And she recounted her memories, happy as well as troubling, and she filled Melanie in about the murder, still unsolved to this day. She broke down several times, but for the most part Katie was in full control of herself.

When she had finished, Melanie blew her nose and patted her eyes with tissues. 'I said before, and I'll say it again, it's a dreadful burden for you to carry, Katie.'

'Grandma Catriona from Ireland always says God *never* gives us a burden that's too heavy to carry, but I'm not so sure I subscribe to that,' Katie murmured.

'That's faith for you. Perhaps your grandmother's lucky that she has it. But I know what you mean. However, somehow we all cope with problems, don't we?' Melanie sighed, and rose. She walked over to Katie, put an arm around her shoulders. 'I'm really glad you told me all this, and it will remain a confidence with me. Don't worry, I'm not going to discuss what you've said with Jack. This is private, between us.'

'Thank you. Thanks for everything.'

'I do want you to do something for me, Katie.'

'Tell me. I'll do whatever you want.'

'I think you should take the weekend off. Skip tomorrow's rehearsals. Rest on Saturday and Sunday. Be back here on Monday morning.'

'But what will Jack say?'

'Leave Jack to me. Don't worry about him. Or the play. You're word-perfect, and you have the part down pat. I have great confidence in you, and missing a couple of rehearsals is not going to hurt you. It'll probably do you good.'

'But are you sure . . . I don't want him to be . . .'

'Difficult?' Melanie smiled at her. 'Jack's one of your biggest fans even though he doesn't show it. That's his way. No favourites. Anyway, the buck stops here, you know, with me. I'm the producer, and I'm telling you to take the weekend off.'

Her bedroom was much the same as it had always been, with the same colour scheme and the same furniture. Her father repainted it from time to time, to keep it fresh, but it was always done in the same dusty pink on the walls, with pristine white paint on the windows and doors. She loved this unusual dusty pink colour, and her father had once explained that it was a warm pink toned down with grey which made it soft and muted. 'Easy on the eye,' was the way her father put it, and she knew he took special care with her room.

She was glad to be back at home in Malvern for the weekend. This house had always been important to her; it was home; she had grown up in it and it spelled safety, security, and boundless love to her. The love from her parents and Niall and little Fin. Not so little any more, she thought, with a half smile. He was six feet one and gorgeous. She hung up a pair of grey flannel trousers and a heathery-coloured tweed jacket which she had brought with her for the weekend, then emptied her small suitcase.

When everything was put away, she glanced at the bed-side clock, saw that it was four-thirty. Her mother had gone shopping and wouldn't be back for an hour at least, so she went over to her carryall and took out her diary. She suddenly noticed that its green leather looked slightly worn, but then again, it was five years old. Time for a new one soon; this one was already almost filled up.

Sitting down at the desk facing out over the back garden, Katie opened the diary and began to write.

January 21st 2000   *Malvern*
                                                    Connecticut

I felt very guilty when I got back to the apartment earlier today. I had upset Jack and Melanie, but what happened at the theatre was not of my own volition. It just happened. And I couldn't stop it at first. I could no more have stopped it than I could have flown to the moon.

Xenia once said Verity was impeccable. And now I really understand what she meant. Also, I can now say that of Melanie Dawson. She, too, is impeccable. Talking to her helped me. She was sympathetic, understanding, and kind. Impeccable. I love that word. And Melanie is impeccable in every sense of it.

I had no choice but to take the weekend off, but I did feel guilty about it when I left the theatre. Even worse by the time I got back to West End Avenue. Mom was so surprised to see me when I walked in, and she immediately looked crestfallen, as if she thought I'd been fired. Once I'd explained that I hadn't felt well on stage and had been sent home until Monday morning she cheered up, and insisted I drive up to Malvern. I didn't need any persuading to go home with her. A chance to see Dad and Niall was irresistible. Unlike some people, I had a very happy childhood, and I don't hate my parents or my siblings, and none of my extended family. I love them all, and I think they're all wonderful. Human, of course, with human frailties. But wonderful.

Going home to Malvern was also a chance to go and see Carly at the hospice. I went to see her this past Christmas when I first got back from London. I hadn't seen her in over a year, and she hadn't changed at all. She was just the same as she's been for the last ten years.

I didn't expect Carly to be any different now. But I had a

real need to go and see her, a pressing need. I wanted to hold her hand and talk to her as I had in the past. I wanted to let the love I felt for her spread over her, in the hope that she would somehow feel it, and that it might help her.

On the drive up from the city, I told all this to Mom. She confided that she believed Carly knew when she was there, she didn't know why she believed it, but she did. And she said Carly would know I was with her in the room. Because she would feel my love flowing to her. I wanted to believe my mother, needed to believe her, I suppose. She's a Celt, very fey at times, and very much in touch with herself and her feelings.

I dozed part of the way. I always do in cars. It must be something to do with the motion . . . it sort of lulls me to sleep. Anyway, I slept my way to New Milford, and then I awakened. We'd just left the town behind when it hit me. All of a sudden I understood the flashback, understood what it was all about.

It should have been the three of us up on that stage, doing this play about the Brontë sisters. Three sisters so close and loving, just like the three of us had been all those years. And we had always dreamed of acting together in a Broadway play.

As Mom drove us back to Malvern it was crystal-clear. So simple. Yet it hadn't been at eleven o'clock this morning. There is another thing. Charlotte has the same colouring as Carly and Petra is a blonde just like Denise. In their sweaters and skirts at rehearsal they had reminded me of them . . . and something had been triggered.

I needed to write this down, to see it on paper. Writing helps me to understand things, to make order out of chaos. If I didn't act I think I would be a writer. I enjoy it. But would I enjoy it professionally? I'm not sure.

Mom was surprised when I didn't go to the supermarket with her because she knows I love the local supermarkets up here. I always have. Just as I like bookshops. I'm a bit of a browser in both. I didn't go because writing in my diary was more important. Pressing.

I was really surprised when Melanie told me that Jack Martin was a fan of mine. He's a brilliant director, but has a reputation for being difficult. Very irascible. However, I do know he likes my interpretation of Emily, different as it is from Janette Nerren's in London.

Rex truly helped me to understand Emily. He gave me a book about her that contains what he considers to be one of her great epic poems, one of six. It was composed when she was twenty-six, just a year and a half younger than me. I'll be twenty-eight this year. Anyway, Rex said the poem delineates the obsession with memory that Emily had. I only know one thing, I love it, too.

Katie stopped writing, put down her pen, and went to find her carryall. She rummaged around in it, found the book Rex had given her and took it back to the desk. Opening the book, she found the poem, which she knew was one of Emily's most famous, and propped the book against the base of the lamp. She read it through quietly to herself, and then she slowly began to copy it into her diary, wanting to have it there, so she could read it whenever she wished.

Cold in the earth, and the deep snow piled above thee!
Far, far removed, cold in the dreary grave!
Have I forgot, my only Love, to love thee,
Severed at last by Time's all-wearing wave?

Now, when alone, do my thoughts no longer hover
Over the mountains on Angora's shore;
Resting their wings where heath and fern-leaves cover
That noble heart for ever, ever more?

Cold in the earth, and fifteen wild Decembers
From those brown hills have melted into spring –
Faithful indeed is the spirit that remembers
After such years of change and suffering!

Sweet Love of youth, forgive if I forget thee
While the World's tide is bearing me along:
Sterner desires and darker hopes beset me,
Hopes which obscure but cannot do thee wrong.

No other Sun has lightened up my heaven;
No other Star has ever shone for me:
All my life's bliss from thy dear life was given –
All my life's bliss is in the grave with thee.

But when the days of golden dreams had perished
And even Despair was powerless to destroy,
Then did I learn how existence could be cherished,
Strengthened and fed without the aid of joy;

Then did I check the tears of useless passion,
Weaned my young soul from yearning after thine;
Sternly denied its burning wish to hasten
Down to that tomb already more than mine!

And even then, I dare not let it languish.
Dare not indulge in Memory's rapturous pain;
Once drinking deep of that divinest anguish,
How could I seek the empty world again?

Once she had copied it, Katie sat back, staring at
the poem, thinking of all the things Rex had explained
about it. She loved it most for the use of the language, the
cadence, the rhythm, and the emotions it evoked in her.
Rex had told her that the woman voicing the thoughts
in the poem was Lady Rosa of Alcona, a character

borrowed from Emily's juvenile writings. *Memory*, Katie thought. It's about the memory of a dead lover, and yet in me it also evokes thoughts of Denise and Carly . . .

Picking up her pen, Katie continued writing in her diary:

I told Melanie I'd never been to a psychiatrist to talk about my traumatic experience, when my girlfriends were attacked, and I don't intend to go. I must work things out for myself. I think I'm getting there at long last. I feel comfortable living in New York now, and I'm very preoccupied with the play, with my work, and work is a wonderful healer. As my mother has always told me.

I want to see Carly more than I have. I shall go to the hospice tomorrow, and then again on Sunday before I go back to Manhattan. Mom said she'd drive me in, but I can always take the bus to the city.

I'm glad I now understand the flashback, and what brought it on. I thought for a moment in the theatre that I was going crazy. Although I've been rehearsing with Georgette and Petra for some weeks, we were working in the rehearsal hall at 890 Broadway that once belonged to Michael Bennett. It's only these last few days that we've been in the theatre, and being on a stage with my co-stars definitely took me back in time. Took me back to the old barn . . . triggered my memories so vividly I was reliving that last day. But I'm all right, in good shape . . . as long as I understand what makes things happen and why, I can cope.

I feel that I must go forward now. Put the past behind me as much as I can . . .

Katie heard the door slam, and she closed her diary, put it away in the desk drawer, went out of the bedroom. She was running down the stairs to greet her mother when she heard the door close a second time, and a voice calling, 'It's me, Mom!'

Her mother answered, 'Hello, Niall. Katie's here from New York.'

And a moment later she was rushing into her brother's arms, laughing as he swung her around, lifting her feet off the floor.

'Katie! It's great to see you!' he exclaimed as he put her down and hugged her to him. 'And what brings you home? I thought you were busy on Broadway, becoming a star?'

She grinned at him. 'I got the weekend off. A short rest before plunging into dress rehearsals next week.'

'Is that the famous voice of Katie Byrne I hear?' a strong masculine voice asked

Katie swung her head, saw her father and ran across the kitchen to him. 'Yes, it's me, Dad!' she said, laughing again.

Michael Byrne put his arms around his daughter and

held her close to him for a long moment, thanking God, as he did very often, that she was alive.

The four of them sat around the kitchen table having a cup of tea.

There was a lot of talk about the play, and opening night, and the party afterwards at Tavern on the Green.

Her father and brother asked Katie questions about the production, opening night, and a variety of other things to do with her Broadway debut. She answered them as best she could.

Maureen poured tea, passed the currant cake, and smiled contentedly, happy that they were all together for the weekend. Having Katie here was an unexpected bonus. And if only Fin were present, the circle would be complete, she thought. But he had gone back to Oxford earlier in the month, to continue his studies at the university. But Michael had bought him a ticket to come back for the opening of *Charlotte and Her Sisters*, although this was a secret from Katie. A surprise.

At one moment, Katie sat back in the kitchen chair, listening to her father and mother discussing the arrangements for the weekend in New York when the play opened. As she looked from one parent to the other, she couldn't help thinking how well they had weathered the years.

Her father's dark hair was touched with silver, and

he was a little more weather-beaten from being outside so much on building sites. But he was as handsome at fifty-seven as he had been ten years earlier.

And her mother looked wonderful, Katie thought. She was slender, and her face was remarkably unlined. If her bright-blue eyes had faded ever so slightly, her hair was still that lovely, burnished red of her youth, with not a grey hair visible, even though she was now fifty-five. Katie sometimes wondered if her mother touched it up at the hairdressers. But even if she did, what did it matter? Maureen had always been a beautiful woman. There was no other person like her mother, as far as Katie was concerned.

As for Niall, he was a younger replica of their father. A true Byrne. Black Irish. They had always been similar in appearance, but to Katie that resemblance seemed more marked than ever these days. Niall was fit and in good shape, with a trim athletic body, which Katie knew came from dedicated physical activity and consistent working out. Tanned from being outdoors on sites, like their father, his handsome face was rugged, and his thick black hair flowed back from a broad brow. No wonder women fell for him.

A carbon copy of Dad, Katie thought. But although they looked alike they were quite different in personality. Niall was not quite as outgoing or as charming as their father, and over Christmas she had even thought he had become somewhat introverted.

Like her mother, Katie often wondered why Niall wasn't married. Suddenly, she thought of Denise. She truly believed her brother had always had a thing about her girlfriend. But was he still carrying a torch for her? Now after all these years? After her death?

Katie had no answers for herself.

Chapter Twenty-nine

Niall had offered to drive Katie to the hospice to see Carly, and so they set off on Saturday morning just after nine o'clock. It was a beautiful day, with a blue sky, no clouds, a bright sun and no snow, which had been predicted by the television weatherman the night before.

As they came out of the house together, Niall turned to Katie and said, 'I just bought myself a new car, shall we take it?'

'Why not? And what is it?'

'A BMW, and it's a beauty.'

'My, aren't we getting fancy, Niall Byrne!'

Her brother laughed. 'No, not fancy, just practical. It's a good car, the best, and it's my only indulgence in life, if you can call it that. I consider it an essential, especially for business.'

'Don't you use a pickup truck any more?'

'Sure I do. Every day. For working on sites. But when I go to New York, or up to Litchfield, places like that I'll take the car.'

By this time they were in the garage, and after opening the door for her, Niall hurried around to the other side and got in. He backed out slowly, and within seconds they were on the main road heading towards Warren and New Preston just beyond.

They drove in silence for a while, and then suddenly Katie asked, 'Why do you still live at home, Niall? Why haven't you found a place of your own?'

'A number of reasons. First of all, I didn't want to leave Mom and Dad alone . . . you're gone, Fin's gone, and I felt they needed me to be around, especially Mom. But there are other reasons.'

'Such as what?'

He looked at her quickly, out of the corner of his eye, and began to laugh. 'Living at home with my parents is protection.'

'From whom, for heaven's sake?'

'Women.'

Katie chuckled. '*You*. Needing protection? Come on!'

He smiled knowingly, muttered, 'Sure I need protection. I don't want to find myself getting pushed into a permanent live-in relationship. Or any kind of permanent relationship, for that matter.'

'Nobody special then?'

He shook his head, kept his eyes straight ahead on the road, obviously not wishing to continue this conversation.

Katie said, 'But listen, Niall, you've dated quite a few

women from time to time. So I'm assuming they all have their own places?'

'Sure they do.'

She noticed the sly smile playing around his mouth and she punched his arm lightly. 'You're a devil. But seriously, Mom would love you to settle down.'

'I am settled down. With them. And they love it.'

'She'd love a grandchild more.'

'And what's wrong with you? The same rules apply.'

'I know, but I haven't met anyone that really interests me. Unfortunately.'

'What happened to that guy we called The Face?'

'Long gone and forgotten. Anyway, he's getting married.'

'Bully for him.'

'So you plan on being a bachelor?'

'Yes, why not? The world is full of bachelors.'

Katie realized he wanted her to drop this topic, and so she did. She sat back in the deep leather car seat, thinking about the visit to Carly. She always got butterflies in her stomach, never knowing what to expect. And yet she did know, because nothing ever changed. 'Oh Niall, stop at that plant place, in New Milford, please. I need to buy flowers for Carly,' she suddenly exclaimed.

The man came barrelling through the swing doors, almost knocking Katie down in the process. She stepped back swiftly, dropping the bunch of flowers, backing away to avoid collision.

After stepping on them, the man said, 'Oh my God, I'm sorry, so sorry. My apologies. Here, let me retrieve the flowers.' He gave her a weak smile as he bent down to pick them up.

Katie stood staring at him, thinking what a clumsy fool he was.

Straightening, the man said again, 'I'm so sorry.' He tried to rearrange the crumpled paper around the flowers and dusted them off, adding, 'I shouldn't be rushing around like this in a hospital, of all places.'

'That's right,' Katie said, glaring at him.

He attempted another smile as he handed her the bunch of flowers. 'Not too badly damaged, I don't think.'

Katie accepted the flowers silently, looking down at the blooms. But he was correct, the flowers were intact.

He suddenly said, 'Oh my God, you're Katie Byrne!'

Katie looked at him coldly. 'Yes, I am.'

He stuck out his hand. 'Christopher Saunders.'

Katie had no alternative but to shake his hand, and as she did, she said, 'But I don't know you, do I?'

'No, no, you don't. But I saw you in an off-Broadway show a couple of years ago. It was the revival of *A Lion in Winter*. You played Alice.'

'*The Lion in Winter*,' she corrected. 'And yes I did have the part of Alais.'

'And I saw your picture in *The New York Times*, one day last week. You're in Melanie Dawson's new play, the Charlotte Brontë play.'

Katie nodded, trying to edge away, wanting to get to Carly's room. Clutching the bunch of flowers tightly, she tried to step around him.

'I hope to come to one of the previews.'

'Yes, good,' she answered, nodding.

'You're playing Emily. I bet you can really get your teeth into that part. She was quite the enigma, wasn't she?'

Katie was startled by this comment, and for the first time she really looked at him, half smiling as she did. 'Yes,' she muttered

He smiled back, a wide, generous smile, showing very white teeth, and his brown eyes were warm, and slightly questioning.

Her eyes locked on his and she found she couldn't look away. He was very good-looking in a sort of freshly-scrubbed, collegiate way, and he was staring at her so intently Katie grew uncomfortable.

Finally, she said, 'I have to go.'

'Oh yes, of course. I'm delaying you. Sorry again about almost knocking you down. See you at the play.'

She stepped around him and went through the swing doors, walking rapidly down the corridor, thinking there was something quite disconcerting about him. *Christopher Saunders*. The name didn't ring a bell.

One of the young women at the nurses' station recognized her, and came over, smiling. 'Hello, Miss Byrne. You've come to see Carly.'

'Yes, I have, Jane. How is she?'

'More or less the same. Shall I take the flowers, put them in water for you?'

'Thanks.' Katie smiled and handed them to her, then opened the door and went into Carly's room. It was filled with bright sunlight, and there were several vases of flowers on the chest against the wall.

Carly lay on her back in the hospital bed, the feeding tube in place. Her eyes were open, as they sometimes were, and Katie looked down into them, seeking a spark, a hint of life. But they were blank, like a blind person's eyes. Those beautiful eyes, wide open but seeing nothing, were startling in that pale face. It, too, was passive, bland, showing no animation whatsoever. And very little ageing.

Katie sat down in the chair near the bed, put her shoulder bag on the floor, and then reached out for Carly's hand. It was cool, unresponsive as she held it in hers. Katie stroked it, slightly tightened her grip. 'Hi, Carly, it's me, *Katie*. I'm here from New York. I wanted to see you, Carly, to tell you I love you, and that I miss you. I wish you could hear me. Perhaps you can.'

There was a noise behind her, and Katie swung her head as Jane, the nurse, came in with the vase of flowers.

'I'll put them with the others,' she murmured, did so, and left.

Katie looked into Carly's face, and continued talking to her in a soft and loving voice. 'We're in the theatre now, Carly, after weeks in the rehearsal hall. It's very exciting to be on stage at last. Thrilling, really. And next week we start dress rehearsals. I told you when I was here in December, I'm playing Emily Brontë. I have the second lead. And I'm on Broadway. It's what *we* always dreamed about. Mom keeps saying that I'll have my name in lights at last. But I don't think it'll actually be in lights. Georgette Allison's, yes, and Harrison Jordan's too. They're the stars. But nobody's ever heard of me.'

Except for Christopher Saunders, she thought, and pushed the compelling image of his face away from her. Leaning forward, she stroked Carly's pale, passive face, and went on, 'The play's at the Ethel Barrymore Theatre on West 47th Street. Just over a thousand seats. Imagine, Carly, a thousand people at a time in the audience. I wish you could be one of them.'

Katie leaned back in the chair, and closed her eyes, swallowing hard, trying to keep the sorrow from erupting, as it was now threatening to do. It was more than sorrow, though, she knew that. It was frustration and anger as well. There was a man out there who should be paying for this, paying for what he'd done to Carly. And to Denise. There's no justice. None at all, she thought.

Sitting up straighter, Katie concentrated on Carly once

more. 'I think about you all the time, Carly. You and Denise are always in my thoughts. I told you when I came at Christmas that I took this part for both of you as well as for myself. I was a bit ambivalent about it, and then I realized I was afraid of failing. And I thought if Carly and Denise were here with me I wouldn't be afraid at all. And one day I understood that you *are* with me. In my heart and in my mind, and you always will be. Xenia helped me to make the decision to do the play. You'd like her a lot, Carly. She's different from the three of us, yet like us, one of us. She's the only friend I've ever had in all these years since you and Denise were . . .'

Katie stopped, choked up again.

She sat for a long time, holding Carly's hand, stroking it, squeezing it from time to time, and talking to her quietly. She recited some Shakespeare, because Carly had always loved his work, and whispered part of Emily Brontë's poem, *Cold in the Earth*.

But eventually she fell silent, and after a short while she stood up, leaned over the bed and kissed Carly on her cheek. 'I have to go now, Carly darling, but I'll come back soon.' Blinking back the tears, Katie found her bag on the floor, and went out, closing the door behind her quietly. For a moment or two, she leaned against the wall, trying to compose herself, but the tears suddenly flowed, and she fumbled in her shoulder bag for a tissue.

'Are you all right?'

Startled, Katie glanced up and saw Dr James Nelson standing outside another patient's door, holding a chart in his hand. She had met him briefly at Christmas. He was new at the New Milford Hospital, where he was head of Neurology. And he also supervised the Neurological Wing at the hospice. Her mother had told her he had worked here for about a year.

'I'm okay, Dr Nelson,' she replied. 'I still get a bit upset when I see Carly like this . . . lying there in a coma.'

'That's quite understandable, Miss Byrne.'

'Oh please call me Katie, everybody does.'

He inclined his head. 'How's the play coming along?'

'Very well, thanks.'

Katie moved away from Carly's door, and he fell into step with her. He was tall and thin, sandy-haired, an attractive-looking man, in his mid-thirties, she thought, and she had liked him the first time she met him. He inspired confidence with his competent and very direct manner, quiet and thoughtful demeanour.

They walked along the corridor together, making for the front lobby. It was he who broke the silence when he suddenly said in his quiet voice, 'Carly's not actually in a coma, you know.'

Katie stopped dead in her tracks, and so did he. She swung to him, stared up into his face. 'What do you mean?' she asked, her voice rising an octave.

'Carly was in a *true* coma for about five or six weeks after she first suffered her injuries,' he explained. 'She then went into what is known as a vegetative state, and she's been in that vegetative state ever since.'

'But nobody told me that!' Katie exclaimed, still staring at him. 'And what does it mean? Why is it *different* from a coma?'

'From a medical standpoint, a person is in a coma when his or her eye opening, verbal response, and motor response, on the Glasgow Coma Scale, total eight or less. And it's typical for a patient's eyes to be closed, and he or she is never awake. Do you understand, Katie?'

'Yes, so far.'

'Now, a *vegetative state* is a condition in which the patient's eyes are frequently wide open, and the sleep/wake cycles are intact. However, the patient does not speak, and does not exhibit any behaviour that indicates an awareness of loved ones, or an awareness of the environment in which he or she is living. Do you follow me still?'

'Oh yes, I do.'

'Good. By the way, the term vegetative state was coined by two doctors, Jennett and Plum, at the Royal Hospital for Neuro-disability in Putney, London, in order to provide a clinical diagnosis based on behavioural observations of patients. Let me put this as simply as possible, in layman's terms. The word *vegetative* was very specifically chosen to describe *merely physical life*, or existence if you like, *devoid* of sensation and thought. I'm sure you're understanding all this, Katie.'

'Yes, I am, Dr Nelson. But there is one thing I'd like to know. Could Carly come out of this vegetative state?'

'I obviously can't predict anything like that,' he said, shaking his head.

'But has anybody ever come out of it?'

'To my knowledge, no.'

'Does Mrs Smith know Carly's not actually in a *coma*, as such?' Katie asked, her brows drawing together in a puzzled frown.

The doctor nodded. 'I did explain this to Carly's mother last year. I pretty much said what I've just said to you. But to be very honest, I think she really believes Carly is in a *true* coma, and nothing will change her mind.'

'I see.' Katie bit her lip, looking reflective. After a split second, she said, 'I haven't seen Mrs Smith for a very long time. I called her when I came back from London at Christmas and left a message, but she never got back to me. And she hasn't responded to any of the overtures my parents have made. But I do know my mother's run into her once or twice here. I can't imagine why she didn't say anything to Mom . . . about this vegetative state Carly's in, as opposed to a real coma.'

James Nelson was silent for a moment, wondering the same thing. Finally, he responded. 'Katie, I honestly don't think Mrs Smith understands the difference. She's just convinced Carly is in a deep coma . . .' He looked at Katie helplessly, and shook his head. 'It's odd, I admit that.'

'Thanks for explaining all this to me, Dr Nelson. I realize Carly is still truly out of it, that her condition is terrible, irreversible, but on the other hand it doesn't seem quite as bad as a coma.'

Katie hesitated on the steps of the hospice, shading her eyes against the sun with her hand, looking for Niall. But the BMW was nowhere in sight. It was such a sunny morning, mild even, and so she went and sat on the low wall to wait for him. She knew her brother wouldn't be very long. Like her, he was always fairly prompt.

A moment later a shadow fell across her, and she turned her head slightly, then lifted it, found herself staring up at Christopher Saunders, who was hovering over her anxiously.

'Hello again,' he said, gazing down at her with that same intensity of earlier, the huge smile on his face touching his eyes, filling them with warmth and laughter.

'Hi,' Katie murmured, gazing back at him, wondering if he had been hanging around waiting for her.

As if reading her mind, he said, 'I've been waiting for you. I hope you don't mind, but I did want to apologize to you again. I'm such a clumsy fool. I could have hurt you, the way I came hurtling through those doors.'

'It's okay,' she said and finally pulled her gaze away

from his, not wishing to look into those mesmerizing eyes any longer. There was something very compelling about this man, and it troubled her. She didn't want to be compelled by anybody, least of all this stranger.

'I hope the person you came to see didn't mind squashed flowers, and that he or she is feeling better,' he said, sounding as if he really cared.

Katie sighed. 'She won't ever get any better, I suppose. And she didn't notice the flowers, as far as I know. But at least Dr Nelson told me a few things that made me feel, well, less depressed about her.'

'Jamie's the best doctor in the world, you know. Brilliant guy. So it's a neurological problem, is it?'

'Yes. You call him Jamie. Is he a friend of yours?'

'Sure is. My best buddy. We grew up together, went to the same school in New York. Trinity.'

'Oh, I see. So that's why you're here. Or did you also come to visit a patient?'

'No, I brought something for Jamie from New York.'

'Oh.'

'I'm sorry someone in your family is ill,' Christopher now said, trying to make further conversation with her. 'It's very worrying, I know.'

'It's not a family member, it's my best friend. Or she was my best friend until she was violently beaten and went into a coma. Now she doesn't even know me.'

'Oh my God, how awful!'

'Dr Nelson says she's not in a *true* coma, but is actually

343

locked in something called a vegetative state. But in a way, that doesn't give me much hope, because she's still lost to the world. And she will be for the rest of her life.'

'I'm so sorry.' Christopher again sounded genuinely sympathetic, and he went on, after a brief pause, 'How did it happen? Was your friend mugged, or what?'

When she didn't answer, he sat down on the wall next to her, and murmured, 'I'm sorry. I don't mean to pry.'

'She was beaten on the head by a fiendish psychopath, beaten until she was unconscious. And my other best girlfriend was raped and murdered by the same guy. At the same time.'

Christopher was staring at her stupefied, an expression of total horror settling on his face. There was a long moment before he responded. Then he finally said, 'How truly horrible. I'm very, very sorry. It's a pretty rotten thing for you to have to cope with.'

'Yes, it is. But at least I'm okay physically and mentally. *I* didn't get hurt. Not like them.'

They sat together in silence. Neither of them felt like talking. And so they fell down into their own thoughts for a short while.

Katie could not believe she had told a total stranger about Carly and Denise, and she was startled, furious with herself for being so indiscreet, for confiding in him.

Christopher Saunders, for his part, was reeling from the things she had just said. He wondered whether or not she had been present, had been somehow hurt but had now recovered. He didn't dare to ask her what she'd meant. He wanted to invite her for a drink, or better still, lunch, but he was afraid to do so. After all, she had seemed cold earlier, standoffish. On the other hand, he *had* almost trampled her underfoot. Nevertheless, he didn't want to say the wrong thing, and blow it. *Blow what?* he asked himself, suddenly baffled. He didn't even know Katie Byrne. But he wanted to, and badly. She's prickly, he thought, and hurting inside. She needs careful handling. I hope I get the chance. He remembered only too well how much he had been taken with her when he had seen her in the revival off-Broadway, in the play about the Plantagenets, one of his favourite historical families. Dysfunctional, all of them, to say the least.

Glancing at him, Katie asked, out of the blue, 'Is Dr Nelson married?'

'No, he's not. And neither am I. Are you?'

'No.'

'Listen, Katie . . . you don't mind if I call you Katie, do you?'

'No, everyone calls me Katie.'

'Listen, would you like to go for a drink?'

'I don't drink.'

'A coffee then? Or better still, how about lunch?'

'Oh no, I can't, my mother's holding lunch for me.'

'Where do you live? Can I drive you home?'

'Thanks, that's nice of you to offer, but someone's picking me up. Oh look, there he is now. Nice talking to you, Christopher. Bye.'

She jumped up off the wall and hurried over to the BMW, which was pulling up just ahead of them.

Christopher, following her down the short path, was filled with disappointment, and he chastised himself for being so stupid. It was more than likely this woman was taken. She might not be married, but she most certainly would have a boyfriend. She was far too beautiful, special and talented to be on her own. His disappointment spiralled.

'Hi, Christopher,' Niall exclaimed, as he got out of the BMW. 'I didn't know you knew my sister Katie.'

As they shook hands, Christopher felt a surge of relief rush through him. 'I don't, not really, we just met at the hospital. I was there to see my buddy, James Nelson.'

'I hear he's a great guy,' Niall said. 'Great doctor.'

'Goodbye again, Christopher, nice talking to you,' Katie muttered and got into the car swiftly, putting the door between them.

As he closed the door for her, he said, 'My friends call me Chris.'

Niall said, 'See ya, Chris!'

'Sure thing, Niall,' Christopher replied, and stepped away from the kerb as the BMW pulled away.

*   *   *

'How do you know Christopher Saunders?' Katie asked, settling in the seat, glancing across at her brother.

'We did his parents' house, Dad and I, the company. You know, we did a restoration and remodelling job.'

'Oh, I see. Where do his parents live?'

'In Washington. They bought that big old barn of a place that once belonged to Jessica Rennard, and then to her niece, Patty. It was really dilapidated, but the basic bones were good, and it has spectacular views, plenty of land attached.'

'Is it the place we always believed was haunted?'

'That's it.' Niall laughed. 'You should see it now, Katie, Mrs Saunders has a great eye. It's gorgeous. Mind you, we gave her the canvas to work with.'

'Do they live there all the time? Or do they commute?'

'A bit of both. In the summer they spend a lot of time up here. But yeah, I guess they commute. They have an apartment in New York.'

'And Christopher? How did you get to know him?'

'Because he was always around. I'm going back about four years now. He and his sister, Charlene, seemed to have quite a lot of input in the design of the house, if I remember correctly.'

'Oh, so he must live in New York too, I guess?'

'I don't know.' Niall frowned. 'Yeah, possibly. But there was some talk about a job abroad.'

'What does he do?'

'I don't know. Something *odd*, though. Hey, Katie, why all the questions about this guy? You got a yen for him?'

'Don't be so stupid, Niall Byrne!'

Chapter Thirty

'Everything sounds so exciting, Katie.' Xenia smiled across the dinner table at her friend, and added, 'Aren't you glad now that you took the part?'

'Of course I am, and it's thanks to you that I did. And thanks to Rex, as well. Because he gave me such great insight into Emily Brontë, and that helped me to have confidence in myself, the confidence I was lacking.'

'I knew he'd be able to help you, and I was really pleased that he came to spend the weekend with us at Burton Leyburn.'

'I'd love to know the truth about everybody there,' Katie ventured, eyeing Xenia speculatively. 'There seem to be so many mysteries, and everybody's very intriguing, to say the least.'

'They are indeed, and of course there are many mysteries,' Xenia confirmed in a very matter-of-fact voice, then she added, with a small, knowing smile, 'One day I'll tell you everything, reveal all of their secrets.'

'Oh come on, don't be a spoilsport, Xenia, tell me now.'

'It would take far too long.'

'Shame. I'd love to hear. But another time, yes? Promise?'

'I promise. How are rehearsals going?'

'Very well. It's the final dress rehearsal tomorrow night, then previews for three weeks until the opening in February. Mom says you told her you're definitely coming.'

'As I said to your mother, I'll be there with bells on.'

Katie smiled at her. 'I'm glad. I want you to be in the audience so much.'

'You told me on the phone that Melanie's been very kind to you . . . in what way?'

'She's been extremely helpful in that she encouraged me to give my own interpretation, for one thing. Now she says I'm not only word perfect, but that I've got the part down pat. And the director seems to agree.'

'Hey, that's praise indeed, Melanie's tough. A great producer, but tough.'

'She has to be, there's a lot of money at stake, and she has investors to answer to, a fiscal responsibility, is how she puts it. And actually, she's as tough on me as she is on everyone else. She doesn't play favourites.' Katie took a sip of white wine, and continued, 'It's very hard work, and there have been days when I've been totally exhausted. But that's just the way it is. Acting is so much harder than most people think, especially civilians.'

'Civilians meaning us chickens, the non-theatricals, right?'

Katie laughed at Xenia's expression. 'Yes, that's who civilians are, non-theatricals. But Chris says the public are not supposed to know how hard the work is. He says the illusion of ease and naturalness has to be preserved.'

'Who's Chris?' Xenia asked, frowning slightly in puzzlement, not having heard the name before.

'A friend. A new friend. He's very nice.' Under Xenia's sudden, intense scrutiny Katie felt herself growing warm, felt the flush rising from her neck to flood her pale face.

'Ho hum!' Xenia cried. 'Why, you're actually blushing, Katie. I've never seen you do that before. So Chris is the new boyfriend, eh?'

'Oh I wouldn't say that!' Katie exclaimed. 'I only met him last weekend. Last Saturday. He's not a *boyfriend* as such, but a *friend*.'

'Where did you meet him?' Xenia probed, intrigued.

'At home. In Connecticut, I mean. I went to the hospice to see Carly. That's where I met him.'

'How is she? Just the same, I suppose.'

'Yes. But the doctor told me she's not actually in a *true* coma, but that she is locked in a vegetative state.'

'What's a vegetative state?'

Katie explained, and then went on, 'Anyway, Dr Nelson's a friend of Chris's, and Chris practically knocked me over coming through some swing doors. So he waited for me to come out, to apologize again.'

'I'll bet he did!'

'Why do you say that? And in that tone?'

Xenia shook her head, staring at Katie in astonishment. 'Haven't you looked at yourself lately? Katie, you're gorgeous.'

'Oh come on, I'm not.'

'All that fabulous red hair, those sapphire-blue eyes, cheekbones to die for. It's my turn to say, *oh come on*. Anyway, getting back to Chris. He waited for you outside the hospital, and then what?'

'We sat on a wall and chatted. I was expecting Niall. He was coming to pick me up. Chris wanted to take me to lunch, but I couldn't go. Anyway, when Niall arrived it turned out they knew each other. His parents bought an old wreck of a house in Connecticut . . . in Washington, and it was Niall and my father who did the restoration and remodelling, and our landscaping company did the grounds.'

'So he's a family friend?'

'Well, he knows Niall and Dad.'

'So have you seen him again?'

'Yes.'

'In New York presumably?' Xenia raised a brow.

'Yes. The thing is, he phoned me later on Saturday afternoon, and asked me out that evening. I didn't want to go. Then Mom got in the middle, and she made me call him back and ask him to supper. So I did. He accepted and then that evening he offered me a lift to the city on Sunday afternoon, and I sort of felt . . . well, obligated to accept, because otherwise Mom was going to have to drive me in. So it kind of took off from there.'

'Took off? What do you mean?'

Katie bit her lip, and shook her head. 'He's very much a sort of a take-charge person, not domineering or a control freak, but down to earth and practical. And when we got back to New York he said let's go and have dinner, you've got to eat, keep your strength up, etc . . . and so we went to Elaine's and had spaghetti.'

'And then?'

'There's no *and then*, Xenia. He drove me home to the West Side.'

'Have you seen him since?'

'Yes. He was waiting for me when I came out of rehearsals. Waiting to take me to dinner.'

'When? On Monday?'

'Monday, Tuesday, Wednesday, and Thursday.'

'Ho hum indeed!' Xenia cried, her eyes twinkling, her face lighting up with pleasure. 'And tonight you dumped him for me.'

Katie smiled, and said, 'I didn't really dump him, Xenia, because I invited him to join us for coffee. I knew you wouldn't mind, and I do want you to meet him.'

'I can't wait. Now, tell me all about him.'

'He's thirty-three, and he's an ecologist. He's based in

Argentina, in Buenos Aires, that's where he lives. But he keeps a small apartment in New York.'

'Oh dear, don't tell me this is going to be a long-distance romance. Problems, problems, Katie.'

'It's not a romance.'

'Oh come on, don't be so ridiculous! This is me you're talking to. Of course it's going to be a romance, and I personally think it's wonderful. How do you feel about him?'

'I like him a lot. He's a really nice person, and intelligent, very well read, interesting to talk to. He's very knowledgeable about a lot of things, Xenia. I mean, who'd expect someone like Chris to know all about those nineteenth-century novelists, the Brontës, but he does, and he knows British history. He reads a lot, and he writes. He started out thinking he'd be a writer and journalist, but then he got caught up in ecology.'

'He wants to save the planet? Well, I do too. My hat's off to him.'

'Mine too,' Katie agreed. 'And let's face it, the planet does *need* saving.'

Xenia nodded, looked thoughtful for a moment or two, then she murmured, 'You've always been so wary about men, very cautious. Yet you don't seem to be worrying about Chris.'

'I know, and I find that strange,' Katie quietly confided. 'I'm usually so on edge when I meet a new man who shows interest in me. But with Chris I've felt so at ease, right from the beginning.' She grinned. 'It's only a week, but I *have* seen him every night, and I feel I know him . . .'

'And?'

'No *and*. We're just good friends.'

Xenia laughed lightly. 'But you could be more?'

'I think so,' Katie confessed, and suddenly looked bashful.

The waiter arrived with their black sea bass on a bed of leeks, and they fell silent while the food was being served. But once they were alone, Katie glanced around her, then said, 'It's so nice of you to bring me here, Xenia. I like Le Cirque and I love the food. I've only been twice before, though. Once with Aunt Bridget and my parents, and on Wednesday with Chris.'

'Goodness, Katie, Le Cirque twice in one week! Aren't we getting posh.'

Katie smiled, and dug her fork into the bass, made no comment.

Xenia said, 'I'm very partial to this place myself, and I felt like giving us both a treat. You're about to open in a play that I know is going to be a big hit, and we've just signed a big contract to do four parties a year for a beauty product company.

'Which company is it?'

'Peter Thomas Roth, who makes clinical skin care products. They're really great, and he's very go-ahead, not only in his products, but also in his promotion. He's going to give four really big, and rather fancy, parties a year, and Celebrations has been hired to create them.'

'Congratulations, Xenia!' Katie cried, lifting her glass of wine. 'This is great news.'

Xenia did the same, and they clinked glasses. Xenia grinned and said, 'Thanks. I have a feeling the year 2000 is going to be good for the two of us.'

The two women had just finished their main course when Christopher Saunders was shown to their table.

After the introductions had been made by Katie, Christopher took a chair opposite the banquette where they were seated, and ordered a cup of coffee.

Xenia liked the look of him at once. He was of medium height and build, slender really, with dark-brown hair and warm brown eyes, and she found his looks attractive. He was handsome in a clean-cut, boyish way, and extremely well dressed in an impeccably-tailored dark-navy suit that smacked of Savile Row to her, a pale-blue shirt and a blue-on-blue striped tie. Old money, privileged background, waspy upbringing, she decided as she listened to him talking to Katie.

'Would you like to come too, Xenia?' Katie asked.

'I'm so sorry, I'm afraid I was day-dreaming, and I missed that, Katie. What were you talking about?'

'Tomorrow night: it's the final dress rehearsal. It's what they call an *invited dress*. In other words, the actors can invite family or friends. I decided not to even mention it to Mom and Dad, because I really do prefer them to come on opening night. But I just invited Chris, and I'd like you to come too, if you can.'

'I'd love it. I'm not going back to London until Sunday morning, and I'm free Saturday night. I wouldn't miss it for the world. Thanks, Katie.'

'Shall I come and pick you up, Xenia?' Chris asked. 'We might as well go together, don't you think?'

'Yes, I'd like that. Thanks.' Xenia smiled at him, then turned to Katie. 'Just think, I'll be able to tell Rex about your performance. He's been dying to know how it's all been going. In fact, everyone at the hall will be anxious to know about you, Katie.'

Unexpectedly, Katie thought about Dodie, the house-keeper, and she went very still inside, remembering her words that Saturday night at Burton Leyburn Hall.

Xenia said, 'What's wrong? You've got a funny look on your face, Katie.'

'I suddenly thought of Dodie, and those things she said to me when I was in Yorkshire with you. I told you at the time.'

Xenia nodded, but made no comment, knowing Katie had more to say.

'If you remember, she said I should go home, that my future was there, and that I was needed. When she used the word *home* I assumed she meant America, or perhaps New York. But now I think she meant *home*. Where I grew up. In other words, my parents' home in Malvern.'

'Who's Dodie?' Chris asked.

'Oh, she's my sister-in-law's housekeeper, and she thinks she's psychic. She's a bit daft in the head,' Xenia explained.

Looking thoughtful for a moment, Chris then said, 'When a person thinks they are psychic, they usually are. They know when they have The Gift.'

Both women stared at him.

Chris said, 'I'm sure this Dodie is psychic. Of course, she could be daft in the head, as well. One thing doesn't preclude the other.'

Katie and Xenia laughed, and Katie said, 'Dodie told me my future was here, and it *is*, if you think about the play. She also said I was needed, and I think I am. And if –'

'Absolutely!' Chris interjected. 'Carly needs you, your mother needs you, and I need you.'

Katie gaped at him, and so did Xenia.

Immediately aware of their surprised expressions, Chris laughed, and addressed Xenia. 'How about that, hey? What a declaration for a man to make to a woman he's only known for six days. Although it does seem much longer.' He smiled at Katie. 'And it happens to be true.'

Chapter Thirty-one

Katie sat at the dressing table, checking her make-up and wig. She thought, as she stared in the glass, that she had a slight look of Emily Brontë, and this pleased her. She knew it was the wig that created the effect, and she was glad she had chosen this particular style.

The wig had a middle parting, with soft waves and curls on each side, which touched her temples and face; once she had put it on, her appearance had definitely changed, no question about that.

Katie smiled to herself, aware that she now looked like a woman of the nineteenth century, which was important. Victorian, of course. And she also knew that she could walk out on that stage and be Emily. In a few moments she would be doing just that.

It was Sunday evening, February 20th in the year 2000, opening night of *Charlotte and Her Sisters* at the Barrymore Theatre on West 47th Street. And she was opening in a play on Broadway. Finally. At long last.

She slid out one of the drawers in the dressing table, and looked down at the photograph which lay there. It was of Carly, Denise and herself, taken on her sixteenth birthday. She nodded. Tonight was as much for them as it was for her.

Rising, Katie straightened the skirt of her long, dark-blue dress, looked in the mirror for a final check, and walked across the dressing-room floor.

There was a knock on the door. 'Five minutes, Miss Byrne!' the call boy shouted a split second before she opened it and went out.

Charlotte and Branwell were on the stage in this first scene of the first act, and Katie moved towards the wings, stood waiting for her cue. She was nervous, shaking inside. It was stage fright. Fear of failing out there. So many actors suffered from it. Richard Burton had, she knew that. His stage fright had been so acute in the first play he had ever done, someone had given him a glass of brandy to calm him. And that was how his drinking had started.

She shook this thought off, concentrated on the words being said on stage, and suddenly she was on. For a split second she was frozen in the wings, then the adrenaline kicked in, and she moved forward, found herself out there, centre stage, under the bright lights. And the words came easily, flowed out of her.

'More bills, and more bill-collectors, Branwell,' she said with cool deliberation. She was Emily, facing Branwell down. 'We are *all* going to end up in debtor's prison if we're not careful. It won't only be you, brother dear. And then where will this family be? And what about poor Father? Brought to shame and dishonour by a profligate, dissolute son. Oh, and one other thing, Branwell. Do not send Anne to get your opium for you ever again. I forbid it.'

She sailed through the scenes, all six of them.

Blackout. Curtain. End of Act One.

As the curtain came down the applause was deafening, and every single actor knew it was going to be as big a hit as the London production in the West End.

Katie rushed off stage to her dressing room, to change her costume and retouch her make-up. All she could think about was the next act. It was even more complex than the first, and she was hardly off stage. Furthermore, she had a death scene.

Act Two could make or break her.

Of course it made her.

The party was in full swing when Katie arrived at Tavern on the Green with Christopher Saunders. He had waited for her while she had toned down her stage make-up, done her hair and changed into her dress for the evening. It was long, made of purple velvet and had an old-fashioned look about it which she loved. Her only jewellery was a pair of amethyst drop earrings which Chris had given her yesterday, much to her surprise and delight.

Christopher had brought her over to the restaurant in Central Park in a chauffeur-driven car which he had hired for the evening. 'Katie, you were miraculous,' he had told her in the dressing room, and he had kept on saying it all the way from the theatre.

'Everyone was good,' she murmured just before they alighted from the car.

Leaning into her, he kissed her cheek. 'But you stole the show, darling girl, whether you want to admit it or not.'

Melanie and Harry Dawson, and Jack Martin, the director, were waiting at the entrance, and they congratulated her yet again, told her what a great performance she'd given. Smiling, but filling up with nervous tension, she put her arm through Christopher's, and taking several deep breaths she walked into the room with him.

More deafening applause. And then her family were surrounding her. Two sets of grandparents, aunts and uncles, her mother and father and Niall. And suddenly she spotted her brother Finian.

'Oh, *Fin*!' she cried, 'you came all the way from Oxford!'

'Sure did, Katie,' he said, hugging her to him. 'How could I miss this. The first of many big hits for you, I know.'

Her Aunt Bridget was squeezing in between them, looking ravishing in red silk with her red hair swept up into an elegant chignon. 'You knocked 'em dead, Katie mine. Congratulations.'

Katie nodded, turned, her eyes seeking her mother. At once, Maureen came forward and they embraced. Her mother said, through her tears, 'I'm so proud of you, mavourneen, you were just extraordinary up there on that stage.'

'Thanks, Mom.' She beckoned to her father, who was standing just behind her mother. 'Did you enjoy the play, Dad?'

'I did, Katie.' He hugged her tightly. 'But you've always been a star, as far as I'm concerned. Congratulations, honey.'

'Hey, what about me? Don't I get a chance to kiss her?' Niall exclaimed. Katie brought him into the circle, then embraced her brother. And as she did she realized that somehow Chris had managed to remain glued to her side through all the excitement.

'I've a surprise for you,' Chris now said, and taking hold of her hand, he led her through the family group. As they parted to let her pass, she found herself staring at Xenia. Katie's expression was one of total astonishment as she viewed the people standing there with her.

'You were fabulous.' Xenia smiled at her. 'Congratulations.'

'You were wonderful,' Verity exclaimed.

'You *were* Emily,' Lavinia said.

'Thank you, Katie, for understanding everything I told you about Emily. Lavinia's correct, you *were* her, and I can only say, you deserve every award that's going. Many, many congratulations, Katie.' As he spoke, Rex walked towards her, put his arms around her, and held her. Against her hair, he whispered, 'You've stolen this show, you know, my dear.'

'Phew!' she exclaimed a moment later, her eyes sweeping over them. 'How did you all get here?'

'On a plane,' Lavinia said.

'They were so desperate to come to the opening, to root for you, Katie, I finally phoned Melanie from London. She was happy to invite them.' Xenia threw Katie an odd look. 'And she certainly seemed to know the name Rex Bellamy.'

'Oh yes, I'd told her about him weeks ago, how he'd helped me.' Katie gave Rex a loving smile. 'And thank you for that, Rex, and thanks, all of you, for coming to New York to support me. I'm so touched.'

Katie introduced Christopher to them, and she was chatting to Verity when Xenia took hold of her arm. 'Katie, there's my client Peter Thomas Roth and his wife over there. They're with Melanie. Oh, look, they're heading this way.'

A moment later, Melanie was introducing the Roths to Katie and Christopher, and Xenia introduced her group from England.

Melanie said, 'Peter is one of my backers, Katie, and

he's glowing tonight because he feels we've got a big hit. I think we do, too. I *hope* we do.'

'What a great performance you gave, Katie,' Peter said. 'You were spellbinding.'

'Thank you,' Katie murmured, smiling back at him.

'Yes, you were superb as Emily,' Noreen Roth interjected. 'I think you'll get a Tony nomination for your performance, and you deserve it.'

They talked about the play for a moment or two longer, and then Melanie drew Katie aside and said, 'I thought you'd like to know that Jenny Hargreaves gave birth to a little girl. Tonight. In Yorkshire. Prematurely. And that's why she's not here to see her play open on Broadway. But you knew she was pregnant, I think I told you that.'

Katie nodded. 'I'm so pleased for her. Perhaps I can send her a message. Or flowers. Something.'

'Of course, that's no problem. Oh and Katie.'

'Yes, Melanie?'

'She's named the baby Emily.'

Katie simply smiled, her bright-blue eyes full of happiness.

The centre of interest shifted as the other actors began to arrive and mingle with everyone in the big room. Katie and Chris circulated with her family and friends, and Katie kept accepting congratulations, smiling broadly, enjoying every moment of this very special evening.

*　　*　　*

It was a foregone conclusion that Chris would spend the night with her. And once they arrived at the apartment building on West End Avenue he let the car go.

They went up to the apartment in silence, not speaking in the lift. Nor did they say a word when they entered the small entrance hall of her apartment.

He held her with his eyes.

She stared back at him.

Suddenly, they moved at the same time, came into each other's arms. Chris held her tightly against him. Katie clung to him. He kissed her neck and her cheek, but a moment later he held her away by the shoulders, looking deeply into her lovely eyes.

There was a small silence as they gazed at each other as if mesmerized, frozen in place in the foyer.

Finally Chris spoke. 'I meant what I said four weeks ago, Katie. That night at Le Cirque with Xenia. I do need you. Very much.'

'I knew you weren't speaking lightly. That's not you.'

'I've fallen in love with you.'

'Yes, I know you have, Chris.'

'And you, Katie, what do you feel?'

'The same. I love you.'

A faint smile crossed his face, and was instantly gone. He took hold of her hand and led her into the living room. Katie flung her purple velvet stole on a chair, and the two of them sank down onto the loveseat. Chris leaned into her, kissed her lightly on her mouth. A second later, he said, 'You're the best thing that's ever happened to me, Katie Byrne.'

She rested her head against his chest, enjoying this closeness. 'You're very special to me, Chris. As no one else has ever been.'

He put his arms around her and began to kiss her ardently. She returned his kisses with equal passion, and her hands went up onto his neck and into his hair. They kissed for a long time, and then he stood up, gave her his hand; Katie took it and rose, and together they went into the adjoining bedroom.

They shed their clothes and found each other in the dim light of the bedroom. Chris embraced her, held her in the circle of his arms, then led her to the bed; they lay down on it, facing each other, and their eyes locked. They gazed at each other for a long time.

Eventually Chris reached out and stroked her face, saying nothing, and then he bent his head, kissed her breasts with tenderness. It was the first time they had made love, yet they seemed to know each other instinctively.

Her hands stroked the back of his neck, and he felt her fingers strong and supple on his skin. And her body was strong and supple under his touch, long and lithe and beautiful. She was the most beautiful woman he had ever known, ever wanted, and he knew full well that without her his life would be nothing.

But he did not say a word, he just went on kissing

her tenderly, stroking her inner thigh, slowly moving his hand towards the core of her.

Katie felt tense and excited, filled with a longing for Chris, a yearning she had known since their first meeting. But there was also a sense of peace within her as well, because she knew this man was ideal for her. He was the man she had always been searching for, and she knew she loved him deeply.

Chris moved abruptly, pushed himself up on one elbow, looked down at her.

She stared up at him expectantly.

Chris reached out, turned on the bedside lamp. 'I want to see your face,' he murmured softly, touching her cheek.

Her eyes were wide and very blue. She half smiled at him.

Chris brought his mouth to hers. His tongue touched hers, lingered next to hers, and it was a moment of absolute intimacy, like he had never known, the prelude to passion.

Gently he turned her on her back, and moved onto her slender body, fitting his close to hers. How well they fitted together, he thought. His passion soared, he felt as though he would burst with desire. He moved swiftly then, taking her to him, and she called out sharply, said his name as he entered her.

Katie felt as though her mind had emptied itself of everything except her thoughts of Chris; her desire for him was paramount. Her arms and legs were wrapped around him, as if never to let him go, and she felt herself becoming part of him, as they moved, found their own rhythm. And as they flowed together to become one, Katie thought her heart was exploding as she was carried along on a wave of ecstasy.

Chapter Thirty-two

The drive from Manhattan to Malvern had taken her exactly two hours, give or take a few minutes, and Katie was pleased she had done it in record time. It was just turning ten o'clock on the dashboard clock when she parked outside the garage at her parents' house.

'It's only me, Mom,' she called out as she went through the back entrance and into the kitchen.

Maureen looked up, a startled expression on her face. She was standing at one of the kitchen counters, chopping apples, and she put the knife down, exclaimed, 'Katie! Goodness, I didn't expect you so soon.' She glanced down at herself, and added, 'Oh dear, and here I am in my pinny. Whatever will Chris think.'

Katie burst out laughing. 'Mom, he wouldn't think anything untoward if he saw you in your pinafore. I'm sure his mother wears one too. She's not that grand. But he's not with me, I drove up by myself.'

Maureen frowned and shook her head. 'But I thought he was coming up with you today. For lunch. That's what he said last week, at the opening. "I'll see you next Monday, in a week. I'm driving Katie up to see Carly." That's exactly what he said, mavourneen. And I said I'd make lunch for you. So what happened?'

Katie put her jacket and handbag on a chair, and stood leaning against the counter, regarding her mother, a loving smile ringing her face. 'He decided he'd better go to this meeting in Boston today after all. He'd told them he wouldn't be coming, but he changed his mind.'

'Who's *them*?' Maureen gave her a long look, her eyes narrowed slightly.

'The people he works with. The ecology organization.'

'Is it Greenpeace?'

'No, no, it's an organization called PlanetEarth, all one word. And there's a division of it called Saving PlanetEarth, and that's the one Chris runs in South America.'

'You know, Katie, you've never told me *exactly* what it is Chris does.'

'Well, in the last ten years he's become an expert on rain forests, and what he does is try to save them. Because they are vital to life on earth.'

Maureen nodded. 'Yes, I guess I somehow know that, honey. And I think what he does is admirable.'

'Chris told me that sixty per cent of the world's rain forests have been lost to agricultural and timber interests, and that most industrial nations have cleared all their original forests. Except for Canada and Russia.

Isn't that something, Mom? It's incredible when you think about it. Really bad news.'

Maureen nodded. 'Do you want a cup of coffee, Katie? I only just made it.'

'I wouldn't say no. Thanks. Let's both have a cup.' Katie walked across to the kitchen table and sat down, and a moment later her mother joined her with two mugs of steaming coffee.

'It's good, Mom, just what I needed,' Katie said, after taking several sips.

'Do you want to eat anything, mavourneen?'

'No, I'm not hungry.'

'I've been thinking about Chris, you know, and 'tis a pity he has to leave, has to go back to Argentina.'

Katie stared at her mother, but didn't say anything. She wondered what was coming next.

Maureen said, 'I like him a lot, and so does your father. And Niall. Although I don't suppose our opinions matter. When you're in love you're in love, no matter what anyone else thinks or says. 'Tis true, you know, Katie, love is blind. But fortunately, everyone likes Christopher Saunders, and your father and I approve of him.'

Katie beamed. 'I'm glad, Mom.'

'But there's a real problem ... that long-distance problem, Katie.'

'That's true. Chris has to leave in two weeks.'

'Does he get a lot of time off? I mean, he's been here over two months.'

'He will have been here for about that length of time when he leaves. A month was his vacation time, and then he had a month to do his business here,' Katie explained.

'I see.' Maureen sipped her coffee, looking sad and reflective.

Katie did not miss the thoughtful look on her mother's face, the sadness in her blue eyes, and she said swiftly, 'What's the matter, Momma, why are you looking so sad?'

'Because I know you're in love with him. You are, aren't you?'

Katie nodded.

'And 'tis a certainty he's in love with you, even Bridget and my mother noticed that he just dotes on you. He couldn't take his eyes off you at the opening-night party last Sunday. But he has to go away, doesn't he? He lives there, you live here, and you're at the beginning of a big career in the theatre. Even *The New York Times* critic says that, and some of the other reviewers did, too. So I'm sad because I don't think your romance is going to get a chance to flower.'

'But it has already flowered, Momma.'

'Flowers don't continue to grow and flourish if they don't get watered and nurtured,' Maureen pointed out.

'I know.'

'Have you discussed it?'

'Not really, Mom. I guess we both know there is this

awful problem of being in two different countries, but we avoid talking about it. I think it's because we just want to enjoy each other while we can.'

'I understand what you're saying, but it's not very realistic of you.'

Katie sighed. 'Chris says life has a way of taking care of itself.'

'Too true, but it's not always in the way we want. Take my word for it.'

When Katie was totally silent, and sat staring into her mug of coffee, Maureen went on, 'Would you be prepared to give up the play? Go to Argentina to live with Chris?'

'You know very well I can't. I signed a contract for a year.'

'*You* know full well what I'm getting at, Katie.'

'Okay, so I do. But I can't answer you, because I don't know.'

Katie thought about this conversation as she drove over to the hospice in Chris's car an hour later. Her mother was right, but she didn't want to face making such a difficult decision. And she was quite certain, deep inside, that Chris was avoiding doing that himself.

Later, I'll think about it later, she told herself, and endeavoured to push thoughts of Chris's return to South America to one side. Right now she was on the way to see Carly, and that was her chief consideration. She wanted to tell her friend about the opening a week ago, and the party afterwards at Tavern on the Green.

Twenty minutes later Katie was walking into the front lobby of the hospice, and hurrying down the corridor to Carly's room. As usual, she ran into the young nurse, Jane, who was one of the day nurses, and they exchanged greetings. Seconds later Katie was leaning over Carly, kissing her on the cheek.

There was no response, and so Katie pulled the chair closer to the bed, sat down and reached for Carly's hand. It was warm, not as cool as it generally was, and Katie glanced at Carly's face. Her violet-blue eyes were open, but there was no sign of life, and her face was as bland and as passive as always.

Katie made herself comfortable in the chair, and took a deep breath. Then she began to talk to Carly.

'I wish you could have been there on opening night, Carly. You and Denise. You would have loved it. I looked at the picture of the three of us before I went on, and you know what, you and Denise helped to carry me through the play. Of course I did it for myself, but I did it for you too. I wanted to fulfil your childhood dream as well as mine. There's something else I have to tell you, Carly. I had a touch of stage fright. I've never really had it before, but last Sunday night I was stricken. At least for a moment or two, and I thought of Richard Burton as I stood in the wings. Do you remember when we read his biography, the one by Melvyn Bragg, and we discovered how he had suffered terribly with stage fright, had started his drinking habit, having a quick nip before he went on stage. And you made me laugh when you brought me a bottle of whiskey to the school concert. Except that it wasn't whiskey at all, but cold tea. Oh, Carly, I do miss you so. And I miss your funny jokes.

'I wish you could have heard the applause. One thousand and fifty people applauding us last Sunday, and we took so many curtains. The play is a big hit, and it looks as if it's going to run for a year, maybe longer, according to Melanie. The reviews were wonderful and I got quite a lot of attention.

'The whole family came to the opening, Carly. Mom and Dad, Niall, and Fin, who flew in from London. All the aunts and uncles, and four grandparents. You would have loved it.

'There was a party afterward at Tavern on the Green. Black tie, everyone dressed up in evening gowns. Mine was made of purple velvet. When I saw the dress hanging in the shop, I thought of pansies, and of your eyes. I wish you could have seen it. I wish you could have been there. I wish you could hear me, Carly. I'd give anything for that.'

Katie stopped and stood up. The sun was flooding the room, blinding her, and she walked over to the venetian blinds, adjusted them so that the sun was filtered.

'Can . . . hear . . . you . . .'

Katie stiffened.

The low, rasping voice said again, 'Can . . . hear . . .'

Katie swung around, rushed back to the bed, stared down at Carly, hardly daring to believe that she had actually spoken. At once, Katie saw that the eyes were different, not so flat and dead. There *was* a spark there, a hint of life.

Bending over the bed, Katie said urgently, 'Did you speak to me, Carly? Blink if you did.'

Nothing happened. The life seemed to seep out of those pansy-violet eyes. They went dead again.

Katie said, 'Carly, listen to me. Listen hard. It's me. *Katie*. Blink if you understand what I'm saying.' Her eyes were riveted to Carly's and when Carly did finally blink several times, Katie shouted, 'Carly! Carly! You blinked.'

Carly blinked again, rapidly, and opened her mouth, tried to speak. Closed it. Then she said slowly, in a mumble, 'Ka . . . tie.'

'Oh, my God! Carly, you said my name! Oh God, oh God! This is a *miracle*.'

Katie looked at the door as it flew open and Jane poked her head inside. 'Is something wrong?'

'No, no, everything's right! Very, very right. Jane, come over here. Carly blinked. She spoke. Honestly she did.'

Astonishment washed over the nurse's face, and she ran to the bed, stared down at Carly, then turned to

Katie. 'Are you sure? She looks the way she's always looked for the five years that I've been here.'

'Ka . . . tie,' Carly said again in the same unsteady and raspy mumble.

'Good Lord, she spoke your name, Miss Byrne! I can't believe it. This is incredible!' Jane was thunderstruck and gaping at Katie.

'Please, Jane, go and get Dr Nelson. I don't want to leave Carly.'

Jane nodded, and rushed out of the room.

Katie leaned over the bed again, and took hold of Carly's hand. It had the same warmth, and she wondered if this meant anything.

'Can you squeeze my hand, Carly? Can you try?'

Watching attentively, Katie saw the fingers move very slightly, but they were not strong enough to grasp her hand. Nevertheless, there was movement there, and this hadn't happened before.

The door opened and Dr James Nelson came in, obviously concerned and worried. 'What is it, Katie? Jane here tells me that Carly spoke to you. Is that true?' He looked doubtful.

'It is, Dr Nelson, it really is. She said she could hear me, and she said my name.'

James Nelson threw Katie a curious look, again as if he really didn't give credence to what she was saying, and hurried over to the bed so that he could examine Carly. He took out his small light and looked into each eye. He then felt her pulse, and listened to her heartbeat.

Straightening, he swung his head to Katie, and asked, 'Can you tell me exactly what happened, Katie, please?'

'Yes, of course. The first thing that struck me when I arrived was that her hand was warm. Usually it's so cool. Anyway, I looked at her as I always do, and there was no sign of life at all. Her eyes were wide open, as they usually are, but they were dead, flat. So I sat and talked to her, told her all about the play, the opening, the party afterwards. There was nothing, not one flicker of life, of understanding. It was suddenly really sunny in the room, brilliant sun was coming in through the open blinds. So I got up to adjust them. Oh, one thing I forgot, Dr Nelson, just before I stood, I said I wished she could hear me.'

Katie paused, cleared her throat. 'Anyway, I'd just adjusted the blinds when I heard this voice. It was low, rasping. It was Carly, Dr Nelson. She said, very slowly, in a mumble, "Can . . . hear . . . you." Just like that. I was stunned, I didn't believe it. I ran to the bed, and I asked her to blink if she knew it was me. At first she didn't seem able to do that, and then suddenly she blinked several times. A moment later she said my name . . . broken up. *Ka . . . tie.* That was how she said it.'

The doctor shook his head. 'I don't understand this . . .' His voice trailed off, and for a moment he appeared baffled, at a loss.

Jane, who had returned to the room with him, said, 'It's true, Dr Nelson. I heard Carly speak, too. I heard her say "Katie", in the way Miss Byrne described.'

'Ka . . . tie . . .' Carly mumbled.

James Nelson focused all of his attention on Carly. Bending over her, he took hold of her hand. He enunciated clearly, slowly, 'Carly, squeeze my hand if you can hear me.'

After a moment he saw the fingers move, but just barely. His astonishment was obvious. He said, 'Blink, Carly, if you can.'

After a second or two Carly blinked.

James Nelson stared down at her, and he saw the flicker of life there in those lovely eyes. It was the most extraordinary moment of his career.

Turning to Katie and Jane, he nodded. 'This is extraordinary. A medical first, I'm sure. Carly's been in a vegetative state for ten years. I've never heard of anyone coming out of it after so long. I must admit, I'm flabbergasted.'

'What do you think happened to bring her out of it, Dr Nelson?' Katie asked.

'I don't know. It's not that we've done anything different, there's not much we *can* do for her –' He broke off abruptly, and stared at Katie, frowning. 'Oh my God, I recently started her on a drug called amantadine, which guards against pulmonary infection. Especially in bed-ridden patients. I wanted to protect Carly . . .' He paused thoughtfully. 'It can be an arousal agent, that I do know. Then again, she may have had a brain-stem blockage that has gradually cleared up. Maybe it's both things working in combination. But whatever, this is great news. As I said, it's possibly a medical first. But I do think she's going to take a while to get back to normal, if she ever is actually normal in the true sense of that word.'

Jane, who had been silent, now said, 'We've moved her legs and her arms for the last five years, that I know. And although her muscles have atrophied, we've tried to give her some help.'

'Yes, I'm aware of that, Jane. It's been good therapy for her. Nevertheless, I do think it's going to take a while before she walks again.'

Jane nodded in agreement. 'Yes, but she's young, Dr Nelson.'

'Parts of her brain seem to have woken up. And I'm sure some of her motor skills will start coming back, however slowly. And eventually her speech and memory,' the doctor explained.

'She seems to know I'm *me*,' Katie murmured.

'Yes, she apparently does, and that is very important, very promising.' He glanced over at Carly again, and then moved across the floor quickly. 'I had better go and phone her mother. Mrs Smith will be overjoyed when she hears the news. And I must talk to the head of the hospice.' As he finished speaking he opened the door.

Katie hurried after him. 'Dr Nelson, please wait. I must speak to you.'

He paused in the corridor. 'Yes, Katie, what is it?'

Closing the door and swallowing hard, Katie said, 'You can't really tell anyone about this, about the sudden signs of life in Carly.'

'Whyever not? It's a . . . a miracle, however it's happened. A first, as far as I know. As I just told you.'

'Carly is the only eye witness to a horrible murder, Dr Nelson. Before she was struck down she saw the killer, the man who attacked her and Denise Matthews. Because there was some sort of struggle in the barn, before the two girls ran out into the wood. Denise is dead, so she can't identify her murderer. But Carly can.'

James Nelson was silent, but he paled, understanding the implications behind her words.

Katie said, 'Carly could be in grave danger. There's still a killer out there. That's why you've got to keep this a secret. And you've got to call the police.'

Forty-five minutes later Mac MacDonald was sitting with Katie and Dr Nelson in the latter's office in the Neurological Wing.

'Thanks, Katie, you've told that very clearly,' Mac said, and turned his attention to the doctor. 'And so have you, Dr Nelson. Thanks. But tell me, in your considered opinion, do you think Carly will recover completely?'

'It's truly hard to say. I haven't had a chance to think clearly. This just happened, less than an hour ago. She might, of course. Then again, she might not. It could go either way.' Dr Nelson paused for a moment, and then added, 'The thing that makes me feel somewhat positive about Carly's eventual recovery is that she said Katie's name, and several times. Which to me means that there's memory intact. I think that perhaps parts of her brain have been awakened.'

'By the amantadine?' Mac asked.

'Possibly. Although I gave it to her to prevent pulmonary infection, as I explained to you.'

'I understand. What I'm getting at is will Carly be able to remember what happened to her ten years ago? At the barn, and later in the wood? Will she remember who her attacker was?'

'It's possible,' Dr Nelson answered. 'As I said, she seems to know Katie. However, the attack on her was so horrendous, caused such trauma physically and mentally, she may have blocked it out. I just can't say. I can't predict anything.'

Mac was silent for a second or two, and then he said, 'I'm going to make the assumption that she *will* remember everything, whether it's this week or next month. And therefore I have to take certain steps, Dr Nelson.' He gave the doctor a penetrating look, and continued, 'This sudden development in Carly's condition must be kept under wraps. The perp's out there, and I don't want him to know about this change in Carly. He thinks he's safe, that he got away with murder. Now, maybe he hasn't. I don't want him coming after Carly. So I must ask you to keep quiet about what's happened here today.'

Dr Nelson nodded, looking worried.

'I realize this is medically important to you, doctor,' Mac went on. 'A first, a medical breakthrough, perhaps. But by waiting to tell the world we protect Carly. No press announcements. Understood?'

'Of course,' James Nelson responded.

'There would be a feeding frenzy if the media got wind of this. Also, you must talk to the staff here. There cannot be any leaks. Not one. And I'm taking further precautions. I'm leaving those two officers now outside her room here at the hospice. There're going to be permanent guards outside her door. Just to be on the safe side.'

'I think that's wise,' Dr Nelson said. 'And I'll talk to the staff immediately, caution them about talking. There'll be no problem.'

'Good.' Mac MacDonald stood up. 'Now I'm going over to see Carly's mother, to explain to Mrs Smith that she has to keep this development a secret for the moment.'

'Thanks, Mac, for coming so quickly,' Katie said, also rising.

He threw Katie a knowing look. 'I've waited ten years

to solve this case, and I think I will now, with Carly's help and a little luck.'

'I'll walk with you to the door.' Katie followed him across the office. She glanced at James Nelson. 'Thanks, Dr Nelson, and I'll come back tomorrow morning, before I return to New York.'

'I'll see you then, Katie.'

James Nelson rose, walked over to the door, and shook Mac's hand. 'If there are any developments I'll call you immediately.'

'Thanks. I'd appreciate that.'

Katie and Mac MacDonald walked to the front entrance in silence, but when they were outside, Mac turned to Katie and said, 'I'm sorry, Katie, but right now you can't talk either. So not a word to your parents.'

Katie stared at him, frowning. 'Okay, I understand. It's so easy to let something slip. Careless talk costs lives.'

It was his turn to stare. 'That's a good line, where did you get it?'

'I saw it on a World War Two poster at a house in Yorkshire recently. The owners have a whole collection of war-time memorabilia. It seemed so . . . apt.'

He nodded, smiled at her. 'Your father's very proud of you, Katie. Bursting with pride.'

She returned his smile, thinking he looked much the same as he always had. Ten years had brought a few silver hairs and even a few lines around his eyes and his mouth, but he was still a very good-looking man. 'How's Allegra?' she asked, suddenly thinking of the Medical Examiner, knowing they were close, although they had never married.

'She's great and she'll be real happy about this development, I can tell you that. We've got the DNA taken from Denise's body at the time of her murder stored away. If Carly comes up with a name, and we arrest the perp, all we need is a DNA match to convict.'

'You mean DNA samples last that long?'

'Sure they do, Katie. They last forever.'

Chapter Thirty-three

Pushing pots of theatrical make-up to one side, Katie found space on the dressing table for her diary. After opening it, she sat back in the chair for a moment, thinking, and then she began to write.

March 1st, 2000   *Barrymore Theatre*
                                     New York

Today is Wednesday matinée day, and since I never leave the theatre on matinée days, I have time to put a few things down here.

Opening in a Broadway play is really the most exciting thing that has ever happened to me. Just stupendous. But what's also very exciting to me is the sudden change in Carly's condition. When she spoke to me earlier this week, I was flabbergasted. In fact, as she spoke my name I was the one who became speechless! What a wonderful breakthrough this is. I'm sure Carly is going to recover, if not completely, certainly enough to live a halfway decent life. James Nelson tends to agree. He's still stunned himself, puzzled as well, and not sure what started this sudden change in Carly. The amantadine is one factor, he believes. When Carly's up to it he's going to do some extensive neurological tests on her. She'll also start undergoing intensive speech and physical therapy. Dr Nelson told me that she might be physically disabled and mentally challenged after ten years in a vegetative state. But my money's on Carly. She was always a fighter, and she'll fight now. And I'm going to be there to help her.

I'm frustrated a bit because I can't tell Mom and Dad and Niall. I was bursting with the news on Monday night, but I managed to keep my mouth shut. I can't put Carly at risk, and talking might do that. Not that my parents would let anything slip, but I told Mac I wouldn't say anything to them. And I can't break my word to him. Dad has always said he's a good cop and a good guy. He was startled when he saw Carly. He thought she hadn't changed much at all, that she was still like a beautiful young girl. That's true, although she has a few lines on her face now. So do I. Mac didn't question her, or say a word to her at the hospice on Monday. Anyway, Carly was out of it again, and there was no point in him hanging around. But once she shows more improvement, he's going over to the hospice with Detective Groome, hoping to get a lead on the murderer. For years I've wondered who did it, and I never could come up with a name. That name is locked in Carly's brain, but maybe it will be revealed now. I was really startled when Mac told me DNA samples last forever. I never knew that. I guess most people don't either.

I'm going to go back to Malvern next Monday. If Chris can't lend me his car, I'll rent one. I must go and see Carly again, to encourage her. Dr Nelson thinks it's vital I do this, because I'm the one she remembers. How could we ever forget each other? We were together most of our lives, on a day-to-day basis, until we were seventeen. I'm in her system, just as she's in mine. There's a very strong bond between us. It's a bond that can't be broken, so James Nelson says.

Going back to opening night, that was such a wonderful experience for me. Full of excitement, and success. The critics liked me, mentioned me, went so far as to say I had a big future as an actress. My mother was all puffed up with pride and excitement, and said she felt justified for her constant belief in me. She looked wonderful in her long black Trigère gown, and so did Aunt Bridget in her slinky red silk gown and diamond earrings. I was really proud of my mother and my aunt, and of all the women in our family, who had made a big effort to look their best. Even the two grandmas were all fancied up in evening dresses. As for Xenia and my English friends, they looked sensational. Of course, Lavinia was Audrey Hepburn personified, in a slender column of black silk, with long black gloves, chandelier earrings and her hair piled on top of her head. Verity was her usual glamorous self, also in black, a three-quarter-length lace sheath, and her usual pearls. Xenia had outdone herself, was in royal-blue silk with blue earrings. She told me they weren't real sapphires, but they looked like it to me. All of the men in my life looked handsome, especially Dad, Niall, and Christopher.

What to do about Chris?

My mother put a bug in my ear when she said I had to face the fact . . . mainly that we live in different countries. I've thought about this endlessly for the last two days. Could I ever live in Argentina? I don't know. Chris says it's beautiful, that it's known as the Paris of South America. But I'm an actress, and so I need to be in New York or London, where there are theatres. There are theatres in Buenos Aires, I'm sure, but I don't speak Spanish.

I asked Chris last night if he will always make his home in Argentina and he said he didn't know. He gave me a funny look, so I decided to drop the subject. He's picking me up for dinner after the show again tonight, but I'm not going to say anything about the future. After all, he hasn't mentioned it. He does keep saying he's in love with me, and that he needs me, wants me in his life forever. But he hasn't said anything about getting married. Do I want to marry him? I don't know. What I'm certain of is that I'm in love with him, and that we get on so well it's incredible. I wish he could come back to live in New York, but I suppose he has to be near rain forests.

The strange thing is I feel as if I've known Chris all my life, when in fact it's only been five weeks. He told me the other evening that you can know someone for years and never know them, and that time as such is not a factor, not meaningful. I guess he's right. Aunt Bridget says we're the same blood type. She doesn't mean that actually, it's just an expression she's used for years to describe a couple of men she's been involved with. She's the big success in our family, New York's top real-estate broker, one of the biggest, with her own company. Water finds its own level is another one of her expressions, and by that she means Chris and I will work everything out somehow. I hope so.

Katie put the pen down, closed her diary and slipped it into the carryall at her feet. She drank some bottled water, ate the sandwich she had brought with her from home, and then went over to the daybed. She liked to have a short rest before the evening performance; it always refreshed her, and she was able to walk on stage feeling energized. Two shows a day were taxing for most actors, and she was no exception to the rule.

'Where do you want to go for supper?' Chris asked later that evening, as he helped her into a yellow cab.

'I don't know really, what about Fiorella's? I like it there, and so do you.'

'Great, Katie.' He leaned forward and told the driver where to go, and then sat back next to her, took hold of her hand. 'How did it go tonight? How was the audience?' he asked, his voice warm and loving.

She smiled at him in the dim light of the cab. He had come to understand that audiences were very different, and sometimes affected an actor's performance. You had to rise above a bad audience, and she had explained that to him. 'It was good, and the same this afternoon,' she replied. 'I didn't have any problems.'

'I spoke to Jamie Nelson tonight, Katie.'

Katie felt herself stiffening, and she held her breath for a moment. 'Oh, and how is he?' Surely Dr Nelson hadn't mentioned anything about Carly?

'He's great. He said he saw you on Monday.'

'That's right. I guess I forgot to tell you.'

'He said he'd like to see the play, Katie. So I invited him down for the Friday-night performance, and dinner afterwards. Is that all right with you? You won't be too tired, will you?'

'No, I won't, and that's fine. I'll arrange a house seat for him. Or will he be bringing someone with him?'

'I'm not sure, sweetheart, but I can buy the ticket or tickets, you don't have to bother Melanie.'

Katie laughed. 'There aren't any tickets to buy, Chris. Have you forgotten, we're sold out for months to come.'

'It did slip my mind for a minute.' He leaned into her and kissed her cheek. 'I guess you'll have to get house seats then.'

They had been sitting at the table in Fiorella's for about twenty minutes, sipping their drinks, when Chris said suddenly, 'I spoke to Boston today, Katie. I have to leave on Sunday.'

She looked across the table at him, and asked, 'Leave for Boston? Or Argentina?'

'Argentina, darling.' He smiled faintly.

'I guess I've been expecting it,' she murmured softly, and lifted her glass of Fiji water. 'How long will you be away?'

'Six months. I'll be back in New York in August. For a couple of weeks.' He reached out, put his hand over hers resting on the table. 'I could probably fly in for a weekend, maybe even two. How about you? Could you come down to Buenos Aires for a long weekend?'

Katie stared at him askance. 'Of course not, Chris! I'm in a hit play. I'm the *second lead*. I can't have any time off *now*. And not even in the foreseeable future. I thought I'd made that clear to you.'

'Yes, you had, but you do all these matinées, sometimes two performances a day, doesn't Melanie think you're entitled to a little break now and again? All of you, not just you, Katie?'

'Of course she doesn't think that, no producer does, and that's not what Broadway's about, having weekends off, and all that jazz. Yes, if a play has a very long run, the stars do sometimes take off a couple of days now and again. But this one only opened on February the twentieth.'

He nodded. 'Okay, okay, don't get het up. I guess I'm an ignoramus when it comes to show business.'

'I'm not het up, Chris.'

'You sound it. And I don't know why you're always so very defensive about Melanie Dawson.'

'I'm not defensive about her!' Katie snapped. 'I'm merely explaining the rules . . . of the game, if you like. Anyway, Melanie's been wonderful to me, given me my great chance.'

'You'd have made it anyway, eventually. You're so talented someone would have discovered you. One day.'

'Maybe, maybe not. There's a lot of undiscovered talent out there. Anyway, Melanie's been a true friend to me, she's always kept an eye out for me, and given me other chances, which I didn't accept. As you well know.'

He nodded, and opened his mouth to make a fast retort when their food arrived. And so he closed his mouth, said nothing, and began to eat the lasagna in silence when it was served.

Katie cut into the piece of chicken, seething inside. For a reason she couldn't understand he seemed determined to pick a fight with her tonight. She couldn't help wondering once more if James Nelson had said something to him about Carly? Perhaps he had, and perhaps Chris was angry with her for not trusting him, not confiding. But then again, Nelson had promised Mac MacDonald he wouldn't let it leak out, primarily for Carly's safety. Anyway, wouldn't it be unethical to discuss a patient with a friend? No, she told herself now, James Nelson hasn't said a thing. Chris is in a bad mood, that's what this is all about. He's probably upset because he has to leave New York, leave me.

She voiced this thought when she said quietly, 'You're upset because you have to leave, Chris. Don't let's quarrel like this. Not tonight.'

'We're not quarrelling, are we?' he asked, lifting his head, staring across at her, putting his fork down.

'Not really, I suppose, but we're having heated words.' She touched his hand. 'Please, Chris, let's enjoy the last few days you have in New York.'

'Okay,' he muttered, and forced a smile, began to eat again.

Katie looked at him surreptitiously from underneath her eyelids, and she couldn't help thinking that he not only sounded sulky, but looked it. She held her tongue, and picked at the chicken.

Once he had finished eating, Chris took a swallow of red wine, and threw her a long, speculative look. He said, 'Do you think this is going to last? That we're going to last, with me there, you here?'

'I don't see why not. We're both working hard. I'll see you in August . . .' Her voice trailed off. She suddenly felt he was challenging her and she wasn't sure why. She exclaimed, 'We've never discussed the future, you and I. And I've never mentioned marriage. Neither have you.'

'I thought it was a foregone conclusion,' he exclaimed, staring hard at her. 'You must know I want us to get married.'

'Well, I can't read your mind!'

'But surely you know how I feel?'

'Yes.' Katie also put her knife and fork down and sat back on the banquette, looked at Chris. 'And I hope *you* know how *I* feel. I love you, Christopher Saunders.'

He smiled, his eyes warm. 'And I love you too, Katie Byrne. But I'm not sure this is going to work out. Long-distance love affairs are pretty tough, you know. They often do fall apart despite the intentions of the participants.'

'My mother said the same thing, only the other day. I told her we'd never discussed it, and we haven't, not until tonight.'

'I guess we were both putting it off, because we couldn't bear to look at the situation. Listen to me, Katie,' he leaned forward as he spoke, and went on quickly, 'this contract of yours is for a year. I think we could handle a year apart, if I come back once or twice, don't you? Then after that you can move to Argentina.'

Katie gaped at him. She was affronted, and slowly shook her head. 'But I'm an actress, Chris, that's what I do, that's who I am. It's my identity. Take my acting away, and I'm no longer Katie Byrne.'

'Of course you are, silly,' he said, smiling at her, squeezing her hand.

'No, I'm not!' she cried, pulling her hand away from his. 'Without my acting I'm nobody. Just another woman with red hair and blue eyes.'

'Beautiful eyes,' he said, realizing his mistake, now

trying to cajole her into a better mood. She was very angry. He'd never seen this side of her.

'Stop trying to flirt with me. This is serious. I can say the same thing to you, Chris. When your contract runs out, you could move back here.'

'But Katie, my job's in South America.'

'And mine is on Broadway. Or in the West End. Or L.A. You see, my work is in the English-speaking theatre, Chris. I'm an actor. That's what I do, what I want to do. And if I'm not doing it, then I'm no longer the woman you love. I'm a different person.'

'And I'm an ecologist, and take that away from me, and I'm not the same either. I believe in my work.'

'That's true, I'm sure,' she said softly.

'Then we're at an impasse.'

'I suppose we are.'

'I truly thought you'd move to Buenos Aires next year.'

'I can't.'

He reached for his wallet. 'I'm not hungry any more. Shall we go?'

'Yes. I'll get a cab. I'm very tired tonight, after two shows today, Chris. And I'd like to be alone.'

'No problem,' he snapped, throwing her a furious look. 'But I will take you home. I'm not going to let you wander the streets alone.'

She cried herself to sleep. She knew it was over between them, knew he wouldn't call her tomorrow, and that

James Nelson wouldn't be coming in to see the play. Chris was out of her life.

He was stubborn. She had spotted that about him right at the beginning of their relationship; and he was a little spoilt, if the truth be known. He wanted his own way. He'd probably always had it, starting with his mother and his sister, Charlene, and the other women he'd known before her. He was without a doubt the most attractive and appealing man she had ever met: warm, loving, intelligent and kind. And other women must have seen the same things in him, and *spoiled him*.

Yes, it was over, because he expected her to bow to his will; she couldn't do that. She was as stubborn as he was, perhaps. And probably as spoiled as he was, too. Spoiled by her parents and her family.

How can I go and live in Argentina? Katie asked herself. Aside from my acting, there's also Carly. Now that there had been this radical change in Carly's condition she couldn't leave her friend alone. Abandon her. All right, in a year Carly would be much better than she was now, provided everything went well. But even so, *she* was all Carly had. Well, there was Janet Smith, but Carly and her mother had never been all that close. And she couldn't leave Carly after the ten years that had been lost to her.

Katie buried her head in the pillow and wept fresh tears. It would be hard, too, to leave her family; they had always been so close. No, she and Chris would never make it, and that was that.

It's over, she whispered into her damp pillow.

Chapter Thirty-four

It's like spring today, Katie thought, as she walked slowly around her mother's back garden. Some of the trees and bushes were sprouting tiny green shoots, and the daffodils were pushing up under the trees at the end of the garden.

There was a feeling of regrowth, of renewal in the air on this bright, sunny April day, and Katie felt better than she had for the last few weeks. To her surprise, Chris had called her before leaving for Argentina, just to say goodbye and wish her well. She had caught a note of despair and sadness in his voice, and she had been sweet with him on the phone, but she had not given him an opportunity to continue their last disastrous discussion. Since then she had not heard a word.

Almost a month, she thought. He's been gone almost a month, and he hasn't been in touch. So it's over, just as I believed that night at Fiorella's. Well, so much for that.

'Katie! I'm back!' her mother called, and she swung around, walked up the path to the back door, where her mother was standing.

'You've been quick,' Katie said, coming to a standstill at the back door. 'You must have flown there and back. How's Grandma Catriona?'

'Oh, she's fine, darling, just a bad cold, that's all. She sends her love. I explained why you didn't go with me, that I didn't want to expose you to germs.'

Katie laughed. 'Honestly, Mom, you don't have to wrap me up in cotton wool!' Glancing at the garden, she went on, 'Everything looks beautiful. And you seem to be winning your battle with the deer.'

'I am, finally. I've been using a new spray to stop them eating everything. 'Tis a shame really, the poor things are hungry in the winter, but I can't let them eat my entire garden, now can I?'

Katie shook her head, smiling, and followed her mother into the kitchen. 'I've made some coffee,' she said. 'I'll have a cup with you before I go to the hospice to see Carly.'

'You've been very devoted, Katie, going every Monday and Tuesday, giving up your bit of free time to see her. It's a good thing the theatre's dark on Mondays.'

'I was away for a year in London, Mom, so I want to make it up to her.'

'Shall I go with you today?' Maureen asked, carrying two mugs of coffee over to the kitchen table.

'Oh no, it's not necessary, but thanks anyway. You were so devoted last year, going once a month to see her. Now it's my turn. I'm happy to take over.' Katie sat down at the table and poured milk into her mug of coffee. The last thing she wanted was her mother going to the hospice again. Maureen did not know of the recent change in Carly's condition, and Katie wanted to keep her in the dark for as long as possible. The fewer people who knew, the better. Mac MacDonald had made it clear he wanted Carly absolutely protected. The secret had remained a secret thus far. And there had been no leaks from the hospice.

'Have you heard from Chris?' Maureen asked as she joined Katie at the table.

'No, I haven't. I don't suppose I will, Mom. We sort of came to an impasse that evening, and there's really no way anything can change. Chris knows that as much as I do.'

''Tis a shame, mavourneen, I must admit that. We all liked him so much. But there you are, it wasn't meant to be, Katie.' Maureen sat back in the chair, staring at her daughter intently, studying her.

'What is it?' Katie asked after a moment, and gave a small baffled laugh. 'Do I have a smudge on my face or what?'

'No, no. I was just thinking how well you look, Katie mine. Beautiful if the truth be known. You've blossomed since you went into the play. And you have so much going for you, a big career ahead of you, friends and family who love you. So you mustn't fret for Chris.'

'I'm not fretting, Momma. I miss him, I love him, but

I'm practical enough to get on with my life. What's the alternative?'

'There isn't one, and I'm glad you've got your head screwed on the right way, Katie. You've never been one to mope, flop around feeling sorry for yourself, thank the Lord. Anyway, you're busy with the play, and will be for a long time. And one day you'll meet another nice man. There must be one out there for you, darlin'.'

'I hope so,' Katie responded, and reached out, squeezed her mother's hand. 'Thanks for being so supportive. You and Dad have been great these last few weeks.'

As Katie parked outside the hospital an hour later she saw James Nelson crossing the road, heading for the nearby hospice, his white coat flapping around him in the breeze. She got out of the rented car quickly, snatched up her carryall, and called out, 'Dr Nelson! Hi!'

He swung his head and lifted his hand in a wave when he saw her.

A moment later Katie was by his side. 'I decided to stop in again today, on my way back to New York. I think the more Carly sees me the better, don't you?'

'Absolutely. And she's making remarkable progress. Didn't you notice that when you were here yesterday?'

'I did. In the week I was gone she's made all kinds of strides. I couldn't believe it yesterday when I saw her sitting up.'

'I didn't expect Carly to do as well as she has,' Dr Nelson confided, opening the door for her, ushering her into the front lobby. 'That's something I've got to admit to you, Katie. I've come to the conclusion that she may have been in a *semi*-vegetative state, but aware of much more that was going on around her longer than anyone realized.'

Katie nodded. 'So your prognosis is good?'

'Yes, it is. I think Carly will make an excellent recovery. There will be challenges she'll have to deal with, but there's a great chance she will be fully mobile eventually, and that most of her motor skills will return.'

'That's wonderful news!' Katie exclaimed, her eyes lighting up.

He smiled at Katie, put his hand on her shoulder. 'You've been a really good friend and I know your continuing presence here has worked wonders for Carly. You're helping her memory to come back, of that I'm certain.'

'Talking to her about the past, showing her photographs, playing music she knows, I think all those things have been a factor, don't you?'

'Yes. Just keep on doing all of it.' He turned to go into his office, and said, 'I'll see you next week, I presume.'

'You presume correctly, Dr Nelson.'

Katie hurried along the corridor to Carly's room, went in and closed the door. As always, she went straight to the bed. The difference now was that Carly was propped up against the pillows and the feeding tube had gone. Dr Nelson had put her on soft foods, and she was managing to eat quite well. Another surprise for everyone who looked after her.

'Here I am again, Carly,' Katie exclaimed as she leaned over the bed, and kissed her on the cheek, squeezed her arm lightly. She drew away, looked into Carly's eyes, and saw the lovely bright spark of life in them.

Katie beamed at her girlfriend. 'I'm so happy, Carly, *so happy*. You're getting better very quickly, you know. Much quicker than anyone ever expected. *You are doing very well*. Do you understand me?'

Carly attempted a smile, and then blinked her eyes. 'Katie . . . Hi . . .'

'Good girl.' Katie took hold of her hand. There was a light pressure of Carly's fingers against hers, and Katie was overjoyed again. 'I'll be taking you out on the town dancing before you know it!'

Carly made a small gurgling noise in her throat, and Katie frowned, stared at her. 'Are you all right?'

'Den . . . ise,' Carly said in that low mumble, and stared at Katie, her eyes frantic.

'*Denise*. Is that what you're saying?' Katie asked, leaning closer to her.

Carly blinked rapidly. It had become one of her ways of communicating. 'Denise . . . okay?' she enunciated more clearly.

Katie suddenly remembered that she had been unconscious in the wood. She didn't know Denise was dead.
Oh my God. How can I tell her that? It could set her
back, and she's doing so well. Katie had always had an
ability for thinking on her feet, and now she said swiftly,
'Yes, Denise *was* hurt, Carly.'

'*Oooh*.' The noise Carly made was more like a groan,
and her face crumpled slightly. Tears came into her
violet-blue eyes and rolled down her cheeks. 'Poor . . .
Denise . . .'

'Oh darling, yes, poor Denise,' Katie murmured, her
own eyes filling. She went to get the box of tissues;
returning to the bedside, she patted Carly's cheeks,
drying her tears, and then her own.

There was a silence for a while.

Katie sat next to the bed, holding Carly's hand,
stroking it, wanting to comfort her friend.

There was a sudden, unexpected change in Carly. She
tried to move up, lifted her head off the pillows, and
her eyes were agitated. 'Denise . . . me . . . run . . .
Katie!'

Startled, Katie leaned in closer. 'You and Denise ran?
That's what you're saying, isn't it? You and Denise ran
into the wood.'

Carly blinked rapidly. 'Yes . . .'

Taking a deep breath, Katie said carefully, 'Who did
you run away from?'

A blank look settled on Carly's face. She stared back at

Katie. Her mouth moved in agitation and then stopped. But her eyes were bright with life again.

'*A man was chasing you*. Who was it? Tell me, Carly.' Katie took her hand again and squeezed it. 'I'm here. Nothing can hurt you now.'

'Denise hurt . . .'

'Yes, Denise *was* hurt, and so were you. Who was the man who hurt Denise?'

'Ha . . . nk . . . Hank . . . hurt . . . Denise . . . hurt . . . me.'

'Hank? Are you saying Hank?'

Carly blinked. 'Hank . . .' she said again, and lay staring at Katie.

Katie was puzzled. She bit her lip, racked her brains, wondering who Carly meant. She didn't know anyone called Hank. 'Hank *who*, Carly? What's his last name?'

'Hank . . . Thurl . . . o.'

'Hank Thurloe!' Katie cried. 'Do you mean Hank Thurloe?'

'Yes . . .'

'Oh my God!' Katie was momentarily stunned, and she sat very still in the chair, her eyes riveted on Carly. After a moment she recovered, and said again, '*Hank Thurloe?* Hank Thurloe hurt Denise and you?'

Again Carly said, very clearly, 'Yes . . . Katie . . .

An hour later Katie was greeting Mac MacDonald in James Nelson's office at the hospice. Mac was accompanied by

Detective Groome, who had worked on the Matthews murder case with him ten years ago.

'Sorry we took so long to get here from Litchfield, but the traffic was bad,' Mac said to her. 'And it was lucky you called when you did. I was just leaving to drive up to Sharon.'

'This last hour has seemed like an eternity,' Katie exclaimed, then turned to Dave Groome. 'Nice to see you, Detective.'

'It's good to see you, too, Katie. You look great.'

'Thanks. Listen, Mac, I'm going to cut to the chase. As I told you on the phone, Carly's regained some of her memory. Enough of it to tell me who it was who assaulted them.'

Mac looked at her keenly. 'Who was it, Katie?' His voice was urgent.

'Someone called Hank Thurloe.'

'Who is he? Was he at school with you?'

'Yes, but he was a senior, and he'd been gone about two years in 1989. He was the school football hero, the big jock, the big romeo. All the girls were crazy about him –'

'Was Denise crazy about him?' Mac cut in peremptorily.

'No, no, he was ahead of us in school. As I just said. And then he left. But the other girls, the older girls, thought he was glamorous. They had crushes on him. He's good-looking, or he was then.'

'Tell me everything you know about him,' Mac said.

'Okay. Let me try and remember.' Katie's brow furrowed and she bit her lip, thinking hard. 'Well, his family were affluent, that I do know. They had a very nice house in Kent, an old farmhouse. Between Kent and Cornwall Bridge. His father had some sort of business in New Milford. A printing business, I think.'

'There's still a printer's called Thurloe in New Milford,' Detective Groome volunteered.

'Then it must be his father's business,' Katie said.

'Can you give me a description of Hank Thurloe?' Mac now asked, trying to keep the excitement out of his voice. He knew he was going to solve this case after all these years, and he felt a rush of adrenaline. Finally he was going to get justice for Denise Matthews and Carly Smith. At long last.

'Yes. As he was then,' Katie replied. 'He was tall, well built, heavy-set really. His hair was light-brown. I don't recall what colour his eyes were. I mean, you have to know someone well to remember that.'

Mac nodded. 'How did he dress? You said his family was affluent, so no doubt he favoured good clothes.'

'That's right, Mac. Jeans, of course, but cashmere sweaters in winter, nice sports shirts in summer. I remember about his clothes because Niall always thought Hank looked out of place. He said Hank was showing off, trying to impress. Especially the girls.'

Mac nodded, thinking of Allegra's profile ten years ago. My God, she had been right on the button. She had described Hank Thurloe when she had given him a partial profile of the perp. She had said he was tall, well built, with brown hair, and that he must've worn cashmere sweaters. There had been cashmere threads on Denise's body and brown hair, as well. Not to mention the skin particles under her nails. DNA was going to help him put Hank Thurloe behind bars, of that he had no doubt now.

Mac said to Katie, 'Let's go to Carly's room. I want her to tell me herself. I want her to name Hank Thurloe.'

The days that followed this dramatic turn of events were filled with tension for Katie.

She threw herself into the play, glad she had her work to lose herself in, because it helped to keep worry at bay.

Nevertheless, there were moments when she did find herself worrying – about Carly, and about Hank Thurloe being found and arrested.

But she had infinite faith in Mac MacDonald. She knew how committed he was, and that he wanted this unsolved case to be solved. As he had said to her after they had visited Carly's room: 'I want to be able to write *case closed* on this particular file. I want Carly to live without fear in the future, and Denise to rest in peace in her grave.'

Mac had telephoned her once during the week to tell

her that they had located Hank Thurloe. He was married with two children and lived just outside Litchfield. She had hung up the phone thinking how close this was to Malvern; her mother had been right, the murderer had not moved away. He was right on their doorstep.

The log fire blazed up the big chimney, the antique Victorian lamps threw lambent light across the walls, and the sense of warmth, comfort and welcoming hospitality seemed more pronounced than ever.

Michael and Maureen Byrne, and Katie, sat at the table in their big country kitchen with Mac MacDonald and Allegra Marsh, mugs of coffee in front of them. It was a Monday afternoon, and Mac and Allegra had stopped at the house in Malvern to fill them in about the murder case.

'As I told you a month ago, Katie, it didn't take us long to locate Hank Thurloe. He's an accountant, and has his own small company. His father's retired now, and it's his brother Andy who runs the printing business. It was through his brother that we found him.'

'Did he seem normal?' Katie asked, riddled with curiosity. 'Or was he weird?'

'He did appear to be normal on the surface, but we soon discovered he wasn't. In any case, I went to see him with Dave Groome, and I told him we were starting new investigations into a ten-year-old unsolved murder case, because of fresh evidence that had come to light. I told him the name of the deceased, and I asked him if he would be willing to give us a sample of his blood for a DNA test. I explained that if he wasn't willing I'd have to get a warrant.'

'And he agreed?'

'Oh yes, he was quite willing.'

Katie frowned. 'Is that a normal reaction?' she asked, staring across at Mac.

'Yes, I think it is, because he didn't know he was at risk. The average person doesn't understand much about DNA. For instance, you yourself didn't know that DNA samples last forever, Katie. And most people don't know that either.'

'They don't realize that DNA is a genetic fingerprint which makes each one of us unique,' Allegra interjected. 'DNA is never wrong, and a person truly can be identified by a small sample of DNA, and that's what Mac and I did with Hank Thurloe. We matched him up to the DNA samples taken from Denise's body, which have been kept in storage at headquarters all these years. It was *his* seminal fluid, *his* skin under her fingernails, *his* blood, *his* pubic hair, and hair from *his* head. It was even his saliva on a cigarette stub found at the crime scene. We got him on the DNA match.'

'And so he's arrested and in jail,' Michael stated.

'Yes. He's been charged and he's awaiting trial,' Mac said.

'He couldn't get off, could he?' Maureen asked, looking at the detective worriedly.

'No way, Maureen. The evidence is overwhelming. But in any case, he confessed.'

Katie was startled and exclaimed, 'He told you he raped and strangled Denise? I can't believe it!'

'Believe it, Katie,' Mac replied. 'He sure as hell confessed. He went berserk a few days after he was arrested, and threw a crazy fit. It wasn't an act, either. He was really out of control. Underneath that jock exterior, the football hero image, there's a psychopath. He ranted and raved about Denise, about her belonging to him. He had a sexual fixation about her. He's a sicko.'

'Did he tell you what happened that day?' Katie asked, leaning forward intently, staring at Mac and Allegra.

'Part of it, yes,' Mac replied. 'And I've also managed to re-create the scene to a certain extent in my own mind. Hank went to the barn with some intent. *He* says he went to talk to Denise. Seemingly, he'd noticed her in his last year at school, really fallen hard for her. He told me at one point that he loved her blonde beauty. Anyway, he wanted to make a date with her, but when he asked her to go out with him, she said no. She rejected him. He took hold of her arm, trying to persuade her to leave with him then, to go somewhere that night for a cup of coffee. He told me over and over again that he meant her no harm. But she pushed him away, a struggle broke out between them, and then apparently

Carly rushed to Denise's defence. There was something of a scuffle between the three of them in the barn and then the girls ran outside. He says he ran after them.

'It's my belief he had become angry, inflamed by that time, and I think he went over the edge,' Mac continued. 'In the wood, he saw Carly first. According to Thurloe, he tried to push her out of the way, but she picked up a log and hit him with it. He grabbed it from her, beat her over the head with it, and knocked her unconscious. Then he went after Denise. That was his intent . . . having sexual relations with her.'

'But why did he have to kill her?' Katie cried.

'I think everything escalated. Obviously he had the need to cover up. He says he panicked. He'd forced her, *raped* her. He knew Denise could bring rape charges against him, and he couldn't face that. It seems he was newly engaged to a girl from a prominent Sharon family, Martha Eddington, whom he subsequently married. So he was in a state of panic, alarm, couldn't risk being identified as a rapist. And that's why he strangled her.'

'Oh my God!' Maureen cried, covering her mouth with her hand. Michael put his arm around her, trying to comfort her.

'And he attacked Carly because she got in the way?' Katie gave Mac a long look.

'Yes, he did. It was always Denise he wanted, Denise he'd watched and stalked for years.'

'Was I ever in danger, Mac?' Katie now asked quietly.

'No, I don't believe you were.'

'But what about my school bag? The way all three of the bags were lined up in a row?'

'I told you at the time that we never found any trace evidence on it. Only your fingerprints and those of Carly and Denise.'

'But he could have worn gloves, couldn't he?'

'Yes, Katie, he could. But it's my belief the girls found your bag in the dressing area, put it with theirs, intending to bring it to you.'

Katie nodded. 'I guess you're right. Do you think Thurloe was still in the wood that night? I mean when Niall and I got there, and started calling out their names?'

'I do, yes. And there's no doubt you saved Carly's life. He had probably gone back to see if she was dead, realized she was still breathing and hit her again with the log. Then when he heard you and Niall, heard your voices, he ran away, bolted through the bushes, taking that log with him. We never found it.'

'And he thought he'd killed Carly in the last attack?' Katie said.

Mac nodded. 'I'm sure he did.'

'But she didn't die,' Michael said. 'Why didn't he come after her in the hospital?'

'Because she was in a coma,' Allegra answered. 'If you remember, there were a lot of stories in the newspapers, and on TV, a lot of media attention was given to the murder, and the attack on Carly, at the time. The prognosis was very grim. The doctors looking after Carly said she was in a coma and would be for the rest of her life. He believed he was home free.'

'It's amazing how she suddenly came out of it,' Maureen ventured, addressing Allegra. 'I was stunned when Katie told me today.'

'I'm sorry, Mom, but I'd promised Mac I wouldn't say anything. We had to protect Carly.'

'Did he ever kill again?' Michael asked.

'I don't think he did.' Mac shook his head. 'He's not a serial killer as far as I know.'

'How can you be sure?' Maureen asked.

It was Allegra who answered. 'Because his DNA, his genetic fingerprint, is now in the DNA criminal databank. And he's not been matched up to any similar murders of young women. And that's a nationwide databank.'

Maureen simply nodded her head.

'Will I have to give evidence at the trial?'

'Yes, Katie,' Mac responded. 'And so will Carly, if she's able to when the trial starts.'

'Allegra, can you explain how Carly suddenly came out of the coma?' Maureen frowned as she spoke to the Medical Examiner. 'I still don't really understand.'

'I'll try, Maureen. I've done a little more investigating into coma in the last few weeks, and I think what happened is that Carly was probably wrongly diagnosed right at the outset. It was an easy mistake for anyone to make. You see, she *was* in a coma when she was taken to the hospital after the attack. Now, a *true* coma usually lasts about six to eight weeks, although it has been known to last two years. But if it's two years there's usually real brain damage when a patient comes out of it. I tend to agree with Dr Nelson, who now thinks Carly was in a coma, then subsequently went into a *semi*-vegetative state. She may have been aware of a lot of things going on around her for years, but was unable to make this known to her nurses, because she couldn't speak, had no motor skills. I also go along with Dr Nelson's theory that she may have had some sort of brain-stem blockage that kept stimulation from getting to her brain until that moment when she spoke to Katie.'

'And what about the amantadine he gave her?' Katie said.

'That may well have been a factor. I just heard the other day of a similar case, of a woman coming out of a coma in New Mexico,' Allegra explained. 'And she had also been given amantadine to prevent pulmonary infection. By the way, that woman had been in a semi-vegetative state for fifteen years.'

'How amazing!' Katie exclaimed. 'And just think, Hank Thurloe would have got away with murder if Carly's memory hadn't come back.'

'Absolutely correct,' Allegra agreed. 'Because we've

always needed a suspect to match up to the DNA samples I took from Denise's body, and which we've held all these years. But blood doesn't lie ... DNA doesn't lie.'

'What'll happen to Thurloe?' Michael stared across the table at Mac.

'Hank Thurloe will spend the rest of his life in jail. And without any possibility of parole, of that I am certain,' Mac answered.

Later that same day Katie drove over to the hospice to see Carly. She sat with her for a while, holding her hand and talking to her. And then, at one moment, when Carly seemed more relaxed and aware, Katie said, 'I've just been with Mac MacDonald, the detective who came to see you about a month ago. Do you remember him?'

Carly blinked. 'Yes ... Katie.'

'He wanted you to know that they've arrested Hank Thurloe for attacking you. He's in prison.'

A small smile touched Carly's mouth and her eyes seemed much brighter all of a sudden.

Katie was about to explain to her that Denise was dead, and then she instantly changed her mind. There was no need to tell her this now. That bad news could wait until Carly had improved further. It would be such a painful thing for her to hear, and Katie did not want her to have a setback at this stage of her recovery.

Instead, she leaned forward, and put her arms around Carly, held her close. And against her hair she whispered, 'Justice has been done, Carly, and you have nothing to fear now.'

Chapter Thirty-five

The curtain calls seemed to go on forever. Katie was aware that the entire cast had given of their very best, and that the audience had loved them, and loved the play. It had been a sensational performance.

She knew that she herself had given her *all*. Every ounce of her talent and skill had gone into making Emily Brontë a living, breathing person on this stage. She had brought her to life in a way she never had before. She had actually become Emily for two hours tonight.

Carly was out there in the audience with Niall and their parents, and in a certain way she had played to Carly, and to her alone, because she had wanted to excel for her friend.

After she had taken her last bow, Katie hurried off the stage, almost running back to her dressing room. She knew she had to tone down her stage make-up and change into her own clothes as quickly as she could. Her parents were taking them all to supper at Circo on West 55th Street, and she wanted to join them without delay. Mostly because she wanted to see Carly, to hear what she had to say about the play. And her performance, of course.

Once she had taken off some of her theatrical make-up, Katie brushed her hair, and then got dressed in the pale-grey cotton suit she had worn to the theatre earlier. It was fairly cool for June, and as she pulled on the white tee-shirt she decided she had made the perfect choice. Within minutes she was slipping on the jacket, picking up her red shoulder bag, and running down to the stage door.

As she stepped out into the alley she collided with a man, and stepped back, began to apologize. And then she stopped, stood gaping. It was Christopher Saunders.

'Now it's *your* turn to knock *me* down,' he said. 'Remember how I collided with you at the hospice?'

Katie opened her mouth to make a sharp retort. But no words came out. How could they? Chris had pulled her into his arms and was kissing her.

Finally managing to push him away, Katie exclaimed, 'What a nerve you've got, Christopher Saunders! You come back here after all these months of silence, and think you can just pick up where you left off.'

'Yes, I do, because I love you. And you love me.'

'Not any more I don't!'

'Liar.'

'I'm not a liar!'

'Yes, you are. I know you love me because your mother told me.'

'My mother. What's she got to do with this?'

'I guess she wants me for a son-in-law.'

'I'll never marry you.'

'Oh yes you will, and the sooner the better, as far as I'm concerned.'

'Oh go back to your rain forests, and good riddance!' Katie cried.

'I can't go back to my rain forests because I've given them up.'

'What?'

'You heard me. I've given them up. For love.'

'You have? But you *love* your rain forests.'

'True. But I also love the Everglades and they're also endangered, and let's face it, Katie mine, Florida's much closer than Argentina.'

Katie had been rendered speechless, and she stood gazing at him, thinking how wonderful he looked in his navy-blue blazer and grey slacks.

Chris said, 'Did you understand? I've left Argentina, Katie. I've come back to New York. I'm going to live here. With you. If you'll have me.'

'Oh.'

'Don't say *oh*. Say yes.'

'*Yes*!'

He pulled her into his arms and kissed her again. She clung to him. After a moment he drew away from her, and stared into her face. 'You mean it, don't you? You will marry me, Katie?'

She nodded. 'Yes, of course I will . . .' She gave him a penetrating look, her head on one side. 'What made you do this, Chris?'

'You did, Katie.'

'Me. How?' she asked, her bafflement obvious.

'I came to New York in May. On business. And of course I had to see you. But I knew you would give me short shrift, so I didn't call you. Instead I came to see the play again. I suddenly understood everything you'd said to me when we broke up. I wondered how I'd ever expected you to give up your acting. It is *you*, Katie, I know that now. And it would be very selfish of me to take you away from the stage. You're a natural, and far too good, too brilliant. I'm a dedicated ecologist, you know that. But I can be an ecologist in lots of places. So I decided to swap rain forests for the Everglades. In a nutshell, I asked for a transfer. And I finally got it. I'm here to stay.'

'Oh Chris.'

'We'd better not stand here talking. We've the rest of our lives to do that. Everyone's waiting for us at Circo.'

'My God, you're all in cahoots!'

'Just about. Come on, darling, I've a car waiting.'

Her parents beamed at them when Chris and Katie came to the table in Circo. So did Carly and Niall.

Carly turned slightly in her wheelchair, and said, 'You

were . . . great . . . Katie.' She spoke carefully, slowly, but her speech was much improved, almost back to normal after months of therapy.

'Thanks, Carly.' Katie bent over her, kissed her on the cheek. 'I'm so glad you finally got to see the play.'

Carly nodded. 'You were . . . always . . . the *best*. Even then . . . Before . . .'

'We were all good, darling,' Katie murmured. 'You and me and Denise were the best. The three of us.'

Carly merely smiled, and moved her wheelchair so that Katie and Chris could sit down together on the banquette.

Maureen said, 'We've ordered champagne, Katie and Chris. Because we have so much to celebrate.'

As she spoke, Michael beckoned to the waiter, who came to the table and opened the bottle of Dom Perignon. There was a pop when the cork came out of the bottle, and then the sparkling wine was being poured into their glasses.

Katie looked at each person sitting with her at the table. Her mother. Her father. Her brother. Her best friend. And the man she was going to marry.

'It is *very much* a celebration. A celebration of life,' Katie said.

Acknowledgements

I would like to mention a number of people who have helped me during the research and writing of this book. Most particularly, I am indebted to Lieutenant Eric C. Smith, Commanding Officer, Western District Major Crime Squad, Connecticut State Police, for walking me through police procedures at major crime scenes and events thereafter. My thanks to Bette Bartush, Connecticut State Police, for explaining other police procedures; to Arthur H. Diedrick, Chairman of Development, Office of the Governor of the State of Connecticut, for advice about matters pertaining to that state; to Fran Weissler for clarifying certain aspects of the Broadway theatre; to Rosemarie Cerutti and Susan Zito of Bradford Enterprises for help with many different aspects of this book, and to Liz Ferris for a marathon typing job meticulously done so quickly. My editors Deb Futter of Doubleday, New York, and Patricia Parkin of HarperCollins, London, are sounding boards par excellence, and my thanks to them. Last, but by no means least, I must express my gratitude to my husband Robert Bradford for his belief that I could write a mystery and for his constant encouragement for me to do so.

A Woman of Substance
Barbara Taylor Bradford

In 1905 a young kitchen maid leaves Fairley Hall. Emma Harte is sixteen, single and pregnant.

By 1968 she is one of the richest women in the world, ruler of a business empire stretching from Yorkshire to the glittering cities of America and the rugged vastness of Australia.

But what is the price she has paid?

A magnificent dynastic saga, *A Woman of Substance* is as impossible to put down as it is to forget. This multi-million copy bestseller is truly a novel of our times.

'An extravagant, absorbing novel of love, courage, ambition, war, death and passion'
New York Times

'A spellbinding family saga . . . A *tour de force*'
Annabel

'A rags-to-riches blockbuster . . . brilliantly told'
Manchester Evening News

ISBN 0 586 20831 3

Hold the Dream
Barbara Taylor Bradford

Emma Harte was the heroine of Barbara Taylor Bradford's multi-million copy bestseller, *A Woman of Substance*.

Now she is eighty years old and ready to hand over the reins of the vast business empire she has created.

To her favourite grandchild, Paula McGill Fairley, Emma bequeaths her mighty retailing empire with these heartfelt words: 'I charge you to hold my dream.'

A towering international success and the glorious sequel to *A Woman of Substance*, this is the powerfully moving tale of one woman's determination to 'hold the dream' which was entrusted to her – and in so doing find the happiness and passion which is her legacy.

'The storyteller of substance'   *The Times*

'A must for all Barbara Taylor Bradford fans'   *Woman*

'I enjoyed every word'   *Daily Express*

'The novel every woman is going to take on holiday'
                    Daily Mail

ISBN 0 586 05849 4

To Be the Best
Barbara Taylor Bradford

The enthralling sequel to Barbara Taylor Bradford's universally loved novels, *A Woman of Substance* and *Hold the Dream*.

Set in Yorkshire, Australia, Hong Kong and America, this remarkable contemporary novel continues the story of an unorthodox and endlessly fascinating family. As the spirit of Emma Harte lives on in her granddaughter, Paula O'Neill, an engrossing drama is played out in the glamorous arena of the wealthy and privileged, underscored by a cut-throat world of jealousy and treachery.

Paula must act with daring and courage to preserve her formidable grandmother's glittering empire from unscrupulous enemies so that Emma's precious dream lives on for the next generation . . .

'A compulsive read'   *Daily Mail*

'Will keep you up till all hours, reading just one more chapter before you can bear to turn out the bedside light'   *Prima*

ISBN 0 586 07034 6

Voice of the Heart
Barbara Taylor Bradford

Katharine Tempest, world-famous actress and star – a dark-haired beauty with a volcanic temperament.

Francesca Cunningham, blonde, cool, distant – the aristocratic writer of bestselling historical romances.

Yet their lives were inextricably intertwined over two decades and more.

Voice of the Heart is the spellbinding story of two unique and brilliant women – and of the charismatic men whom they loved and lost – and to whom they ransomed their hearts.

'It really keeps you turning the pages, wondering just why it is that two beautiful and successful women who were once great friends are now sworn enemies'   *Daily Express*

'Extremely well told . . . riveting . . . enchanting'
Yorkshire Post

ISBN 0 586 05848 6

Her Own Rules

Barbara Taylor Bradford

Meredith Stratton is forty-four and a successful business-woman.

The owner of six elegant international inns, she is about to celebrate her only daughter's engagement. At this seemingly happy time in her life, Meredith begins to suffer from a strange illness that baffles everyone. Her doctor cannot find a cause for her debilitating symptoms, and, desperate for answers, she seeks the help of a psychiatrist. Through therapy, Meredith peels back the layers of her life to discover the truth behind her most careful creation – herself.

Secrets, survival, redemption and love abound in this compelling story of a woman who uncovers the key to her tormented past, and finds the courage to live by her own rules.

'Barbara Taylor Bradford is a wonderful storyteller who can convey the power of love. The warmth and compassion of her tale brought tears to my jaded old eyes.'

Sunday Express

ISBN: 0 586 21741 X

Dangerous to Know

Barbara Taylor Bradford

Sebastian, the fifty-six-year-old patriarch of the Locke clan, is handsome, charismatic, a man of immense charm and intelligence. He heads up the philanthropic Locke Foundation, funded by the vast family fortune built by his forefathers. Committed to relieving the suffering of those in genuine need, Locke travels the globe, personally giving away millions a year to the poor, the sick, and the victims of natural disasters and wars. He is seen as a beacon of light in today's darkly violent world. That is why the police are so baffled when Sebastian is found dead in mysterious circumstances. Has he been murdered, and if so who would want to kill the world's greatest philanthropist? Could such an upstanding man have enemies?

Vivienne Trent, an American journalist, met Locke as a child, married him, divorced him, but stayed close to him. Aware that there was another side to this enigmatic man, she sets out to find the truth about his death and about Locke himself.

'Few novelists are as consummate as Barbara Taylor Bradford at keeping the reader turning the page. She is one of the world's best at spinning yarns.' *Guardian*

ISBN: 0 586 21739 8